'My mind is officially blown! This clever, twisty debut really delivers. Gripping, well written and intriguing on every level'
Sarah Pearse, author of *The Sanatorium*

'Guy Morpuss is set to become a powerhouse in speculative crime. Tense, dark, gritty and high-concept, it's a feast of a book'
Helen Fields, author of *Perfect Crime*

'*Five Minds* spearheads an exciting new trend in speculative fiction, with a mind-stretching and irresistible premise deftly spun into a twisty, page-turning action-thriller. Clever, cool and thoroughly entertaining'
Philippa East, author of *Little White Lies*

'Consider my single mind blown! An astonishing and original concept, deftly executed. This novel cries out for a screen adaptation'
David Jackson, author of *The Resident*

'A whip-smart, searing debut with a story which grinds into the mind like cursed clockwork. I really loved it'
Matt Wesolowski, author of *Six Stories*

'A brilliantly inventive, pacy debut with a great premise. A *Maze Runner*-type world of complex death games and riddles that keep you guessing to the very end. If you liked *The Seven Deaths of Evelyn Hardcastle*, you'll love this'
Eve Smith, author of *The Waiting Rooms*

T0017465

FIVE MINDS

GUY MORPUSS

This paperback edition first published in 2022
First published in Great Britain in 2021 by
VIPER, part of Serpent's Tail,
an imprint of Profile Books Ltd
29 Cloth Fair
London
ECIA 7JQ
www.serpentstail.com

1 3 5 7 9 10 8 6 4 2

Printed and bound in Great Britain by
CPI Group (UK) Ltd, Croydon, CRO 4YY

A CIP catalogue record for this book is available from the British Library.

ISBN 978 1 78816 5686
Export ISBN 978 1 78816 5679
eISBN 978 1 78283 7268

FSC
www.fsc.org
MIX
Paper from
responsible sources
FSC® C171272

FIVE
MINDS

To Julie, El and Zog

ARE YOU READY TO DIE?

NEED TO EARN TIME?
BORED WITH THE REAL WORLD?

ESCAPE TO OAKBURY FLATS DEATH PARK

Walk the tightrope between life and death
Indulge your wildest fantasies . . . or most morbid desires

DREAMS OF REALITY INC™ PROMISES YOU

* State-of-the-art game booths
* Forty-seven arenas
* Over 150 unique and personalised games
* Every genre — historic, fantasy, futuristic, role-playing and more!
* No limits on time earned — leave with a new life
* Concessionary rates for end-of-lifers*

IT'S BETTER TO BURN OUT THAN TO FADE AWAY

* T & Cs apply

Terms and Conditions

1. Players must be 21 (twenty-one) or over.

2. **WARNING**: Probable side effects of participation in games include death, loss of limb(s), paralysis, post-traumatic stress disorder or catatonia.

3. Body disposal fee of 1 (one) month required to be deposited before entry. Refund available on exit if unused. In the event of death, credit will be given for any body parts that remain in saleable condition.

4. 'End-of-lifers' may enter the park for a reduced fee of 2 (two) months, and clause 6 below does not apply to them.

5. In these conditions, for the purposes of clauses 4 and 6, 'end-of-lifers' means:
   a. **HEDONISTS** in their final year of life (41–42 years of age);
   b. **ANDROIDS** in their final year of life (79–80 years of age);
   c. **COMMUNES** in the last year of their fifth life (141–142 years of age);
   d. **WORKERS** (having no fixed expiration date) cannot qualify as End-of-Lifers.

6. **IMPORTANT NOTICE**: Before entry, CGov requires players to provide psychological certification confirming that they have fully understood and been counselled as to the risks of entering the park. Communes must provide such certification (separately) in relation to at least three (3) of their five (5) personalities.

7. **WARNING**:
   a. By entering into the park you confirm and acknowledge that you understand that death in the game booths is permanent.
   b. This condition does not apply to communes in their first 4 (four) lives, who upon death will forfeit any time remaining in their current life and any time won in the park. Other lives will not be affected.

8. Dreams of Reality Inc™ is not affiliated with any arenas and accepts no liability for death or physical/mental injury to players, howsoever caused.

ALEX

What to call it?

Waking. Suiting up. Slipping on the skin. Uploading, downloading. Body bounce. Mindswap.

Schizos are still searching for a word that makes it feel better, more glamorous. Normal, even. But there isn't one. It doesn't matter what name you use, it still seems like someone's dragging your brain from the base of your spine to your skull – and then kicking it for good measure.

Once the shock has passed, my first question is: where exactly has Sierra left us? The good thing is that there are only so many places you can dump a body in a death park.

We had voted four-to-one to take this trip. The others had thought it a chance to add value and have some fun before the first trade-in. I had voted no. But there was at least one aspect I appreciated: being in a contained environment limited Sierra's options.

The protocols are clear: before dropping out, you leave the host in a safe place, lying down, alone. A locked door, food and

3

water nearby. In twenty-five years I could count on the fingers of one hand the number of times all those had coincided. I've woken indoors, outdoors, in prison cells, on public transport, half lying in a frozen pond, and on one memorable occasion on the deck of a freighter starting a ten-day transatlantic voyage.

No amount of time fines seem to make any difference to Sierra. Sometimes I think she's trying to kill us.

My second question on waking is: what level of ethanol is flowing through my bloodstream? You'd have thought that someone who lives their life in four-hour slots wouldn't want to waste half their time in a drunken stupor. But we all fight our demons in different ways. And Sierra's demons are different from the rest of ours.

Even with my eyes shut I could tell the answer to the first question. I was in the same place as the previous three days. Voices, laughter, music, the clink of glasses: the Diamond Room at the Excelsior, the only upmarket bar in the death park. Quite why Sierra had started frequenting it I wasn't sure, but it was a step up from her usual haunts.

The answer to the second question was 0.235 per cent blood alcohol. That's a bottle of whisky in four hours. Or three bottles of champagne. Good going even by Sierra's standards. Serious intoxication, but not the sort of level that would have had alerts sounding and the autonomous control systems kicking in. I brought the inhibitors and reclean up. Twenty-five years ago they were state-of-the-art, but they'd been well used and we hadn't spent much on them in the last few years. Now using them felt like someone was scouring my veins from the inside while shaving my eyeballs with a potato peeler.

I sat still for a minute while they did their work. Eyes closed. Considering. That was two breaches of protocol on waking. Should I let it slide? What was the point of taking some of Sierra's time? She was never going to change. Then again, why should I let her get away with it? At the very least, the others ought to know.

I logged on.

Re: Sierra. Breach of Protocol 2.08: unsafe wake. Breach of Protocol 3.17: ethanol 0.235 per cent. Data file attached. Request: One-hour time fine. Votes to be logged by end of cycle. Alex.

I was about to log off, but then added a personal message.

FFS Sierra, I'm sick of clearing up after you. Do this to yourself if you want, but don't drag the rest of us into it. Make sure we're clean and safe before you drop out. We need to see a new attitude in our next life, or I will be voting for some serious downtime. A.

I breathed out, calmer now, and with alcohol levels falling fast.

I opened my eyes.

I was slumped in a corner seat, humanity swirling around me, an upturned champagne flute dangling from one hand. I let it fall to the sodden carpet.

A low table separated me from a blonde woman in a green dress who was looking at me expectantly. She smiled. My heart sank. What had Sierra left me with now?

'Alex Du Bois,' she said. 'You're back. I'm Jessica.'

A message from Sierra appeared.

You're welcome, Alex. Don't screw this up. Or do, first, if you have
the time. You can probably still remember how. She is rather lovely,
although we know from Montreal that blondes aren't your type.
She's rich and she's greedy. And not as good as she thinks. We need
this. Sierra. x

I sighed and scanned the woman.

JESSICA ENGELS
Hedonist
Expiry: 42 years
Age: 41.98 years
Credit: 3.27 years

'I don't know what Sierra's promised you, but I'm not interested,' I said.

She pouted. 'Sierra told me you'd be fun. She said you like
playing games.'

'Usually. But I don't like the stakes on offer in the park.'

'Then why did you come?'

'I wasn't given a choice. But it doesn't mean that I have to
play their sick games.'

'Not entirely true.' She leaned across the table and touched
my hand. 'Sierra signed you up. See.'

Challenge accepted. New York Treasure Hunt: Jessica Engels
(hedonist) vs Alex Du Bois (commune), to be completed within 24h.

What was Sierra thinking? This wasn't part of the plan.

I sat back. 'You're obviously good at this, Jessica. No one earns three years in a death park unless they have some skill; and a lot of luck. Your luck won't hold, though. I don't want to be the one to kill you. Cash in and go home.'

'She didn't tell me you were scared.'

'Tired. Not scared,' I said. 'This body is almost done, and until we trade in it's worth virtually nothing. What will you get if you beat us? A few months? If I lose it's a couple of weeks in stasis and then we're back in a shiny new body. If you lose, you're gone for good. You're chasing scraps of time, and the odds aren't in your favour. We'll just waste it, anyway. Mike wants enhanced quadriceps so he can run faster. Ben wants new gaming implants. It's all frivolous stuff. But it's all you have. Take your time, walk away, and live it.'

Jessica hesitated. There was a flicker of fear behind her eyes, but then the smile was back. She shook her head.

'Spoken like someone who knows they're going to lose,' she said. 'We have a deal. You play or you forfeit. Which is it?' She stood, and stretched out a hand.

I took it, not because I like human contact, but because I like information. If I was going to have to do this I wanted to know as much as I could. Her hand was warm and slightly sweaty. Ninety-eight beats per minute – too high for someone who had been sitting down. She was scared. Good.

She frowned. 'You look the same as her … but different somehow. Your eyes show someone else. You schizos might be used to it, swapping minds every few hours, but it's weird to watch.'

'Not as weird as you heds – giving up half your life for a few years of luxury.'

'You gave up your body.'

I laughed. 'If you'd seen it you would have known it wasn't worth much. And I don't need it. Whatever happens today, I'll still be here long after you're gone.'

She looked away and bit her upper lip. Her grip remained firm.

We threaded our way through the crowd looking like lovers after a quarrel, keen to find somewhere quiet to make up.

But I had no intention of taking up Sierra's suggestion of romance before work. I was going to kill Jessica as quickly as I could.

•

The nearest arena was two blocks away, on the ground floor of a crumbling high-rise. No one wants to live in a death park, so apart from the basics they are not well maintained.

It was dark outside, with most of the streetlights broken. A drone screamed low overhead, its spotlight catching us for a moment. It circled once, then moved on.

We picked our way carefully through the potholed remains of what had once been the main street, concrete dust crunching under our feet. Across from the arena was a club – flashing lights and the beat of music emerging through cracked windows. People partying while they waited to die.

The doors to the arena slid open at our approach and the stench of sweat and death hit us. There was a souvenir stall just inside, selling T-shirts and hoodies emblazoned with slogans such as: GREETINGS FROM THE DEATH PARK and I CAME, I SAW, I KILLED. One I didn't get: REVILLAGIGEDO ISLAND: COME FOR THE NAME, STAY FOR THE GAME. What was that about?

The reception desk was staffed by a girl with pink hair and a T-shirt that said ARENA X: COME DIE WITH US! She looked up and scanned us.

'Ms Engels. Mr Du Bois. Welcome to Arena X.' A hatch opened in the counter in front of her. 'You'll want these.'

She reached in and handed each of us a pair of trainers.

'Ms Engels, Room D. Mr Du Bois, Room L. The hunt will start five minutes after you enter. Our fee to the winner will be ten per cent. You also get a choice of a T-shirt or branded water bottle. For the loser,' she pulled a face, 'well, body disposal is free.' It seemed a well-practised line.

I followed Jessica past the counter and down a corridor lined with doors on either side. As we reached a door marked D, it slid open. Jessica hesitated, as though about to say something, but then stepped inside. I walked on. What do you say to someone you are about to kill?

Room L was a standard games booth. About three metres in diameter, the walls, floor and ceiling all black. A small seat protruded from one wall next to an open drawer. I sat down and changed my shoes, dropping my own into the drawer. It slid shut. I stood, and the seat retracted into the wall.

A screen lit up, with a countdown reading '4:28'. I walked across to it, feeling the floor flex beneath my feet.

Welcome, Mr Du Bois

Game:	The Treasure Hunt
Winner:	First to the prize, or last to die
Stages:	Three
Location:	New York City
Transport:	Not permitted

To preserve the integrity of the game, any attempt to record events will lead to an immediate forfeit.

A new screen appeared:

In this game you may make the following choices as to appearance and resources:

1. a. Male; b. female.

2. a. Athletic kit; b. business suit.

3. a. Five units local currency; b. one-minute freeze.

I hesitated over the first option. Bluff or double bluff? The games booth would read my mind, not my body. I'd appear in the game as Alex, not Mike. So there was no chance of Jessica recognising me. I'd stick with male.

The second was easier. Unless I was being dropped in the middle of a sports ground a suit would hide me better.

As to the third, a clever opponent will never let you use the freeze. Some money gives you flexibility.

So a, b, a, then.

I stepped back. The screen went blank, leaving only the countdown.

2:48

I stood in the centre of the room, closed my eyes, and got my balance. My mouth went dry and the adrenaline started to flow. I pushed it down slightly. But if you're not nervous you shouldn't be competing.

So far we had played and won a few games and were just under a year in credit. You tend to start slowly in the death parks, fighting for scraps until you've built up a decent stake of time. We'd arrived with two weeks, and there weren't many who wanted to play for that little. In fairness to Sierra, Jessica was our first chance to win big.

As I'd said to Jessica, schizos have an advantage in a death park. If any one of us dies in an arena we all die. But it isn't a real death. We move on to our next body, minds intact. Heds like Jessica – they only have one life. For them death in the arena is permanent. But that didn't mean I wanted to lose. We were in the park to win time.

I opened my eyes.

1:32

I waited for the room to go black.

•

Bright sunlight overhead, flickering through metal cables. Wooden boards at my feet, with glimpses of water far below. The roar of traffic around me. The acrid smell of exhaust fumes.

The New York skyline ahead.

I am running uphill, weaving between pedestrians. Ahead of me stands a tall stone tower. A bicycle shoots past on my right, bell ringing: 'Stay on your own side!'

I'm on the Brooklyn Bridge, running west towards downtown Manhattan.

No sign of Jessica, but they seldom start us together. Half a mile to my right is the blue and white of Manhattan Bridge. I can see a subway train heading east and a runner heading west. I squint, but these lenses aren't good enough. Maybe Jessica – or maybe just some random citizen out for exercise. I can't control what Jessica does, but it would be good to know where she is.

I can run for ever, thanks to Mike and his insane obsession with fitness. But this is not just about running. If it was, Mike could have done it.

I slow slightly and wait for the first clue. It flashes up on my right lens.

Stage One: An Eastern leader, with twittering sparrows; find the blind player.

I'm just south of Chinatown. There aren't going to be any Eastern leaders walking around, so I guess I'm looking for a statue. I pull up the map on my lens – Confucius Plaza, complete with a statue of the great man, is five minutes away. That sounds promising.

To be safe, I set a search running for other nearby statues, and turn to the second part of the clue.

Search "twittering sparrows"

There is a moment's pause, then the result appears on my lens.

The first shuffle of the tiles in the game of mah-jong.

I pass through the left arch of the tower and on to the long concrete walkway that leads down to City Hall. I increase my pace, dodging a group of tourists.

Another search tells me that the game of mah-jong is traditionally said to have been invented by Confucius. It all fits. Am I looking for a blind mah-jong player by the statue?

At the end of the bridge I cut right, past the courthouse, and down a side street.

It's not far to the plaza, but this feels far too easy.

I slow to a walk as I go back through the clues. If Jessica is nearby I'd rather she didn't realise it is me. Hopefully I look like just another anonymous lawyer in a dark suit, out for a stroll in the sunshine. A slightly sweaty lawyer. Maybe I've had a tough day in court. I see no sign of Jessica. Most of the people on the street are Chinese, so she ought to stand out. Then again, as Alex, so will I, which might give her a clue. Mike would have blended right in.

I find five dollars in my jacket pocket. For cover I buy a bottle of water and a small roll from a food vendor. Now I am just another anonymous lawyer out having his lunch.

As I chew the unappetising roll the results of my search for statues pop up. Just north of me, in Columbus Park, is a statue of Sun Yat-sen, first president of China. An Eastern leader. I may not have heard of him, but according to my search the park is home to locals playing mah-jong, cards and chess.

So which is it? I pull up a picture of Confucius Plaza. There is an open square, a statue of Confucius, but not much else. It looks more like a thoroughfare than somewhere to sit and play games. And noisy. Not the sort of place a blind player would choose.

I make my decision. I bin the roll, turn north into Columbus Park, and hope I've got it right. I try to look unhurried as I step on to the grass.

Where is the blind player? There is a group of boys playing basketball on a concrete court. It won't be one of them. A man and woman are practising what looks like t'ai chi with swords. Not them. More promisingly, clustered in a corner under a shady tree are groups of people playing cards and chess.

I stroll towards them, drinking my water.

At a stone chess table, opponents face off, one leaning forward, the other looking half asleep, eyes closed. The blind player? He says something and his opponent moves a piece for him.

Yes.

I look around. I don't want Jessica copying me. But no one else seems interested in the players.

I hesitate for a moment. If I get it wrong there is a time penalty. Then I walk over and lightly touch the man's shoulder. The scene freezes.

I let out a small sigh of relief, then look around again. Still no sign of Jessica. Is she ahead of me, or behind? The second clue flashes up.

Stage Two: Pier 54, a great ship sinks, touch the right anchor.

My map shows that Pier 54 is on the west side of Manhattan, on the Hudson River a good two miles away. It's a long way to go, especially as we are not allowed transport. Surely it's too obvious to suppose that I have to go to the pier and find an anchor. And what is the great ship?

Search "pier 54 new york" + "ship sinking"

After a moment the results appear:

Two matches:

1. RMS *Lusitania* departed Pier 54 New York, 1 May 1915, sunk by German U-boat 7 May 1915; 1,198 killed.

2. RMS *Carpathia* docked Pier 54 New York, 18 April 1912, with 712 survivors from the sinking of RMS *Titanic*.

It could be either. Touching the anchor suggests a physical memorial of some sort. Presumably both ship's anchors are at the bottom of the Atlantic Ocean. I search, but can't find any memorials in New York to the *Lusitania*. There are several for the *Titanic*. Less than half a mile away is the Titanic Memorial Lighthouse. Do I go north to Pier 54 and look for an anchor? Or south to the lighthouse?

It's got to be the lighthouse. Pier 54 itself is too obvious.

I glance behind me. There is still no sign of anyone interested in the chess players. I stuff the empty water bottle into my pocket, and start running. Left, then right, and under Brooklyn Bridge.

I duck down a side street and see the lighthouse ahead. It's in a park, a narrow triangle of land between two streets, with a few trees and benches. A disappointing memorial to the deaths of 1,600 people.

But more importantly for me the park contains no anchors. I walk over to the lighthouse, and circle it, looking for an engraving of an anchor. None.

There is a cobbled street next to the park, and beyond it a sign for the Seaport Museum. Between the trees I see rusty metal. An anchor? I move closer. Two anchors, framing the steps leading up to the museum.

Got it.

I walk over.

A young woman in bright yoga kit and a Yankees baseball cap is negotiating a child's pushchair down the steps of the museum. 'Could you give me a hand?' she asks.

Unthinking, courtesy kicks in. I reach over to grab the bottom of the pushchair, but then recoil an instant too late. Her eyes meet mine and I realise that she's a much younger version of Jessica. She lets the pushchair fall, and as I tangle with it she puts a hand on my shoulder, and whispers 'freeze'.

I curse. How could I be so stupid? I can't move and a timer in my lens starts counting down from sixty seconds.

Jessica smiles. 'Thanks, sweetie.' She steps out of my vision and I hear her sprint away over the cobbles. West, maybe.

It feels like the longest minute of my life. I spend the time wondering where Jessica got a pushchair. Did she just steal someone's child from the Seaport Museum?

Now I know that she is ahead of me, and well ahead.

'Zero.'

I jerk back to life. I know it's a simulation, and I know I'm in a hurry, but I can't stop myself checking the pushchair for a child. It's empty. I touch the right-hand anchor. Again, the scene freezes.

Stage Two complete.

Now I know what Jessica looks like, but she's long gone. The third clue appears.

Stage Three: 77, a flight to nowhere, pass through the water.

A flight to nowhere suggests the World Trade Center attacks of 11 September 2001. Two planes that crashed into the twin towers. The nearby memorial pools are well known, vast waterfalls where the north and south towers once stood. That could be 'through the water'.

But surely no one would put a prize in a national memorial, even in a simulation. And what does '77' mean? Besides, if it is one of the pools, which one?

I set up a search for a connection between 77 and 9/11; then, in case I am wrong about 9/11, a wider search with the entire clue.

With nothing else to go on I start running west towards the memorial site.

Traffic is backed up on Broadway. I dodge through, trying to catch up. Trying not to end it all by getting run over. To my left is a building that looks like a giant white hedgehog. I run past it. Heads turn, and a guard starts towards me. This is a place of contemplation, not a place to be running. Someone shouts.

I ignore them.

I still don't know which pool, though. If it is either of them. As I slow to a walk the results of my first search appear.

Search "77" + "9/11" + "world trade center memorial pools"

American Airlines Flight 77, hijacked on 11 September 2001, crashed into the Pentagon, killing all 64 people on board and 125 people on the ground. Names of the dead are inscribed on the South Pool of the National September 11 Memorial, Manhattan.

That must be it. The south pool. But it still doesn't feel right.

I turn left and walk past the underground museum to the south pool. There is a crowd at one corner.

'She jumped in!' someone shouts. 'Where's she gone?' A police officer has his gun drawn, pointing into the pool. But there is no one to be seen.

Seriously? The prize is down there? The clues fit. But my gut still tells me no.

Either way, Jessica is ahead of me. I have to decide now.

It looks a long way down, but I see no other option. With a silent apology I vault on to the surrounding nameplates, hang by my fingertips, and let go. The waterfall runs down the black slate side of the pool. I am soaked, I can see nothing, and have no grip. I hit the base of the pool hard, and find myself kneeling in a foot of water with a strong current pushing me towards the central well. There are people shouting at me from above, but I can't hear their words over the roar of the water.

I struggle to my feet. The police officer is waving his gun at me. Surely he isn't going to shoot me? Maybe they think I've jumped in to save Jessica. So I'm a hero. I turn my back on him. There's only one way to go. Jessica must have gone into the central well.

I slip and swim my way towards it. I try to pause at the edge, to see how far the drop is, but I misjudge it and the current pushes me over. I tumble into a deeper pool and take a gasp of breath as I am sucked under. It is dark here. I can't see or feel anything. I'm being pulled deeper.

This can't be right.

I hit what must be the floor. I edge my way along it, following the current. I still can't see anything, but it feels as though I am in a tunnel of some sort.

My lungs are burning, but I push forward. If this is right there must be a way out soon. The clue said to pass through the water.

Incongruously the results of my second search flash up before my eyes.

In 1969 a replica First World War Sopwith Camel fighter plane was installed on the roof of an office block at 77 Water Street.

There is a photo of a small aircraft at the end of an impossibly short green runway on the roof of a tall building, with '77' written on the runway in large white numbers. It's a flight that will never take off.

Idiot. I should have gone with my instincts. No one puts a prize in the bottom of a national memorial. And this fits the clue. It was a flight to nowhere – singular – not flights.

Did Jessica get this right? Was the story about her jumping some sort of set-up? Has she gone to 77 Water Street?

I try to turn round, to swim against the current, but it is far too strong. Even if I can get back to the pool I have no idea how I will get out. The walls are slick granite. And if Jessica got it right I am too far behind anyway.

My head hits the roof and I start to panic. I'm pushed back until my feet hit something. Something soft. And it is clawing at my legs.

For a moment I imagine some multi-limbed sea creature. Then I realise that Jessica made the same mistake I did. She is pulling herself up my legs, or pulling me towards her, for what purpose I don't know. Perhaps just the desperate desire to cling to life, any life, for a moment longer.

There is only one way out of this now. I kick backwards with what little strength I have left, and her grip loosens. We are both dying, but I have a slight edge. I reach into my pocket and fumble for the empty water bottle I put there earlier. I struggle to loosen the lid.

The breath explodes from my lungs and I bring the bottle to my lips, swallowing half water and half air, trying not to choke.

It is just enough.

Jessica's grip goes and she is swept away into the darkness. Despite everything, I feel sorry for her. No one deserves to die like this, and it feels sick to die in a memorial to so many dead. We were misled on purpose.

But Jessica's death means I live.

My lungs are going to collapse. As I am about to give up and take a breath of the icy water, I am blinded by light.

•

Game terminated.

•

I was lying, gasping, on the floor of the game booth. Water was rapidly draining away beneath me.

I was shivering, whether from cold or shock I wasn't sure. I turned my head and threw up.

So I had won, and we were still alive.

Unlike Jessica. Left floating in the water where she had drowned in Room D. But at least body disposal was free. Lucky Jessica.

I rolled on to my back. As my eyes adjusted to the light I realised that there was a message on the screen.

Victory by death

Congratulations, Mr Du Bois.

You have been credited with 2.69 years.

You have ten minutes to leave the booth.

Or what? Would they turn the water on again? I wasn't going to wait to find out.

A door had opened on one side of the room, revealing a shower and a new set of clothes.

By the time I was clean and dressed I had thrown up twice more. At least the shaking had stopped.

I binned my wet clothes and stepped out into the corridor.

I returned the trainers to the girl at the entrance. She seemed unperturbed by the death going on around her.

She gave me a slight smile. 'Well done, Mr Du Bois. Ms Engels had credit of 3.29 years. We have deducted our ten per cent fee. There is also a local fine of one hundred days for culturally insensitive intrusion. Your final credit is 2.69 years.'

That seemed like a scam to me. A fine for breach of local laws in a simulation made no sense.

'One hundred days?' I asked. 'That seems steep. I know it's wrong to jump into a national memorial, but it was just a simulation. And your clue was deliberately ambiguous. We both got it wrong. This must happen all the time – it's just a way for the arena to steal credit.'

She smiled. 'I'm sorry. I don't write the games or make the rules.' She leaned across the counter and said quietly, 'I'll tell you what, you can have a T-shirt *and* a water bottle.'

There was no point in arguing. I took my gifts and headed outside.

It had not been worth the 2.69 years. I would remember Jessica for longer than that. I could still hear the roar of water in my ears and feel the frantic clawing at my legs. Normally you don't get that close to death in the games. Your own or anyone else's. This had been *much* too personal. Too many people died in the death parks who didn't deserve to.

I checked the time. I had just over an hour left. For once I needed a drink, and I didn't care what it cost. I headed back towards the Excelsior.

•

The Diamond Room was still going strong. If anything, it seemed busier than when I'd left. I found a seat out of the way and ordered a whisky. The hand that raised the glass to my mouth was shaking.

Forget Jessica. She'd have killed me if she could. Jessica died because of Sierra – she was the one who had signed me up for the game. I'd had no choice.

Half the drink went down my front, but I felt a bit better once I had finished it, and ordered another. That was the last, though. I needed to find somewhere safe to drop out for Kate.

I had almost finished the second glass when someone slid into the seat opposite me. A slim blonde woman in a black dress that clung to every contour. For a moment I thought it was Jessica, and sat up sharply, spilling more of my drink.

She looked across at me and flashed perfect white teeth. Her eyes met mine in a blank stare, then looked down coyly. 'Do you want to have some fun?' she asked.

Most definitely not. I wasn't going to crown a thoroughly awful day with some soulless coupling with a sex dandi. Take an andi, leave out the mind to keep it dumb, insert some low-level AI, and you have a walking, talking sex toy that will comply with your every whim. Or rent her out to get some return on your investment. I sighed. Humanity could safely be relied on to pervert just about anything.

I shook my head and stood up. 'No thanks.'

She didn't react. It seemed that she had not been programmed to show disappointment.

As I left I logged on.

All. Thanks, Sierra. Next time, ask before you sign me up for something. As you can tell from the fact that you are waking up, we are still alive. Just. Your 'rather lovely' girl isn't. She was tricky but I found a way to beat her. This will cover Mike's new legs. We might prefer new lungs (we almost drowned). Someone else can do the next one. Alex.

KATE

I woke feeling great.

I always did. Between Alex and me there was almost four hours R & R. A real rest while nanomes swarmed through us checking, patching, fixing, healing. And some real sleep. Not the brief upload/download that the others got.

Besides, I followed Alex. There was a benefit to coming after the fat kid with an inferiority complex. Or rather, the once fat kid now living in the athlete's body, who still didn't think he was good enough. Who thought that the way to be loved was to be best at everything. Kind, sweet, loyal Alex.

I looked around. I was lying in the middle of a large bed in what appeared to have once been an expensive hotel suite. It was now pretty run-down. Wallpaper peeling, a cracked mirror on the opposite wall, a layer of dust over everything, and a smell of damp.

On the bedside table to my right was a water bottle and a paper bag. I sat up and took a gulp of the water. I spluttered and almost dropped the bottle as it sprouted ears and a mouth and started singing something about Arena X. Wherever that was.

I banged the lid shut. The mouth blew me a kiss, then disappeared. The ears folded in after it. I looked down and realised I was wearing a T-shirt with the same logo.

For God's sake, Alex. Who picks up this tat?

I looked suspiciously at the paper bag, then opened it cautiously. Chocolate chip cookies, my favourite. And they weren't singing. Much better. Alex always looked after me.

I got out of bed and wandered over to the window to see where I was.

Somewhere high. The sun was rising between distant tower blocks, but nowhere was higher than me. The death park was spread out below. Derelict buildings stretching to the razor-wire fence. This would have been a city suburb before humanity sorted out its overpopulation problem. Now it was just a death park. Abandoned. Only the arenas, bars and clubs were still open. The rest was left to rot.

Anywhere else these buildings would long ago have been demolished. As the population fell there was less and less need for high-rise living, and the concrete tower blocks would have been turned into sustainable eco-homes. Eventually that would happen even in the death parks. The green of the outside world would consume these islands of concrete for ever. For the moment, however, they were a lingering reminder of forgotten times.

I logged on.

Morning, Katie. I thought you would enjoy the view. Although I am

not sure it was worth climbing twenty floors given the state I was in. The door lock isn't working, but the lifts aren't either, so I reckon you are pretty safe. I found you some cookies – enjoy.

We almost died last night. Sierra's drinking is slowing me down. She entered me in a game without even asking us. And couldn't resist getting a dig in about Montreal again [attached]. Can't she just let it go?

Love you, Alex.

Sweet, needy, bitchy Alex. He needed to let Sierra's antics wash over him. She felt no guilt, and every time he reacted to her she got what she wanted. We all needed to forget what had happened in Montreal and move on.

There was a group message from Alex complaining about Sierra being drunk in a bar again. What did he expect? Why we had put them together I couldn't remember. She had probably seemed exciting to him when he was seventeen. But being next to one another in the cycle did not mean that you got to do anything together. It just meant that the one who followed got to clean up the other's mess. And Sierra left *a lot* of mess.

He wanted an hour of her time. She was never going to change, however much we fined her. If three months in stasis hadn't done any good then losing the odd hour certainly wouldn't. I hesitated, then voted yes. The less time Sierra had in the death park the more chance we had of winning.

There was a second message from Alex telling us all, in his usual passive-aggressive way, how brilliantly he had done in the game. Alex the reluctant killer. I was sure he had surprised himself.

Alex, sweetie. Thanks for the munchies. You are too kind. I hate the stupid singing water bottle. Well done last night. It sounds like a tough one. Don't let S wind you up like that. We can't change what happened in Montreal. I know you've moved on – so don't let her drag you back again. It's what she wants. I've given you the hour. Hope the others agree. K. xxx

I skimmed through the rest of my messages. The downside to being first in the cycle was that I had to deal with most of the group admin. Only one message was of interest.

HIGH PRIORITY, DO NOT IGNORE: CGov to K. Weston. You have been selected to serve for one month with immediate effect as a Ruler of Choice. Congratulations. This is your chance to participate in the front line of democracy and shape the decisions for the future.

Your term will start immediately upon receipt.

Failure to carry out your civic duty will result in time penalties.

If you have any questions about the process, consult the attached file.

You will be reimbursed all time spent in performing your civic duty.

Under Protocol 2.1.7384 you are required to advise us immediately if you are mentally unstable, incapable or imminently dead.

I smiled to myself. Normally this would have been the last thing I wanted. I had been chosen once before. It sounded more exciting than the reality. As a Ruler of Choice you are one of millions who spend hours each day making tiresome decisions about spending, taxes, local law enforcement, and other tedious subjects. Decisions made by the public, not faceless politicians. Some people enjoyed the feeling of power. I didn't. It's particularly bad if you are a schizo, because time reimbursed gets spread between the group. So in fact I would only get back one-fifth of the time wasted. There are so few communes that no one seems concerned to correct this inequity.

But on this occasion I had an answer. I shot back a reply.

CGov. Sadly I will be unable to fulfil my civic duty, as I am imminently dead. I am part of a commune with ten days left to live. I will in the next month be undergoing transfer to a new body. Also, I am currently in a death park – so death may be even more imminent. Please confirm my removal. Kate Weston.

That would show them.

Alex had left a pack of new clothes at the foot of the bed. As I stripped off the stupid T-shirt and started to dress I was alerted to a call.

06:17: Identity withheld.

I hesitated, then answered. Voice calls were unusual, and I was curious.

'Who is this?'

'Ms Weston, my name is Amy Bird. You don't know me, but I would like to meet you.' Her voice was smooth and soft. 'I have an offer for you.'

'Is this a challenge? We have plenty of those. Post it and I will get back to you.'

'It's not a challenge I can post,' she said. 'There are . . . unconventional elements.'

'I'm not getting us involved in anything illegal,' I said. 'Try someone else. There are more than enough low-lifes in the park.'

Her voice hardened. 'It's you that I want, Ms Weston. I'm willing to offer you twenty years for almost nothing in return. Your boy Alex nearly got killed last night for a fraction of that.'

'What? How do you know about that?' Games are meant to be private. But there have always been stories of black-market gambling syndicates streaming games and staking fortunes on who lives and dies. Or voyeurs watching because they find real death better entertainment than make-believe.

'I know a lot about you, Ms Weston, and your commune. I could just wait a few hours and make the same offer to Mike. We both know he doesn't want to lose this body. It was his, after all. Offer him twenty years to spend on the next one and he'll grab it. Wouldn't you rather be the one to get the time for your group?'

She was right. Mike would jump at the chance. And *twenty years*. We were here fighting over scraps and this woman was offering almost a lifetime. But no one offers twenty years for nothing. Still, better that I met her than leave it to Mike.

'Where and when?' I asked. 'I don't have a lot of time.'

'That's the problem with you schizos,' she said. 'Always in a hurry. You have three hours and forty-two minutes. That's more than enough. We will meet opposite the Borth Street Arena at seven.'

She cut the call without waiting for my response.

It was an easy walk to the arena through streets that were mostly deserted at that time of morning. The only other person I saw was a thin man in a long coat with a suitcase at his feet, standing at the end of an alley. He smiled, his teeth flashing.

'Hey,' he shouted. 'Are you playing today? I've got what you need to win. Brain boosters, muscle boosters, endurance, uppers, downers. Whatever you want, I've got it. All genuine and guaranteed to work. My prices are low. It could be the difference between life and death.'

I shook my head. 'No thanks.'

'C'mon, make me an offer. It's good stuff. I never get any complaints.'

I laughed. 'The ones who *would* complain are dead.'

He chuckled in response. 'Well, don't come back crying if you die today.' He made a show of looking at the contents of his suitcase. 'I don't think I've got anything labelled "resurrection".'

I smiled and walked on.

I hadn't been to the Borth Street Arena before. It looked even seedier than most, a single-storey prefab painted black and covered in graffiti. The plot next to it was empty and overgrown, and on the other side stood a towering high-rise. Opposite sat a run-down park with six-foot-high weeds and a rusty playground.

Despite what she said, we would not have been meeting here if what Ms Bird had planned was above board.

A woman was sitting on a bench beside the remains of a swing. I scanned her.

AMY BIRD

Android

Expiry: 80 years

Age: 67 years

Credit: 7.5 years

So she had thirteen years left, and a credit of 7.5 years – just over twenty, and she was offering to give it all to me. Which couldn't be right. Despite the name, no one comes to a death park to kill themselves.

She was older than she had sounded on the call. But that made sense, because although she was sixty-seven she didn't look it. She had kept the visual age of her body at around forty. Some andis are vain like that. She was tall and well-muscled, with short dark hair and bright blue eyes. Her physique was emphasised by the close-fitting trouser suit that she wore, black apart from ornate red buttons on the cuffs. Alex would have liked her.

She stood as I approached, and offered her hand. It felt warm, normal, but as usual with an andi her movements and expressions were just a little too perfect. Her smile didn't touch her eyes.

I repressed a shudder.

'Ms Weston, thank you for coming.'

'This is an odd place to meet, Ms Bird.'

'Please. Sit.' She waited for me to do so and then resumed her seat.

'What is it you want?' I asked.

'It is not what I want, it is what I can give you,' she replied. 'I have a unique but lucrative proposition for you.'

'You said you would give me twenty years. Which is all you

have. I don't trust andis at the best of times, and this makes no sense. If you're looking to kill yourself you should have done that when you were seventeen. You missed your chance.'

'I don't want to kill myself,' she said. 'I want to get out of this body. For that I need your help.'

'Why? And, more importantly, how? We both know it's not possible to just jump from one body to another when you feel like it.'

'As to why, to get revenge on my bastard of a husband. As to how, that's where you come in. I need a schizo, and there aren't many of you around.' She paused, and turned to me. For the first time there seemed to be some emotion in her eyes. Pleading. 'Look – give me two minutes of your time. Let me explain. If you don't want to help I'll find someone else who wants to earn an easy twenty years.'

'Make it quick,' I said. 'I still don't like the sound of this.' Two minutes for twenty years seemed a reasonable trade. I could still walk away.

'All right. The short version, then.' She nodded, as though composing her thoughts, and then continued. 'Ms Weston, being a schizo, you probably haven't had many relationships, and those you have had were doubtless short and shallow. We andis, on the other hand, tend to fall in love slowly but bond for life. Knowing that you have eighty years to live makes it easier. We are proof that it is the head not the heart that falls in love. Or so I believed.' She snorted. 'I won't bore you with the details, but I've been married now for twenty-four years. And I look the same today as I did when we got married. That should have been my first clue.'

'What do you mean?' I asked.

'It wasn't my choice,' she said bitterly. 'It's a foolish vanity to keep your body young while your mind ages. What's the point, when anyone can scan you and see your real age? But my husband – Charlie – insisted. Said he loved me for what I was. It turned out he loved the person he remembered, and not what I had become. It's got to the point where I want to leave him.'

'So.' I shrugged. 'Leave him. What's the problem?'

'If I do, I'll die,' she said.

'He's threatened to kill you? That's illegal. Leave him and report him.'

'It's not that simple,' she responded. 'What he's threatened is immoral, but not illegal. You will have seen that I have time in credit. I didn't win that here. A long time ago Charlie and I visited another death park. It was foolish, given how much time we still had and what was at stake. But we were young and we felt invulnerable. It turned out we *were* invulnerable, because we won and kept on winning. Charlie played most of the games. He was younger, stronger and faster. We agreed to share what we had won. So that we could grow old together.' She laughed bitterly at that. 'As you know, the parks are one of the few places where you can gift time. So he gave me half his winnings – twenty years. We had to record it legally, and it included a term that if we ever separated I had to give it back. I thought nothing of it at the time. I probably didn't even read it.'

'But you've spent most of it,' I said. 'You've only got 7.5 extra years left.'

'And that's the problem. If I have to repay twenty years I'll be

34

dead in six months. It's cruel. It seems he'll either have me tied to him or dead. He should have just bought himself a sex dandi.'

'It can't be legal,' I said.

'I've wasted plenty of time on the best lawyers, who've told me it is.'

'Look, I'm sorry for you. It's tough, but you don't seem to have much choice. Leave him and die, or stick with him and live. I don't see how I can help you.'

'There is a third option,' she said. 'I have . . .' she paused, 'friends. Friends with particular skills. They have procured another body, a recycled dandi.' She smiled. 'It's an aged body; Charlie would hate it. It has a little time credit. Enough for me to live a few more years on my own, in happiness. I can't take my time with me, but I *can* move my mind across. That's what I need you for.'

'Why me?'

'As I said, I need a schizo,' she said. 'You have, in that fine body of Mike's, five minds. But as with all schizos there is space for one more that you don't use. The sixth space is what controls your body, keeps it alive, performs routine maintenance during downtime at the end of each cycle. It's mostly empty. I want to borrow that space for twenty-four hours. In return you can have my twenty years. To all appearances you will have won it fair and square in a game and I will be dead. Charlie will be furious, but there's nothing he can do. We play, you win, and this body dies.'

I was concerned that she seemed to know more about how schizos worked than I did. 'Even if I agreed, how would that help you?' I asked. 'Your mind dies with your body. Only your time passes to me.'

'Not so.' She gestured across the street. 'My friends have

made special arrangements for me in that arena. With your consent to access the sixth space, when I die my mind will move there. Tomorrow you will be contacted and told where to find my new body, and they will make the transfer to the dandi. I have to trust you to do so since you will already have my time. But I imagine you will want to be rid of me anyway.'

This sounded dangerous, and I was far from convinced it was legal. She seemed genuine, and I felt sorry for her. But if we agreed and got caught there was a risk of some serious time fines. Then again, twenty years is twenty years.

She turned to me and put a hand on my arm. 'Will you help me, Ms Weston? Please?'

'I don't know,' I said. 'I'll have to ask the others. It will need a vote so you'll have to wait one cycle. I make no promises.'

'No,' she said, and her grip on my arm tightened. 'There's no time for that. Charlie knows I'm here, and he has people who will follow me and bring me back. This offer won't be here at the end of your cycle. I can't risk waiting that long. If you can't do it I'll have to try another schizo.'

I looked into her artificial eyes but could read nothing. I've never trusted andis. Who chooses to give up being human? Sure, I gave up my body, but I was still a person. Different sex, different race, but living, breathing flesh. Not something grown in a vat with a brain stuck inside.

Was I being scammed? This was a big decision that ought to be put to the group. But I knew what would happen if we voted. Mike and Sierra would be blinded by the amount of time on offer, and would say yes. Ben would be cautious, want to know much more, and would delay so long that we missed the chance.

Alex would agree to do whatever I suggested. So it would come down to me anyway.

But I would have valued their counsel.

Twenty years.

If I said yes we could pack up and leave with more time than we knew how to spend. And it would all be down to me.

I hesitated. 'Why me? Why not wait and go to Mike, or Sierra?'

'I need you,' she said. 'You're first in the cycle, you have the admin access codes, and are the only one who can let me into the sixth space without a full vote. There's no time for a full vote.'

She was right. Again, I was disturbed by just how much she knew about how schizos work.

'Give me a moment. I need to think.' I shook my arm free, stood up and walked away, circling through the long grass around the playground. I wanted those twenty years. I wanted to help her. She'd been wronged, and revenge sounded good.

Why was I having to make this decision alone? I knew what Mike, Sierra and Ben would have said. That didn't help. What would Alex have advised? He'd have told me to forget revenge and focus on the time that we could win. He hadn't wanted to come here, so he would have seen a chance to win big and get out. He would have told me to ignore the emotions and take the deal.

I walked back to the bench.

'All right, Ms Bird. I'm not sure I trust you, and if this is all part of some elaborate scam then we will come after you. But let's do this before I change my mind.'

The arena was unlike any I had ever seen. The door was rusty, and it screeched as Bird pulled it open. There was no one inside, just four rooms with faded numbers: 1 to 4.

'Are you sure this works?' I asked. 'It doesn't look very safe.'

'It's fine,' she said. 'I've made special arrangements for us to use it free from interference. I'll use Room 1; you use 2. Once this is over, leave straight away. My body will be removed later, after you've gone.'

'All right.' I swallowed hard. This no longer seemed like such a good idea. Maybe I was being tricked and she was actually after our time. I again regretted not getting the others' views.

'How's this going to work?' I asked. 'You say I'll win your time, but how do we guarantee that?'

'You will still need to play. It needs to look real in case anyone ever checks. However, all you need to do is beat me. I'll make sure that you do.'

It was too late to go back now. I had agreed to the game. It was play or forfeit. I stepped into Room 2.

While the rest of the building was decrepit, the game booth looked normal and functional. The door slid shut behind me, and a screen lit up.

Welcome, Ms Weston

Game:	The Search for Cupid
Objective:	Win the board
Stages:	One
Location:	Rugaard Castle, Denmark

A countdown appeared on the screen.

5:00

Then I received a message from Amy Bird:

Ms Weston, before we begin I need access.

With some misgivings, I sent her the codes.

•

I am standing with my back to a rough stone wall. My arms are above my head, my wrists shackled to an iron ring. The room is dimly lit, circular, unfurnished apart from a wooden desk and two chairs. There is a single, narrow window opposite me – too high for me to see anything other than a sky filled with black clouds. It is open, with a cold wind blowing through.

Amy Bird is seated at the desk.

'Kate,' she says. 'I wasn't sure you would fall for that.'

'What do you mean?' Fear rises in my throat. This feels wrong. 'What is going on? Is this the game?'

'This is the game,' she says, gesturing to a wooden box on the desk. The lid is closed, so I can't tell what it is inside. 'This . . . and that.' She points to the window and holds up her hand, as though for silence. From outside I hear a loud thump, wood striking wood, a scream, and then a cheer.

'What was that?' I ask.

'The gallows. Seventeenth-century Denmark is a barbarous

place. They haven't yet mastered the art of the long drop. So death tends to either be by slow strangulation or the head being ripped off. From the crowd reaction that sounded like a ripper to me – a quick death, at least.'

'What's all this about? What's the game?'

She ignores me. 'Did you know, people sometimes paid for others to pull on their legs to make death quick? Or got their relatives to do it.' She walks over the window and looks out. 'I was wrong. It's a strangler. A shame you can't see this, really, because that's what you are trying to avoid. The kicking legs are particularly evocative.'

'Let me go,' I snarl, pulling against the chains. 'I didn't agree to this.'

She turns back to me. 'Interesting that you have lived for twenty-five years in a man's body but manifest here as female. As the young Kate. More pleasant for me, I suppose.'

I glance down and realise that she is right. At least as far as I can see. I appear to be in the body of young woman, dressed in a rough brown shirt, dark leggings and muddy leather boots.

She, in contrast, is dressed as she was in the park. She doesn't seem to be fully in the game.

'What do you want from me?' I ask. 'Was that story outside all a lie?'

'Not entirely. Mostly what I want is what I told you – access to your minds.' She walks across to me, and stops with her face inches from mine. I try to shrink further into the wall. I turn my head away but she grips my chin with one hand and turns it back.

'There are things I'd like to do to you,' she says. 'But we're going to have to wait.' She strokes my cheek with one finger, and looks me up and down. 'Not just female, but a seventeen-year-old girl. I mustn't be misled by your apparent innocence, attractive though it is.' Her thumb runs lightly across my lips. She stares into my eyes. Her hands move lower, down the front of my shirt and come to rest on my waist. She leans in closer, her lips brushing mine.

A spark runs down my spine. But this is all wrong. She's an andi. I jerk back and my head strikes the stone wall painfully. 'Stop it,' I say angrily. 'What the hell are you doing?'

Her tongue flicks across my upper lip. I have nowhere to go. I close my eyes.

Then she steps away, and laughs. 'Don't pretend you aren't interested, Kate. But you're right, we don't have time for this now. We need to play the game. There are things I need to do first.' She gestures to the box on the desk. 'I suggest you spend your time learning the rules.'

She moves back towards me, and for a moment I think she is going to try to kiss me again. Then she reaches above my head, clicks something, and steps away. My hands are free. My arms fall to my side, throbbing painfully as the blood returns to them.

'Where are we?' I ask.

'I told you,' says Bird. 'Denmark, in the seventeenth century. Rugaard Castle, to be precise.' She steps over to the door. 'I'll be back shortly.' She opens the door and passes through quickly. I hear it lock behind her.

I rub my arms and the pain begins to subside. My back and shoulders feel stiff.

I walk over to the window and look out. I appear to be in the tower of a small castle. Below is a stone-flagged courtyard, dominated by a wooden gallows. The trapdoor is open, and a hooded body hangs by its neck, swinging in the wind. No longer kicking. The body is small and looks to be that of a woman, hands tied behind her back. The crowd I heard cheering has dispersed. The courtyard is empty apart from the body and a masked man whom I take to be the executioner. As I watch he unties the rope supporting the body and carefully lowers it to the ground.

I shiver. I have seen enough. I reach out to pull the window shut. It catches the wind and closes with a bang.

The executioner looks up from where he is crouched over the body with a knife. He sees me in the window and mimes drawing the knife across his throat. He smiles at me.

I step back quickly, out of sight.

This isn't helping. I try the door, but it is firmly locked.

I turn to the desk. The box contains a pair of dice, small metal figurines of men and women, and a hinged wooden board. I open the board and set it down on the desk. It is headed *The Royal Pastime of Cupid, or The Entertaining Game of the Snake*. The board is dominated by a brightly painted coiled snake, its crowned head at one end, its tail at the other. Its body consists of sixty-three numbered spaces, starting at its head and spiralling into the centre of the board. The path ends at a formal garden containing a statue of Cupid, poised with bow and arrow, couples walking arm in arm. Every seventh space contains a smaller picture of Cupid. Other spaces contain a bridge, a fountain, a wood, and an image of Death standing next to a coffin.

The rules are printed down both edges of the board. As far as I can tell it seems entirely to be a game of chance, depending upon the luck of the dice. If I am to play Bird at this I don't see how she can be sure that I will win.

My thoughts are interrupted by the sound of the door being unlocked. It opens, and Amy Bird steps through, followed by a priest in a black robe and a skullcap. Bird is now wearing rough clothing that matches mine. Unseen by the priest, she winks at me and sits in the chair opposite.

The priest stands next to the desk. His hands are folded in front of him, clasping a copy of the Bible. His expression is grave. He looks from one to the other.

'Mistress Weston, Mistress Bird,' he says. 'You have each been tried by Baron Arenfeldt and found guilty of witchcraft, consorting with the Unnamed One. In his generosity the Baron has sentenced you to be hanged, not burned at the stake. In yet a further sign of his generosity, and against my advice, the Baron is prepared to offer clemency to one of you. Whichever one of you defeats the other in this game will be spared. I am here to ensure fair play. May God's mercy be with you.'

'Let's get this done,' says Bird.

I take a female figure, Bird a male one, and we place them at the serpent's head.

'You start,' says Bird, handing me the dice. As I roll them she turns to the priest. 'It's stuffy in here, Father, could you open the window for us?' He nods and steps over to it.

I roll a one and a three. As the priest's back is turned Bird reaches over and changes the one to a four. I am about to protest but Bird puts a finger to her lips, for silence. The priest turns back and raises an eyebrow. 'A lucky seven,' he says. 'And four and three. You must be blessed.'

I look at the rules again: 'He that throws first of all 7 must take notice of what he hath thrown for if it be 1 and 6 he goes forward to 16, if it be 2 and 5 to 25, if it be 4 and 3 he goes to 43.'

Surprised, I move my figure to forty-three. With one throw, and some help from Bird, I am already two-thirds of the way round the board.

She throws a five, lands on a bridge, and moves her piece to a chair on the twelfth space. It's too quick for me to follow, but I look up at the priest, who nods.

I roll a six, and land on a Cupid at forty-nine. This one I do remember: 'He that throws upon Cupid, must not rest there but go as many forward as he hath thrown.' I move forward another six, passing over a tangled wood.

Bird rolls an eight. She is still a long way behind.

My biggest risk now is Death standing next to the coffin: 'He that throws upon 59, where the coffin stands must give way to the corpse, pay for the grave and begin the game again in his turn.' I hold my breath as the dice bounce around, settling on eleven. I move my figure to the garden at sixty-three, and sit back, relieved. I am finished. Bird was right – this was easy.

'Not so fast,' says the priest. He points to the final rule printed on the board: 'He that comes first into the delightful Garden of Cupid where 63 is, he hath won the Game, but if he throws above the Number 63, then he must go so far backward as he hath exceeded the number.'

Cursing under my breath I move my figure back to sixty, one away from Death.

Bird rolls an eight, lands on a Cupid and moves a further eight.

As I pick up the dice again a squall hits the window and rain-drops blow in. Bird catches my eye. 'Sorry, Father,' she says, 'but we're getting wet now. Would you mind closing it?'

The priest sighs but steps over to the window again. I throw the dice. Before they have finished moving Bird has turned them to a two and a one, giving me the three that I need. Once more I move my figure to the garden in the centre of the board. Bird may be helping me, as she said she would, but I still don't trust her.

The priest turns back, seemingly surprised that it has ended so quickly. He lays a hand on my shoulder. 'You are truly blessed, Daughter. It is not God's will that you die today.' He turns to Bird. 'You, my child, must come with me.'

She looks across at me, and smiles. 'Well done. You beat the bad guy. Sort of. Now I must go and die. Enjoy the rest of your lives.' She and the priest leave the room.

The door is left open. It seems I have won. Why has Bird done this? Why did she behave so strangely at the start of the game?

A spiral staircase leads downwards. A door at the bottom opens into the courtyard containing the gallows. Rain is being driven into my face by a gusting wind. It's a grim day to die. The corpse that was on the ground has gone. Amy Bird and the priest are standing by the wooden steps at the foot of the gal-lows. The executioner is behind her, tying her hands.

I'm not staying to watch. I can still taste her kiss, stale on my lips. Whatever she is really up to, I don't want to see her die. I turn my back on them and walk out through the gate to the courtyard.

•

I was back in Room 2, damp from the rain, but alive. I was struggling to understand what had happened to me. It was all very odd. Bird had had me at her mercy, but instead of taking advantage she had fixed the game so that I won. And then she had died. It didn't make any sense.

A message appeared on the screen.

Victory

Congratulations, Ms Weston.
You have been credited with 20.5 years.
You have five minutes to leave the booth.

I might have won, but something was wrong. What had Bird meant when she said that she wanted to do things to me? There was something strangely intimate and familiar in her behaviour. I felt as though I had been double-crossed, but she had done what she promised and let me win. I had got all her time. I was confused and slightly afraid.

Something wasn't right.

I left the room quickly and went over to Room 1. It was locked, but rusting, and I easily wrenched it open.

The room was empty. No body. No Amy, alive or dead. She couldn't have been removed that quickly. The room felt unused. It had been raining in the game, but the floor and walls were dry. Had she really died? Had I even being playing her at all? But if not, how had we got a credit of over twenty years?

I checked the other two rooms, but there was no sign of her there either.

09:28 – I had thirty-two minutes left, so no time to look into this. I needed to move fast. It was pointless to ask Mike to do anything, as he had a race to run. Equally pointless to ask Sierra. For other reasons.

I left the arena and headed back towards the centre of the death park, where I knew I could find a cheap bed and safety. It might have been free but I was not going back to Alex's stupid high-rise.

As I walked I composed a message to Ben. He was going to have to work out what had just happened to us. And more importantly, why?

MIKE

I was in a locker bed with just enough room to sit up without banging my head. Typical Kate, never spending any more time than necessary.

My electrolyte drink and protein smoothie were by my side. Reasons to be cheerful.

I stretched, feeling the ripple of muscles loosening from my head down to my toes.

This always was the perfect body.

I was in great shape when we all met, twenty-five years ago. There was never any doubt who we were going to choose as host. For all Kate's angular charms, and Sierra's sensuous curves, they were never in the running. And Alex was a joke. As wide as he was tall, and most of it fat. Ben the opposite, beanpole thin and without a muscle in sight.

In twenty-five years our body had only got better, thanks mostly to me. It was the product of at least two hours of gym per cycle. Sometimes Ben complained that I left us exhausted, but that was a small price to pay for what he got in return. And it wasn't as though he ever did anything other than sit around and play games. The height of activity for Ben was to venture outside and go to a public game booth.

Our stats were impressive. 6 foot 2 of lean muscle, with a resting heart rate of 41. A 10 kilometre pb of 30:32. We could swim 100 metres in 51.2 seconds.

Those were world-class times, and no thanks to the others. If Sierra hadn't spent her time poisoning us with alcohol, and Ben had occasionally got up out of his seat, we would have been even better.

True, it was getting old, but I was still going to be sorry to say goodbye. Although the prospect of a blank canvas to start all over again thrilled me. It was the reason why, at seventeen, I'd chosen to be a schizo. I'd be the one athlete who never slowed down with age.

As I drank I sent a message.

All. We need to get on and make a decision about our next body. I have produced a shortlist of four for you to vote on [file attached]. This is important. We don't want to leave it to the last minute. Two male, two female. I don't mind which. Let's get it down to two by next cycle. I am also going to put together a list of suggested enhancements, and cost them. Mike.

I checked my messages. There was one from Alex saying that he had almost drowned but won two-and-a-half years. Impressive. He also wanted us to punish Sierra. I replied.

Alex, I'm voting in favour but we can't just keep taking Sierra's time whenever she screws up. We know she's not like us, and she needs our help. She's been going through a rough patch and being here

with so many bars and clubs probably isn't helping. Try to have a bit
of compassion. Mike.

Then one from Kate.

Hi chaps, weird cycle. If you check our credit you will see that I
acquired 20.5 years! That's not a joke. Some mad andi offered me
that to play a game against her, which she said I couldn't lose. And
I couldn't. She helped me win. It didn't make much sense. Who
comes to a death park with twenty years? And gives it all away?
Anyway, now it belongs to us. Let's not waste it. Mike has some
race that he says he can't lose, but after that I suggest we cash out.
Vote on that by next cycle. K.

I found that hard to believe. How had Kate won more than
twenty years? But our credit showed 24.2 years. So it was true.
This changed everything.

All. Scrub my earlier message. Just seen Kate's. Way to go Kate!!
With that sort of time we can be looking at something pre-treated
from EliteCorps. I will take a look and circulate a shortlist later.
Good one, Kate.

I logged on quickly, excited.

Welcome to EliteCorps, the place to come if you want to have the
best body your time can buy. We deal in trade-in, rebirth or new
purchases. We offer full genetic mapping and guaranteed disease-
free for twenty-five years. If *you* are not happy, *we* are not happy.

Choose from one of our three base models, and then select your desired enhancements: THE ATHLETE, THE GENIUS or THE ALL-ROUNDER.

There were bound to be arguments as to which one we chose. But I knew what I wanted. With an EliteCorps Athlete base model, improved by me, we could come to the death parks whenever we liked, and win. By the start of our third life we would have more time than we could possibly spend.

THE ATHLETE

Get a seventeen-year-old body that has been carefully nurtured from birth, with a scientifically proven diet and years of careful coaching. We guarantee at least five years of dedicated coaching to the sport of your choice. Order in advance and we will train the body to your requirements (non-refundable deposit required).

We also provide a ten-year post-purchase coaching service to maintain you in optimum shape, which can be extended on an annual basis at low cost.

And don't think that because you have chosen the Athlete that you are compromising on brain power. You may not be getting the extreme levels of the Genius, but we guarantee a base IQ of at least 120. (Actual levels will depend upon the implanted mind(s).)

That is just the start. Choose the enhancements you want to add, mental or physical, HERE. We are currently offering two-for-one on retractable webbing – buy the hands and get the feet for free.

Base body cost is 18.5 years. Enhancements priced individually.
Contact us now to discuss the package you want and multi-deals.

Fun as this was, I realised I did not have time for it. I was going to have to wait. Last cycle I had signed up to a 10k knock-out race that started at 11:30. I needed to eat, warm up, get to the arena and win it.

I finished up my drinks, got dressed, and headed out.

•

'Welcome to the Safari Elimination 10k.' The announcer is a tall man dressed all in black, with an old-fashioned jacket with long tails. He wears a top hat. 'This is winner takes all. Ten will die. One will live.'

He looks at the athletes in front of him. We are an odd-looking group. Seven men and four women. Many look as though they can barely run a hundred metres, let alone ten thousand. One of the men is twice my size, grossly overweight, and wearing a vest saying 'Mr Flabby'. My guess is that he will be one of the fastest – the disadvantage of simulated runs is that you can choose whatever appearance you want and it becomes a game of bluff and double bluff before the start.

I see no point in playing those games. I don't need to. I have stuck with my normal appearance. I prefer to intimidate rather than bluff.

We are gathered in a grassy clearing in the middle of a forest. It is enclosed by a fence. In front of us is a metal gate, and behind us another one. Both are presently locked.

'This is a race with a difference,' says the announcer. 'You will leave through that gate.' He points to the one in front of us. 'You will complete a circuit through the park of precisely one kilometre, and will return through that gate.' He indicates the one behind us. 'At the end of each circuit, after the last runner has re-entered, there will be a two-minute break before the next lap begins. So the quicker you get here the longer you can rest.' He pauses.

'There is one other thing. Although we're in the middle of a safari park with wild animals, you will be safe for the first 900 metres of each loop. The last hundred metres is along a wooden bridge that brings you back to the gate. The bridge carries you across a river swarming with crocodiles. As the last runner crosses, the treads of the bridge will collapse behind him, or her. On the first loop, ten of you will be allowed back through the gate before it seals shut. The last runner will fall into the river below and meet the crocodiles.'

He smiles to us. 'And so on. Until only one of you is left. You have between you brought to the race a total of 32.2 years. That is unusually high,' he says, glancing over at me. 'Deducting our small fee for organising this event, that leaves a winner's prize of twenty-eight years.' He pauses, and looks around the group. 'Run like your life depends upon it. Because it does.'

I have done these events before. Sometimes in real life, sometimes simulated. The theatrics of this one are a bit unnecessary, but I can see that it makes for a good race. Run to the death. Win or get eaten. The basics are the same: tactics and pacing. It holds no fears for me.

'The race will begin in one minute. Make your preparations. Make your peace.'

There is a tension in the air. Jackets are discarded, laces tightened, muscles flexed. One of the female runners jumps up and down on the spot – wasted energy.

I find a place near the back of the pack, and wait.

A klaxon sounds, the gate swings open, and we are off.

A group of three leaps out ahead, quickly opening up a lead of ten metres or more. We let them go. There are no prizes for winning the first circuit; or any of the others until the last one. It is all about not coming last. There is no point in wasting energy trying to come first in a race that you don't need to win.

Behind the three leaders there is then a group of five, and just behind them Mr Flabby and me. The pace is very easy. I glance across at him, and he is moving smoothly. I was right.

We pass along a dusty track through the forest, the only sounds the distant roar of animals, the light pounding of shoes on dirt, and heavy breathing.

After little more than a minute we burst out of the forest on to open grassland, and the path turns to the left. A few hundred metres ahead I can see a wooden tower, no doubt the start of the bridge. I edge closer behind the group of five ahead. Mr Flabby follows me.

The entrance to the bridge looks narrow, no more than three people across. I don't want to be stuck at the back at that point. I accelerate slightly, overtaking a dark-haired man who is breathing heavily.

Then we are on the bridge. It is narrow and noisy, our feet echoing off the wooden slats. I can hear a crashing behind me as slats swing down. There is water below us, but no sign of the crocodiles. There are seven ahead of me. Eighth is comfortable enough. I don't want to show my hand yet. Then the gate is ahead. I plunge through it, with another at my heels.

I hear a scream behind me, and turn to see the dark-haired man crash into the gate and then fall away. The floor of the bridge has entirely disappeared. There is splashing and screaming for a moment, and then silence.

That was perhaps a little closer than I would have liked.

I look around the clearing. There are ten of us gasping for breath, looking slightly shocked.

'Two minutes,' says the man in the top hat.

I feel fine. That was easy. My heart rate has dropped and my breathing is almost normal. I grab my bottle and take in a quick burst of electrolytes.

'One minute.'

We all edge closer to the gate. Ready to go again.

The klaxon sounds, the gate opens, and we are off.

Again the same three head out first. Stupid tactics. I stick in the middle of the main group and finish up sixth. Feeling good. We lose one of the women on the bridge this time round.

And so on, another five times. Two out of the three leaders have gone by then, tired from their early efforts at pointless victories. One remains, plus a blonde woman in black leggings and a vest, Mr Flabby, and me. I have the measure of them. The one-time leader is puffing hard. He finished second to last on the previous circuit. He looks across at me and I catch fear in his eyes. The woman won, but is trying to hide the fact that she is limping slightly. Mr Flabby still looks comfortable, but I am confident I can take him.

We go again, the one-time leader slipping as we enter the

bridge, and falling victim to the crocodiles. The blonde woman wins again, and I finish just behind her. But I can tell she is hurting more now.

'So,' says the announcer in the top hat, 'we are down to the final three. Well done to you. Who will it be? Two minutes and we start again.'

I am puzzled as he walks over to me and puts a hand on my arm. The scene freezes. The forest falls quiet. Everyone stops moving. Apart from him.

'Mr Ganzorig.' He pauses, struck by a thought. 'That's a fine Mongol name you have there. Your parents stayed with the traditions even as the blood of the Khan thinned. But I'll stick with Mike, if I may. It's easier.'

'What . . .' I'm surprised at the extent of his knowledge. Most people just assume I'm Chinese. But what's going on? 'What is this?' I ask. 'This is quite irregular.'

'Indeed it is, Mike. This is all rather irregular.' He smiles. 'But entertaining.' He turns away from the others, as though he has a secret to tell me. 'Perhaps you should call me Amy.'

I am confused. 'What are you?' I ask. 'You're meant to just be some AI routine. You're not even real.'

'Things are, as you say, irregular. Let me just say that I am a friend – no, an acquaintance – of Kate's. We did a deal, she and I, and she gave me access to places where she shouldn't really have allowed anyone. Especially me. It was silly of her, but greed overcame fear. So I have changed the rules a little for this game. I am sure you think of yourself as pretty much unbeatable, and rightly so in normal circumstances. But there are two things you should know about this race. First, as I am sure you have

57

guessed, *he* is not all that he appears.' He gestures to Mr Flabby. 'He is certainly as good as you, probably better. We shall find out shortly.

'Second, and as important, the consequences of losing this race are rather more severe than you might realise. If you lose, you will be wiped. Your commune won't just lose its time and be reborn in a week or so. That may still happen to the others, but it will be without you. Lose this race, Mike, and it is all over for you. Mindwiped.'

What? This can't be right. *Mindwiped?* My mind erased. Not saved in stasis. Not transferred to another body. Deliberately destroyed. When a mind is wiped it's lost for ever.

I'd be dead.

'But there are rules,' I say. 'The worst that can happen to a schizo here is that we lose *this* life. No one can *die*.'

'What can I say, Mike? The rules have changed.' He shrugs. 'Oh, look, we're about to start. No time to chat. Perhaps the threat of death, real death, will sharpen your mind and speed your legs.'

He walks back to the gate and everything returns to normal. The noises of the forest, the sounds of breathing.

'One minute left,' he announces.

My thoughts are racing. This can't be right. If a schizo dies in a game then all five minds are preserved, ready to be implanted into a new body. Yes, you lose all the time you've won already, and what little time you have left – in our case just ten days. But your mind doesn't die. That's impossible. A schizo still has other lives left to live.

If I am being told the truth then somehow, in a way I don't

understand, Kate's deal with this Amy person has enabled him – her – to change the rules. What was Kate thinking, letting this happen? Or is this just some ploy to make me panic and lose the challenge? Is this someone's way of unsettling me and winning all our time?

I don't believe that there is anyone in the park who can beat me in a fair race. I am fitter, stronger and faster than anyone here. Whoever Mr Flabby is must know that. This is their only way of beating me, to make me believe that I will die if I lose. Well I'm not going to lose.

Before I have a chance to worry more the klaxon goes, and we are off.

Whatever happens I am not troubled about this circuit. I know that the blonde woman is finished. There are really only two of us left. So even if what I have just been told is true – which seems bizarre – it won't matter on this circuit. But it can't be true. That is not how it works.

I am breathing hard by the time we reach the bridge, but ahead of the other two. For the first time in the race I win a circuit. The blonde woman disappears behind us.

'Two minutes,' says the man in the top hat.

Mr Flabby is standing next to him, bent over, hands on his knees, breathing hard. I walk over to them. He's good, but I don't believe he's as good as me. I hold out my hand: 'May the best man win.'

He straightens up, ignoring my outstretched arm.

I laugh. 'Fine. Give my regards to the crocodiles.'

He looks at me with contempt. '*Zalupa. Svoloch.*' He spits out the words with a heavy accent.

The announcer coughs. 'My Russian is a little rusty, Mike. But I think that loosely translates as "bastard scumbag".'

'Dickhead,' I say.

The announcer blinks. 'Excuse me?'

'*Zalupa*,' I say. 'Dickhead, not bastard. It's one thing you learn from two weeks spent on a freighter with a crew from Kazakhstan.'

I turn back to Mr Flabby. '*Mudak*,' I say, and spit on the ground in front of him.

He flinches, and I walk away smiling.

My breathing is almost normal, my heart rate below 100. But adrenaline is coursing through my body, and is hard to damp down. I can feel panic rising. I know that I am the best here, but still something isn't right about this. Even before I'm running my heart rate is starting to rise.

The klaxon sounds for the last time.

We are both being cagey. I let Mr Flabby take the lead, but then he drops the pace and I overtake him. I have no need to turn to look where he is as I can hear him on my shoulder, treading lightly but breathing hard.

We leave the forest and run out into the sunlight of the grassland for the last time. I cough in the dusty air and miss a stride. A toe clips my heel and I stumble. Does he believe that the only way to beat me is to trip me up? That's not going to work. I cut right and let him take the lead. I'd rather have him where I can see him.

We hit the bridge shoulder to shoulder and it's starting to hurt. But I'm still sure that I have him. We are halfway along the bridge as I take a small lead. I push on, gaining in confidence. I can see the gate ahead. I can hear the slats falling away behind me, heavy wooden boards slamming down. Closer this time. Each piece of wood is creeping up on me, chasing me down. This time I can feel every thump.

Then one foot slips on the damp wood, and I struggle to gain traction.

Suddenly he is level again. I am gasping. I can't breathe and my heart feels as though it is jammed in my throat. There is no one faster than me, but he's pulling ahead. He can't be.

Then he turns towards me and smiles.

'Now . . .' he gasps. 'Now . . . who eez sheet-head?'

And I know that I am dead.

BEN

Everything was wrong. All the numbers were wrong.

Mike knows very well that I dislike change. He's always careful where he leaves me. He looks after me.

Normally I enjoy uploading, unlike Alex. It's the sense of slipping into a clean new skin. You are being poured into a familiar body, settling down until you have filled it to the tips of your fingers and toes and the top of your head. I imagine pouring water into a glass, level with the rim but not spilling a drop. Precise. To me it's a comforting feeling of coming home.

But not this time.

I was crumpled on the ground, one arm awkwardly trapped under my body, staring at a wet, black floor. As I sat up I realised that I was in a game booth.

What? This couldn't be right.

Out of habit, I checked the time. I like to see '14:00' roll across my lenses as I wake. It's a number that feels comfortable. A nice, soft, familiar number to start the day.

But this time it was wrong.

12:29?

That's not a number I like. I don't like three – it's hard, black, spiky. So I don't like nine either. Three threes. Horrible. And 12:29 was all wrong. It wasn't a number that I should have been seeing. This was one of Mike's numbers. Somehow I was in his time.

What was I doing in the wrong time, and how had I got there? I had no recollection of coming to an arena.

I didn't dare to move until 12:29 had become 12:30. Slightly better. I could ignore the three by focusing on the soft numbers around it.

I struggled to my feet, slipping on the wet floor. There was a message on a screen on the wall.

Game aborted
You have ten minutes to leave the booth.

What did that mean? I had played thousands of games in my time and had never heard of one being aborted. Besides which, I hadn't played the game. Mike had.

A shower cubicle opened up in one wall. I had no time for that. I hated the feel of wet clothes on my skin, but I needed to get out of there.

I opened the door and staggered down the corridor, struggling to make my legs work. Someone said something as I passed through the entrance lobby, but I ignored them and stepped outside.

I blinked in the harsh sunlight reflecting off a ruined concrete building across the street. Even the sun felt wrong. It was too low in the sky. I shouldn't have been seeing it like this.

There was movement to my right. A man in a long white robe, the hem grey with concrete dust, was standing just outside the doors of the arena. He was waving a black book in his right hand.

'It's time to repent, my friend,' he said. 'You may have won the game, but at what price to your soul? The Lord does not approve of this unnatural trade in time. It is a sin to gamble with what the Lord gave you. Your lifespan is preordained and you cannot run from death for ever. You must embrace it when your time comes.'

I looked at him in bemusement. When I didn't reply he walked over to me, put a hand on my shoulder, and stared into my eyes. His gaze was strangely hypnotic.

'You do not look well, my friend. Your body may have survived but your spirit is being torn apart. Do not fear death. As our Lord said, the body that is born is perishable, but it is raised up imperishable. It is born in weakness, but raised in power. You are born in a natural body, but raised in a spiritual body. Come with me, my friend. We can help you.'

His words were soothing. Another time I might have stayed and listened. Not because I believed any of his religious nonsense, but because I liked the rhythm of his voice.

I needed to be on my own, though. To work out what had happened to us.

I shrugged off his grip and turned away.

He let me go. 'It's your choice, Brother, but you will be back. You won't find peace in these dens of iniquity. Remember the Lord is always watching over you.'

His timing was unfortunate. As he said that a drone sped down the street towards us, paused overhead, studying us, then shot off in another direction. I rather doubted whether it was being driven by the Lord. Besides, unless the Lord could tell me what I was doing in Mike's time he wasn't much use to me. What I needed was peace and quiet.

The nearest motel was two blocks away. It was cheap and run-down, but it would do. It was fully automated, so I didn't need to speak to anyone to check in, which was good.

Once I had showered and printed a change of clothes I felt a little better.

I sat cross-legged on the bed and logged on. First things first, had I got anything from Mike that would explain this?

There were two messages, but nothing that helped. There was yet another request for us to choose our new body. He was becoming obsessed. Then one saying that he was looking at EliteCorps bodies. That made no sense at all. We couldn't afford an EliteCorps body.

I checked where we were: 24.2 years. *What?* We had been playing cheap games for scraps of time, and had had almost nothing last cycle.

I backed up through my messages.

There were two from Alex. The first complaining about Sierra – again. I sympathised. What she had done to him was unforgiveable. But when you are going to be living with someone for the next hundred years forgiveness is the only option. He was still cross with me for telling him that after Montreal. Their constant bickering was a pain.

Alex's second message was more positive, telling us that he had won 2.69 years. Which was a good win, but didn't explain how we had got to more than twenty-four years.

Then there was a personal message from Kate to me.

Ben. I've either done something stupid or brilliant. I'm not sure which yet. I'm about to send a group message that tells you how I got us twenty years, but it doesn't tell the full story. I need you to do a bit of digging.

I got approached by this andi who said she was trying to get revenge on her husband, and she was offering me twenty years to help. She said she wanted to move her mind into a new body, and needed our help. She seemed a bit highly strung, but it sounded believable and she had the twenty years, so I agreed. We played a game, which she let me win, but she said some crazy things to me. I was tied up and it was all weirdly sexual. I thought I had been scammed and she was going to kill us and take our time. But then she let me win anyway, so it seemed all right. But then I looked for her body and she was gone. I don't know if she lived. Or how she lived since we have her time.

She was really creepy. Even more than most andis. And the thing is, I had to give her some admin access to make this work. I am worried she might have been into places she shouldn't have.

Can you take a look for her round the park? See if you can find her, and who she is, or was? I don't want the others to know about this unless they have to. But I'm scared we haven't seen the last of her. Now we've got so much time we should get out of the park as soon as we can.

See the attached file for her details.

Cheers, Kate.

So that explained the twenty-four years. But in answering one problem it presented me with another. Weighing it up, I could understand why Kate had done what she had in return for twenty years. It would have made sense to her, but it was a risk that I would never have taken. The bold die young. The whole point of being a schizo is not to die young.

And, unlike the white-robed evangelist at the arena, I didn't believe that the Lord would be raising me up into a spiritual body after I died. I preferred to be the one to choose my next body.

Kate should never have given up admin access without a full vote. She shouldn't have changed the system. This was annoying. I'd been concerned about coming to the death park. The thing that had made me vote yes was the thought of playing the latest games in the best arenas. Now that we were here I didn't want to get distracted from that. So I wasn't keen on leaving either, despite the time we now had in hand.

I read Kate's group message but it didn't tell me anything new. There was nothing more from anyone. Mike must have done his challenge, but there was no message from him saying what had happened, nor any record of it. If he had won then we would have more than 24.2 years now.

But if he had died we would all have ended up in stasis, and I wouldn't have woken in the park. Those were the rules. But if he had lived what was I doing in his time? I checked again: 13:32 – another number that wasn't mine. Too many threes. I shuddered. I shouldn't have been awake for another twenty-eight minutes. Had Kate, or Mike, or this mysterious andi somehow screwed with the cycle?

There were some dark places I could have gone to watch

68

Mike's game live. But, given the harsh penalties, no one would have been stupid enough to save a copy.

I sat back and breathed out heavily. Where to start?

Alex's game appeared irrelevant to events. All the odd things that had happened had been after Alex had dropped out. The only lead I had was Kate's mysterious andi.

I opened the file.

Amy Bird, a sixty-seven-year-old andi. So thirteen years left to live. She also had 7.5 years that she had earned somewhere. Her visual age was around forty, and she was pretty in a slightly nerdy way. There was no record of her having played any games in the park, but since most games are private that didn't mean much.

I started with a general search. She was showing as alive, which made no sense at all. Kate said that she had beaten the andi in a game, and we had clearly taken all her time. So how was she still alive, and where was she?

I toyed with the idea of calling her. If she answered I could find her easily. But that would let her know we were after her. It was better to be cautious at this stage. I'm not big on confrontation.

I closed my eyes and began to dig deeper. Now I was going to places where I shouldn't be. Get caught here and I would be looking at some serious time in stasis. But I wasn't going to get caught. I knew my way round the systems better than those who designed and policed them.

An hour later I sat up, stretched, and ordered some food from the primitive wall console. My eyes were sore, my lenses blurred. While I waited for my food to print I reflected on what I had learned about Amy Bird.

She didn't exist.

Sure, there was a superficial record that came up for anyone who did a basic search for her. It showed she was what she claimed to be: an andi with a little over thirteen years left, married to Charles Bugard, no children. She had led a thoroughly uneventful life. There was nothing to raise any alarms.

But it was all an illusion. Beneath that she didn't exist. All of her records had been created two months ago. Before then there was nothing.

So what was she?

It would have been easy enough for someone to send a dandi to deliver a message. But no dandi had AI anywhere near good enough to fool Kate into thinking it was real. And no one would bother to fake a backstory for a dandi. No – there had to be a human mind inside the body.

I wasn't panicking – yet – but this was worrying. There aren't many who can create a false history that stands up to even cursory scrutiny. And most of them work for CGov. What could we have done to get them interested in us? If it wasn't CGov that was probably worse. Any private individuals who could do this were not going to be operating legally.

A panel beeped and opened, and my noodles popped out. As I ate I pondered my next move. The official records were getting me nowhere. There were two options left: look for Mike or look for the andi. Visual records are hard to fake. Of the two, Mike would be easier. I didn't know where we had been overnight, but I could track back to Kate and follow from there. I knew she had played a game that morning.

By the time my noodle wrappings were in the disposal unit I had a picture of Kate entering an arena in Borth Street at 7:32. She was accompanied by a dark-haired woman, a match for Kate's photo of Amy Bird. They were talking. She looked real enough. I moved forward. No one entered or left until 9:14, when the door slid open and Bird left, moving fast. Fifteen minutes later Kate followed.

For someone whom Kate was meant to have killed, the andi looked very much alive.

Through various cameras I got a disjointed record of Kate walking down Borth Street and entering a locker motel at 9:43.

At 10:38 Mike emerged, dressed to race. He crossed the street to a diner, where he spent twenty minutes eating; then reappeared and jogged slowly away.

At 11:22 I caught him entering the arena on Kingston Street where I had woken. This was a top-of-the-range, multi-room arena. A big step up from the dive that Kate had visited earlier. I was about to flick forward when I saw a familiar figure going into the arena after him – Amy Bird, still very much alive.

Then nothing until 12:00, when the white-robed evangelist took his place outside the door. Bird emerged at 12:30, talking to a woman I had not seen before. They were moving fast, and brushed past the evangelist, disappearing up the street.

Five minutes later I appeared, looking somewhat worse for wear, befuddled by my confrontation with the Lord's apostle. The circle was complete.

I tried to find the drone that had buzzed us in the street. Nothing. I'd assumed it was ParkGov security, so it should have been easy enough for me to trace. ParkGov had been running a drone a few blocks away at the time, but nothing matching the one I'd seen. Why would anyone be running private drones round the park? Odd.

So that was it for Mike. He went into the arena, he ran a race, but he never left. I was the one who did. Yet somehow we weren't dead, and hadn't lost our time.

I backtracked, and started a visual search for Amy Bird.

I eventually picked her up four days earlier, exiting the door of the Death's Head, a bar in one of the more run-down parts of the park. She was alone. I backed up. She had entered it twenty minutes earlier.

She seemed to have made a real effort not to be seen. Or she stayed inside a lot. I didn't find her again that day.

She reappeared a day later, once waiting outside an arena, a second time back at the Death's Head, entering this time, and exiting after fifteen minutes. That was it until I got back to what I had already seen: her entering the arena with Kate, exiting it alone, and then at the arena where Mike had his race.

I sat back. There was not a lot to go on. The lack of sightings for Bird was unusual. Somehow she had stayed hidden despite being in the confines of a death park. Was it possible that someone was deleting sightings of her, or faking them, or both? That would be difficult.

I dug into the data behind the videos. It all looked real. And apart from me, no one had viewed any of the videos of Bird outside the Death's Head. The ones where she was with Kate also looked real enough.

Although there was a difference. The video of Kate and Bird at Borth Street had been viewed 104 times since that morning. But the video of Bird leaving the arena, on her own, hadn't been viewed by anyone other than me. I quickly flicked through the others. The same pattern continued. Kate leaving the arena had been viewed 108 times. My staggering out of Kingston Street after Mike's game, 112. Bird leaving five minutes before me, zero views.

Were we being watched? Why by so many people? I tried to track back to see who they were, but came up against a wall that was going to take much more time than I had to break down.

It was 17:14. This had taken far longer than expected. What could I usefully do? Someone needed to visit the Death's Head and try to find out what Bird had been doing there. Andis don't need to drink, and seldom have alcohol. The type of people who choose to be andis don't like losing control. Besides, who goes to a bar to drink on their own for twenty minutes? Other than Sierra, perhaps. Bird must have met someone there.

I didn't have time to visit the bar myself. Could I trust Sierra to do it? Or wait for Alex, or even Kate? But this was urgent. We needed to find out what had happened to Mike. There were too many odd things going on.

I composed a few quick messages.

Mike, I haven't heard from you since your race, and something has gone badly wrong. I woke in a game booth during your cycle. Let me (and the others) know what is happening asap, Ben.

All. This is weird. Something has happened to Mike. I haven't heard from him since his race, and I woke during his time. This isn't right. If he messaged any of you, let the rest of us know asap. Something feels wrong. There's lots of strange things going on. B.

Kate, everything is wrong today. I don't like it. I woke during Mike's time, in a game booth. I haven't heard from Mike. I have done some digging. The last I can find of Mike he was entering the arena for his race followed shortly after by your andi, Amy Bird. She definitely isn't dead. And officially she didn't exist until two months ago. She looks real, but all her records are faked. I don't know what went on in the arena with Mike but the next thing I know is that I am uploading ninety-one minutes early. I don't like that. Your twenty years is going to come at a price. I don't have time to follow up the leads on the andi. I am going to have to get Sierra to do it. I know she's unreliable, but we don't have a choice. I'll ask her to let you know what she finds. Tell me next cycle where you get to. Hopefully by then this will all have blown over, and Mike will be back in touch. We need to get everything back to normal again. I don't like all this change. I woke at 12:29! It was horrible. I've set up an alert so that we'll be told if Bird is detected in the park again. Keep it to yourself – it's not entirely legal . . . Ben.

Sierra. This is important. I have made this highest priority so read it before you do anything else.

Things are happening that I don't understand. Kate may have got scammed by some andi and Mike has disappeared. I have run out of time. I need you to go to a bar called the Death's Head and find out what you can about this andi [file attached]. She calls herself Amy Bird. She's the one Kate got the twenty years from, so she ought to be dead but isn't. She's been hanging round that bar quite a lot, so maybe someone knows her there.

Whatever you find out let Kate know.

Please take this seriously. I think Mike might have been mindwiped. Any one of us could be next. IT COULD BE YOU NEXT, SIERRA! Even if you don't care about helping the rest of us, do this for yourself. Ben.

Finally, because I didn't trust Sierra to do anything, I sent Alex a copy of my messages and a picture of the woman I had seen leaving the arena with Amy Bird. I didn't have time this cycle to track her myself, but maybe Alex could find her.

SIERRA

Endless messages from the others. *Again*. Why? Didn't they realise that I had no interest at all in what they did with their time in my body? All I wanted was that it was there when I needed it.

The longer this went on the more I realised I had made the wrong choice when I was seventeen. I should have chosen to be a hed. One short life to live in luxury. No need to work, no need to care about anyone else, and then it would all be over. No need to deal with people who had become more difficult to control as they got older.

I was in a cheap motel near the centre of the park. Good. There were fifteen bars within a 500-metre walk. Nice forward planning, Ben.

I chose one on the basis of proximity, not clientele. It was mostly empty that early in the evening. Most people don't live a four-hour day.

By 18:08 I was sitting in a booth with a glass of whisky in one hand, and some reconstituted sludge on a plate in front of me masquerading as breakfast. This wasn't the sort of bar that did champagne. Besides, that's a social drink. Whisky is for when you want to be on your own.

After a couple of fingers of Scotch I began to feel well enough to start deleting everyone's messages.

Ben had sent one with high priority, which he insisted I read first. So I ignored it.

Alex had sent me three messages. The first two were bleating about the fact that I had left him hungover in a champagne bar. He was threatening to try to get me put in stasis again. As if three months hadn't been enough. I deleted his messages unfinished. I can't be bothered to read things that criticise me.

The third said that he had won the game I set up for him. Typical Alex. No gratitude. I had left him in a bar with a half-cut, oversexed hed with low self-esteem, and all he had done was kill her. And then he'd whined about it.

There were a couple of messages from Mike about choosing the body for our next round. Boring. It could wait.

An odd one from Kate saying that she had won us more than twenty years. That seemed unlikely, but it was there to see. Typical that she'd fallen on her feet again.

Finally I got to Ben's high-priority. It required two reads and another glass of whisky before I made much sense of it. Mike hadn't checked in after his race, and Kate had been scared by an andi. Hardly reasons to panic. These things happen, although admittedly not usually with a time glitch on top. It was likely to all be fixed by next cycle. I didn't see why I should be chasing after some andi just to keep Mike and Kate happy.

Although Ben seemed to be taking it seriously. And he

believed that there was a risk to me. Was he just trying to scare me into doing something? I pulled up the photo of the andi. She didn't look dangerous, but if she had managed to wipe Mike and spook Kate then she must be. I like dangerous people. They tend to be interesting. But if Mike really had gone then I didn't want to be next. It seemed so unlikely, though.

All it required me to do was walk down the road to another bar, have a few drinks and ask about the andi.

An hour later I was still sitting in the same place. In that time I had fended off the advances of two dandis and declined an invitation to watch a death match. Or maybe it had been to participate in one. I hadn't been listening too closely.

The whisky bottle was empty. Time to order more or move on. Which was it to be?

The more I thought about it, the more Kate's andi interested me. If she was a threat to me then I needed to know. If she wasn't then maybe there was some fun to be had.

I pushed myself up off the table and took a leisurely if not entirely straight course towards the door. I could have flushed the alcohol out of my body, but what would have been the fun in that?

•

The Death's Head was less than five minutes' walk away. It was about as seedy as a bar could get without being shut down. The fittings were old and broken. It was dark and stank of stale alcohol. It was packed. Busier than the last bar, with noise echoing off concrete walls. More up my street with a few drinks inside me.

I found a seat on the end of a bench in a dark corner, ordered a bottle, and sat back. The bar was full of people who seemed to have given up on winning any more time, and who were here to use up their bodies as fast as possible. There were several obvious heds, still young enough to look good, but winding down fast with an air of panic. A few workers, old beyond their years, nothing to look forward to. Mostly they were huddled over, nursing their drinks and talking in low tones. No obvious andis, which was a shame, as that was what I wanted. Unlikely to be any schizos, as there are so few of us.

The man next to me shifted along, bumping my elbow and spilling half my drink.

'Hey, dickhead!' I shouted. He muttered something and looked away.

'What did you say?' I asked.

He ignored me. 'Hey, have you gone deaf?' I poked his shoulder.

He turned back and looked me up and down. It seemed he'd already come off second-best in a recent fight. His right eye was swollen and half-closed. He held up his hands. 'Sorry, too many people in here.'

I nodded. No one wants to pick a fight with six foot of solid muscle.

Not a great start, but perhaps he could tell me something. I turned to scan him.

Nothing.

He scowled. 'What's your problem? You know we don't do that here.' He squeezed past me and walked away.

The red-headed woman who had been sitting next to him slid closer and leaned in. 'Ignore him,' she said. 'He doesn't like the idea of dying, so he's too scared to play any games. I don't know why we came to the park. It cost us two months just to get in and we haven't won anything yet. He's not happy that I want to play when he doesn't. So he sits here and drinks instead.' She looked around. 'As do most of the others. What's the point?'

I topped up her glass from my bottle.

'So what's your story?' she asked. 'Have you had any luck in the games?'

'I'm doing OK,' I said. 'I've played a few and won a few. That's not why I'm here, though. I had a run-in with an andi last night and I know she comes here sometimes. I'm trying to find her to have a little chat. There might be some time in it for you if you know her. Have you been here much?'

She looked interested. 'I've not. But Karl has practically lived here for the last week.' She glared over at the bar, where her part-ner was leaning, staring at us. 'Why do you want to find this andi? Are you looking to buy from her?' She leaned closer and said quietly. 'You don't need her for that. Karl and I can get you what you need. And we'll guarantee to beat the andi's price.'

'I need the andi, not what she's selling,' I said.

She shrugged. 'Have it your way. Do you have a picture of her?'

'I do,' I said. 'But you'll have to open up to let me send it.'

'No one here shows themselves,' she said. 'We'll have to do this the old-fashioned way.' Eyes fixed on the bar, she reached across and held my hand. I sent over the picture of the andi that Kate had given me.

She paused, then shook her head. 'Means nothing to me. Wait, I'll see if Karl knows. His desperate need for time will overcome his distaste for you.' She looked across at him and inclined her head. There was a moment of silent communication.

He stiffened, and set his drink down on the bar. His face went blank. He shook his head. But Karl was a terrible liar. The andi meant something to him.

'No,' said the woman. 'He says he doesn't know her.'

Karl nodded towards the door. For a moment I thought that he was calling me out. I was halfway to my feet when I realised he was indicating to his girlfriend that they were going.

'Sorry.' She stood and squeezed past me. 'Time for us to leave.'

I nodded. 'Thanks for trying.'

One thing I am good at is reading people. I've told enough good lies to recognise a bad one. Karl knew the andi. The fact that I was asking about her was of interest to someone, and Karl was busy selling me out. He wanted the two of them gone before any trouble started. He caught the woman's elbow and pushed her ahead of him through the crowd.

I hesitated over whether to follow them. But Karl was not going to lead me to anyone. He had done what he needed to and trouble was on its way here. I was sure that whatever was coming would be more entertaining than Karl and his girl-friend. All I had to do was wait.

It didn't take long. I was halfway through my next drink when I felt a change in the atmosphere. There was shuffling as the crowd moved aside.

With good reason. The andi who pushed through them

82

was at least six inches taller than me and half as wide again. It was all muscle. And he had a friend. They looked as though they had come out of the same vat, pre-cultured andis built for violence. No one got that way through training alone.

They walked slowly over to where I sat and stopped, looming over me. The first one spoke, his voice a deep rumble. 'Mr Guskov wants to speak to you.'

'Do I have a choice?' I asked. Knowing the answer.

The giant's thickset features contorted in what it took me a moment to realise was a smile. 'There is always a choice, Ms Summers. You can walk with us to see the boss. Or Stas here can break your legs and carry you there. Which is it?'

Well, I'd wanted information and excitement. The mysterious Mr Guskov might offer me both. I knocked back the last of my drink and stood. 'Let's go.'

What troubled me more than meeting their boss was the fact that they knew who I was. I couldn't scan them, so how did they know me?

The first andi led the way, with Stas following. I was the meat in the middle. Instead of leaving the bar we headed deeper into it, coming to a door in the back wall marked PRIVATE. We passed through, into a dimly lit concrete passageway. The sounds of the bar faded away and we came to a stairwell.

'Up,' said the andi.

We emerged in another passage, and stopped outside a wooden door. The andi paused, evidently communicating with someone. Then the door opened and he stepped through. Stas gestured for me to follow.

Unlike the rest of the building, this room was smart and

expensively furnished. The walls were wood-panelled. There was carpeting, and a large wooden desk in the centre, two leather armchairs in front. It looked like an executive's office from some old-time movie. There was a large window opposite, but it was too dark to see much outside.

Mr Guskov was dwarfed by the desk behind which he sat. He was a thin man, probably a good foot shorter than me. His hair was white and carefully combed to one side. He wore small gold-rimmed glasses, through which he squinted at me. The hair and the glasses were clearly affectations – he could have fixed them easily. Although I couldn't scan him, he had to be a worker. He was too old for a hed or a schizo, and no one would make an andi as weak-looking as he was.

'Sit.' He gestured to the chairs in front of him.

I hesitated, glancing over my shoulder. I could have snapped Guskov in half with one arm. But then I'd have needed to dispose of the andis standing either side of the door.

I sat.

He studied me for a moment, then nodded to the andis. 'Stas, wait outside. Vincent, stay.'

The andi left, halving the odds against me. Although I still didn't fancy my chances of fighting my way out.

'So, Ms Summers, I understand you are looking for me,' Guskov said in a thin and raspy voice.

'Not really,' I said. 'I was just asking around about an andi who had caused some trouble, and that seems to have led me to you.'

'What's she done?'

'That's something I need to discuss with her,' I said. 'If you can help me find her, great. If not, I'll get out of your way.'

He sat back, and blinked, looking at me reflectively.

'I'm sure I could find her for you, but it's really not my problem. I told you last time that my involvement is strictly limited. I'm not here to babysit you. I wanted to see you because I assumed there was something we needed to work out, that there was a problem with my merchandise. Is there? I have a reputation here. I always honour my deals. Everyone knows that my word is my bond. So if there is a problem I will sort it.'

It was my turn to be puzzled. If I said yes I was going to have to explain, and I had no idea what we were talking about. What was the merchandise that he thought he had sold me?

'Well, is there a problem?' he asked again.

'Not that I know of,' I said.

'Then why are you here?'

'I didn't ask to speak to you,' I said. 'All I'm trying to do is find this andi, Amy Bird. Let me show you.' I leaned forward, half out of my seat, and offered my hand.

He shrank back, and a pair of meaty hands seized my shoulders, pushing me back into the chair.

'Stay away from me,' Guskov rasped. 'What game are you playing? If Bird's causing trouble that's not my problem. What were you doing, coming here and causing a scene? This isn't how I do business.'

'I'm not the one causing a scene,' I said. 'I just came here for a drink and you set your grunts on me.' Vincent muttered something, but at a gesture from Guskov his grip relaxed.

'I'll be watching you,' said Guskov, frowning. 'Don't cause me any more trouble. We had a deal. I expect you to keep your side of the bargain. Or there will be consequences.'

'But—' I began.

He shook his head. 'We'll speak again when I need you. Good day, Ms Summers.'

Vincent ushered me out of the door, and he and Stas escorted me back to the bar in silence.

My bottle was where I had left it, untouched. It seemed that my association with Guskov – good or bad – was protection enough.

I turned to the andis. 'Fancy a drink, boys? Do you know where I can find Bird?'

They ignored me and pushed their way through the crowd. I sat down, waving the bottle at their retreating backs. 'Your loss.'

A few faces turned towards me, but clearly decided I was safest left alone. No one returned to the table.

I sat back.

I had bought enough recreational highs in my time to know what Guskov's merchandise was likely to be. And in the past few days one of us had been here and done a deal with him.

Who, and why?

There was no way it was Alex. Mr Square, who broke into a cold sweat jaywalking. Could Kate be a secret user? Dull, virtuous Kate. That seemed even less likely. Ben? Sometimes the quiet ones are the ones who surprise you. Maybe he was taking something for his anxiety. But Ben was the one who'd sent me here to investigate in the first place. So it seemed unlikely to be him. Mike would never put drugs in his hallowed body. Unless they were performance boosters. There were enough people competing for there to be a market. Mike had some big races lined up, which he had said he was confident of winning. But could he have decided to tip the odds in his favour? Was this connected in some way with his disappearance? And how was the andi linked to all this? Why had my questions about her triggered this reaction? Too many questions and no answers.

Did I even care? What did it matter to me if Mike or Ben, or even Alex or Kate, was hooked on something illegal? I had put enough drugs into this body in the past and it was still working fine. Besides, it only needed to last another ten days, so it was the ideal time to be trying new things.

Against that, what if Mike really had been wiped, and I was next? Guskov had seemed dangerous enough that I could believe that his andi might have done something to Mike.

I needed to find out what he was selling. That would likely tell me who had been buying from him. While I didn't much care if the others were convinced I had been buying drugs, there would be some satisfaction in telling smug Alex and Kate that this time it wasn't my fault.

Guskov wasn't going to tell me what he was selling, but I knew someone who would. If I could find out where Karl had gone I had no doubt I could beat the information out of him.

I sobered up and left, ignoring the stares and muttered complaints as I pushed through the crowd.

•

I hadn't thought that Karl and his girlfriend would go far from the Death's Head, so my plan had been to search the local bars.

There was no need.

I was barely a minute's walk from the bar when I heard a hissed, 'Hey.' I turned sharply, expecting trouble.

It was Karl's girlfriend, leaning against a broken wall in the shadows. She was alone. Now that I had left the bar I was no longer blocked. I scanned her: Vicky Earl, a hed days away from death. She had just under a week left. With that little time she was going to struggle to find anyone willing to play her, even if she wanted to. No one would think it worth the risk. I guessed that she and Karl were getting scraps of time from Guskov in return for dealing.

I walked over to her.

'What are you selling?' I asked.

Her eyes widened. 'What? I didn't come here to sell you anything. Karl wants to meet you.'

'Why?'

'You want to know about the andi. What's it worth to you?'

'What can you tell me?'

'Not me,' she said. 'It's Karl. But he needs to know it's worth his while.'

'You've got no time at all,' I said. 'Every day is a bonus for you. I might be able to give you a couple of days if Karl can tell me something useful.'

'It's worth more than that.' She hesitated. 'He wants at least a month.'

'Fuck off. Nothing you can tell me about the andi is worth that.' I turned to leave.

'Wait,' she said. 'It's not just the andi Karl can tell you about.'

'What else?'

'He says he knows things about you. Things you'll want to know. That you *need* to know.'

'Like what?' I asked.

She smiled. She thought she had me. 'No. I've told you too much already. Karl says to meet him thirty minutes from now. Here.' She held out her hand and I tapped it lightly to get the coordinates. 'You pay him a month and he tells you.'

I checked the time. I still had well over an hour before dropping out.

'All right,' I said. 'It had better be worth it.'

I had to admit that she had me hooked now. What could Karl possibly know about us that would be worth that much?

TWENTY-FIVE YEARS EARLIER

FIVE INTO ONE

DEPOPULATION ACT NOTICE

By order of Central Government and in accordance with the
Depopulation and Environmental Accord Acts ('the Acts'), you
KATHERINE WESTON
now being 17 years of age, are required to report to
ENTON GRANGE TRANSITION CENTRE
within <u>no more than 28 days</u> of receipt of this notice.

Whereupon you will further be required, within no more than 7
days of your arrival at the stated location, to make your binding
election under the Acts.

This notice constitutes statutory notification of your right and
obligation under the Acts to elect for one and one only of the

following four options (italicised terms being as defined in the Acts), namely: (i) to exchange your current body for that of an *android*; (ii) to join a *commune*; or to remain in your current body as (iii) a *hedonist*; or (iv) a *worker*.

Failure to report to the location notified above within the time stated above will render you a fugitive under the Acts and liable to arrest and trial before a court of summary jurisdiction, which court will have the power to make your statutory election for you in accordance with the overriding objectives specified in the Acts.

Time will start to run from receipt of this notice, whose receipt has automatically been reported and logged.

If within 7 days of your arrival at the location notified above you fail to make an election you will be deemed irrevocably to have surrendered your right of election to the Minister of Depopulation, who may exercise that right or delegate its exercise in accordance with the Acts.

The hall was packed, filled with the chatter of over-excited and nervous teenagers. Rows of hard plastic chairs faced a temporary stage. Kate had never before seen so many people gathered in one place. She guessed that there were over a thousand seventeen-year-olds squeezed into the hall. In her village five people counted as a crowd. The noise was overwhelming.

She'd got there early, found a seat at the back, and waited as the hall filled up. Now she was stiff and fidgety.

She had spoken to no one. Just sat watching the empty stage at the far end of the hall.

At 10:00 precisely the lights dimmed and a tall grey-haired woman in a dark suit stepped on to the stage. She paused for a moment, then walked with precise steps to the podium in the centre. She waited for silence. Her image and voice were projected round the hall.

'Good morning, children,' she said. 'And that is the last time that you will be called that. From tomorrow you are all classified as adults. Tomorrow you begin your lives.

'Before you do that you must each make a choice. No doubt most of you will have been thinking about this for many years, and many of you will have made your choice already. You have all had the opportunity, over the past few days, to discuss your options with our counsellors. But we are legally required to give you one last chance to change your mind.

'When we eradicated disease we drove back death. Soon there was little to kill us beyond bad luck and old age. Very old age. The result was a population explosion. A planet that was already on its knees was about to be crippled. Humans make up less than one hundredth of one per cent of the planet's biomass but have devastated more of it than any other creature or natural disaster. Nothing compares to our powers of destruction. Research showed that the most environmentally damaging act that any human could commit was to have children. Every human added further to the intolerable burden that we were imposing. Which eventually would kill us all.'

There was a low murmuring amongst her audience. Like Kate, they would have heard all this before. Many times. They just wanted to get it done.

The speaker hurried on. 'We can't stop having children. We need them. We need you. So we came up with our greatest achievement of all.' Her voice lowered. 'Fair use.'

She paused and looked around. 'Everyone is entitled to fair use of resources. No one is entitled to more than their fair share. Everyone is allocated the same share at birth. For the first seventeen years of your lives you have been housed, educated, fed, watered and nurtured. You have bought those services with some of your time allocation.

'Now you must choose where you go from here. You have five options. Don't criticise anyone for their choices. There are certain stereotypes but they are wrong.

'First, you may choose to be a worker. If you do, very little will change. You will be taken from here and educated for the next five years. After that you will be found a job and will earn time. You will spend that time. You will live your life and pass on. Some deride workers as dull and unimaginative. Some say that people choose to remain workers from fear of the other choices. Those criticisms are unfair and wrong. It is an honourable and honest choice and I commend it to you. Unlike all other choices, there is no set limit on your time here. You have no expiry date. Some workers – a very few – may even outlive communal bodies. From past experience around one-third of you will choose to be workers.

'Second, you may choose to be an android. Make that choice and your mind will be removed from its current body, so expensive to feed, house and maintain – so wasteful of resources. The essence of your mind will be uploaded into an android body that is virtually indistinguishable from the real thing. Your new body will seem exactly the same to you as your current one. An android can do anything that a human can. But its drain on resources is minimal. You won't need to eat or drink. All you need is a little power, occasional upkeep, and that is it. You will never get ill. Not only that. In return for your commitment to fair use you will be allocated eighty years of time. You will live till then and pass on.

'Some are frightened of this choice. They fear that it will change them, make them less human. But there is nothing to be scared of. It is a fine choice.' She paused. 'It was mine.'

Well that explains her cold, precise manner, thought Kate. Typical andi. No longer human, but always believing themselves better than everyone else.

'It's also a myth that androids are in some way superhuman. We are not.' She cracked a weak smile. 'I can't jump over buildings or run any faster than you can. We are just like normal humans. But better, in some ways.

'Don't confuse sentient andis with non-sentients – what you know as dandis. Dumb andis. Those are just andi bodies with basic artificial intelligence that are used for dangerous jobs, or by some of the very rich as their personal servants, or,' she screwed up her face in an expression of distaste, 'for less salubrious functions. Dandis are entirely different. They have no minds.

'It may surprise you to know that becoming an android is a popular choice. Again, around one-third of you will choose that. It makes good sense.

'Third,' she said, 'you may choose to be a hedonist. That is an unfortunate pejorative term, but it has stuck. It is a choice of sacrifice, and should not be criticised. You will be given a very generous allowance, a fine home, and you will never have to work. But in return your time here is limited to a further twenty-five years. At age forty-two you will pass on. Think carefully if this is your choice. What seems like a good idea now may not look the same in twenty-five years. There is no going back. Around a quarter of you will choose this.

'Fourth, you may choose to join a communal body – what you may know as schizos. Another word that's best avoided.' She shook her head. 'It's a derogatory term, but unfortunately it has stuck. Try as we might, we've never managed to come up with anything better. Those of you who choose this will be allocated a group by reference to aptitude, intelligence and grades.

'In recognition of the significant sacrifice that you will be making – the removal of four wasteful bodies from society – you will each be allocated twenty-five years, and housed and fed. Enough to keep you comfortable. You may work if you wish, to earn extra time, but you will not need to. At the end of each life – after twenty-five years – you will be returned here for your old host to be recycled and your minds moved to a new host. Communes are the most long-lived of all. You will not pass on until you are 142, at the end of your fifth life. Communes are the rarest of all. Fewer than one in ten of you will choose that, and it takes five of you to make one commune. But for some it is definitely the right choice. It means that you will see a time that none of the rest of us will see.

'There is a final option. You may not wish to travel down any of the other paths. You may feel that your greatest contribution to society is to cease to be a burden upon it now. If so, you may choose to terminate both your body and mind. That is a selfless choice, and one that is much admired. But it is not one that you should take lightly. It avoids society wasting its resources on those who may choose to discard their lives at some future point. If it is your choice you will not be allowed to make it today. You will, depending upon the individual, undergo weeks or even months of counselling first. Only when it is right for you and society will you be permitted to take that path.

'One last point. Generally you may not buy or sell time, or give it away. Otherwise the strong would prey on the weak. There is one place you may do so: the temporal reassignment challenge facilities. What you know as death parks. You may enter these by choice at any time. Most only do so when they are near the end of their time, when the potential rewards out-weigh the risks. There you may play games to acquire the rem-nants of people's time. It is a choice you will not need to make for many years, and most choose never to enter. Be warned that most who do, die.'

She paused again and looked around.

'Today your choice is very different. More pleasant. You will have until 14:00 to report that choice. If you already know, you may tell us now. If you are uncertain there will be staff and counsellors available for the next few hours to assist.

'I wish you well. Choose carefully. You are choosing how you will live. You are choosing when you will die.'

•

'Mike. Mike Ganzorig.' The tall, well-muscled youth held out his hand. His grip was firm and reassuring. He smiled at Kate's puzzled frown, a twinkle in his hazel eyes. 'It's Mongol. Genghis Khan and all that.'

'Ah ... right,' Kate said, thrown by his odd introduction. 'I'm Kate. Kate Weston. Not Mongol.' In other circumstances she would have been pleased to be alone in a room with this handsome young man who looked as though he'd just stepped off a fashion runway. But this was different. It was not a date, but something far more intimate. Of all the boys that she ever met, this was one that Kate knew she could never go out with. It felt weird.

His grin widened, showing perfect white teeth. He seemed at ease, but sensing her nerves. 'So, is this your first time?'

She laughed, but was spared answering as the door opened and three more people walked in.

The first was a blonde girl with flawless skin and a cat-like grace. She paused in the doorway, looked Mike up and down, and glided over with a smile. She stood on tiptoe to kiss him lightly on the cheek.

'Sierra Summers,' she said. 'You must be Michael.'

He grinned back. 'Call me Mike.'

She nodded to Kate, slightly dismissively.

'Nice to meet you too,' said Kate.

Sierra was followed by a short boy with a mop of dark curly hair. It would have been generous to call him overweight. He was sweating despite the coolness of the room, a dark patch staining the front of his shirt. It was rare to see anyone that size. Kate wondered how his parents had afforded the monthly fines that would have been levied for 'chronic overconsumption of resources'. Perhaps he'd got a medical exemption. Perhaps that was why he wanted to become a schizo.

He looked around quickly. 'Hello, all. I'm Alex,' he said.

Last in was a boy who looked no older than twelve. He was painfully thin, his face hidden under a black hood, head bent down, his pale skin and glasses barely visible. It wasn't obvious whether that was because he didn't want to meet their gaze, or because he was being careful to avoid stepping on the cracks between the tiles. He was muttering under his breath and seemed to be counting. He stopped and looked up briefly. 'Ben,' he said quietly.

Sierra pulled a face, and grimaced towards Mike. He shook his head.

Kate found it hard to believe that these were the four people with whom she had been selected to spend the rest of her life. Was it too late to change her mind? Could she ask for a different group? Mike was all right, but Sierra seemed contemptuous of her. Alex looked as though he had no self-control. And she didn't know what to make of Ben.

'I suggest we get started,' Mike said. 'There's a lot for us to do today.'

The only furnishings were a table and five chairs. There was also a screen on the wall. Until they were adults they would not get implants or lenses.

As they sat, the screen came to life. It was the same woman who had addressed them in the hall. This time her message was pre-recorded.

'Congratulations on your choice. In this short presentation you will receive some additional information specific to your future.

'You will now have got to know the other four members of your commune.' She smiled. 'If you are anything like nine-ty-nine per cent of the people who come through these rooms you are probably looking at the other four and thinking some-one has made a terrible mistake. How can you possibly have been matched with people who are so different from you?'

There was nervous laughter round the room. Kate glanced at the others. Clearly they felt the same as she did.

'You have to trust us. We have been doing this for a long time, and we know what works. In the early days we used to match people by interests, similarities, male with male, female with female. But it often didn't work. It is sometimes possible to unwind a commune, but even when it works it leaves deep mental scarring. In the early days we found that we were doing it all too often. Putting people together who are similar doesn't work. As with everything in life, you need balance. You five have been carefully chosen to achieve that balance. You are dif-ferent, but because you are different it will work.

'We no longer offer the option of unwinding. It is too easy to take that choice as a way out when things get a bit difficult. We have discovered that it is better to leave things as they are, and for the commune to find its own solutions over time.

'That is not to say that you won't have disagreements. But as with any relationship you will have to learn to compromise. Sometimes you will give and sometimes you will take. There is a reason that there are five of you. You will decide things by majority vote. With five you will reach decisions, even if not all of you agree with all of them.

'You will make your first decision today. A decision that will remain with you for the next twenty-five years – who is to be your first host? You may keep one of your current hosts, or you may select one provided by us, at a cost. Those that you do not use will be reused or recycled. You will receive time credit for them. The basic credit is three years for each body. However, particularly desirable bodies may receive remote bids from third parties. You will be able to check bids shortly. Whatever total credit you receive you will be able to spend now, if you wish, on certain limited enhancements that are available. Or you can keep it for the future.

'A few practicalities. Many people think of communes like a collective mind. That is incorrect. You remain separate individuals. Though you will share one body you will have no direct contact with the others. You can send each other messages during your part of the cycle, but you cannot speak directly. You cannot read one another's minds. You will have no contact except what you want to have. You will not know what the others have done in their time unless they tell you.

'You will need to work out a balance, a way of cooperation. You are sharing a host and must treat the others fairly. You must respect the host. There are protocols that will bind each of you. Any breach of the protocols will be punishable by loss of time, at the discretion of the group. Hopefully you will have no need of that.

'There are a few other decisions that you must make today. You must choose the order in which you cycle. The cycle begins at 6:00 in the morning and ends at 2:00 the next morning. Try to choose a place that fits with your personality. One of you will not see the sun for the next twenty-five years. So don't choose the last slot if that would worry you. Two of you will only ever see daylight. These choices, once made, will be fixed for this lifetime. You can change them when you move to your next host.

'The reality is that you will spend this first lifetime working things out, and deciding how to do things better in your next host. I wish you well with your choices and your life.

'As well as learning about one another you will need to learn about yourselves, and how to make your new life work. Relationships are never easy for members of a commune. Most people don't want to be with someone who is only around for four hours a day. Keep in mind that people may see you as older than you are. Because you are only living four hours each day, in your early lives you will be much younger in life experience and emotional development than you appear. When you near the end of your first life others will see a body that is more than forty years old, but not realise that it houses twenty-year-old minds. You must learn how to deal with that.

'You have until the end of today to make your choices. If you need assistance, please ask. You will stay here overnight and tomorrow we will carry out the medical procedures necessary to add your implants and create the commune. After a few days' rest you will be sent out to your new lives. As one.'

The screen went blank. They were silent for a moment, seemingly overwhelmed by their choices.

Kate spoke first. 'God, she's cold. Who'd choose to be an andi? You might as well dump your mind in stasis and never come out again. I don't care what she says, it doesn't seem human.'

Sierra shrugged. 'It's not for me. This is what I've always wanted. Four hours on suits me fine. That's longer than most relationships I've had.'

The others laughed, although with differing degrees of sincerity. *She must have started young,* thought Kate.

'Logically,' said Ben, 'becoming a schizo is the only choice that makes sense.' His voice was soft, and muffled beneath his hood. Kate strained to hear him. She was surprised that he had spoken at all. 'You get to live the longest, you are given a new body every twenty-five years, and you don't have to work. If you run the numbers, it's a no-brainer. Besides, 142 is a great number. If it wasn't for seventy-one it would be a prime number. I like that. It makes sense to live to 142 – it's two prime numbers.'

'No offence,' said Kate, 'but I'm surprised you didn't choose to be an android. Logic is what they are best at.'

'That's a myth,' he replied. 'Android minds are no different from ours. They think the same as everyone else.' He paused. 'It was my second choice. I considered it for a long time. But the maths doesn't work. I'd have got another sixty-three years, whereas as a schizo I get almost twice that. Who knows what will happen in that time?'

'And androids are freaks,' said Sierra. 'Schizos are cool. Mysterious. People find them intriguing.'

'Not wanting to argue,' said Alex, turning to Ben. 'But the maths isn't that obvious. We get another 125 years, but only four hours a day, so in total only around twenty years each'

'It's 20.83 recurring,' said Ben. 'But we don't lose time to sleep. To keep the maths simple let's assume the average person spends one-third of each day sleeping. That means we are effectively getting six hours per day, so your 20.83 becomes 31.25 . . .'

He trailed off as Sierra yawned audibly.

'Look,' he finished quickly. 'The point is that it's the only way for certain of living for another 125 years. By then who knows what other options might be available. We may be able to download permanently into andi bodies, or into stasis. We might live for ever. I'd happily do this without you lot if I could. But at the moment it's the only option to live that long.'

'Fine,' said Sierra, holding up a hand. 'Let's quit the geek fest and get on with things that matter.'

'True,' said Mike. 'Interesting though this is, we don't need to debate why we're here. We've all made our decisions. There's a lot we need to get through today.'

'You're right,' said Kate. 'There's no going back now. So where do we start?'

'The first question is whose body we use,' said Mike. 'Can I start by making a pitch for mine? It speaks for itself. I think I can safely say that I am the fittest person in this building. I have been a competitive athlete now for seven years. Swimming, running, rowing, cycling – I've won them all since the age of ten. I train at least two hours a day, and I would keep up a significant workout regime if you choose me. I can give you my stats if you want.'

No one else spoke. Although she had prepared for this for years, Kate now found the discussion bizarre.

Eventually Sierra reached over and put her hand on Mike's biceps. 'So, are we allowed to test the goods first?'

'What exactly do you have in mind?' Kate asked waspishly.

'I want to get some idea of what we're buying into,' said Sierra. 'This is a big decision. We can't just return Mike's body if we get it wrong. Or at least not for twenty-five years.'

She slipped a hand between the buttons of Mike's shirt. He made no effort to stop her. 'Wow,' she said. 'Is there any fat on those abs, Mike?'

He smiled and gently pulled her hand away. 'Overall, I have just under ten per cent body fat,' he said. 'I wasn't joking when I offered you my stats. Although I can't tell you the precise fat-to-muscle ratio on my abs.'

Kate looked around. 'If you two are quite finished, are there any other volunteers?'

'How about me?' said Sierra. 'I may not have Mike's abs but I do have certain other attributes. This body has served me well, and I'm sure that there's a lot the five of us could do with it.' She smiled at Ben, and ran her tongue around her lips. 'And let's face it, choosing me is the best chance nerd boy here has of ever getting close to a body like mine.'

'Sierra,' said Kate. 'I don't know what you are trying to prove, but this isn't helping.'

'Just trying to liven you all up a bit. You'll get used to me over 125 years.'

'Let's just get on and choose a body,' said Mike. 'I can certainly see the attraction of yours, but mine is likely to last the twenty-five years better. Don't forget it's high usage, twenty hours a day.' He paused, then smiled. 'Besides, someone as adventurous as you might enjoy seeing what things are like from the other side. Particularly when you get to be in a body with as much stamina as mine.'

'That could be fun,' admitted Sierra. 'I'd be happy enough in your body for our first life. And Alex and Ben won't know what's hit them when they have women falling at their feet – probably men as well.'

'I'll make it easy for you,' said Alex. 'I'm not offering mine. We can sell it back.'

'Let's hope they pay by the kilo,' Sierra said sharply.

Kate gasped. Alex reddened and looked down.

'Come on,' said Sierra, looking around. 'I'm only saying what we were all thinking. Alex knows his body is useless. None of us wants to spend twenty-five years in that. Let's at least be honest with one another.'

Kate glared at Sierra. 'For God's sake, Sierra. There's a difference between being honest and deliberately nasty. Alex has told us he doesn't want us to use his body. Let's just accept that and move on.'

'Well, why don't we take a look what people are offering?' said Sierra. She nodded to the screen. 'You heard the woman. People will be bidding for any bodies that we don't want. We ought to know what they're worth so we can decide.'

Kate hesitated. This was unlikely to help Alex. But she had to admit Sierra was right. Before they made a final choice they ought to know what credit they could earn.

'All right.' Kate stepped up to the screen and cycled through the menu until she found an option headed 'LIVE AUCTION'. She tapped on it.

Kate Weston – 4.1 years
Sierra Summers – 6.3 years
Michael Ganzorig – 7.8 years
Benjamin White – no bids [3 years]
Alex Du Bois – no bids [3 years]

Sierra snorted. 'Well the geek squad is bringing in the credits. What a surprise.'

Kate glared at her.

Ben shrugged. 'Our bodies are just empty vessels. It is vanity to think otherwise. It's only our minds that matter.'

Alex was staring at his feet and looked as though he was trying hard not to cry. 'I don't want to be here,' he muttered.

Kate sighed and crouched down in front of him, taking his hand. He flinched.

'Look, Alex, we're all a bit tense,' Kate said. 'It's a big day, and *some* of us are saying things we'll regret later.' She met Sierra's gaze, daring her to speak. Sierra raised an eyebrow, and shrugged.

'I understand,' said Alex, gulping hard. 'It's just, people have always bullied me about my size. I want to just get rid of this body and start again.' His shoulders shook and he started crying.

'Christ, what a loser,' muttered Sierra under her breath.

Kate turned to her angrily. 'Stop it.' She stood and took

Alex's hand. 'Give us a minute. Come on, Alex,' she said softly, and led him outside.

•

There was a small canteen nearby. A few tables were occupied by counsellors in earnest discussion with the undecided. Kate sat Alex at an empty table and went to get him a glass of water. Judging by his size he found food a comfort. She printed him a sticky pastry. That ought to do. And grabbed some tissues.

By the time she got back to him he had calmed down a bit. He blew his nose noisily and left the dirty tissues on the table. Disgusting. Then devoured the pastry in three bites.

'Thanks,' he said around mouthfuls.

Kate cringed. 'Are you feeling better?'

'A bit. This just isn't what I expected. Sierra is so . . . so horrible. I thought we'd all be nice to each other. That I'd finally have some friends. This feels all wrong. I don't even know why someone like her chose to be a schizo. She seems perfect to be a hed.'

'You saw the presentation. We're meant to be different. I'm sure we all have different reasons for our choice. From what I've seen of her I'm guessing Sierra wants to live life at full speed but have someone else take responsibility for the boring bits. Mike seems nice, but you can tell that he's vain. I guess he doesn't want to ever grow old.' She looked across at him. 'What are your reasons?'

'Isn't it obvious?' he said. 'Look at me. Sierra is right. I'm disgusting. I've ruined this body and I just want to be rid of it.'

Kate couldn't disagree with him with any pretence of being honest. 'So why not an andi?' she asked.

'I've spent all my life alone,' said Alex. 'I wanted to be part of something. Maybe it was a stupid choice. But maybe not.'

He reached across the table and held Kate's hand. She found it uncomfortable. Moist and slightly clammy. He didn't seem to understand normal social conventions. But she couldn't pull away without hurting his feelings more.

'What about you?' he asked. 'Why is someone like you becoming a schizo? Why would someone as pretty as you give up their body?'

Kate was embarrassed at his clumsy flattery. In other circumstances she would have thought he was hitting on her, but he was just trying to be sweet. She hesitated before replying. Maybe it would help to take his mind off his own problems.

'If I tell you, please don't tell the others. I don't want them all knowing.'

He nodded.

'For me it was a process of elimination,' she said. 'I grew up in a small village with a few hundred people. Nearly all workers. It was so dull. My mother was a single parent and spent the best years of her life juggling work with looking after me. Don't believe what that andi told us in the hall. Being a worker isn't a good choice. The name tells you everything. You work and work and work. Then you die. So I ruled that out. And I could never be a hed. I'd spend my whole life worrying about dying at forty-two. I don't know how they sleep at night.

'I was never going to be an andi.' She hesitated again. Should she share this with him? It seemed to be helping. He seemed calmer now, although he still hadn't let go of her hand. She plunged on. 'My father was an andi. My mother wouldn't talk much about him. They met when she was working in the city, young and impressionable. He was much older. Andis can have children the same way we do, but they don't often do so. So I don't know if I was planned or an accident. I never dared to ask. He evidently didn't want me. The relationship didn't last, and they split up when I was still young. I don't remember much about him.'

She tightened her grip on his hand, although she was no longer seeing Alex. 'My clearest memory is of him leaving. I'd just turned four. There was no drama, no shouting. Or not that I remember. I can see him pausing at the door, telling my mother he would send someone to collect his stuff, and saying goodbye in his normal way. He must have discussed it with her in advance, but he said nothing special to me. Not even a hug . . . nothing. I never saw him again.'

Kate blinked furiously. *Don't cry. Not now.* 'Sorry, I'm probably not helping. I didn't mean to tell you that much.'

'No,' said Alex, kindly. He looked intrigued. 'Carry on.'

'That's really it. My mother fled to a small village where no one knew us. Word gets around, though. The first time I heard the phrase "andi-whore" was at school, after my mother dropped me off. I thought it was something special, that it meant I was special. It was only when I repeated it at home that I understood. My mother cried. And it wasn't just the children who called her that. Adults can be just as cruel.' She paused and shook her head. 'It's a long time ago now. There's nothing I can do about it.'

She smiled weakly at Alex. 'So that's me. That's why I'm becoming a schizo. It wasn't really a choice. More about picking what was left. And getting rid of my half-andi body.' She took a deep breath. 'Come on, if you're feeling better we ought to get back. The others will be wondering what we're up to. We still have a lot to get through.'

Alex smiled. 'Thanks for telling me. I promise I won't tell anyone. It can be our secret. Just the two of us. As friends.'

•

Back in the room Mike and Sierra were sitting close, heads together, giggling about something. Ben was standing in front of the screen on the wall, reading lines of code. Mike looked up as they entered.

'You all right?' he asked Alex.

'I'm good. Thanks to Kate.' He looked pointedly at Sierra with an uncharacteristic flash of boldness.

They took their seats.

'Where had we got to?' asked Kate.

'We still haven't decided on a host,' said Mike. 'I'm voting for me. We could make good credit by selling my body, but we'd do better to keep it. I think Sierra is for me as well.' She nodded. 'What about the rest of you?'

'I'd be happy with Mike,' said Ben, softly, still staring at the floor. He looked up slightly, not meeting their eyes. 'Just so you know, I'm super bright. That's why I'm here. We will make a good team if Sierra can just learn to be nice to us. Five is a good number. It feels right.'

'I'll be sorry to say goodbye to this body, but I knew that was part of the deal,' said Kate. 'Mike is a good choice. Unless anyone disagrees, I think we've made our first decision.'

'Sure,' said Alex softly.

Kate went over to the screen and started tapping in their choices. After a moment she said, 'Right, decision made, and we're left with a time credit of 16.4 years. Before we decide whether to spend it, I suggest we work out where we go in the cycle. I'm happy to take the first slot. I've always been a morning person. I'm happy with my own company.'

'Give me one of the night slots,' said Sierra. 'I like the night, clubs, music, drinks. People are what I do best.'

'I want the morning,' said Mike. 'I need the daylight to go work out. I could take the slot after Kate.' There were nods all round. He looked across. 'What about you, Ben?'

'I don't much mind,' Ben said. 'Like Kate, I like to be on my own. But I don't want to never see the sun. The third slot will start at 14:00 – I'd like that.'

'I'd be happy with the last one,' said Alex. 'I stay up late. I could follow Sierra.'

She turned and put a hand on his knee, and winked at him. 'You just want to get close to me, don't you?' For the second time that day Alex blushed. He shied away from her.

'Leave it alone, Sierra,' said Kate wearily. 'If you want to help you could start by saying sorry to Alex.'

Sierra shook her head. 'I never apologise for anything. You'll learn to live with me.'

Kate sighed. She'd have years to sort Sierra out. No need to antagonise her now. 'Let's just move on. We've got a lot to get through. Let me get the cycle order down, and then we can discuss our other choices.'

The rest of the afternoon was spent considering the various

possible enhancements available. Was it better to spend two years on zoom lenses with night vision (Kate and Alex), fourteen months on EPO trickle glands (Mike), thirty months on neural nano implants (Ben and Alex), or three years on an inhibitor/reclean package that would not only speed up the effect of alcohol but also remove it at three times the normal rate (Sierra)?

The arguments ranged back and forth. By the end of the day they were tired, but seemed to have achieved consensus.

Kate, standing at the screen, made their final choices.

Mike gave Kate a high five.

'Nice one,' he said, looking around. 'See you all tomorrow. The first day of the rest of our lives.'

ALEX

DAY TWO
21:00–02:00

Sierra lies.

Know one thing about her, know that.

She flirts and charms. Manipulates and controls. But most of all she lies. Big lies, little lies, lies for a reason, and lies for no reason at all. Catch her out and she is utterly shameless. 'So what? I lie to get what I want. Why doesn't everyone?'

The worst of her lies seem to be reserved for me. That was the start of all our troubles.

So I usually assume that what she is saying isn't true.

Alex. I'm telling you this but you can't tell anyone else. I don't know who we can trust. Mike has gone missing and Kate has got involved in some dodgy deal with an andi called Amy Bird [see attached]. I tracked her to a bar but once I started asking questions I got hit on by shorty and his grunts [attached]. His name is Guskov and he seems to be some sort of drug dealer.

The thing is, he knew us. He said that one of us bought something from him. I'm thinking maybe he uses the andi to do his deals remotely, so they can't be traced back to him. I know you won't have been buying drugs, and it wasn't me, but it's got to be one of us? Maybe Mike bought some boosters, told Kate, and something went wrong with the deal.

I've arranged to meet this dealer called Karl who works for Guskov [attached]. He says he can tell me things about the andi and us. I'm hoping he can tell me what they sold to us. If it's performance boosters then we know it's Mike, which might explain why he disappeared.

I'm going to be short of time so don't whine to me if I have to drop out in a bar again. This time you can't blame me. I am trying to sort out the mess the others have made.

S.

I wasn't in a bar.

I was sitting in the dark in an abandoned warehouse, my back to a pile of overgrown rubble. Moonlight streamed in through what had once been the roof several storeys above me.

I didn't need the moon or my enhanced vision to tell that the shape on the floor in front of me had been human. Once. Now it lay like a broken doll, neck at an odd angle that no living person could tolerate, face turned towards me.

Karl's career as a drug dealer was over. He wasn't going to be telling anyone anything.

I felt sick, a cold sweat was on my arms. I'd never seen a dead body before. What should I do? Who to tell? Who could I trust?

The warehouse seemed deserted. There was no sign of anyone nearby, so I was safe for the moment. Before doing anything I skimmed the rest of my messages.

There was one from Kate that confirmed parts of what Sierra had said about the andi. A couple from Mike about choosing a new body. A private message from Mike saying he needed my support with buying an EliteCorps athlete, as Ben and Sierra wouldn't agree. None of that mattered for now.

There was another message from Mike telling me I ought to be more compassionate towards Sierra. Yeah, right.

Then nothing more from Mike.

Lastly one from Ben.

Alex. Strange things are happening, my friend. Kate has told you part of it, but not everything. See her message to me [attached].

I have sent Sierra to try to track down this andi of Kate's. Hopefully she will do it, and will have some news for you. If not you are going to have to find the andi.

We also need to know who this is [attached]. I found her leaving the arena where Mike did his race, together with the andi, shortly before I woke up at the wrong time.

Hopefully this is all about nothing, and by the time I'm next round Mike will have been in contact. It's not what we need, though, ten days before a new life.

I don't like any of this. We need to get things back to normal.

Ben.

As was obvious, things were anything but normal. I could answer some of Ben's queries, but not all. What to tell him?

First things first. I stood and walked over to the body, kneeling beside it. With difficulty I turned him over, trying not to look at the face as his head flopped to the other side. I swallowed hard to keep down the remains of whatever Sierra had been drinking. My throat tasted like acid. Real death was very different from the games. Even Jessica hadn't felt as bad as this.

Steeling myself, I rifled quickly through the pockets of his coat. They were stuffed with small packets, each containing a single black pill.

Perfect. I didn't know exactly what they were, but I had little doubt that they would prove to the others that Sierra was using again. I took one and stuffed it in my pocket.

The discovery of the pills also solved the problem of what to do with the body. I had contemplated calling ParkGov and putting the blame on Sierra. The trouble was that if she was hauled in for questioning we all were. Odds were that we all got locked up. And what would I say? That I was here sitting next to a cooling corpse, that he might have been killed by someone I was sharing a body with, and could they please come and arrest us? Once they had stopped laughing they would be here in a shot to take me away, plans ruined.

Better just to leave Karl where he was. If he was found with his pockets full of recreational drugs, ParkGov would just assume it was a deal gone wrong and leave it there. Case closed. There were enough bodies produced in a death park on a daily basis. No one was going to investigate the death of a drug-dealing hed with days left to live.

No. There was no point in calling the authorities. We needed to deal with this ourselves.

•

I retreated to my high-rise block to work out what to do next. It was quite a climb, but I needed somewhere safe and free from disturbance.

I sat cross-legged on the bed in the dark, staring out of the window at the moonlight on the ruined buildings below.

What to tell the others? What was it safe for me to say? The official line was that all messages were encrypted and confidential. No one believed that. Messages containing words such as 'murdered', 'killed' or 'dead' might well trigger an alert that had ParkGov hauling us in for questioning. I might be right that no one was going to care about a drug dealer who was days away from death. But it still wasn't worth taking the risk. Murder is murder.

I started with the easiest one.

Ben. We have to assume Mike lost his race, and that is why you woke early. If you ever watched anything other than games you would have recognised the woman leaving the arena with Bird as Svetlana Gurushkin, a former elite marathon runner. She hit the headlines a couple of years ago after she signed up to be the face of Siber-X, an energy drink said to be sourced from the spring waters of the Ural Mountains in Siberia. It turned out that the springs were next to an abandoned nuclear power plant, and the secret ingredient of Siber-X was depleted Uranium-235. The last I heard, Gurushkin was bankrupt and in jail. I don't know how she ended up running a race against Mike. Presumably someone has slipped her a chunk of time. He wouldn't have stood a chance against her, even in retirement.

But if he died in the game then we all ought to be out of here, waking up after a couple of weeks in stasis and arguing about what body to choose for our next life. And we'd have lost all our time. But we're still here and Mike has gone missing. I don't understand how that is possible.

Sierra traced Bird to the bar where you saw her, but then got leaned on by some drug dealer. See her message to me [attached]. I didn't hear from her after that, so don't know what Karl told her at the meeting. But he won't be troubling us again. In my pocket is a pill that he was selling. We really need to know what it is. It seems to me that either Sierra or Mike has been buying stuff they shouldn't. Sierra may be using again, or Mike may have decided he needed a performance boost. Sierra says she didn't, but we know how far we can believe what she says. If we knew what was in the pill then we would know which. But I don't know how we get it analysed without someone asking questions.

I don't understand where Bird comes into this. Why did she get in touch with Kate instead of Sierra or Mike? Why did Kate give her access? Is there something Kate isn't telling us?

None of this makes sense for a minor drug deal gone wrong. If Mike or Sierra didn't pay I could understand if one of us woke up in a back alley with a broken nose, or some ribs kicked in. This seems way too elaborate.

Did Sierra see something she hasn't told us?

We need to find Bird again. I'm running out of time. Not much more I can do this cycle. Let me know what you can find out.

Alex.

Next a message to Mike, copied to the others.

Mike, we need to hear from you. Get in touch asap. Alex.

Then one to Kate.

Kate. As you'll have seen, there's lots of odd things happened since your encounter with Bird. Mike's gone missing. I'm copying you a message from Sierra where she tracked Bird to a local bar [attached]. It seems as though someone (Sierra?) bought some drugs from this dealer earlier, and Bird was somehow involved.

Or could it be Mike? Or Ben, even? Something weird happened in Mike's game, and if anyone could manipulate a game it would be Ben.

There's a pill in my pocket that came from the dealer, Karl, that Sierra mentions meeting. If you can find out what it is that might tell us who was buying from them.

I've got to drop out any minute. Let me know what you find.

A.

Finally a private message to Sierra, copied to Kate and Ben.

Sierra. I found Karl but didn't learn anything useful – as you will have guessed. What were you doing dropping out in a warehouse?

Please be honest for once – are you using again? Is this all down to you? It might not just be Mike. We are all at risk now.

Alex.

I wasn't going to say anything more to her. Generally the less information you give Sierra, the better. I hadn't trusted Sierra from the first day I met her.

KATE

Things seemed to have gone to hell since my last cycle. There was a brief moment of first waking when I enjoyed the feeling of another morning, before the memory of the previous day's events came crashing down on me.

It didn't get any better as I waded through my messages.

I started with a high priority from CGov, telling me that on this occasion my imminent death excused me from public service, but that they would be in touch again once I was in my new body. Great.

But probably the least of my worries.

There were forty-seven challenges to various forms of death match. The lists would have been updated overnight, and with twenty-four years we were now a juicy target for everyone. There was a message from ParkGov reminding us that we were here to play, and if we didn't complete at least one challenge per cycle we would forfeit time and be assigned one at random. I didn't remember that being in the rules. Maybe they only bothered to enforce it once you'd acquired enough time to become an interesting target. We could presumably still leave the park before midnight and avoid competing. Alex was going to have to make that decision.

Most worrying was the fact that no one had heard from Mike since his race. There was an excited message from him about the twenty years I had won, and potential new bodies. And then nothing.

My heart sank as I read on through the various messages from Ben and Alex. Mike had been suckered into a race that he couldn't win. But we were still here, and had all our time, which made no sense at all. I could raise a query with ParkGov about Mike's race, but if he'd lost, that risked alerting them to the fact that something had gone wrong. The likelihood was that they would deem us losers and take away all the time we had won.

Poor Ben. He hated change. This would be killing him.

All of this was somehow connected with Amy Bird. As I'd guessed, she was still alive. I'd been right to be suspicious of her, and should never have taken the challenge. Had I killed Mike by giving her access? What had Mike or Sierra got involved in with the andi? It all seemed too elaborate for a drug deal gone wrong. As Alex suggested, if anyone could manipulate a game it would be Ben. But why? Could he and Mike be up to something?

I felt in my pocket and pulled out a packet containing a small black pill. It could have been anything. I found it hard to believe that this could be causing all our troubles. Had we stumbled across something much bigger? Was Guskov behind all this?

If Bird had been telling me the truth then we would be carrying an extra mind, and I could expect to be contacted by someone this cycle to tell me how to remove it. I hadn't been entirely honest with the others about what I agreed to with Bird, as they would have been horrified at the idea of me letting in a sixth person, even if only for a day and with no control. Although I doubted now whether any of what Bird had told me was true.

I logged on through my admin codes. There was no record of the sixth space ever having been accessed, let alone recently. So good news and bad news. We weren't carrying anyone extra, but the andi's story had been lies from beginning to end.

I couldn't tell whether Mike was still with us. Although I had access to restricted areas, privacy controls meant that I didn't know who occupied which space. Each space showed traffic and I couldn't differentiate between messages going in and out, so it told me nothing. For all I could tell, Mike was in there but keeping quiet, screaming his head off unheard, or gone for good.

This was getting us nowhere. I needed to find another way. Tracking down Amy Bird seemed like a long shot. If Ben couldn't find her then I wasn't going to.

The only other lead we had was the pill. I couldn't go to the authorities with it. Equally, I wasn't going to find the answer cruising the bars at seven in the morning.

I sat staring at the pill as though it could provide a solution.

Then it struck me who might know the answer.

•

As I'd hoped, halfway to Borth Street the man in the long coat was in the same spot as the day before at the end of the alley.

Again, business seemed quiet, and he perked up as I walked over. Up close I saw his face was lined. His long black hair, down to his shoulders, made him look younger than he was.

'Hey, what can I do for you today?' he asked. 'What game are you playing? Give me the name and I'll tell you what you need.'

'I'm not playing,' I said. 'I'm looking for information.' I looked down at his suitcase, coloured packets and bottles of pills neatly arrayed. 'Is this stuff legal?'

'Hey! What sort of a question is that?' He kicked the lid of the suitcase shut and I heard the whirring of a locking mechanism. No doubt he could send a signal that would incinerate the contents of the suitcase, destroying any evidence. I'd obviously come to the right man.

'Relax,' I said quickly. Making him destroy his drugs by mistake wasn't going to get us off to a good start. 'I got passed something last night that I'm pretty sure isn't legal. I was hoping you could tell me what it is.'

'And what makes you think I'd know?'

I said nothing, just looked down at his suitcase again.

'All right,' he said. 'I might be able to help you. But not here.' He glanced left and right. 'We're being watched all the time. How much is it worth to you?'

'It depends on what you can tell me. But it'll be more than you're making standing here at seven in the morning with no customers.'

He considered for a moment. 'All right. Meet me at 8:30, at this address.' He touched his hand to mine. 'Tell them you're there to see Godfried.' He paused. 'That's me.'

'Fine. See you there.'

I killed time by finding somewhere for breakfast, then took a leisurely stroll to the address he'd given me. It was a nondescript brown door in yet another crumbling concrete monolith. There was an old-fashioned intercom next to the door. I pressed the button.

'Yes?'

'I'm here to see Godfried.'

'Come up.' The door buzzed open.

I stepped into a dimly lit corridor that led to a flight of stairs. At the top a middle-aged woman was sitting behind a desk. She looked up at me, and nodded to her right. 'Carry on through – God's in the bar.'

To my surprise the corridor opened out into a large, circular room with high ceilings and elaborate chandeliers. A long curved bar ran along one edge. Along the opposite edge was a row of red-leather booths. Dotted around the rest of the room were low tables and armchairs, separated from one another by small trees in pots. This was by far the nicest place I'd been in the death park.

The bar was dark and deserted at that time of morning. It took me a moment to find Godfried. He was sitting in one of the armchairs, suitcase at his side. He'd discarded his coat.

He rose at my approach and shook my hand.

'So, Ms Weston,' he said. 'What will you have? I can recommend the Admiral Nelson. You're paying.'

I looked down at his glass. 'Rum? At 8:30 in the morning? I'm fine, thanks.'

'Gods, woman,' he said. 'If I wanted to be told when I could drink I'd have got married.'

I shrugged and sat down across from him.

He gestured to the room. 'What do you think?'

'It's incredible. What's somewhere like this doing in the middle of a death park?'

'It's a club, of sorts,' he said. 'Invitation only. You can do things here that you aren't allowed to do in the games.'

'Like what?'

'Pretty much anything. You want to gamble with your time, see if you can win big? The casino is through there.' He pointed to an unmarked door next to the bar. 'That's tame, though. Suppose you've given up on ever leaving the park and want to drift towards death in the most pleasant way possible. There's an opium den. You rapidly get into a death spiral, trading more and more of your time for drugs, until eventually you have nothing left. I'm told it's a pleasant way to go.

'There's a lot here that isn't nearly as pleasant. There are some for whom killing in the arenas isn't enough any more. Maybe it never was. For them it's the act of killing that matters, not winning time. They want to kill without risk to themselves. Let's say you've got a few days left to live and you know the odds of getting any more in the arenas are low. They'll offer you what's known as the mini-hed package. You live here for thirty days, all the alcohol, drugs, gambling, whores, whatever you want. But you never leave. At the end of the thirty days you're stuck in a room with some rich psychopath to die as part of his – or her – twisted fantasies.

'There's plenty more like that. There are game booths here where you can play games that are banned in the arenas. Basically, whatever sick desires you have, if you've got enough credit you'll find someone in the park who's willing to act it out with you. It makes what I do look innocent.' He paused, and took a drink.

'So why are you a member if you find it all so distasteful?' I asked.

'I'm more on the service side of things. There's good business to be had here at night. I don't come here for pleasure. Unlike others.' He nodded to one of the booths opposite the bar. 'The good doctor over there, for instance.'

I turned in surprise. I'd thought we were alone. Half hidden in the darkness of the booth was a pale-faced man wearing an old-fashioned three-piece suit. He had a short dark beard, and piercing blue eyes that were staring at me. He smiled slightly as my gaze met his, but made no effort to look away. I shivered and turned back to Godfried. But I could still feel those eyes on me.

'Ugh,' I said, beginning to wish I'd taken up the offer of a drink. 'Who is he?'

'Doctor Bernard. He practically lives here. He's been in the park for years. Much longer than I have. Rumour is that he fled here because he's wanted for horrible crimes. Or he worked for a secret government agency, and left when they wouldn't let him carry out his more extreme experiments. I don't know which is true, but from what I've seen I can believe either story. He seems to have limitless amounts of time, and he's sponsored some of the most gruesome acts here.' Godfried paused, and took another drink.

'Years ago, before my time, they staged a live chess tournament that lasted a month. Paid for, it was said, by the doctor. A board was painted on the floor – you can still see traces of it.

Two players at either end, and the pieces were live humans. The doctor always played white. Every time a piece was captured they got taken to the side of the board and had their heads chopped off. People came here instead of playing in the game booths. The potential rewards were much better. You could choose which piece you wanted to be. If you lived through the game there were big rewards. Apparently the trick was to study the players and try to work out which pieces were most likely to survive. Do you choose to be a lowly pawn, skulking around the edges of the board hoping you'll be overlooked? Or go for broke and be the queen? Ultimate power, but everyone's gunning for you. A bit like life, really. By the end of the month the bodies were stacking up round the back like empties. It drew too much attention and the owners decided it was a one-off.' He paused again, and looked at me.

'But you're not here for a history lesson, Ms Weston. What do you want from me?'

'I want to know what this is,' I said, reaching into my pocket and passing over the packet containing the pill.

He glanced at it and put it on the table next to his drink. 'Where did you get it?'

'Someone gave it to me in a bar last night. They said I should take it if I wanted a good time.'

His smile vanished, and his voice became hard. 'That seems most unlikely, Ms Weston. Where did you really get it?'

I hesitated. What could I safely tell him? 'Someone . . . someone I know acquired it.'

'Where? Only one group that sells this stuff in the park. There's a rumour going round that someone knocked off one of their dealers last night. Then you show up asking questions about their product. Where did you get it?'

'I can't tell you any more than that,' I said. 'If I'd killed a dealer I'd hardly be going round the park asking people to identify their merchandise, would I? All I want to know is what it is. If you can tell me, fine, I'll pay you for that information. If you can't then I'll be off.' I reached forward to pick up the pill.

He put his hand on mine to stop me, then sat back.

'On second thoughts,' he said, 'I don't want to know where you got it. You're mixed up in some serious shit here, and the less I'm told the better. I'll tell you what you want to know. But the price has just gone up. I'm going to need to pay off a couple of people here to pretend they didn't see me with you. It'll cost you four months.'

'*Four months?*' I said. 'I'm not trying to buy your first-born child. This information is worth a few days, at most. I'll find someone else to tell me.'

'Fine with me. You go out and keep asking these questions, and I'll be along later to collect your body. I could probably get more than four months by selling you out, but I don't want anyone to know I'm involved in this. That's the price.' He picked up the packet and tossed it back to me. 'Have your pill back if you don't want to know.'

'All right,' I said. 'I pay you afterwards. If what you tell me is worth it.' Although Godfried seemed nice enough, in an immoral sort of way, I didn't like dealing with him. What he was doing was illegal. Mike, or Sierra, shouldn't have put us in this position.

'You'll pay me afterwards or be leaving here in a body bag.

I have friends here; you don't. How much do you know about andis?'

'As much as anyone, I suppose. They tend to be cold, unemotional freaks, driven by logic and little else. What have andis got to do with this?'

'Everything,' he said. 'No one would have given you that pill, and they certainly wouldn't have told you it would get you high. That's not what it is. And anyway, it only works on andis. The whole point of andis is that they're low-maintenance. They consume almost nothing. But they can mimic us if they want to. They can eat and drink, although they don't need to. If they do they need to excrete it. They can sweat. They can cry. All of that leads to mineral imbalances in their bodies over time. These pills correct that. If you're an andi you need to take one every month or so. Why this couldn't just be fixed with some trickle gland I don't know. Some say it's CGov's way of controlling the andis, since they're the only official source of these pills.'

'So why are people selling them illegally in the park?' I asked. 'Is there a shortage?'

'No. Not for official andis. They get given them free every month from authorised clinics. For unofficial andis it's a different story.'

'For what?' I asked. 'I've never heard of an "unofficial" andi. I thought you made your choice at seventeen and that was it.'

'They only exist in places like this. They can never leave. As I said, there are a lot of desperate people in the death parks. Not everyone is here to play in the games. Or they come here to play and then they get scared. Too frightened of death. Strictly speaking, if you don't work in the park you can't stay here unless you regularly compete. But that's a rule that only tends to get enforced against players with big credit scores, to keep things interesting. Like the doctor, I've been here for years. And there are plenty of others like us. Some people use their remaining time to buy a second-hand andi body, and their mind is moved into it. I don't know how it works, exactly. Whether someone manages to skim off the occasional body from the arenas before recycling. Or they're somehow converting dandis. One way or another they have access to andi bodies.' He paused and knocked back the last of his rum.

'It's just another form of death sentence,' he said. 'A slower one. They can't leave the park because they have no status and they'd immediately be picked up and erased. They no longer have an expiry date, but they also don't have much credit left. And a death park is a pretty grim place to be without credit. So they usually end up dying somewhere like this. In the meantime they need to buy these pills to stay alive. That's why there's a black market for them. Whatever your choices, you get screwed from every side in the park.'

'Are you sure that's what it is?' I said. Why would any of us have been buying pills for andis?

He stood up. 'I know what that pill is. Hundred per cent. I've told you all that I can. Please transfer the time and we'll be done with this. I don't know what you're mixed up in, but good luck.' He reached out a hand to me.

'Thanks.' I transferred the time. It was expensive, but he'd done what he'd promised.

He picked up his coat and suitcase, and made his way towards the door. Then turned back to me with a broad smile. 'You can settle my bar bill on the way out.'

I nodded, my mind on other things. I was more confused than ever. There was no neat answer to this. Mike hadn't been buying illegal boosters, and Sierra wasn't using again. Why would either of them – or Alex or Ben, for that matter – have been buying pills to treat a condition they didn't have? We didn't know anyone in the park, let alone any andis, so they couldn't have been buying pills for someone else. Unless they were for Amy Bird. But why would any of us have been buying pills for an andi who clearly already had her own connections to the park underworld? We'd only just arrived.

This Guskov might have had a strong interest in protecting his secrecy, but why would Mike or Sierra have had anything to do with him?

And we still weren't any closer to knowing where Mike was. Was he dead? Was it even possible for one part of a schizo to die? I ran a search to try to find out if one mind in a schizo can be erased, and if so what happens. There was nothing useful, which suggested it wasn't possible. In the end I gave up and posted a question to CGov on an anonymous message board. I wanted to know the answer, but I didn't want them knowing it came from me. We had enough difficulties already without having the authorities breathing down our neck.

What should I tell the others? Which of them could I trust? I'd never seen eye-to-eye with Sierra, but there was nothing to suggest she was behind any of this. If she had been, why would she have told us that Guskov seemed to have dealt with one of us already? Unless it was some elaborate double-bluff. All Ben lived for was the game booths, so why would he want to be rid of any of us? Or Alex? It was hard to see why, or how, he'd have done anything to Mike.

In the end I messaged Ben and Alex with an update, leaving Sierra out of the loop. I had to trust someone.

Ben/Alex. I've found out what the pills are. They're something and is need to take to stay alive. None of us would have needed that, so I don't understand why we would have been buying them off Guskov or Bird. I've got nowhere towards finding Bird. Hopefully, Ben, you'll be waking up after Mike, and everything will be back to normal. If not, the two of you need to find Bird somehow. She needs to be made to tell us what she did and how we unwind it. K.

As I got up to leave I heard my name called quietly from across the room.

'Ms Weston.' It was the doctor. His voice was a soft hiss, barely audible. He curled a long finger, beckoning me over.

I crossed reluctantly to the booth. He looked me up and down.

'It is a pleasure to meet you in person, Ms Weston,' he said. His eyes looked excited, greedy almost. 'Such a pleasure.'

'Have we met before?' I asked.

'No.'

'So what do you want from me?'

'Nothing. Yet. I wanted to wish you well with the rest of your games.'

I was being dismissed. Which I didn't mind. But creepy as he was, maybe I could learn something from him. Confirm what

Godfried had told me. I dug in my pocket for the pill.

'You're a doctor, aren't you? Can you tell me what this is?'

He didn't even glance at it. His sharp blue eyes remained fixed on mine.

'I can't help you with that,' he said. 'Not my speciality.'

'Which is?' I asked.

'Pathology,' he hissed.

BEN

It was 11:00. I was in Mike's time again. So it hadn't been a glitch last cycle. He wasn't just keeping quiet. I didn't like this time. I don't like change.

I had a message from Alex telling me that Sierra hadn't managed to find Bird, and speculating that Mike or Sierra had been buying illegal drugs. Then one from Kate saying that the drugs were something to do with andis, so there was no reason for any of us to be buying them. They didn't seem to be any further forward. All that we knew was that we were somehow mixed up with a drug dealer.

Given Sierra's history, and her inability to tell the truth, my instinct was that it must be something to do with her. But if so, why had they gone after Mike? That suggested that he was the one that knew something. How did they know that he had not shared it with the rest of us? Did that mean we were all at risk? And I still didn't understand why Kate had allowed the andi Bird to access our minds. That in itself was suspicious. And what about Alex? He was quick to blame Sierra for everything.

Still too many questions. The one person who could tell us something useful was Bird. We needed to find her.

I checked the searches that I had set up in the previous cycle. There were two alerts.

The first was at 20:14 – there was a short clip of Amy Bird emerging from a narrow alley next to the Death's Head. She turned away from the bar, seemingly in a hurry, and I lost her. That couldn't be a coincidence. If Sierra was telling the truth, that was when she had been in the bar talking to Guskov. Had she also met Bird and not told us?

I traced the original feed and let it run on. At 20:26 I saw us – Sierra – leave the Death's Head, heading in the same direction as Bird.

The second alert was almost an hour later – 21:14 – around a kilometre away. It came from a ParkGov drone that had been passing down a deserted street, razorwire fence on one side, a crumbling warehouse on the other. As it raced past, a figure emerged from the warehouse. The drone stopped and circled back, a spotlight snapping on. Amy Bird glanced up, then quickly down, one hand shielding her eyes. She stepped back through the door into the warehouse.

The drone hovered for a long moment, seemingly hesitating over whether to follow her inside. Then its AI evidently decided that it had seen nothing suspicious, and continued down the street, accelerating hard.

I rewound the clip. There was no question it was Bird. What was she doing there? I scouted round for other cameras, but there were none.

I relaxed my criteria and started getting more hits. But after watching my thirtieth clip of an andi that looked a bit like Bird but wasn't, I gave up. She had gone to ground somewhere.

Out of interest I went back to the clip of Sierra leaving the bar. Number of views: 110. Whereas the drone's clip of Bird had been viewed only twice. That was consistent with what I had observed in the previous cycle. Who was watching us? And why?

I turned my attention to Guskov. With his distinctive appearance and bodyguards he ought to have been easy to find. I started near the Death's Head, since we knew he had been there recently, and that was where I had first picked up Bird. Nothing. He must have had a more discreet method of entry and exit than she did. I widened the search.

An hour later I had a whole lot of nothing, plus tired eyes and a headache. Guskov knew how to avoid leaving a trail.

We had a choice. Pack up and leave with our time before the end of the cycle, to avoid having to fight any further challenges. Or stick around and try to find Mike. I didn't want to abandon him until we had lost all hope.

We were running out of ideas, and I wasn't sure where to go next.

But before I did anything I needed to eat. Kate seemed to have forgotten that. Or maybe she normally left it to Mike. It was the first time I had ever followed her. She had left me in a cheap locker motel which was so old fashioned it didn't even have a room printer.

I headed out, cutting across an overgrown lot between two high-rises to get to a diner. It was deserted outside. People who go to death parks don't tend to go for walks for their health.

Our body moves gracefully and quietly, even when I am

controlling it, so I heard the movement behind me moments before a slab-like hand landed on my shoulder. I tried, and failed, to shrug it off.

A deep voice rumbled behind me. 'Mr White. We need you.'

The hand released me and I turned quickly, backing away.

I recognised the two of them immediately from Sierra's description. Vincent and Stas, Guskov's bodyguards. I tried to scan them: nothing. I tried to send a call for help but realised I was blocked. And who would I call anyway?

The thick features of the first andi crumpled into a smile.

'No one's coming to help you. Don't run away.'

'What do you want with me?' I asked.

'I have an invitation for you, Mr White. Our employer would like to ask you a few questions,' he growled.

Whatever the reason for Guskov summoning us back, I wasn't keen on answering his questions. I didn't have much choice, though. Given a head start, I was confident I could outrun these hulks, but they were too close and I didn't rate my chances of out-fighting them.

'Well,' said the first andi. 'Are you coming with us? Or,' he smiled again, 'are we going to have some fun first? I'd enjoy breaking that pretty nose of yours.'

'What does Mr Guskov want to talk about?' I asked. 'And where are we going?'

'You'll find out when we get there. It's not far.'

I resigned myself. They walked close on either side, with no chance for me to escape. There was no one around to help, but even if there had been I didn't imagine a passer-by would get involved.

After five minutes we turned down an alley lined with rubble, cutting between two streets, and I realised that we were heading back to the Death's Head. The lead andi pushed through the doors and into the empty bar. His colleague followed close behind. I was led along a passageway, up some stairs – fourteen, which was a good number – and stopped outside a wooden door. The first andi opened it.

'After you.'

Guskov was seated behind a large desk. He looked up as I entered. The window behind him provided a view of a small park with a dried-up lake. I pondered my chances of diving through the window before the andis got to me. Not high. Besides, there were three panels of glass in the window. That didn't bode as well as the stairs.

'Back so soon,' said Guskov. 'Please. Sit.'

I gave up on the idea of escape, and sat down. One of the andis shut the door.

Guskov looked me up and down. 'So, Mr White. You schizos aren't easy to deal with. We don't get many of your sort here. Was it really Ms Summers that I spoke to yesterday?'

I didn't see much point in lying about that. I didn't know why he had called us back, but I doubted it was to offer afternoon tea. 'Yes, that was Sierra.'

'So was she the one who lured one of my employees into an abandoned warehouse and murdered him?' he asked. 'Or was that you? I have a reputation for many things, most of them not good, but one thing I am known for is protecting my people.'

Oh, God. As if we didn't have enough problems. None of the others had said anything about a dead dealer. Then again, Alex had said something about Karl 'not troubling us again'. Was that some cryptic reference to him being dead? If so, who killed him? Alex? Sierra? Why would either of them have done that?

I realised that my chances of getting out of this room alive had dropped dramatically. Or rather, our chances of getting out alive. Die in an arena and if you are schizo you move on to your next life. It's inconvenient but not deadly. Die anywhere else and that's it. Real death for all of us. There's no machine around to catch your minds and preserve them for transfer to a new body.

'I've no idea what you're talking about,' I said. 'I haven't killed anyone. And I've no reason to suppose that anyone else in our commune has. But I wouldn't know. I don't know what Sierra does when she is in here, any more than she knows what I get up to. Legally, we're separate people. I'm no more responsible for what Sierra does than she is for me.'

Guskov sat back and looked at me quizzically. 'Interesting,' he said. 'I had expected a denial. It's an odd life that you schizos choose. Trusting your existence to others over whom you have no control. I appreciate that legally you and this Sierra are different. But as you might have guessed, the law isn't always enforced in the park. My employee had his neck broken. It must have taken someone of considerable strength and speed to do that. You appear to have both.' He looked over my head at the andis. 'Stas, get the girl.'

Stas stepped outside. We sat in silence until he returned, dragging a reluctant woman by one arm. 'Let me go!' she shouted, making a futile effort to pull herself free. Stas turned her to face me.

She might once have been attractive, but her red hair was

142

dishevelled, her eyes puffy, her cheeks tear-stained. She lurched forward when she saw me, straining against her captor.

'That's him . . . her,' she shouted. 'She's the one Karl arranged to meet last night. She killed him.'

'That's what we are finding out,' said Guskov, calmly. 'That's all I wanted. Take her back out.'

'No,' she screamed, as Stas half carried her towards the door. 'Check her clothes. That'll prove it.'

'I'll decide that,' said Guskov, watching silently as she kicked against Stas and cursed them both.

When the door had closed he turned back to me.

'So, Mr White, it's not looking good, is it? Your Ms Summers arranges to meet my employee, and shortly after he's dead. And then I hear that this morning you're sniffing around the park with one of my pills, asking about my merchandise. That was unwise.' He paused, and sighed.

'It all points to you, doesn't it? The trouble is that I'm a simple man. Unlike the authorities I don't have the ability to extract one mind from your body and erase it, or put it in a stasis tank for a hundred years. Even if I did, it's not a very visual punishment. It doesn't send the same message as hanging you from the ceiling while my pet doctor shaves slices off you until you can no longer scream. Karl may not have been worth much but I need to be seen to be protecting my people. It makes them nervous when one of them dies and I don't kill someone in response.'

This was looking bad.

'Wait,' I said. 'What did she mean? Check my clothes?'

Guskov pushed his glasses up his nose, blinking through

them at me. Then he tossed something across the desk to me. I caught it awkwardly. It was a bright red button, thread hanging from it.

'She meant that. Recognise it?'

'No,' I said. 'It's nothing to do with us.' Although as I said that I realised that it did trigger some memory. I had seen it somewhere, and recently. 'Why does it matter?'

'My dead employee was clutching this in his hand when we found him. It seems reasonable to assume he tore it off whoever killed him.'

'Hang on,' I said, turning the button over in my hand. Trying to remember. It was so close. I shut my eyes and I could see it. *Yes – that was it.* 'I know who it was,' I said quickly. 'Give me a moment.' I pulled up one of the clips I'd been viewing earlier, and there it was. A row of red buttons on the cuff of a black sleeve.

I looked up at Guskov. 'I can't send you this. I'm blocked. But I need to show you.'

'Show Vincent,' he said.

The andi walked over to me and we touched fingers. Vincent stood still for a moment, then nodded and walked round the desk to Guskov. He passed on the clip.

It was Amy Bird, the previous night, emerging from the alley next to the Death's Head. While Guskov was viewing it I found the footage from the drone, showing her briefly stepping out of the warehouse. I paused the clip as she raised an arm to shield herself from the drone, and zoomed in. One of the buttons was missing, a torn thread all that remained. *Yes.*

'There's one more,' I said, holding out my hand to Vincent.

We went through the same procedure. 'Check the coordinates. Is that where your dealer's body was found?'

Guskov sat back, lips pursed, pushing his glasses up his nose again. He said nothing. To me it seemed clear. But he didn't seem convinced.

'Look,' I said. 'It's obviously your andi, Amy Bird, who did this. I don't know why, but it's nothing to do with us. Maybe this dealer of yours, Karl, stepped out of line, and Bird thought you wouldn't care if she disposed of him. Maybe she was worried that Karl was going to tell Sierra about your pill operation. There's nothing to prove that Sierra was involved.'

'Proof?' said Guskov. 'That isn't how things work round here, Mr White. You sound like a lawyer. I don't like lawyers.' He grimaced, as though the idea of dealing with them caused him physical pain. 'You are also badly misinformed. This Bird, as you call her, is not "my andi". And I don't make my living selling pills. Showing me that Bird killed Karl really doesn't help you.' He stared at me, tapping his fingers on the wooden desk.

'What did you sell us if it wasn't pills?' I asked.

I was finding it hard to think with the noise from the beating of his fingers on the desk. Each tap drove a nail into my brain. I started hitting my hand against the side of my leg in the same rhythm, to drown out the sound. Sometimes it helps.

He looked at me oddly, and stopped. I breathed out. He leaned forward and rested his chin on steepled fingers, staring at me through the gold-rimmed glasses. My life was being weighed. His expression didn't change until eventually he laughed coldly. 'Perhaps you are as naïve as you pretend to be,' he said. 'That makes it even better. Come with me. I'm going to show you something. Then I will decide what to do with you.'

Vincent opened the door. The three of us followed yet another corridor and went down four flights of stairs. There was a smell of damp. It was colder now. After a minute we came to a heavy metal door, which the andi opened. Lights flickered on in the room beyond.

We stepped into a vast, cold, windowless space. The roof was the height of the building, several storeys high, dark apart from occasional skylights. It stretched a good hundred metres back, crisscrossed with metal gantries and stairs, many rusted and hanging at odd angles. Ground level was a jumble of machinery. It was a mess. I don't like mess.

The only nods to modernity were the lights and two rows of what looked like glass coffins in a corner of the room near the door that had been cleared of debris. There were ten in each row, neatly ordered. Twenty in total. Excellent.

'What is this place?' I asked.

'It was once a meatpacking factory,' he said. 'In the days when we still did that. Look.' He pointed to large hooks hanging from an overhead conveyer belt. 'Now it is my storeroom. It has a natural coolness that helps in ensuring that my ... merchandise doesn't spoil.' He gestured to either side. 'This is what I sell, and this is what you – one of you – bought from me.'

I walked over and peered through the glass lid of the nearest coffin. A blank but surprisingly lifelike face stared back at me. The body was coated in a layer of slime.

'What are they?' I asked. 'Bodies?'

'Andis,' said Guskov. 'After people die in the arenas the occasional andi goes missing on the way to recycling. Not enough to be a problem, but enough to make a profit. They end up here. The pills are just a sideline. Mostly my andis are bought by those who come to the park and then realise that they are too scared to play but don't want to die. So I give them a body with no end date. I shouldn't say this, but most regret their purchase. A death park is a grim place to live. What I really provide them with is the chance to live a little longer and drink themselves to death in one of the bars I own. So I win all round. Sometimes I even get the same body back to sell all over again.' He chuckled to himself. 'I ought to get some sort of eco award for all the recycling I do. Or sometimes I sell them as dandis. They've all got basic AI and it's easy enough to turn on the personality that the customer wants: personal butler, sex slave, whatever.'

'Are you saying that one of us bought an andi from you?' I asked. 'We've only been in the park a week. That doesn't make any sense.'

'That is all I can tell you. One of you bought Bird. The andi that you have been trying to find belongs to you, not me.'

'Why would any of us want an andi?' I said. 'It makes no sense.'

'Are you doubting my word?' he asked sharply.

'Of course not,' I said quickly. 'So who is Bird? We know she's an andi, but whose mind is inside?'

'How would I know?' said Guskov. 'She was a dandi when she walked away from here. Basic AI, but nothing more. But dandis don't kill people. And that wasn't a dandi we saw in the clips you showed me.'

It certainly wasn't a dandi that had scammed Kate into giving up the access codes. That had been a human mind. I still couldn't understand what one of us had been doing buying an andi almost as soon as we got to the death park.

Guskov interrupted my thoughts.

'So, what to do with you, Mr White? Who may have killed Karl – or had him killed – but appears to know nothing about it.'

'Wait,' I said. 'It wasn't me. And even if it was Bird it doesn't mean it was one of us. Besides, killing us would cause you trouble. At the moment we have the highest time credit of anyone in the park – more than twenty-four years. We've got dozens of challenges. If we disappear, someone is going to look into it. I know I'm blocked, but I'm sure Vincent was picked up at some point on our walk over here. No doubt you could bury an investigation but it would cost you. Let's not do something we'll both regret.'

Guskov smiled. 'I can say with some confidence that you will regret it more than I do. Vincent has buried many things for me. I'm sure it wouldn't trouble him to add you to the list.'

'That may be true,' I said quickly. 'But you could make a profit from this, and still set an example. If you kill us outside an arena our twenty-four years disappear. Everyone loses. But I could transfer some time to you in compensation for whatever part my associates may have had in your employee's death. We all win.'

He breathed out slowly, studying me. 'I've got a better idea. Vincent, we need to get rid of the girlfriend. Then spread the rumour that she had Karl killed – lover's spat or something. You know the routine.'

'All right, boss,' said Vincent. 'Should I give her to the doctor? He's been asking for someone new, and he'd pay well.'

'No,' said Guskov. 'Too messy. Sell her to an arena. She can be bait in one of the games, and she'll disappear.'

'All right, boss.'

Guskov turned back to me. 'As for you, Mr White, you're right that it would cause me some inconvenience to kill you. At the end of the day I work for profit, and I hate to see waste. I'll make you an offer. I don't want to appear greedy. I will let you go in return for a flat fee of ten years.'

I hesitated before answering. That was a lot of time. But I wasn't sure that I had much choice.

He smiled. 'Choose carefully before you try to bargain with me. You can take the deal or try to fight your way out of here, which would be entertaining in itself. For you it is, quite literally, the offer of a lifetime. In fact, all your lifetimes.'

There was no chance I was going to fight my way out past his two thugs. But *ten years* – that was half a lifetime. No one was going to be happy with me for giving that up. Then again, we'd come by it cheaply, and better to lose it than die. I had no choice.

'All right,' I said reluctantly.

'Good. Let's go back upstairs and sort out the legalities. After that, Mr White, it is probably best that we don't meet again. It might end badly. And not for me.'

SIERRA

DAY THREE
16:00–21:00

My day didn't start well. I woke at the wrong time and no one was telling me anything.

There was nothing from Mike, and despite everything going on I had nothing from Kate or Ben either.

All I had to work out what the hell was going on was an aggressive message from Alex, suggesting that I was using again, and that I was lying to him. I didn't bother to reply.

If they didn't want my help that was their problem.

Then, to entirely ruin my day, a message from ParkGov appeared.

ParkGov to S. Summers and A. Du Bois. One of the conditions of your entry into the park was that you would, if required, complete at least one challenge per cycle. You have yet to accept or complete any challenge this cycle. We have therefore assigned you one at random [details attached]. If you do not complete this challenge by midnight it will count as a forfeit. You may choose to leave the park before midnight, in which event you will be fined

one half of your accrued time for failure to complete a challenge in
this cycle.

Great. How had the others let this happen to us? Kate was
meant to keep on top of this. I already had good ideas as to how
we were going to spend the time that we had. I wasn't going to
give up half of it to the park.

I looked at the challenge.

Revillagigedo Island – Moral Dilemmas

The submarine USS *Marlin* lies trapped under 1,000 feet of water.
You must make a series of command decisions to decide who lives
and who dies. Are you up to the challenge of naval command?

The name was stupid. So unpronounceable it was probably
real. This sounded like a game that could play to my strengths.
One of us was going to have to do it, and there was no way I
was leaving it for Alex. He was too weak. He struggled with any
decisions, let alone tough ones. No. This one was down to me.
This would be the first game I'd played in the park. The others
didn't seem to think I was capable of winning.

I would show them.

•

I was halfway to the arena when a man stepped out in front of
me. He was long-haired, tall and handsome in a rough sort of
way.

'Ms Weston,' he began. Then hesitated. 'No. Ms Summers. You schizos are a confusing lot.'

How did Kate know someone like him?

'Who are you?' I asked. 'What do you want?'

'I'm Godfried,' he said. 'I wanted to talk to Ms Weston. I thought maybe I could help with whatever game you're playing.'

'Why? And how could you help?'

He hesitated again. 'I ... I can give you something that would help you win.'

'Why would you help us?'

'What's the game?'

'It's got some weird name.' I checked again. 'Revillagigedo Island. Do you know it?'

He pulled a face. 'That's a tough one. No one's won that in a long while.' He shook his head. 'There's nothing I've got that will help with that. All I can give you is a piece of advice. You've got to harden your heart. Good luck.'

I walked on. Well that was a useless load of shit. How did any of that help me?

It was easy enough to find the arena. There were several people going in. Why was it so busy? I followed them and crossed over to the reception desk. 'I'm here for the game. What's happening?'

The man behind the desk looked up at me. 'Ms Summers. Let me find you a room. It's busy today. This is the default game ParkGov has allocated. So our fee will be twenty-five per cent.' He paused. 'Room 14. Down the right-hand corridor. Best of luck.'

I nodded, and followed his directions. I wasn't going to need luck.

Welcome, Ms Summers

Game: Revillagigedo Island – Moral Dilemmas
Winner: Any players who complete all stages
Stages: Four
Location: Revillagigedo Island/USS *Marlin*

Ms Summers, in the game that you are about to play you will be presented with various leadership decisions. Importantly, in this game you will not know that you are in a simulation. The scenarios and the choices will seem real to you.

There are fifteen players competing, with accumulated time of 18.5 years. You will not interact with each other, but each of you will face the same scenarios. The winner will be the one who makes the right choices and survives all four stages of the game. The survivor, or survivors, will share the time of those who lose.

Make the wrong decision, or die in the game, and you will die in real life.

The game will commence in two minutes.

18.5 years? That couldn't be right. We were bringing more than twenty-four years on our own. I quickly checked our credit. *14.2 years?* How had that happened? We had lost ten years overnight. And that meant the other players were barely bringing in four years between them. Thanks to Kate failing to choose a game we'd ended up playing the dregs of the death park. It was hardly worth it.

I didn't have time for this. Something had gone wrong. Why wasn't anyone telling me anything?

•

Revillagigedo Island, Alaska. I am seated in the command centre of the United States Navy's Southeast Alaska Acoustic Measurement Facility – SEAFAC. Below me, running fifty miles north and south, is the Behm Canal, a sheltered natural channel separating the island from the mainland.

It is a clear night and the surface of the water is calm.

A calmness that contrasts with what is happening 1,000 feet below aboard the USS *Marlin*, a ballistic missile submarine that had been undergoing acoustic testing in the canal. At 2:28 we received the following transmission:

USS *Marlin* struck unidentified object at 940 feet. Forward
compartments breached and sealed. Forward crew presumed dead.
Unable to surface. Flood doors sealed. Commander and XO only
control room crew alive. Estimate four to five hours' breathable air.
Believe engineering crew in aft compartments alive. Doors sealed,
cannot communicate, but respond to tapping. Advise urgently.
Captain Rogers, CO.

Followed at 2:36 by another message:

Chief Engineer, USS *Marlin*. Urgent assistance requested. Vessel
stopped. Flooding. Emergency power. Engineering crew: nine (one
injured) trapped in aft compartment. Air running out. Estimate no

more than thirty minutes. If divert life support from control room
estimate up to two hours. Please advise urgently. C/E.

I turn to the officer seated to my right. 'Lieutenant, what is
your recommendation?'

She sits up. 'Commander, we launched the rescue submersible at the same time as calling you. It will be at the *Marlin* in
forty-two minutes. That is fifty-one minutes after the incident.
We agree with the chief engineer's estimate that, by then, all
of the crew in the aft compartments will be unconscious if not
dead. They need to be conscious to unlock the escape hatch
from the inside when the submersible docks. If they divert life
support from the control room then the captain and the executive officer will die, but the engineering crew will live. It's a
straight choice, Commander.'

'I asked for your recommendation, Lieutenant.'

She looks away, and hesitates. 'If we do nothing, the captain
and the XO live. If we tell the chief engineer to divert life support then we kill the two of them. We can't be responsible for
doing that.'

'Can't the two in the control room get to engineering?' I ask.

'No,' says the lieutenant. 'The flood doors are shut. With
water coming in and possible contamination they won't be able
to override them.'

'What do we know about Captain Rogers?'

'He is forty-two, career navy man. Worked his way up from
the bottom. He's been a commander now for just over two
years.'

'So, nothing exceptional,' I say. I think for a moment. 'Send two messages. First one: "To Chief Engineer, USS *Marlin*. You are ordered to divert life support from control room to engineering. All in control room believed to be dead now. Submersible will dock at aft escape hatch in approximately thirty-five minutes." The second one: "To Commanding Officer, USS *Marlin*. Message received. Submersible on way and will dock at sail escape hatch in approximately thirty-five minutes. Await further communication.""

The lieutenant looks at me wide-eyed as she types the messages. Well, if she can't cope with this she won't be going any further under my command.

'Don't look so shocked, Lieutenant,' I say. 'It's simple mathematics. Nine live and two die. I would rather the CO and XO don't know what's happening until it's too late. The carbon dioxide will build up and they will gradually fall asleep. If they know it is going to happen they might try something stupid and get everyone killed. Send the orders.'

'Yes, ma'am.'

●

Stage One complete. Twelve players surviving.

●

Revillagigedo Island, Alaska, SEAFAC, 2:37.

The command centre door bangs shut behind me as I stride through, buttoning my jacket and blinking sleep away.

'Lieutenant, report,' I say.

She slides out of the command chair and I take her place.

'Ma'am, we have received two messages from the USS *Marlin*. She has struck an unidentified object and the forward compartments are breached. She has settled on the floor of the channel and cannot surface. Captain Summers reports that he and the XO remain alive and trapped in the control room. The chief engineer reports that he and eight others are sealed in the aft compartment, one badly injured. The rescue submersible will be with them in forty minutes.'

'What are our options?' I ask. 'Can we get them all out?'

'I don't believe so, ma'am. We can get the captain and XO out. But the chief engineer estimates that those in the aft compartment will run out of air in less than thirty minutes. We agree with that estimate. He can divert life support aft but then those in the control room will die.' She hesitates. 'Including your son, ma'am.'

I look up sharply. 'That has nothing to do with this, Lieutenant. You would do well to remember that.'

It's a numbers game. The right decision is to save the engineers. The important question is how this will reflect on me and my career. Save the engineers and I will be known as the hard-ass who did the right thing and sacrificed her own son. I'll make admiral next year. Do nothing and I'll be the officer who couldn't make the tough decision and chose family over the service. I'll never be promoted again. I'll end up being posted to Diego Garcia, the back end of nowhere, as my career slowly dies.

So what do I sacrifice? The career I've spent thirty years pursuing to the exclusion of all else, when I'm about to reach the pinnacle? Or the son who deserted me at fourteen to live with his deadbeat father, and whom I've barely spoken to in the last ten years? The son who will want nothing to do with me if I do save him, because my name will be mud throughout the US Navy.

I make my decision.

'Lieutenant, tell the chief engineer to divert life support aft.'

She stares at me, aghast. I look her in the eye and dare her to protest.

'Yes, ma'am.' She types the message. 'What about your ... what about the officers? What do we say to them?'

I pause. We need to tell them something. I don't want them doing anything stupid and killing everyone. That would be the worst possible outcome for me. 'Tell them that rescue is on its way and to sit tight. By the time they know differently it will be too late.'

'Don't ... don't you want to at least say goodbye?' she asks.

'No. If I do that they will know what's coming.'

I turn away from her shocked look and stare out over the Behm Canal. As my first commander told me, make a decision and move on – never regret.

•

Stage Two complete. Two players surviving.

•

The control room of the USS *Marlin* is unusually quiet. The engines are silent, the vessel still. There is the occasional groan or creak as the hull flexes beneath the tremendous pressures

1,000 feet deep. We struck the ground hard and there is no response from the forward compartments. I suspect that they are flooded, and the crew dead.

Someone is still alive in the aft compartments. We communicated by tapping with a wrench on the sealed flood doors. We believe that the chief engineer and some others are still alive.

In here it's just the XO and me.

I feel calm. If the ship breaks up I will be dead before I know about it. It won't hurt. But I don't want to die. I need to find a way out.

'What are our chances of being rescued?' I ask.

The XO looks up from his screen. 'We have just heard back from command. A rescue sub is on its way. It should be with us in thirty minutes.' He hesitates. 'They confirm that there are nine crew alive aft, including the chief. However, they are not going to survive long enough to be rescued.' He pauses again, and swallows. 'Captain Summers, ma'am . . . they have asked us to consider diverting life support aft so that the chief and his crew can be rescued.'

It takes me a moment to understand. 'They want us to go down with the ship in the best traditions of the service? A noble sacrifice and all that. For eight ratings and a chief I've had to babysit through the dying days of his career.' I laugh. 'That's not going to happen.'

The XO looks frightened. 'I don't want to die, ma'am, but is it right that nine die so we can live? What will everyone think when we are rescued? We will be shunned as cowards.'

He is right about that. This is not going to look good on our records.

'I'll tell you what,' I say. 'Send a message to command saying that we have decided to do the right thing and sacrifice ourselves for the sake of the crew.'

The XO looks surprised at my sudden change of plan. His shoulders slump and he is starting to shiver. I hope he isn't about to cry.

'For God's sake,' I say, 'pull yourself together. I'm not suggesting that we actually do it. In ten minutes you send another signal saying that the systems aren't responding. Put it down to power failure or something. When we board the rescue sub we'll leave the *Marlin*'s escape hatch open so that she floods. By the time they get down here to salvage the ship and recover the bodies no one will be able to prove anything different. We will look like heroes who tried to sacrifice ourselves, but failed. Make the message suitably solemn and noble. We might even get a medal.'

The XO looks at me with a mixture of shock, guilt and gratitude. Someone has to take the tough decisions.

'When we get back don't ever breath a word of this to anyone,' I say. 'It would finish us both off.'

He nods silently. I don't trust him. I am going to have to get him posted somewhere remote when we get out of this.

I sit back and breathe out, waiting for rescue. This is what command is all about: making the best of a bad situation and staying in control.

•

Stage Three complete. Two players surviving.

There are two of us left alive in the control room of the USS *Marlin*. The XO and me. Considering that I am sitting in a submarine with the bows torn away, and the forward and aft compartments flooded, I feel surprisingly calm. I know that there is 1,000 feet of pressure on the already damaged hull, but this isn't my time yet.

The XO's head jerks up as a dull groan echoes from one end of the ship to the other. There is blood dripping from a wound at his temple where he struck the periscope earlier. It doesn't look too serious.

'What's our status?' I ask.

He looks at me, fear in his eyes. 'She is holding so far. I got a signal away to command. If things go to plan I anticipate that they will get a sub down here in thirty minutes or so. Provided the escape hatch works, we should get out of here alive.' He hesitates. 'But we have a bigger problem.'

'What's that?'

'The missile run doesn't seem to have shut down. In fact, according to my screens it has gone active. Missile launch in twelve minutes.'

'That can't be right,' I say. 'It was just a drill, and we never entered the real codes.'

We had been conducting a test exercise with one of our nuclear missiles targeted at Dutch Harbor, Amaknak Island. I'd chosen it for no reason other than that it had been my least favourite posting two years earlier. To actually launch a nuclear missile we would have needed a code from command, plus the codes held by the XO and me. None of which we had entered.

'It looks real enough here,' says the XO.

'How do we stop it?'

'I have tried to abort but nothing happens. The missiles are beyond the flood doors so we can't do it manually.'

I shrug. 'So, nothing we can do then. Most likely it's not real and nothing happens. But even if the accident has somehow triggered a launch we can't stop it. We sit here and wait for rescue.'

'There is one thing we could try,' says the XO. He looks at the escape hatch above us. 'We blow that open. The pressure will tear the ship apart and most likely stop the launch.' He swallows. 'We won't feel a thing. It will be done in an instant.'

I look at him, trying to work out if he is serious.

'How many people live in Dutch Harbor?' I ask.

He looks at me wildly. 'How would I know? I never served there. Probably a few hundred. Certainly more than two. Besides, we don't want to turn it into a nuclear wasteland. It might start a war.' He stands. 'We have to do it.'

'No we don't,' I say. 'Odds are this is all some computer glitch and nothing is going to launch. I'm not killing myself for that. Even if I'm wrong, Dutch was a dull place at the best of times. It will be no great loss to anyone.'

He stares at me. 'We have no choice. We can't take the risk.'

I meet his stare. 'Stand down,' I say. 'That's an order. Disobey and it's mutiny.'

'No,' he says. 'If we are wrong I can't live with that.'

'You won't need to.' I draw my service revolver and sight

between his eyes. At six feet I can't miss. 'You disobeyed a direct order. Take one more step and I shoot.'

'Do that and you'll have done my job for me. The bullet will go straight through me and the hull. By the time I hit the floor this place will be flattened.' He turns back towards the hatch.

He's right. Or I am certainly not prepared to take the risk.

I reverse my grip on the revolver, step up behind him and club him hard on the temple. He slumps to the floor, blood now gushing from his wound. I put the gun away, grab him beneath the armpits, and drag him to the nearest cabin. The ship has settled at an angle, and I am having to pull him uphill, so it is surprisingly hard work.

I drop him on the cabin floor, pull the door shut and jam the lock. Even if he wakes before I am rescued he won't get out. I will leave the emergency hatch open and the sea will ensure that there is nothing left to incriminate me.

I sit back in my chair, waiting for rescue. I check the XO's screen. Two minutes more to find out whether Dutch Harbor will still be there when I reach the surface. Does it matter? I was never going back.

•

Stage Four complete. One player surviving.

•

The man at the reception desk looked at me oddly as I left the arena.

164

'Ms Summers,' he said. 'Congratulations. "Moral Dilemmas." That one requires some tough choices. We normally count on it as a banker for the arena. You're the first person to survive it in a long time.'

It hadn't seemed all that hard to me. Logic and self-preservation at all costs.

'What did I win?' I asked.

He looked down at his screen. 'After deducting what you brought in, and our fee of twenty-five per cent, you win 3.2 years. Well done. We hope to see you again.'

Having risked more than fourteen years, winning 3.2 seemed like a pretty poor return. As usual the arena would be creaming off a nice percentage. Nothing I could do about it, though.

As I turned to go he rummaged around in a drawer and offered me a package. 'Here, take one of our T-shirts. We never sell any.'

I opened it: REVILLAGIGEDO ISLAND: COME FOR THE NAME, STAY FOR THE GAME. There was a picture of a broken submarine on the back.

'Catchy,' I said. 'I'm surprised they haven't sold out.' I dropped it back on the counter. 'Not even for free. What kind of loser ever takes this crap?'

●

I headed for the nearest bar. Before I got too far down the first bottle I composed a message to the others. It was time they realised that I had saved their skins this time.

All. I don't know how you let this happen, but we got assigned a
random challenge by ParkGov [see attached]. The option was to
play it, forfeit, or leave the park today with half our time. So I played
it and won. We are up another 3.2 years. You're welcome. Let's make
sure it doesn't happen again. If we are staying for another cycle we
need to choose a challenge for tomorrow so we don't get one forced
on us. I'm not going through this shit again. Also something odd has
happened. We've lost ten years. Has Ben being renting high-class
whores again? S.

I returned to my bottle.

An hour later I was making good progress towards intoxication when someone pulled back the chair opposite me and sat
down. I looked up to protest that I didn't want company, but
stopped. It was a familiar face.

Amy Bird.

She grinned at me. 'You know, the others are keeping you out
of the loop because they think this is all your fault. There's a lot
they're not telling you, Sierra.'

'Like what?' I asked.

'Where to start? That the drug dealer you followed is dead.
Some of the others are wondering if you killed him.'

I laughed. 'Karl? No great loss. Why should I care? I didn't
kill him.'

'Alex seems to think you might have.'

I shrugged. I'd long ago given up worrying about Alex's opin-
ion of me. He'd lost his sense of humour after Montreal.

'That was just one of the things they forgot to tell you.' Bird
paused. 'What else? Oh, yes. That Mike got set up with a ringer

and lost his race. They know that one of you bought me, but they don't know who, or why. And Ben lost ten years of your time to a local gangster.'

So that explained the time loss. 'Why did he do that?'

'In fairness to him, it was either that or get hung from a meat hook and skinned alive.'

So what did that leave us? Around seventeen years. Still a decent prize.

'I have some messages you ought to see,' Bird said. She reached across and put her hand on mine. 'Have a read.' She looked at the almost empty bottle in front of me. 'Preferably before you have any more to drink. You'll particularly like the one in which Alex speculates that it's all a drug deal of yours that's gone wrong.'

She pushed back her chair and, before I could say anything more, was gone.

So was Mike really dead? He was the only one who was ever nice to me. It didn't seem possible for Mike to have lost a race.

I contemplated the whisky bottle and the messages, and decided that I had time for both.

Whisky first.

I owed it to Mike. A drink to his memory – just in case.

ONE YEAR EARLIER

VINOGRADOV

Alex regarded the seagull through his single open eye. The bird loomed large, hopping from one foot to the other. Its pale feathers shone in the moonlight. It cocked its head, then darted at him.

Alex jerked away from it. And instantly regretted moving. He dry-retched and pain stabbed through his eyes.

The gull jumped backwards, flapping its wings and squawking. It seemed to have been hoping that he was dead, and edible.

Half of him wished that he *was* dead.

The metal floor was rising and falling beneath him. That, the seagull, and the smell of salt in the air made Alex realise that he was on a boat. A mixture of vomit and seawater was surging back and forth across the deck. The gull hopped out of its way and flew up to a railing, turning to observe him.

As the swill moved back towards him, Alex pushed himself upright, ignoring his throbbing head. He rubbed at his right eye, which seemed to be stuck shut.

He looked around. There was sufficient light from the moon

that he didn't need to use his enhanced vision. He had been lying in a narrow gap between the railing on which the gull was perched and a tall metal container. Beyond the railing a dark ocean stretched out as far as he could see.

'What the hell?' he muttered, as he lurched to his feet. He staggered over to the rail, clinging to it as he dry-retched a second time, scaring away the bird. All he could see was water, moonlight reflecting off rolling waves.

Containers blocked his movement in two directions. The only option was to head for the back of the ship. He clung to the railing as he made his way along the narrow passageway, timing his movements to the rise and fall of the deck.

Alex had never been on a ship before. This one seemed massive. Above the row of containers to his right he could just make out some sort of superstructure, lights twinkling. He guessed that was the bridge, where he could find the crew. Assuming it even had a crew. If the ship was run by AI it might be difficult to persuade it to turn round and take him back to land.

He was halfway to the bridge when a gap opened up in the wall of containers to his right. It was narrow, but it seemed like a better route. Alex squeezed down it, emerging into a wider passage that ran the length of the ship.

It was dimly lit, and to his left there was a person walking away from him, towards the bridge. Alex hesitated, then shouted. Whatever he was doing on board, there was no point in hiding.

'Hey, can you help me?'

The crewman stopped, turned, and then ran over.

Alex smiled as best he could, conscious that he wasn't looking his best. One side of him remained encrusted with vomit and seawater. And he stank. He extended his hand. 'Hi, I'm Alex. I'm not sure how I've ended up here, but I need to get back to land. Can you take me to your captain?'

The crewman stared at him blankly for a moment. Alex scanned him. Bugger. He was a dandi – known only as 'Crew 2'. This was hopeless.

'You are not authorised,' said the dandi in flat tones. 'You must follow me. You must come to the captain.'

Well, that was more promising. Provided the captain wasn't also a dandi.

Without waiting for Alex's agreement, the dandi turned on his heel and started towards the bridge. Alex struggled to keep up on the moving deck.

'Hey, where are we?' asked Alex. 'Where are we heading?'

The dandi looked over his shoulder. 'You are on board the container ship *Vinogradov*, bound for Montreal, where we will arrive in ten days.'

Alex stopped. 'Montreal. Ten days? Shit.' He ran to catch up. 'How do I get off?'

The dandi looked at him blankly. 'I am taking you to the captain.'

As they neared the bridge a voice shouted down out of the darkness. 'Dva? What is it? Who have you got there?' A light shone from above, blinding Alex. 'Sierra? *Blyad! Ty che, blyad.* What are you doing here?'

Alex looked up, but could see nothing. But at least this sounded like a person, not a dandi. 'Can I come up?' he asked.

'Of course. Follow Dva.'

The dandi led Alex up steep metal steps to the brightly lit bridge. It was smaller than Alex had expected, a single black chair facing a low bank of screens. The captain closed a door that led out to a gangway looking over the deck. He was short and barrel-chested, stomach straining against his black turtleneck. He had a red cap pulled low over his forehead.

'Sierra ... *Govno.*' He was shaking his head and chuckling. He took a step towards Alex, arms out wide, then stopped. 'You're a mess.'

Alex scanned him. Captain Lesnichy Igorevich, a fifty-eight-year-old worker, originally from Kazakhstan. His English seemed good, which was a relief to Alex, as they'd never bothered to get a translation implant.

'I'm not Sierra. Although she seems to be the one who's got me into this mess. Didn't she tell you she was a schizo? I'm Alex.'

'She did mention it. But I thought I'd never see her again. I met her in a bar in port and she came back here for a some of my special vodka. She was meant to get off the ship well before we left port.' He shook his head. 'She had a lot to drink, though. Shit.' He hesitated, then stuck out a hand. 'I'm Les.'

'Your dandi said we're on our way to Montreal. Is that true?'

Les nodded and rubbed his chin. 'Shit, this is a mess.' He looked across at the dandi, who was standing silently by the steps. 'Dva, go find Tree. He needs some help in the engine room. The recharge link from the panels to the port battery stack is glitching again.'

'Is that your whole crew, two dandis?' Alex asked.

'Pretty much. *Dva* means two in Russian. *Tree* means three. You don't need a big crew. Two dandis isn't much company for a long voyage. I renamed the third dandi, Tasha. She's different. She's here for . . .' He looked away, not meeting Alex's eye. 'She's here for other reasons. If you understand?'

Alex did. He tried not to pull a face, and quickly changed the subject.

'So how do I get off here?' he asked.

'Before Montreal?' asked Les. 'You don't. Unless you fancy a long swim that way.' He gestured vaguely behind them. 'I wouldn't recommend it. Particularly if you space out every four hours.'

Sierra had a lot to answer for this time. She had recently developed a taste for a new drug that was marketed to schizos with the promise that it left no after-effects for the others. That part was true, but it made the generally uninhibited Sierra even less inhibited. There were more unsafe wakes, often in the presence of her latest sexual conquest. This was the worst so far, though. Perhaps the time had come for the rest of them to stop dismissing her actions with a casual, 'That's just Sierra for you.'

'Can't you turn around?' asked Alex. 'Where are we?'

Les glanced at one of his screens. 'The nearest land is Wolf Rock.'

Alex looked at him blankly. 'Where's that? Can you drop me off there?'

Les laughed. 'This ship's probably bigger than the island, and it's surrounded by rocks. There's a lighthouse and not much more. It's at the western end of the English Channel. Between us and Montreal there's several thousand kilometres of ocean. And we won't be turning round. I work to a tight schedule. I can guarantee you can't afford to pay for the time I'd lose to drop you back at port, plus the penalties for arriving late in Montreal.'

He walked over to the chair and slumped into it heavily, sighing. 'No, you're stuck here, Alex. You're going to Montreal. All five of you.'

•

Alex met Les an hour later in a room spanning the width of the ship, one level up from the bridge. There were windows all around, but the view of the dark ocean just reminded Alex that he was stuck on this ship for the next ten days. And then stuck in Montreal.

The captain had summoned Dva back to escort Alex to a cabin and, more importantly, somewhere he could clean up. He felt considerably better once he'd showered, rehydrated, and taken some potent anti-sickness tablets. In the meantime Dva had printed him some black jeans and a polo neck. They fitted him rather better than the ones worn by Les.

The captain was sitting with his back to the door, staring out over the moonlit ocean, a glass of something clear in his hand. He spun his chair around as Alex entered.

'Take a seat.' He raised his drink. 'Dva, get Alex one of these. It's not printed vodka. This came on board with me at Murmansk. A man needs some comforts on these long voyages.'

'Like Tasha,' said Alex.

Les grinned. 'You can judge me once you've spent three weeks crossing the Pacific with nothing for company but two dandis. Dumb bastards aren't much good as conversationalists.

Not that Tasha is. But she has other qualities that take my mind off the loneliness. *Nochnaja babochka* – my night butterfly. Don't call her that,' he added hastily. 'To us Kazakhs it means "whore". Sounds better in translation. Not that she'd care, really.' He paused as Dva handed Alex a drink. 'To Montreal. At least this means I can have some intelligent conversation on the way there.'

'Five of us for the price of one,' said Alex. 'Talking of price, how is this going to work? How are you going to explain our presence to whoever owns this ship? And how are we going to get back?'

'The first?' Les gave a dismissive wave. 'The owners will never know you're here. The second? That's more difficult. I'm not heading back. I've got two weeks pottering down the East Coast, then through to Vladivostok. It'll be two months before I'm even back in Murmansk. Sorry, but you're going to have to find another way home.'

'How?' asked Alex. 'There's no way we can afford to fly.'

Alex had never been on an aircraft, and doubted that he ever would. He could still remember as a young child what had been regarded as the most successful advertising campaign ever. Posters, billboards and onscreen adverts plastering the world for over a year. Plain white backgrounds with a single dead tree or plant, the corpse of an animal or child, and four words: 'You Fly, I Die'. It created a collective guilt. Flying was almost unheard of now, the preserve of the super-rich who could afford the massive carbon offsets.

'You'll have to find someone sailing the other way who's willing to take you,' said Les. 'I'll ask around. But it could take a while. Until then I hope you find something to do in Montreal.'

'Great,' said Alex. 'Sierra's got some apologising to do. Even by her standards this is a good one.'

'She seemed like fun,' said Les.

'Everyone thinks she's fun,' said Alex ruefully. 'Then they get to know her.' He took a sip of the rough vodka. He didn't feel like drinking. Although maybe he needed to, to get through this. 'You'll have plenty of time to do that.'

'How does it work?' asked Les. 'I don't really know any schizos . . . sorry, is that rude? What do you like to be called?'

Alex shrugged. 'It's not a name that we like, but everyone uses it. Even us sometimes. We start the day with Kate. She's probably the nicest. Sierra says she's dull, but that's just because they're so different. Kate gets things done. She's followed by Mike. This is Mike,' he said, gesturing to his body. 'He'll be wanting to build a running track and a weights room on deck. Then comes Ben, who will barely talk to you at all. He lives to play games. If you need any of your systems upgraded he'll delight in doing it for you. Then there's Sierra. You're going to need more vodka if you've got ten days of her.'

'And what about you? What should I know about you?'

'Me?' said Alex, looking down. 'There's nothing to know about me. I just make up the numbers.'

Les raised an eyebrow. 'That sounds rather sad.' He gestured to Dva for a refill. 'Do you want something to eat? How long have you got?'

'Thanks, but no. I'd better get back to my cabin and get a message out to the others so they know what's going on.' He stood. 'Thanks again – you've been really good about this.'

'No problem,' said Les. 'This voyage is going to be more fun than usual.'

•

All. Nice one, Sierra. So I wake up in a pool of vomit on the deck of a container ship bound for Montreal. Now we're all stuck here for ten days. The captain, Les, is from Kazakhstan. He's being pretty understanding. He says he'll drop us in Montreal and try to put us in touch with someone who can give us a ride back. Whatever that costs, you're paying. Let's see what he comes up with. In the meantime, we've got a pretty dull ten days ahead of us. Alex.

The captain seems a real sweetie. Apart from his sex dandi. That's just gross. I'm not sure what he actually does on the ship. He spent most of his time talking to me. He seems rather lonely. No news yet on getting back. What the hell, Sierra??? Kate.

So Dva and Tree have built us an obstacle course over the containers. The course record (me) is 7:22, set third time round. Dva managed 9:40; Tree 10:43. Anyone fancy a challenge? Captain Les declined. Nothing else to do here, though. Mike.

Seriously, Sierra? What were you thinking? I'm starting an eight-day quest through the Caverns of Euronia. I've got a team together.

Message me if you need me for anything. Otherwise let's sort things out once we get to Montreal. Ben.

For God's sake, chill guys. It's like a holiday. It'll be character-building. If you're that bored go play with Natasha. She's cute. And dumb. What more do you want? Lesnichy doesn't mind sharing her. S.

FFS Sierra!! With a sex dandi? That's sick. A.

Not cool, Sierra. Les says still nothing on getting home. We could be stuck in Montreal a while. Kate.

What else is there to do? I don't know what Lesnichy paid for her, but the AI in Natasha is unlike any sex dandi I've seen before. She knows moves even I've not come across. Don't be so dull, Kate. Give it a go. You might learn something. S.

Please, Sierra, cut down on the vodka. I'm asking Les to limit your rations. Alex.

New record – 7:13. Why aren't the rest of you trying it? Mike.

Bored. Bored. Bored. If Lesnichy tells me one more time about how to turn potatoes into alcohol I'm going to throw him overboard. I don't need to know how it's made! And he's starting to get grumpy about sharing Natasha. Says he's worried I'm going to break her. S.

Les has found us a boat back. It's a Kazakh friend of his. They used to sail together. But we're going to be stuck in Montreal for at least two months. There aren't many boats going back that'll take us for free. And stop pissing him off, Sierra. We're depending on his goodwill. Kate.

Well that was weird. I saw my first sunset since I was seventeen. Time's going to shift for all of us as we head west. You'll be waking in the dark, Kate. Alex.

8:43 – how can you be so much faster in the same body, Mike? Kate.

Oh, God! Two more days – shoot me now. I don't want to see another boat as long as I live. And Lesnichy has starting telling me about his first two wives now. Pre-Natasha. He's a dull drunk. S.

All. I've got an idea. I've done some research on Montreal. There's loads we could do there. There's a pretty serious AI scene that Ben would enjoy. And they live for the outdoors, Mike. Why don't we find somewhere to live for a few months, stay out the summer, and head back later? It'll mean we're all on the wrong time, but I'm worst affected – I'll be up in the middle of the night, but I can put up with it for a few months. And I just can't face getting on a ship again any time soon. Votes in next cycle. Kate.

Works for me. 5:00–9:00 is fine. Mike.

OK. Makes no difference to me where/when we are. I still won't have finished Euronia. There's some serious shit going down here, and I've got several days to go. Ben.

I don't care. Just get me away from Lesnichy. He spent the whole afternoon boring me about death parks. He's got a cousin or something he wants us to get in touch with. S.

It's pretty cool seeing daylight again. I could live with this for the summer. Tough on you, Kate – you sure it's good? Alex.

6:58!! New record. M.

One more day. I've found us somewhere to stay in Montreal [attached]. Tell me if you disagree. Alex.

Alex watched as Quebec City slid past on the right-hand side of the ship. He and the captain had climbed to the very top of the bridge superstructure, a small lookout point exposed to the elements, low railings all that prevented a long drop to the deck below. Row after row of containers stretched out ahead of them; beyond that, the fiery reflection of the setting sun in the waters of the St Lawrence Seaway. A cool evening breeze ruffled Alex's hair.

'Well, it's been interesting,' said Les. 'I won't say it's been easy. I don't envy you your life. I genuinely don't know how you do it.'

'You get used to it,' said Alex. 'We learn to forgive one another. Even this.' He gestured to the ship. 'There's no point in spending the next twenty years whining to Sierra about bringing us here. You make the best of it and move on. So we get a summer in Montreal. Not many people are ever going to experience that.'

'It's a weird bunch that you share that body with. Ben I've barely seen at all. Mike spent more of his time challenging my dandis to races than talking to me. Kate – she's an interesting one. She knows more about my own country than I ever will. But she needs to learn to let go a bit. Sierra . . . Whatever you say, she's dangerous. Fun, but dangerous.'

'Reckless,' said Alex. 'But she wouldn't deliberately try to hurt us.'

'Be careful with her,' said Les. 'And what about you? You lied to me on the first day.'

Alex turned to him in surprise. 'What do you mean?'

'You said you were just there to make up the numbers, nothing special. I don't think that's right. You are what holds the group together. You're the strongest of all.'

Alex laughed. 'Thanks, Les, but they'd all get on fine without me.' He quickly changed the subject. 'I hope the others at least thanked you. You've been very generous. We'll miss you in Montreal.'

'I'll miss *some* of you,' said Les. 'What's your plan after Montreal? When you get home.'

'We've got some big decisions to make,' said Alex. 'We're at the end of our first life. This body is almost forty-one years old, so we've got just over a year to go before our first trade-in. We don't have a lot of time in credit. We get a new body for nothing, but there's a lot of argument over what we do about enhancing it. Mike's complaining that he's going to have to start all over again. He's been trying to persuade us to go to a death park. Says that as schizos we haven't got anything to lose.'

Les nodded. 'Sierra told me that. You should consider it. You schizos are oddly suited to it. The downside is small for you. And you have five different skillsets in one person. You can choose who plays what games. Go with your strengths.'

'It doesn't appeal to me,' said Alex. 'Anyway, how does someone who's spent his life travelling the sea know so much about death parks?'

'I have a cousin who works in one.' He laughed. 'Well, not really a cousin. Back in Kazakhstan we're all cousins, brothers, uncles, whatever. I grew up with Valya. We sailed together for a while. Before he left to do ... other things. Not all of them entirely legal. But he'd be a good person to know if you ever went.'

'No thanks,' said Alex. 'Killing people – even end-of-lifers – isn't my thing.'

Les shrugged. 'It's easier than you think.'

Alex looked at him in surprise. 'You've been to a death park?'

'No, but my youth was not entirely blameless. Sometimes there are things you need to do.'

The sun had vanished beneath the horizon. Lights were starting to show on the banks of the river. Alex checked the time.

'I don't have long left, Les. Thanks for everything. It won't be me getting off in the morning. So this is goodbye.'

He turned to the burly captain and extended his hand, but found himself engulfed in a fierce bear hug. It went on for longer than Alex would have liked.

Eventually Les released him, thumping him on the back. 'With you, Alex, it's been a pleasure. Stay in touch.'

ALEX

Sierra had shown a bit more responsibility than usual. I woke in a cheap motel room. Although with a wicked hangover. Worse than ever.

I checked the time. I was awake an hour early. Our schedule had changed with Mike's disappearance. Which made sense.

My second surprise was a message from Sierra saying that she had played and won a game so I didn't have to. I couldn't understand how we'd missed this requirement. Kate was normally on top of these things. But I was beginning to suspect that ParkGov was making up the rules as it went along, trying to keep things interesting by ensuring that the big winners kept risking their time.

I shot back a reply, copied to the others.

Good win there, Sierra, but why follow it up by leaving us drunk
again? I've given up complaining. When this is all over I'm going
to be proposing a formal vote that you be downloaded into rehab
until cured. This can't keep happening.

Mike is still gone. I don't know what is going on but I'm sure you're not telling us the truth about it.

Stop this now, and for once be honest with us. Alex.

Kate had messaged Ben and me to say that she had discovered that the pills being sold by Guskov were for andis; nothing to do with Mike wanting boosters or Sierra being on drugs again. That was disappointing. Although I noticed that she hadn't copied in Sierra.

Then one from Ben. Unlike Kate, he had sent it to all of us. Did he think Mike was still getting messages? Did he trust Sierra? Did he still not see that she was probably behind this?

All. Well that was an interesting cycle. I got picked up by Guskov's thugs and dragged back to the Death's Head. It seems that the dealer Sierra met, Karl, got murdered by someone last night. Guskov thought that Sierra had done it. I found some clips [attached] that made it pretty clear it was Amy Bird. Which was fine until he told us that he actually sells andis, and one of us bought Bird a week ago! I don't know who to trust now, so I'm sending this to all of you.

There's clearly a human mind inside Bird, but I don't see how it can be Mike since Kate met Bird before he disappeared. Guskov either doesn't know where Bird is, or he's not telling us. I've changed things so all of us will get an alert if she's spotted anywhere in the park.

Guskov was pretty odd. Talked big and threatened to have us skinned alive, but then let me go in return for a payment of ten years.

My view is we get out of the park now, and once we're safe, report this to CGov. They can go places even I can't, and work out what actually happened. We're being watched by people, and I haven't got time to find out who, or why. I don't want to abandon Mike but if he's still around CGov must be able to find him.

Votes by next cycle? Ben.

I checked our balance: 17.4 years, which made sense with Ben losing ten years and Sierra's win. I had to admit that for once Sierra had stepped up, even if it was only in her own interests. She was also right that if we were staying we needed to choose our challenge for the next cycle. Which suited me just fine. I didn't want us to throw ourselves on the mercy of CGov.

Ben had already risked attracting their attention by mentioning Karl's murder. That was an uncharacteristic slip. However he seemed to be in a panic. Cutting and running was not the right answer.

What to send to Ben? And Kate? I sat on the edge of the bed thinking for a long time. Not helped by the fuzzy state of my head. It was a shame that hangovers couldn't stick with the mind that had created them. Our body's ability to deal with alcohol seemed to be decreasing with every day left. Or maybe it was Sierra's drinking that was increasing.

Eventually I decided what to say.

Kate/Ben, thanks for the updates. This is all very odd. Well done on talking your way out, Ben. Tough that we lost ten years, but better that than we die outside an arena and end up mindwiped.

I don't know what happened with the challenges on the last cycle, but something went wrong. For once Sierra did something useful, and got us out of it. Although I find it hard to believe that she was motivated by anything other than self-interest.

Looking at the big picture, I don't understand why Mike or Sierra would be buying an andi. They must have done it in the first cycle we were here.

Why use the andi to kill someone? We know Sierra arranged to meet Karl. She hasn't told us what happened, or how she met him without seeing Bird there. It doesn't sound as though Guskov had Karl killed, which makes it more likely it was Sierra. But what could she be trying to hide?

This may sound crazy, but what if Mike and Sierra have been working together? They've always been the closest. He was the one who tried to defend her after Montreal. If it wasn't for him she'd still be in stasis. And it was the two of them who were keenest to come to the death park.

Here's a theory. We know that Sierra would rather not have us around. And Bird told Kate that she wanted to move her mind into another body. What if Sierra decided to move her mind into an andi body and persuaded Mike to help. But something went wrong, and instead of Sierra getting downloaded into the andi, Mike was. Which explains why he's disappeared. Maybe Karl was being paid to help, and Sierra had to dispose of him to keep him quiet. That would explain why Guskov doesn't know what's going on.

> I don't know. Maybe that's too far-fetched. We need to find Bird if
> we are going to solve this. We'll know if Mike's inside her.

> I'll take a look at the challenges for tomorrow and get back to you
> on those. Alex.

I thought carefully before sending it. I was starting to lose
track of who knew what. Keeping secrets amongst ourselves
was difficult. But Kate and Ben needed to know, and I wasn't
going to accuse Sierra to her face, so eventually I sent it.

I started looking through the challenges that had come in.
We were up to ninety-two. Despite what we had lost to Guskov,
we were still probably the richest target in the park.

It didn't take me long to find one that looked perfect for
Kate.

Flight to Danger

On board an aircraft carrying a ticking bomb, you have thirty
minutes to identify the bomber and save the passengers. Can you
do it?

Kate was great at puzzles like that. I accepted the challenge.
Almost immediately a message popped up:

Fancy a game, Alex?

The Dying Spaceship

Trapped aboard a spaceship being sucked into a black hole, can you and your team of marines beat the other team and save the ship? Amy.

This could have been written for Ben. Blasting aliens was the staple diet of the game booths. Ben had played, and won, hundreds of these games. Perfect. It might take a bit of explaining why we had ended up with two challenges, and Ben might not like the fact that the challenger was Amy Bird. But he was, without question, the best in the park at this. I accepted that challenge as well.

Kate/Ben. As I said, we can't leave yet. We still don't know for certain what's happened to Mike, and I'm not abandoning him. So I decided we needed to accept a challenge for the next cycle. We can't risk another random assignment from ParkGov. However, we have ended up with two. Really sorry about that. I found the perfect one for Kate, but after I had accepted it I got a much more interesting one – a challenge from Amy Bird [attached]. It's perfect for you, Ben.

I know it's not ideal to be playing two games tomorrow, and I appreciate that there is some risk, but we can't keep running from Bird. This is our chance to get rid of her once and for all. It's not like Mike's race, where she could bring in a ringer and beat him. We know that there's no one better than Ben at this type of game. He will win. That will solve all our problems.

Good luck, friends. Not that you need it. We are going to win this. By the end of the next cycle things will be a lot clearer.

I can't do much more today. Sierra has fried my brain with alcohol, and there's only so much I can clear. We need to be on best form tomorrow. Alex.

I cleared the rest of my messages. There was only one of any interest.

Amy Bird detected. Two alerts: view?

The first was a still of the andi on a street close to where Sierra had played her last game. It didn't tell us anything useful. The second was much better. It was five minutes later and was taken from a security camera inside a bar. After a couple of seconds the andi entered from the right and crossed over to an occupied table, pulled up a seat and sat down. I zoomed in on the table, and smiled. The angle was from over Bird's shoulder, her back to the camera, but the figure on the other side of the table was well lit and familiar. It was us – or rather, Sierra. They talked for a few minutes, and then Bird reached over and touched Sierra's hand.

Kate/Ben, one last thing. See the attached file. This just came in from Ben's alerts. Check the time stamp – it's Sierra. Bird reappeared and met up with her in a bar. Indiscreet, but Sierra looks pretty wasted. They clearly know each other, and towards the end briefly hold hands. Not sure if it's a gesture of intimacy – am I right that Bird is actually Mike? Or does this show that Sierra is controlling Bird, and they were transferring information? Maybe it was Sierra giving Bird her orders. Whatever is going on, it confirms that Sierra and Bird are working together. Do we confront her with it or wait and see where this goes? Let me know what you think. Alex.

It was all starting to unwind for Sierra. You reap what you sow. And Sierra had sown a lot of poisoned seeds.

KATE

There was a lot to catch up on.

Ben had had a close shave with Guskov, the drug dealer, or, as he had discovered, the andi dealer. He had done well to get us out of there alive. I was annoyed that he had lost ten of the years I had won, but better that than real death. He'd discovered something important, though – one of us had bought the andi, Bird. Why?

We had ended up with a challenge being forced on us by ParkGov. I didn't understand how that could have happened. Surprisingly, Sierra had then stepped up and saved the day.

Alex had decided we ought to stay, but seemed to have messed up and accepted two challenges, one for me and one for Ben. Added to which, Ben's challenge came from Amy Bird, whom I didn't trust at all. But if we didn't play, we forfeited.

Alex was speculating that Bird might be Mike, who had downloaded into the andi. That sounded very far-fetched, and probably impossible. Admittedly, Bird had told me that she had found someone who knew a way of transferring her mind to us and then back again to a different andi body. But Bird had lied to me about many things, so that didn't mean much.

Still, it was worth considering Alex's theory. I preferred to think that Mike was still alive somewhere – even in an andi body – than that he had gone for good. Maybe we could retrieve him.

I ran a search while I read the rest of my messages.

Alex's last message was the most important. It showed Sierra and Bird together in a bar, clearly familiar with one another. I had been trying to keep an open mind, but this seemed to confirm our worst fears. Sierra was up to something. Maybe on her own, maybe with Mike. I ran the image clip a second time, carefully studying Bird in light of Alex's theory. Could that be Mike in Bird's body? There was definitely something intimate in the way they touched. But Sierra acted like that with most people. Or was Sierra controlling Bird in some way? Had we caught her giving Bird instructions?

The results of my search came back. I didn't have time to read them all, but the most promising was a CGov research paper entitled 'The Transfer of Communal Minds to Human/Android Bodies'. I opened it and read the summary.

The first generation of communal bodies gave rise to unanticipated problems. Although the science worked flawlessly, certain psychological difficulties had not been foreseen. A significant minority of commune members regretted their decisions or irretrievably fell out with other members. This led to experiments into whether it was possible to unwind a commune.

Attempts to reverse mind transfers met with mixed results. Out of 412 such procedures, 258 resulted in cognitive damage ranging from catatonia to mild psychosis. Six resulted in death to the entire commune.

In five cases the bodies from which the minds had originally been transferred remained available. In all five cases the unwinding of the commune was successful.

In the remaining 407 cases the original bodies had been disposed of, and the re-transfer was to other bodies (205) or to androids (202). Transfers to android bodies were overwhelmingly more successful (56.5 per cent success rate) than transfers to human bodies (17.1 per cent success rate).

Nevertheless, the high failure rate for both resulted in the programme being shut down, and the option to unwind communes was withdrawn.

This paper explores the reasons for the failure of the programme, and considers whether recent medical improvements could lower the risks of mind transfer from communes to android or human bodies.

We conclude that modern techniques and medicines mean that the risks of transfer could significantly be improved, particularly in respect of transfers to android bodies, where we calculate a potential success rate of up to 92 per cent.

It is beyond the scope of this paper to consider the ethical question of whether reversal should be offered until the success rate has risen to 100 per cent.

I didn't have time to read the full paper, and it probably wouldn't have made much sense to me anyway. However, this did suggest that some of what Bird had told me might have been true.

Maybe Alex's theory as to what had happened to Mike wasn't so far-fetched after all. Although even if it was possible, that didn't explain why Mike or Sierra would have done this.

I was going to have to leave it till later. My challenge was at 8:00. My mind was racing and I needed to calm down. I had time for a walk and some food before going to the arena.

•

Welcome, Ms Weston

Game: Flight to Danger
Objective: Find the bomb
Stages: One
Location: 39,000 feet

There are five players and 32.3 years at stake. You will not be interacting with other players, but each of you will be faced with the same scenario. The survivor, or survivors, will share the time of those who lose.

To preserve game integrity, any attempt to record events or retain memories will lead to an immediate forfeit.

Mandatory CGov Advisory: Please be aware that you are engaging in a simulation. Flying in the era in which this game is set was, and still remains, one of the most environmentally damaging human activities possible.

'Welcome on board, Ms Weston. You are in 3A. Let me show you to your seat.'

The stewardess shows me into the first-class cabin. It is small, with only twelve seats. Mine is at the rear on the left-hand side.

'May I get you a glass of champagne?' asks the stewardess.

I remember that I am here to win a game, not enjoy myself. 'No thanks.'

'Very well, I will leave you to settle in.'

I sit down.

After a few minutes the aircraft begins to move. Five minutes later we are in the air.

The screen in front of me lights up.

Ms Weston, this is a message from the United States Federal Bureau of Investigation. Please do not be alarmed. Do not leave your seat until we have fully briefed you. Be careful in your interaction with other passengers.

We have received information that a bomb has been smuggled on board your aircraft. We believe that it is being carried by one of the first-class passengers. We have been able conclusively to eliminate you from suspicion. We need your help.

Any attempt to search the passengers' luggage is likely to prompt the unknown subject to trigger the bomb. Any change of course or other unusual activity on the part of crew may do the same.

We have been able to obtain limited information on each of the passengers under suspicion, which will be sent to you.

Our informant tells us that the bomb is set to explode thirty minutes from now. Once you have located the bomb please take custody of it. If you choose incorrectly it is likely to alert the unsub and result in early detonation.

Best of luck, Ms Weston.

The seat-belt sign goes off and I decide to visit the toilets to get a look at my fellow passengers.

Seat 1A is occupied by a smartly dressed lady with grey hair, writing something with a silver fountain pen. In seat 2A is a middle-aged man in a dark suit, tapping away at laptop computer. Across the aisle from him, in 2E, is a woman of about my age, dressed in a grey trouser-suit, and sitting next to her is a young girl carefully colouring in a picture of a whale. The final passenger is in seat 3F dark-skinned and dressed in flowing brown robes, clutching what looks like a religious text. He is rocking backwards and forwards and muttering under his breath. This seems clumsy. Am I meant to think that he's a terrorist suicide bomber? Or is it a double-bluff? Is the racist undertone meant to make me dismiss him too quickly as a suspect?

I return to my seat.

My screen has changed. In the top-right corner is a timer, counting down. It reads 26:48. There is then a list of five names. The last one is mine, crossed through. I decide to start with the obvious one.

ABDULLAH IBRAHIM

Seat 3F

Mr Ibrahim is a forty-two-year-old religious scholar who teaches at a university in Karachi, Pakistan. He has a wife and five children who are not traveling with him. He has no known terrorist links. He is avowedly moderate and two years ago was denounced by his university board for trying to establish an exchange program with a Christian university. His brother was arrested three months ago in a protest against the Pakistani government and is currently being held in an undisclosed prison. Mr Ibrahim is returning from a multi-faith peace conference in Washington.

So Abdullah has just gone from being the most obvious suspect to the least likely. Despite his appearance he does not sound like a promising terrorist candidate. Unless his imprisoned brother is being used to coerce him?

THE HONOURABLE ABIGAIL WHISTLER, ASSOCIATE JUSTICE

Seat 1A

Judge Whistler is an Associate Justice of the United States Supreme Court. She is seventy-two years old. She has been a judge for twenty-eight years with, until recently, an unblemished career. She is currently suspended from duty and under investigation by the Judicial Ethics Committee as well as the United States Congress.

Judge Whistler's daughter is a member of a far-right militant organization, CAOG – Christians Against Oppressive Government. They are known to have stockpiled large quantities of arms and explosives against what they foresee as an inevitable future civil war. Numerous members have been convicted of illegal activities and are currently imprisoned.

Judge Whistler has sat on three cases involving CAOG or its members, without disclosing her links to the organization. Some members of CAOG have said that Judge Whistler herself is a covert member. She is known to hold strong religious and right-wing beliefs.

It is widely expected that Judge Whistler will be found to have breached her ethical duties and be required to resign.

Whilst the judge looks like a nice old lady, under the surface she appears to be a religious nut with access to explosives whose career is in ruins. Definitely worth considering.

JAMES BARTON

Seat 2A

Mr Barton was, until recently, the chief executive of a multi-billion-dollar hedge fund operating out of New York. Six months ago his offices were raided by the Securities and Exchange Commission, and multiple breaches of financial regulations and criminal law were identified. He is subject to numerous charges under federal law and is currently out on bail of five million dollars. He is attempting to negotiate a plea bargain with authorities, but will still be looking at likely jail time of ten to twenty years and confiscation of most if not all of his assets.

Mr Barton is married with two young children. Two weeks ago he and his wife took out a ten-million-dollar insurance policy on their lives in favour of their children. They told their insurance broker that since Mr Barton travels a lot they wanted to be certain that the policy would pay out in the event of an aircraft crash.

Suspect Number One, it seems. Although why go to all this trouble? If he wants to kill himself and leave some money for his children why not just jump under a train?

LOUISA AND GEORGINA DE CLERK

Seats 2E and 2F

Ms de Clerk is a thirty-eight-year-old South African socialite and divorcée. Last year, in a bitterly contested divorce, she was awarded sixty million dollars in settlement, together with custody of the couple's four-year-old daughter, Georgina.

Ms de Clerk and her daughter are returning from a scheduled one-week contact visit with Georgina's father.

Not an obvious suspect. What motive would someone who had just received sixty million dollars have for blowing up a plane and killing her daughter and herself?

I really need to know what luggage they are all carrying, but I can't start searching through the overhead lockers. I visit the galley at the front of the cabin on the excuse that I need a glass of water. The air stewardess looks surprised, and tells me to call for her next time. I walk back to my seat as slowly as I can.

The judge has stopped writing and has her eyes closed, her papers stuffed into a wicker bag at her feet. It doesn't look an obvious bomb holder. Barton has put on headphones and is watching something. There is a brown leather briefcase tucked under his footrest. That looks more promising. Why is he keeping it so close?

Louisa de Clerk is reading a book and has in front of her an empty champagne glass and a gin and tonic. Her daughter has given up colouring in and is watching something on a laptop, cuddled up in her oversized seat with a stuffed pink unicorn, wrapped in a blanket. Abdullah Ibrahim continues to pray. He has a soft canvas bag next to him on his seat. He seems to be trying too hard to be a suspect.

It would help if I had some idea of the size of the bomb. How big a bag do they need for it?

I sit back down. My countdown is at 13:12 and I am no further forward. A new message appears on my screen.

We are devoting all available resources to further background investigation of the suspects. Based on your investigations so far please advise which suspects you wish us to prioritize and whether there are any that we can disregard.

I don't have any clear evidence one way or another. I need more information and to get it I am going to have to take a gamble.

Barton, Ibrahim and the judge are all keeping their bags close to them, but the judge's doesn't look like the sort to hide a bomb. And somehow Ibrahim feels like a red herring. He is just too obvious. At the moment if I had to choose it would be Barton.

What about de Clerk? She seems the least suspicious of all, which makes me suspicious of her.

The four names are up on the screen, with a 'yes/no' next to them. More on gut instinct than anything I tap 'no' for Ibrahim and 'yes' for Barton and de Clerk. I can't decide about the judge. I tap 'OK' and the screen disappears.

10:48.

After a minute another screen appears.

We have been able to gather more information about two of the possible suspects.

JAMES BARTON

We have spoken to Mr Barton's wife who said that it was she who encouraged him to take out new life insurance, and it was she who enquired about aircraft crash coverage. She says that she had recently read an article about a CEO who died in a crash and the insurers refused to pay out because of suspected terrorism.

She also told us that Mr Barton is about to agree a plea bargain under which he will be required to serve a four-year prison term and pay a fine of eighty million dollars. He is pleased with the deal and is flying to see his lawyers to finalize the paperwork.

So there goes my Suspect Number One.

LOUISA DE CLERK

Witnesses report that shortly before boarding the flight Ms de Clerk was seen arguing fiercely with a man who matches the description of her former husband. We understand that Mr de Clerk and his second wife met Ms de Clerk at the airport to hand over Georgina. We have traced a vehicle belonging to Mr de Clerk leaving the airport shortly thereafter.

That doesn't take me a lot further, but a row with her ex might explain why she's had a couple of drinks immediately on boarding. That in itself is hardly suspicious.

Please advise which suspects you wish us to prioritize and whether there are any that we can disregard.

I check the time remaining: 7:04. I am taking a chance on dismissing Ibrahim, and now Barton, but I have to make some decisions.

I tell them to focus on de Clerk and the judge, and disregard Barton. I'm flip-flopping on the judge.

I can't get up again without looking suspicious. I need to wait.

5:43

We have further information about two possible suspects.

THE HONOURABLE ABIGAIL WHISTLER, ASSOCIATE JUSTICE

We understand from the Judicial Ethics Committee that based on current evidence they are likely to conclude that Judge Whistler was in breach of her duties in failing to declare her daughter's links to CAOG, but that there is no evidence that the judge herself is a member. The Committee does not think that there is any credible evidence to support that allegation, and considers it highly unlikely that the judge would have access to any form of explosive device. The Committee's current intention is to issue a reprimand and permit her to continue her duties.

So the judge is dropping down my list of suspects as well.

LOUISA DE CLERK

We have now obtained footage of the altercation between Ms de Clerk and her husband. This is being uploaded to you.

We have also traced Mr de Clerk's vehicle, which was involved in a single-vehicle accident approximately five miles from the airport. His vehicle appears to have been driven with intent off the road and into a tree. Mr de Clerk and his second wife died instantly. Officers at the scene believe this is likely to have been a murder–suicide.

4:32

All of which looks suspicious, but still doesn't explain why Ms de Clerk might want to blow up an aircraft with her daughter on board. Am I wrong to ignore Ibrahim? It's getting too late to worry about that.

The image clip isn't great quality. It shows four figures standing near the security gates at the airport. I recognise two of them as Louisa and Georgina de Clerk. The third is a man who must be her ex-husband. Now very ex. Standing just behind him is a red-haired woman who looks as though she doesn't want to be part of the group. She is glancing around her, as though embarrassed by the scene they are causing, and puts a hand on her husband's arm. He shrugs her off. He is arguing with his ex-wife while Georgina clings to her mother's leg. Mr de Clerk moves close up to Louisa and shakes his finger in her face. She pushes him away and turns, taking Georgina by the hand. He stands for a moment then runs after them, pulling something from a backpack. Louisa tries to start through security but he grabs Georgina by the shoulder, crouches down, and hands her what he is carrying. Louisa seizes it from her daughter and throws it across the airport floor. Georgina pulls free from her mother and runs after it, picking it up.

I try to zoom in to see what it is they are fighting over, but the clip won't do that. I play that bit again, and this time I catch a flash of pink. I've seen that shape somewhere before.

And I know where the bomb is.

There is no terrorist. This isn't some fundamentalist plot to blow up an airliner to make a political statement. As I thought, Ibrahim was a red herring. Nor is it a failed businessman looking for insurance money, or a disgraced judge looking to end it all.

This is revenge, driven by the oldest motives of all, love and jealousy. A father who doesn't want to let his daughter go, and who hates her mother. Who would rather see them both dead. Who doesn't care about the hundreds of others who will die with them. Because he knows that by then he too will be dead.

His parting gift to his daughter was meant to kill us all.

1:11

I look up.

I leap out of my seat and cut round the back of row 3 to the other aisle. A stewardess carrying a food tray jumps out of my way and apologises. I run up the aisle to where Georgina is sitting.

She looks up from her computer screen, not understanding why I grab her stuffed pink unicorn and wave it above my head in triumph.

•

Victory

Congratulations, Ms Weston. Thanks to your efforts the crew was able to disable the bomb before it detonated. Two players survived the game.

You have been credited with six years.

You have ten minutes to leave the booth.

•

I found myself back in the arena.

I was relieved to have survived. The first part of Alex's gamble had paid off. But the second part would be harder. Ben would be facing Amy Bird.

BEN

DAY FOUR
11:00–13:10

Alex had set me up with a challenge. I wasn't certain about the wisdom of staying in the park just in the hope of tracking down Mike. It was illogical to suppose that he was still alive.

I brought up the details. It looked like a fairly standard alien shoot-'em-up. These were a staple of the death parks. I could see why Alex had thought this would be good for me. I had spent hours, weeks, years maybe, playing simulations of this kind. Outside the parks I had won some high-profile competitions. I wouldn't know the full details until I got in, but there wasn't going to be anyone in the park who could beat me.

The problem was the challenger: Amy Bird.

Alex had described the challenge as interesting. I would have used other words. High risk. Stupid. Utterly insane, perhaps? What had Alex been thinking? Kate had already played Bird, beaten her, and yet Bird was still alive. Then Bird had beaten Mike, yet *we* were still here. Somehow she wasn't playing by the rules. I was confident I could defeat any normal andi as they wouldn't have the reflexes and experience that I did. All the more so with the second-hand andis being sold in the parks. They probably hadn't been serviced in years.

Bird might be different.

But there was nothing I could do. The challenge had been accepted and my only options were to play or forfeit. I wasn't going to forfeit.

I had thirty minutes to get to the arena, a low-budget place in Borth Street. Ominously, the same place where Bird had played Kate.

I skimmed my messages as I walked there. The results of my search for Bird seemed to show beyond doubt that she was working with Sierra. I struggled to understand why. There was no reason or logic to Sierra's mind and I had long ago given up trying to understand her. But this made even less sense than usual. I found it hard to buy into Alex's theory that they had somehow uploaded Mike's mind into the andi.

I didn't have time to worry about that now. If I didn't beat Sierra's andi we were all going to be out of the park in an hour, minus all the time we had won. At best.

The Borth Street Arena was in one of the most derelict parts of the park that I had seen. Surrounding blocks were overgrown with piles of rubble, and I could hear some creature rustling out of sight. A half-demolished high-rise towered over the single-storey arena, looking as though it might collapse on to it at any moment. That was probably not my biggest risk.

The arena door squealed open reluctantly.

12:26.

Amy Bird was already there, sitting on the unstaffed counter.

I nodded to her. 'Shouldn't there be someone here?' I said.

She jumped down. 'Hello, Ben. I sent them away. I prefer not to be watched.'

'Who are you?' I asked. 'Alex thinks you're Mike.'

'I'm Amy.' She smiled. 'No one else.'

'What did you do to Mike?'

'I didn't do anything,' she said. 'Mike lost a race. You know the rules. He died.'

'If that's true and the rules applied I wouldn't be here now. We would all have gone into stasis. And according to the rules you should be dead – Kate beat you.'

'True,' she said. 'But those were my rules we were playing by.'

'And what now? Are we playing fairly or are you going to twist the rules again?'

'Worried, Ben? This is your sort of game. You should be able to beat me with one arm tied behind your back. I promise you we will play this fairly.'

'We know you're working with Sierra and I know what her promises are worth,' I said. 'Did you tell Mike you were playing fair and then got some ringer in so you could kill him?'

'You worked that out?' she said. 'Clever you. The trouble with Mike was his vanity. He thought he was unbeatable. You may not believe me when I say that I will play fair, but you don't really have much choice. You play the game or forfeit.'

'We don't need to play the game if I kill you here,' I said.

'That would be unwise.' She inclined her head towards a security camera in the corner of the ceiling. 'The authorities would take a dim view of it. You would probably end up mindwiped. Kill me in there,' she nodded towards the rooms, 'and you're a hero who has just won some extra time.'

I doubted whether the camera was working. I hadn't been able to get a feed from it in my searches. But she was right. The risks of killing her here were too high. Besides, I wasn't certain I could bring myself to kill someone in the real world. Dying in a game might have the same result, but it felt very different.

A buzzer sounded.

12:30.

'Now we play, or you forfeit,' said Amy. 'Your choice.'

'Which room?' I asked.

'You're in Room 3,' she said with a smile.

Room 3? That was deliberate. To try to unsettle me. Three was all wrong.

I turned my back on her and stepped inside.

•

Welcome, Mr White

Game: Black Hole Rescue

Winner: First to save the ship

Stages: One

Location: ISS *Makaira*

•

I am standing in the darkened cargo hold of the ISS *Makaira*, which is spinning out of control towards a black hole. The hull has been breached. The crew has been killed by a group of alien terrorists – white-skinned creatures with six-inch claws and pointed teeth that they use for extracting human brains. They are protesting the subjugation of their home world, or their religion, or something. I had skipped over that bit of the briefing as their motivation for eating my brain doesn't seem particularly important.

I am wearing a black spacesuit with various guns and grenades hanging off me. Gravity has failed, and the only things keeping me on the deck are my magnetic combat boots. Which is ironic, as in thirty minutes we will have more gravity than we can possibly handle, torn apart as we are dragged into the black hole. There's me and a team of four marines, brought here in a last-ditch attempt to save the ship. I hear a roar behind me as our landing craft exits through the closing cargo doors. No escape. No going back.

I sigh. This is pretty dull stuff. Clichéd. I have fought this sort of scenario a hundred times. When will they get more imaginative with their writing?

I shake my head. That's not what I need to be focusing on right now. I'm not here to critique the quality of the game.

Bird and her team will be approaching the bridge from the opposite end of the ship. Whichever one of us gets there first will save the ship, stop the fall into the black hole, and win the game. Whoever comes second will die in some convoluted and unlikely plot twist. They always do.

We will move much faster if we can restore gravity. I am guessing that, unrealistically, it is possible to do so in my half of the ship without also helping Bird. It's lazy writing, but that's how these things normally work.

I look around. There is a door to my right with a sign saying

TO ENGINE ROOM. That seems the most likely place to have to go to fix the gravity problem. I signal for my team to follow, and clump over to the door. I can't see their faces behind their helmets, and I don't really need to. They are cyphers, cannon-fodder who will die before we complete this. I decide to name them 1, 2, 3 and 4. I'd really like 3 to die first.

I swing the door open and gesture for one of the marines to dive through. He (or maybe she) does so. I half expect them to be torn in two by a laser beam or a six-inch claw, which is why it never pays to go through first. However, it seems that this time they have a more imaginative death in mind for my can-non-fodder and we all pass through unscathed.

A long corridor stretches out ahead, dimly lit by red emer-gency lighting. It looks safe enough so I take the lead. A minute later we come to a large door with ENGINE ROOM stencilled on it. I push the button to the left of it and the door hisses open. I gesture for the marines to go through.

As Marine 1 does so a thin white alien drops from the ceil-ing and rips his head off. Blood pumps out, a mass of floating droplets in zero gravity. Scientifically inaccurate, but it looks neat. At least they got the effects down. The remaining three marines blast the alien while I spin around and shoot the other two creeping down the corridor behind us. Classic ambush tac-tics. I've done this a million times before. I suppress a yawn.

I duck under the widening pool of floating blood and into the engine room. I sweep the room but there is no sign of any-thing else hostile.

The room is a tall cylinder, with a driveshaft running up the centre. There is a control panel at the base, screens dark. I gesture for the others to remain on watch and walk over to the panel. There is a button marked ENGINE INITIATION. It may be a double-bluff but so far this scenario hasn't been particularly subtle. I know I need to move fast, so I've got to take some chances. I press the button and step back.

The screens light up and a dull thudding reverberates throughout the room. After a moment the lights come fully up and I feel the pull of gravity. There is a thump behind me. I turn to see what remains of Marine 1 crashing to the deck in a mix of flesh and blood and charred alien. His head rolls away into a corner. It's a nice touch.

I check the atmosphere. We now have breathable air, so I unseal and push back my helmet. Peripheral vision is improved. The other three copy me. Two men and a woman. I won't be bonding with them, as I don't rate their life-expectancy.

I look around. The door is the obvious exit. Too obvious. There is a metal ladder running up one wall leading to a hatch high up near the ceiling. I stow my gun and nod to the others. 'Let's go.'

Climbing the ladder is easy as my suit contains small servo motors that enhance my muscles. I pull open the hatch and wriggle into what appears to be an air vent. Conveniently it is just large enough to fit a fully grown male in a spacesuit. They aren't really trying with this one.

I pull myself along until I come to a grille in the floor of the vent. I squint through into a room below containing several aliens sitting around a desk. Their hearing can't be great as they don't seem to have noticed me dragging myself through the metal tube a metre above their heads. They also seem surprisingly untroubled by the fact that gravity has abruptly reasserted its hold on them. They are studying paper plans on the table, pointing at something.

I pause to think. Is this just a red herring and should I carry on? Instinct tells me that I need those plans to progress. I fumble about at my belt until I find something marked 'Stun Grenade'. I manage to pull up one corner of the grille, prime the grenade and roll it through, and quickly reengage my helmet.

There is a flash of light and a blast of sound, and then I dive headfirst through the grille. It's not quite as impressive as I intended. I land on the table, which cracks beneath my weight, and end up with one foot wedged between two bits of broken plastic. But the aliens aren't going anywhere. The stun grenade appears to have triggered some sort of shutdown mode. I shoot them while I extract my foot and try to regain some dignity before my team drops through.

I retract my helmet and pick up the plans. They're torn in half with a boot print in the middle. I piece them together. This is embarrassing. Not quite the image I had been trying to project. It is a schematic of the ship's upper decks. The bridge is obvious, and I work backwards from there towards where I must be. I eventually work it out by matching a number on the wall with some writing on the map that my boot had half obscured. There are two ways of getting to the bridge, with no obvious reason for choosing one over the other. My guess is that one is booby-trapped.

I come up with a plan. I follow one corridor with Marines 2 and 4. Marine 3 takes the other route. In my group Marine 2 takes point, and I hang well back.

With good reason as it turns out. We are barely halfway down the corridor when the lights go out. I dive for the shelter of a bulkhead, my helmet coming back up. There is an explosion ahead, and parts of Marine 2 come whistling past me. Oh well. No point in having cannon-fodder if you don't feed the cannons.

We'll be taking the other corridor then.

We retrace our steps and catch up with Marine 3. The lights are still working here. He is proceeding cautiously, gun barrel sweeping ahead of him. I order 3 to walk backwards behind us, and am rewarded for my caution as an alien leaps out of a doorway behind us, only immediately to be eviscerated by 3. In a repeat of their previous tactics, as Marine 4 turns back to us, two aliens come running down the corridor behind him. Fortunately I am not so naive. By the time 4 turns back, what is left of the aliens is sliding down the walls of the corridor.

The routes meet up again as we come to a door helpfully marked BRIDGE. I set 3 and 4 to watch behind us, and study the door. There is no obvious way of opening it, no helpful button marked 'Push Me'. A screen lights up.

To enter the Bridge you must first solve three riddles.

Of course. If you are flying through the depths of space and liable to face alien attacks, don't make it too easy for the crew. Nothing like body recognition or biometric coding to open doors securely and quickly. Instead have a system that takes minutes to unlock and gives intruders just as much chance as the crew to get in.

Maybe that was why the crew died. They weren't very good at riddles.

I sigh, and check the time. Seventeen minutes have elapsed, so we are well within the parameters. Although I don't know how fast Bird is progressing, which is what really matters. Assuming she is even playing fairly this time.

It takes me a minute to solve their fairly lame riddles, and the door hisses open. I gesture for Marine 3 to go first, and I follow.

To my surprise – and not a little regret – 3 remains alive. There is no obvious opposition. Nor is there any sign of another team of marines, which is what matters most.

There is a flashing screen on a control panel in the centre of the room, with a large red button next to it. I resist the urge to go over and instead look around carefully. I'm guessing that there is one last big bad to kill, then I can press the button and we can all go home. I probably need to trigger the fight by at least looking interested in the button. I take a step towards it.

Everything freezes. The screen stops in mid flash and the room becomes silent. I am frozen in place. For a moment I think that my boots have chosen an unfortunate moment to re-magnetise, but then I realise none of me can move. I hear footsteps behind me, but I can't turn to see who it is.

A figure appears in my peripheral vision and steps in front of me.

Amy Bird.

She doesn't appear to be playing the game. She is dressed as she was earlier, has no spacesuit or weapons, and no team of supporting characters. She turns to me.

'That wasn't really much of a challenge for you, was it, Ben?

Eighteen minutes is pretty impressive.'

I try to say something, if only to shout at her, but my voice is frozen as well. I have no choice but to listen. I don't know if this is Amy Bird or some version of Sierra speaking to me, or if they are even different any more.

'The trouble is, Ben, good as you are, it doesn't really help. You aren't actually playing against me. Our friend Mr Guskov has a number of sidelines. He has a particularly talented doctor working for him. Personally I think Dr Bernard is a psychopath, but he has discovered how to move minds from schizos to andis; and, better yet, how to activate different schizo minds at the same time. Of course you can't release them all into the same body at once – he tried that and it led to catatonic shutdown as they fought for control. But he can drop minds into andis or simulations. As can I, now that I have access to all your minds.

'So you aren't fighting me, Ben. You're fighting yourself. Look.' She waves a hand and an image appears floating in the air in front of me. I can see two figures in spacesuits, fighting their way through a ship's hangar. One shouts something and raises a gun. Then the image fades.

'That's Alex and Kate,' says Bird. 'They aren't as good as you. And their challenges are rather different. But they should finish within the thirty minutes. Don't expect them to come bursting on to the bridge here, though. I have had to keep you on separate ships. It's best that you don't meet. But the set-up is similar. Press the red button and win. Don't press it and die. Real death, Ben. Mindwipe. You won't wake up in a couple of weeks arguing with the others over what body to have. It will all end now.

'But there's a catch. It's not about who presses the button first. It's about who doesn't press it before the thirty minutes is up. Because they will die for sure. But if both teams press it before the game ends, everyone dies.

'I'm going to release you in a moment, and you have a choice to make, Ben. Press the button and you have a chance of living. But only if Kate and Alex fail to complete the game in time, or don't press their button. If neither team presses the button the clock runs out, you get sucked into a black hole, and everyone dies. If one of you presses the button, and the other doesn't, the team to press it lives.

'Your choice, Ben. Press the button if you want a chance at life. But will your friends think you are that selfish, or will they assume you have chosen to let them live? Or will they think that if they are going to die then you might as well too? How much do your friends love you? How well do they know you? How much do you love *them*?'

KATE

For reasons I don't understand I'm dressed in a spacesuit and standing in a dimly lit docking bay blasting aliens. To left and right of me are parked shuttlecraft, leaving a narrow field of fire ahead.

This is meant to be Ben's game. I have no idea what I am doing here, or why. I have no recollection of coming to an arena.

I'm sure Ben could identify with precision the black-barrelled weapon that I am clutching at waist level. He could probably also put a name to the white-skinned, long-clawed aliens that are rushing towards me, pointed teeth showing through rictus grins. All I know is that each time I pull the trigger it gives a satisfying thump and a flash of light incinerates the near-est alien. They seem to be bent on some sort of suicide mission; five bodies are scattered in front of me. Although unarmed, if they get too close their claws and teeth will be more than a match for my gun.

I pull the trigger again, another alien explodes, and the recoil makes me step backwards. I bump into something that moves away from me. I spin around, thinking that one of the aliens has got behind me.

My gun is half-raised, my finger tensing on the trigger, as I realise that it is another figure in a spacesuit, firing in the opposite direction. Their helmet is closed, and I have no idea if I know who he, or she, is. Whoever it is I have to trust that they've got my back.

I turn around and shoot two more aliens at close range. The nearest one explodes over me in a splatter of white goo. I'm not sure if it's blood, brains or internal organs.

I wipe the faceplate of my spacesuit clean with a gloved hand.

In front of me it has gone quiet. There is no sign of any more attackers. Cautiously I look over my shoulder. That way too is empty, apart from gently smoking bodies.

I step to the side, where I can look both ways, and lean back against one of the shuttles. I am sweating inside the suit.

The other figure turns to me, lowers their gun, and fiddles with something on the side of their helmet. The faceplate retracts and the helmet swivels back.

It takes me a moment to realise that it is Alex. Not Alex in Mike's body, and not the Alex I knew when I was seventeen. This Alex is older, lean, his features harder – perhaps how he sees himself now. I don't understand how we can be part of the same game.

But then I don't understand how I am here at all, so anything seems possible.

He gestures to the side of his head, and says something. I can hear nothing. It takes me a moment to realise that he is telling me how to retract my helmet. After some fumbling I find the right button, and am breathing fresh air.

He frowns. 'Kate, is that you?'

'Yes.' I have no idea what I look like in this reality. 'Alex, what are we doing here? This was meant to be Ben's game. How did we get to the arena?'

He shakes his head. 'I don't know. Ben is meant to be playing Amy Bird. Maybe that wasn't such a good idea. She seems to be able to do odd things in the arenas. The first I knew I was standing here with you shooting whatever these things are.' He prods one of the smoking corpses with his toe. 'I did get this message, though.'

You are part of a two-person covert operations team that has been landed aboard the *Queen of Circinus*, an intergalactic cruise liner carrying over 2,000 passengers. A group of alien terrorists has killed the bridge crew and set the ship on a collision course with a black hole. You have thirty minutes in which to find your way to the bridge and change course. Fail to reach the bridge within thirty minutes and you will all die. The aliens are fleeing and will try to stop you. The passengers are unaware of what is going on, and you must try not to cause panic. Avoid or eliminate the aliens, find your way to the bridge by whatever means, and change course.

'So I'm guessing those were the fleeing aliens,' I say, gesturing to the bodies. 'They were leaving as we arrived. How long do we have left?'

'About twenty-eight minutes.'

'Any idea how we get to the bridge? I don't imagine it's going to be as simple as walking along the corridor and finding it.'

'The hangar doors are behind us,' says Alex. 'So I'm guessing the exit is at the other end.'

We step cautiously between the alien corpses, wary of the still-twitching claws. We walk past the shuttlecraft until we come to a door marked LEVEL SIX. Alex presses a button and we pass through into a deserted corridor. It ends at a lift, the doors of which open as we approach. A screen on one wall lights up.

Level One:	Bridge [Restricted Area]
Level Two:	Suites, Cygnus Theatre and Observation Deck
Level Three:	State Rooms and Dining
Level Four:	Cabins
Level Five:	Crew Accommodation [Restricted Area]
Level Six:	Engineering [Restricted Area]

I try to select Level One. The doors close, but the screen flashes red and we don't move. It was never going to be that easy.

'Let's get as close as we can to the bridge,' I say. 'We ought to be able to get to Level Two, and then we just need to find a way up one more level.'

'All right,' says Alex. 'But we can't go stamping round the passenger levels in spacesuits and carrying guns. We're meant to be covert and not panic the passengers. We're going to have to ditch this gear.'

'True, but what if we run into more aliens?'

'Hopefully that was all of them,' says Alex. 'They can't be in the passenger areas or there would be panic already.'

There is no space in the lift, so we open the doors and step back into the corridor. After some awkward fumbling we work out how to remove the spacesuits. We stuff our guns inside the suits and leave them next to a bulkhead.

Underneath, Alex is dressed in a white linen suit with a black shirt. I am wearing a low-cut red dress that stops at mid-thigh. I reach down to pull it lower, but it doesn't have much effect. Why have I chosen to wear this in the game, when I'd never do so in real life? I feel half naked. I glance up and catch Alex looking down the front of my dress. He says nothing, but raises an eyebrow.

'Piss off,' I say, straightening up awkwardly. I'm not enjoying this. Alex's teasing look isn't helping. It may be a game but I don't like him seeing me this way. 'Let's get on with it.'

We take the lift to Level Two and emerge into a brightly lit lobby. There are passengers milling around, and a few uniformed crew members. As we pause to get our bearings, one of them hurries over to us.

'Mr Du Bois, Ms Weston, they are waiting for you.'

'What? Who?' Alex asks.

'You are needed in the theatre,' he says impatiently. 'Come on.' He turns away. As I start to follow him, Alex grabs my arm.

'We don't have time for this, Kate.'

'I think we do,' I say. 'This must be part of the game. Let's at least see where he's taking us. We might be able to find a way to the bridge.'

Alex looks unconvinced, but lets go of me.

The crew member leads us to an unmarked door, and buzzes it open. There is a narrow corridor beyond, which ends in a door. He knocks.

'Can we get to the bridge from here?' I ask.

He looks puzzled. 'Not from here. You don't have time for that now anyway. Maybe afterwards I can show you, if the captain says yes. We're late already.'

The door is opened by a man dressed in a bright purple suit with a ruffled white shirt and a purple bow tie. 'You're late,' he says. 'Come in. Quickly now, show's about to start.'

The room beyond is small, with two couches and a door in the opposite wall.

'What is this?' I ask.

'You'll be on in a moment. Just follow my lead.'

Before we can react he takes a deep breath, opens the other door, and steps through. We hear a round of applause. Alex and I peer around the door.

We are blinded by bright lights shining down on to a stage. Though it is hard to see beyond the lights, there appears to be an audience. There are small black objects fluttering about, which I realise are camera drones.

The man has walked over to a podium in the centre of the stage. There are two smaller ones on either side. He holds up one hand and waits for the applause to subside.

'Good evening, ladies, gentlemen, and others in between! Tonight, as on every night for the next two weeks, our broadcast of *Coupled Up* is brought to you live from the *Queen of Circinus*, the newest and largest of the Circinus Lines' cruise ships. If you want to see the galaxies in comfort and style then come travel with us. For the next two weeks all prizes are kindly sponsored by Circinus Lines, and,' he pauses, 'are doubled in value!' Someone cheers, and there is a round of applause.

'Tonight we have a record audience. We are currently being broadcast to over two and a half billion viewers!' Again there is loud applause.

'I am your host of *Coupled Up*, Jackson James. So . . . let's get coupling!' The audience cheers and claps.

'Let's welcome to the show our first couple. They will be playing for a special prize tonight.' He lifts a small box from his podium and shows it to the audience. 'They've come a long way to be here, so please make them welcome. Our young lovers . . . Alex and Kate!' He turns towards us and waves us on.

'What do we do?' whispers Alex.

'That's got to be the key to the bridge,' I say. 'That's why we've been brought here to play whatever this is. We need to go along with it.'

'Come on,' Jackson says. 'Don't be shy now!' A slow hand-clap starts to go round the audience.

I step through the door and walk over to him. He greets me with a big smile, kisses me on both cheeks, and directs me to the podium to his left. He welcomes Alex with a handshake and sends him to his right.

A camera drone flutters in front of me. It seems to be trying to look down the front of my dress. I try to swat it away, but it dodges my blow. I know this isn't real but my legs are going to collapse at any moment. It all feels deeply unpleasant. Despite what the arenas say about privacy I suspect that we are being watched by hundreds of creeps on illegal streams.

But if we don't play along we're going to lose the game.

Jackson turns back to the audience.

'I'm sure we all know the rules, but for our new viewers a

quick reminder. In the first two rounds our couple have the chance to maximise the time that they will have for the final round. They will start with one minute, but that is probably not enough. Alex and Kate must use the first two rounds to win more time. Win the final round, and win the prize. Lose, and walk away with nothing. Winning depends upon how well they know each other, and how much they think alike.

'By the end of the game we find out whether they are Coupled Up or . . .' He gestures to the audience.

'UNCOUPLED!' they shout back.

Jackson turns to me. 'So, Kate, how long have the two of you been a couple?'

I sense that 'we are not a couple' or 'twenty-five years' is not going to be the right answer. 'Uh . . . six months or so,' I say.

'And how well do you think you know each other?'

'I guess that's what we are going to find out.' I glance across at Alex, who is looking bemused.

Jackson turns to him. 'What about you, Alex? Do you know Kate well?'

He looks embarrassed, and smiles weakly. 'I . . . I'd like to think so, yes.'

'Well, we will start things off gently,' says Jackson. 'For the first round we're going to ask each of you four questions about the other. For each one you get right, you gain five seconds in the final round. Write your answers on the screens in front of you, and they will be revealed together. Are you ready to start?'

We both nod.

'OK. The first four questions are about Alex. Question 1: If Alex could have a superpower, what would it be?'

Really? What is this crap? I have no idea. I glance across at Alex. Obedient as ever, he has his head down and is writing something on his screen.

Jackson catches my eye. 'No peeking now,' he says. 'What's your answer, Kate?'

Somewhat desperately, I write 'Power of Flight'.

'Let's see your answers!' Jackson cries.

Alex has written 'Reading Minds'. Not a great start.

'Never mind,' says Jackson. 'There's still plenty to play for. Question 2: How would Alex least like to die?'

I think back to Alex's recent game, where he complained about nearly drowning. That ought to be fresh in his mind. I write that down. Alex puts 'Burning'. I glare at him, and he shrugs.

'Never mind, Kate,' says Jackson. 'That's two swings and two misses, but let's try and hit this one out of the park! Question 3: What was the name of Alex's first girlfriend?'

Well that one's easy. We both write 'Emily'.

'Yes!' says Jackson. 'We have a match!' The audience cheers. Jackson pauses. 'So Kate, who is Emily?'

I hesitate. We don't want to be going there. 'Just a girlfriend,' I say. 'A while ago.'

'Never mind. As one door closes another opens, eh Alex?' says Jackson. 'That's why you're here with the gorgeous Kate instead! Let's move on to something a little more risqué. Question 4: what is Alex's biggest sexual fantasy? Remember, answer honestly if you want a chance of winning.'

This is not going well. How am I supposed to know? I look across desperately at Alex, but he is staring down at his screen.

'Come on, Kate, is it that difficult?' asks Jackson. 'Or are there so many that you can't choose?'

If Alex is being clever he'll be asking himself what I might put. I remember Montreal. There's only one possibility. I write: 'Sex in the Woods'. Alex has written 'Outdoors'.

'Close enough,' says Jackson. 'So, Alex, has this fantasy been realised?' Alex looks awkward, and starts stammering an answer. Jackson interrupts. 'Perhaps best not to ask. It might not have been with Kate! Let's move on and see if Alex knows more about Kate than she did about him! We'll start with an easy one: what is Kate's favourite food?'

We both put 'chocolate chip cookies', and earn five seconds and another cheer from the audience.

'Question 2: What is Kate's biggest fear?'

I put 'Chaos'. Alex puts 'Losing Control'.

'What do we think?' says Jackson. 'Close enough?' He pauses for a moment, as though consulting with someone. 'All right, we will let you have that one. Question 3: If Kate had a warning label, would it say 'What you see is what you get' or 'Still waters run deep'?'

We both write 'Still Waters'.

'Well done, Alex, you seem to know Kate rather better than she knows you!' Jackson grins at me. 'So, Question 4: Suppose that I offered Kate a kilogram of gold – universal currency, she could go out and buy a small spacecraft with that – would she . . .' he pauses, 'would Kate, for a kilo of gold, run naked across the stage?' The audience laughs. 'Remember, answer honestly, Kate, if you want to win.'

I hesitate, then write my answer.

We both answer 'Yes'. I'm blushing. Someone in the audience whistles. I don't look at Alex.

'So,' says Jackson, smiling, 'we learned something new about the innocent-looking Kate. Well *we* did. Alex already knew that, it seems.' Jackson stops for a moment, then reaches down beside his podium. 'Well, as it happens Kate, I have a kilo of gold right here . . .' The audience laughs again and cheers. My heart stops. 'I'm just teasing, Kate. That dress leaves little enough to the imagination as it is!'

I'm beginning to seriously dislike him. And this show. I know it's not real, but that doesn't make it any better.

I catch Alex's eye. He looks as appalled as I feel. I'm sure he's cross with me for making us take part. But we don't have a choice if we want to get to the bridge.

'Let's move on,' says Jackson. 'At the end of the first round you got six questions right, earning you thirty seconds. Alex showed that he knows his partner perfectly; Kate less so. In the first round it was about how well you know one another. In the second round it's about how much you think the same. There are three questions. For each one you get right you earn ten seconds. Are you ready?'

I nod.

'Question 1: Kate and Alex, you are sailing in a yacht – just the two of you – past a beautiful forested island. You are lying on deck in your swimsuits taking in some sun. But suddenly you hit a reef and your yacht starts sinking. You can swim to the island and just have time to grab two items to take with you. Of these five items, which will you take: a bottle of water, some food, a gun, a firelighter, or a bag of clothes? Remember, no conferring. Choose quickly!' He turns to the audience. 'We can probably discount the clothes. We know where Kate stands on that.' They laugh.

He's really pissing me off now.

'Sorry Kate,' he says. 'But I just can't get that image out of my head!'

I ignore him. It's a forested island, so there's bound to be water. Probably also food of some sort. Surely fire is top of the list. Will Alex think that? And – however much this may satisfy Jackson's lewd asides – I wouldn't care about wandering round in a swimsuit. Would we need a gun?

'Are there any wild—' I start asking, but he interrupts me.

'Sorry, Kate, but I ask the questions, not you. That's all the information you have. Five more seconds to answer.'

I scribble 'fire' and 'gun' on the screen. Alex has done the same.

'Well done!' says Jackson. 'So, you get to the island.' He pauses. 'And here we see the loving couple on the beach.' There are sniggers from the audience, and I look behind me to see a screen at the back of the stage displaying a mock-up of a surprisingly well-toned Alex with an arm around me. I'm wearing a bikini that appears to involve impressive engineering with the minimum possible use of material. Alex's trunks are skimpy too. And packed out.

For God's sake.

I want to punch Jackson on the nose. I'm sure Alex can tell what I'm thinking. He shakes his head and grimaces. I'm hoping he can hold it together long enough to stay on stage and win. If he storms off now, as I know he wants to, we lose.

'So, Question 2,' says Jackson. 'You see smoke in the distance and find a path through the jungle heading in that direction. Unfortunately you have barely managed half a mile when Alex steps into a hole and breaks his ankle. Darkness is falling. As you are trying to decide what to do you hear footsteps on the path. Before you can hide you are met by an improbably handsome islander, who tells you that he lives in a house an hour's walk away.'

The audience laughs. I turn round to see onscreen my scantily clad alter ego gazing up at a muscular blonde man, while Alex lies on the ground. I clench my fists.

'So,' continues Jackson. 'He tells you that he saw your yacht sink and came to help. He offers to take Kate back to his house and look after her for the night.' He pauses and winks at me. 'Of course he does. He says that he and some friends will come back for Alex in the morning. What do you do? Decide that Kate goes with him, as there is no point in both of you spending a miserable night out in the jungle? Or send him on his way and stay together?'

In real life I have no doubt what the answer would be. Alex was the idiot who stuck his foot down the rabbit hole. He can survive a night in the forest. A bit of discomfort might make him more careful next time. I'm sure I can fend off the island Lothario for a night. But that's not the real question. What will Alex expect me to answer? After some hesitation, I write 'stay'.

So does Alex.

'It's going well so far,' says Jackson. 'Love triumphs over lust! So, to Question 3. The islander does return in the morning, but when you get to his house you discover that all is not what it seems. He's operating a drug-smuggling business. He offers to have you both flown to a hospital on the mainland, but only if Alex agrees to wear a plaster-cast made out of cocaine. You'll be rescued, but you'll be smuggling drugs. While he leaves you to decide you see an opportunity to steal a vehicle and escape into the jungle. You'll be together, but there's no knowing when or if you will be able to get off the island. What do you do?'

Well, I suppose at least this one doesn't involve photos of me in bikinis. Small mercies. I'm a pragmatist. I'd be off the island in a shot, cocaine or no cocaine. But Alex isn't. He believes in rules, and he's scared of breaking them. I know what he'll say.

We both write that we would escape into the jungle.

'Love triumphs again!' says Jackson. 'And virtue is rewarded. Two days later you are rescued by a cruise ship and wined and dined all the way home.'

I look behind me and there is a picture of the two of us sitting by a swimming pool drinking champagne. The design of my swimsuit may have changed, but its surface area has not. I sigh. The audience whoops.

'And that's the end of Round 2!' says Jackson. 'You gained thirty seconds in Round 1, out of a possible forty, and the full thirty seconds in Round 2. We add that to your one minute start time for Round 3, giving you two minutes. That's pretty good! Please step this way!'

As he ushers us to one side of the stage he takes the opportunity to place a hand in the small of my back to guide me. Then it slides lower. And squeezes. For a moment I freeze in disbelief. Then I grab his hand and press my thumb hard into the inside of his wrist. I feel something crunch, and he tries to suppress a squeal. His smile slips.

I step away from him as the podiums sink into the stage.

Jackson turns back to the audience and coughs. He is discreetly trying to rub his injured wrist. 'While we set up for Round 3,' he says, 'I should tell you that all of the designer swimwear that we have seen the beautiful Kate modelling . . .' He hesitates for a moment, as though someone is communicating with him, and his smile fades slightly. '. . . and, of course, the handsome Alex too – is available for instant download and printing. Use the code "Coupled Up" and get an extra 10 per cent discount. This special offer is only available until the end of today's show.'

As he speaks, a rectangular glass box descends on wires from above, and settles with a thump. Two black-clad stagehands detach the wires, which retract. One of them opens a glass door in the front of the box.

Jackson gestures for us to follow him.

'So, Round 3,' he says. 'Where you start coupled up and need to get . . .' He points to the crowd.

'UNCOUPLED!' they shout.

I don't have a good feeling about it.

'Please, step inside,' says Jackson.

The glass box is about one metre square and three metres high. Alex walks in and is positioned by the stagehands facing inwards. I follow, and am told to face Alex. They lock a belt round each of our waists, with a metal loop at the back. I am told to put my arms round Alex. Before I know what is happening, my wrists have been cuffed together. As I try to pull them up I realise that the chain has been tied through the loop on the back of Alex's belt. Swiftly they cuff Alex in the same way. We are pulled together, my eyes level with Alex's chin.

I don't like this. Judging by the rest of the show I suppose I should be grateful that they didn't ask me to strip to my underwear first.

I look up. There is a key hanging from the roof of the box. It's a good metre above our heads, and I don't see how we are going to reach it while tied up.

The stagehands move away, and Jackson steps up to the door. 'So here we are,' he says. 'Kate and Alex, coupled up. You have two minutes to escape from the box if you are to win. The time will start when the door closes. The key to the door is up there.' He points to the roof of the box. 'The keys to your handcuffs are here.' He holds them between his fingers. I try to twist towards him, to reach behind Alex to take them.

'It's not that easy, Kate,' he says. He takes one key and slides it into the pocket of Alex's trousers. Then he reaches behind me and I feel him doing something to my hair. 'I hope you lose, bitch,' he hisses into my ear. Then he steps away with a broad smile.

'The key to Alex's cuffs is in his pocket. The key to Kate's is hanging at the back of her head,' he says. 'Careful how you move. If you drop them on the floor you won't be able to reach them. You need to find a way to get both keys, unlock yourselves, and get the key to the box.' A timer flashes up on the screen behind him. He stands to the side of the box. 'Your time starts . . . now!'

The door closes.

I look up at Alex. 'How are we going to do this?'

'You need to get unlocked first,' he says. 'Then you can get my key and unlock me. Turn your head to the left.'

I do so. He pushes through my hair with his mouth. It feels as though he's chewing my hair. Then he starts pulling violently, and I suppress a cry as hair is torn out by its roots.

'Got it,' I hear him mutter through clenched teeth. He twists back in front of me, and I can see the key – and some of my hair – between his lips. He wriggles down until his mouth is level with mine. His lips press against mine. This is horrible. Like kissing your kid brother in the school play, with all your friends laughing and giggling. Alex is struggling to get the key across to me. For a moment our tongues touch. I feel sick. I bite down on the key and pull away from him.

'Move down,' I mutter round the key. I'm trying to focus on what I need to do, rather than my nausea. I only have one chance and I need to be able to see what I am doing.

Alex slides down further. I am uncomfortably aware that his face is buried in my cleavage, pulling my already low-cut dress even lower. Great. But I don't have time to worry how this is looking to the array of camera drones circling the glass box. If we don't get out we're going to die.

I lean as hard as I can into Alex until I can see my hands cuffed behind his back. I twist my arms and cup my hands as best I can. Taking a deep breath I grip the key between my lips and let it drop. It catches a fold on the back of Alex's shirt and spins sideways, away from my hands. I pull hard at Alex's belt, twisting him round, and catch the end of the key between two fingers. Cautiously I transfer it to my thumb and forefinger.

I breathe out again. 'Got it,' I say.

'One minute left!' I hear Jackson announce to the crowd.

I twist the key around and insert it into the lock to my cuffs. The chain is still through the loop of Alex's belt, so I have to waste time undoing both cuffs before I can free my hands.

I reach into Alex's pocket and grab the key to his cuffs. I reach behind me, feeling blindly for the lock.

'Let me have it,' he says. He takes the key from me and after a moment's fumbling has his hands free. We step away from one another.

'Thirty seconds,' says Jackson. 'One key to go.'

I look up. 'You need to boost me up there,' I say. Alex cups his hands, I put a foot into them, and he boosts me hard towards the roof of the box.

Too hard. My head cracks against the glass roof. I manage to touch the key, but can't get a grip on it. It remains in place as I fall painfully back.

'I missed,' I gasp. 'Again.'

'Twenty seconds!' Jackson yells.

Alex lifts me up. This time I manage to get a proper grip on the key. But it's stuck. I twist it and use my full weight to pull it free. I crash down, Alex half catching me.

'Quick,' he shouts.

I push the key into the door lock.

Jackson is standing on the other side of the door. He has a smug grin as I try to turn the key. It doesn't move.

'Five seconds,' he says. 'It's now or never.'

The audience is screaming as I try to turn the key again. It's in the lock, but I can't get it to open. My hands are slippery with sweat.

'Zero,' shouts Jackson, turning to the audience.

Alex slumps against me, his head on my shoulder. 'Shit,' he mutters. 'We failed.'

Then the door opens, and we stagger out, sweaty and dishevelled.

The audience has gone quiet.

Jackson turns back to us, arms outstretched. He shakes his head. 'I'm so sorry, Alex, Kate,' he says oozing false sincerity. 'So close. You had the key, but Kate just couldn't get the door open at the end.'

He walks over to us, ignoring Alex, kissing me on both cheeks. His hands slither up the side of my dress as he pulls back, pausing for a moment as he reaches my breasts.

I've had enough of this.

'You bastard,' I say, pushing him away from me. 'You stopped the door from opening deliberately.'

He grabs me by the upper arms, pulling me back towards him. 'There's only ever one winner here, bitch, and it's not you,' he hisses.

Who programmed him to be such a dickhead? And why? Has Amy Bird made the game glitch?

I'd like to get my hand on the programmers, but he's all there is. I half step back, and as he follows me I bring my knee up hard into his groin.

Jackson releases me and staggers back, his face white.

Someone grabs me from behind. For a moment I think it's Alex, but as I turn to shout at him to let go I realise it is one of the stagehands.

He drags me back to the door we came in.

Someone is shouting, 'Go to the break! . . .'

The audience is screaming and cheering.

The last thing I see before I'm hauled off stage is Jackson writhing on the floor, moaning. He looks as though he's about to throw up.

At least he's finally lost his smug grin.

But it's small comfort.

We lost.

BEN

'I'll leave you to it. Make your choice, Ben,' says Amy Bird.

She walks behind me and a moment later sound returns. I can move. I spin around and see a door sliding shut. I fire a rapid spread of shots through the gap, more in anger than in hope of hitting her. I suspect that it would be pointless to kill her here anyway.

I hear movement behind me. Marine 3 is walking towards the centre of the room.

'What are you doing?' I shout.

'We need to hit the switch to save ourselves,' she says, and reaches for it.

Typical 3. I shoot her through the head, and she folds to the floor. 'You don't even exist,' I mutter. I turn and shoot Marine 4 before he can react. I'm on my own now.

I drop the gun and approach the button. How much do my friends love me? Are they even my friends? Do they even care for me, let alone love me? We share a body, that's all. In fact I probably know them less than anyone else. But I don't have any other friends. Only a list of gamertags identifying allies and enemies that I've never met outside a game booth. Angelofdeath27985 – would you die for me in real life? 101Terminator42 – we may have spent days fighting through the Caverns of Euronia side by side, but will you even notice that BarbarianBen22 is gone, let alone miss him?

The question is whether Alex and Kate will sacrifice themselves for me. There are two of them and one of me, so logic says that I should be the one to make the sacrifice. But if we are all selfless, and no one presses their button, then we all die anyway. Better to at least have a chance of life. But if we all think that then we press both buttons, and we all die.

I try to message Alex. But, unsurprisingly, I'm blocked. That would have been too easy.

What if Alex and Kate don't even finish the game? They aren't as good as me. They might never get to the end. Bird said that they would. But Bird lies.

Logic, not love, is what finally drives me to my conclusion. If I don't press the button there is a chance that two live and one dies. If I do press it there is a chance that we will all die. I can't quantify the chances, so I must treat them equally. And logically it is better that two live than one. Even when the one is me.

I question that. If I'm the one making the decision should I give more weight to my life? Can one ever be greater than two? No, that's not possible. This is not a subjective judgment. I must be rational. My life has been ruled by numbers, seeing patterns in long lines of computer code. Now my life will be ended by numbers. It feels right.

I walk over to the captain's chair and sit down. I stare out at the star field, distorted by the nearing presence of the black hole.

There is an irony in the fact that I'd come to the death park to play the latest state-of-the-art games, and ended up dying after winning one of the lamest space shoot-'em-ups I've played in years.

Now I'm the last living occupant of the ISS *Makaira*. That was stupid of me. I should have kept one of the marines alive. Not 3, obviously.

But 4 would have been good. Then there would be two of us.

ALEX

We find ourselves hustled back the way we came, through the ante-room and down the narrow corridor leading to the Level 2 lobby. Kate is being half-dragged, half-carried by one of the stagehands, kicking and cursing.

I follow, another of Jackson's assistants behind me, hand in the small of my back, pressing me to keep up.

Heads turn as we are virtually thrown into the lobby. Kate's escort steps warily back as she aims a final kick at him. I've never seen her so cross.

I'm trying hard not to laugh.

As the stagehands scuttle back through the door she turns angrily to me.

'What the hell are you grinning at? You were useless in there. Leaving me to deal with that slimy git. And we lost. There's nothing funny about any of this.'

I look around. Half the passengers in the lobby are staring at us. This is not the right place.

'We need to find another way to the bridge,' she says. 'How

long have we got left?'

'About eight minutes. But we don't need to. Come with me.' I take her hand and she reluctantly allows herself to be pulled towards the lift. Away from prying eyes.

'We know this won't work,' she says. 'We tried that before.'

I wait for the lift doors to close. Then I turn to her, triumphantly showing her the keycard hidden in the palm of my free hand.

She stares. 'What? Where did you get that?'

I grin. 'Sorry I couldn't help you, but while you were busy getting vengeful on Jackson I saw the chance to liberate the card. It was a nice diversion. They'll realise eventually, but we'll be gone by then. Maybe this was how the game was meant to play out. To see how we coped with the jammed door. Whatever the reason, we need to move fast.'

I use the card and this time the lights for Level One go green.

Yes.

Kate takes a deep breath. 'Nice. I get to beat up the slimeball and we still get the prize. Good one. But let's get this done before they come after us.'

The bridge is vast and appears to take up most of the level. We have to step over an eviscerated body to exit the lift. The crew member must have been trying to escape when something attacked her from behind. There are other bodies scattered around, none moving. It is obvious that at least one has had its skull ripped open.

The aliens that did this seem to have left. Which is good, as we are unarmed.

There is a large U-shaped console in the centre of the bridge, with three chairs in front of it, one larger than the others. I walk over. The chair appears to contain the bottom half of what used to be the captain. There is a heavy smell of blood.

'So what do we do now?' I ask. 'How do we get this thing to change course?'

Kate comes to join me, and we study the console. Most of the controls look incomprehensible, but there is one panel marked 'Autopilot', with a red on/off button. It is presently turned off.

'Let's turn the autopilot on,' I say. 'Presumably it's designed to avoid crashing into black holes.'

Kate scans the screens. 'I don't see anything else obvious. We've got about five minutes left, but there doesn't seem much point in waiting. If the autopilot doesn't do the trick we have still got time to look for something else.'

She reaches towards the red switch.

And freezes.

'I wouldn't be quite so hasty,' says a voice behind us.

I try to turn, but I am frozen in place. I try to say something, but I can't speak.

Amy Bird steps into view.

'Kate. Alex. Fancy seeing the two of you together. I enjoyed the game show.' She leans back against the console, where we can both see her. To my surprise she is bleeding heavily from a head wound, and limping.

'That little bugger, Ben. His reactions are far quicker than I expected. I hadn't realised quite how much a laser beam would hurt.' She touches the wound on her head, and studies her bloodstained fingers dispassionately. 'We're going to have to make this quick. I need to get this fixed.'

She looks up at us. 'I'll give you the short version. You aren't just playing against the game. You're playing against Ben. He's just finished a similar scenario on a different spaceship. Rather quicker than you, I must say. He's now staring at a similar red button, trying to decide whether to press it. The rules are simple. If you both press your buttons you all die. If neither of you presses your buttons the games carry on, you are sucked into the black hole, and you all die. If one team presses their button and the other doesn't then the team that pressed the button wins, and lives. The other team dies.

'It's that easy. Don't waste your time looking for a win–win outcome. There isn't one. You can't all survive. It's a test of self-sacrifice versus self-preservation. Do you think Ben is self-less, and will let you live? Or does he think that you are? Or will he just press the button anyway to give himself a chance of life? Or to make sure that you die if he does?'

She pushes herself off the console and limps past us. 'Have fun – but you only have four minutes left to decide.'

I hear the bridge door open and close, and then we are free.

For a moment Kate's hand continues towards the red button, then she jerks it back. She looks at me.

'Do we believe her? What do we do?' she asks.

I breathe out sharply. 'How do I know? I don't see what the point would be in her lying to us.'

'We don't know what control she has over the games,' says Kate. 'She can clearly interfere with them in some way, but maybe she can't stop us finishing them. So the only way is to persuade us to make that decision ourselves. She's lied to us enough times before. And we know she's working with Sierra, who lies about everything.'

'True,' I say. 'What if she's not lying this time, though? If what she told us is true, are you willing to kill Ben so that we can live?'

'*If* it's true. Which is a big assumption. If we all do nothing then we all die. The safest thing is to press the button because odds are that Bird is lying or that Ben doesn't press his.'

'But if he thinks the same then we *all* die.' I'm conscious of my voice rising in panic.

'Get a grip. At this rate we're going to run out of time arguing about it,' says Kate. 'We have to press the button.'

'I don't want to kill Ben.'

We stare at each other, neither moving. There is grim determination in Kate's eyes.

We both jump as the bridge lights turn red and start flashing. 'Collision warning,' a voice announces. 'Event horizon detected. One minute to intersect.'

'Fine,' says Kate. 'You don't have to do it. I will.'

Before I can react she steps forward and presses the button.

ONE YEAR EARLIER

MONTREAL

There are two things that schizos don't do well: travel and relationships.

Travel messes with the schedule. Cross too many time zones and everyone is out of place. The barfly becomes a morning person. The athlete is trying to find somewhere to run in the middle of the night.

Relationships that come in four-hour slots are difficult. Most non-schizos want more commitment than that. If you get lucky you can find another schizo and match with someone in the same time slot. Even then the practicalities are difficult. How do you ensure that you are both in the same place at the start of your time?

Which was why Alex counted himself as twice lucky, strolling beside the Lachine Canal, holding hands with Emily.

Things had changed for all of them since coming to Montreal. Kate now operated in the middle of the night, but claimed she didn't mind. Mike could be found in the early hours of the morning running up Mount Royal or alongside the St Lawrence Seaway. To Ben it made no difference where he was, or when, provided he had access to a game centre.

It was Sierra and Alex who were most affected.

Sierra now had the afternoon. The clubs that she would normally have frequented weren't open. Bars that were open tended to be quiet. For a social creature like Sierra it was difficult. But it got her off the new drugs she'd been on before the trip. Although she grumbled about it, she seemed calmer. Mike had suggested that seeing the midday sun for the first time in years might be helping her moods.

Alex had the evening slot. It changed his life.

They had rented a small house in Little Burgundy, near the Lachine Canal. It was surrounded by restaurants and clubs, and even Alex, never the most sociable of people, began to find himself drawn outside on the warm summer evenings. He would sit in a bar by the canal, beer in hand, watching couples strolling along the towpath where ten hours earlier Mike had knocked off a quick ten-miler. He didn't have a problem being alone. That was, after all, the lot of the schizo, and he liked just sitting and watching people.

Until he saw Emily.

She was a waitress in a café on Rue Charlevoix, on the walk back to their house from the canal. It was a wide, pedestrianised boulevard, mature maple trees down the centre, cobblestones on either side. Alex had been walking down it at least once a day for the last month, but had never paid much attention to the little café with the red-striped awning nestled on a street corner.

Until Emily.

He first spotted her clearing a table on the pavement, her

hands full of dirty plates and glasses. A gust of wind blew her dark hair across her face and a napkin flew off a plate and landed on the cobblestones at Alex's feet. He bent to pick it up for her and his heart leaped inexplicably as he looked into her bright blue eyes.

She smiled. '*Merci.*'

'Not . . . ah . . . not a problem,' he muttered, and dropped the napkin back on the pile of plates.

'*Est-ce que*— . . .' she began, then stopped and smiled again. 'Sorry. You speak English. Are you all right?'

Alex was confused. 'What?'

'Your hand,' she said.

He looked down, and realised that the napkin had been covered in bright tomato sauce, which was now smeared across his hand and the cuff of his shirt.

'Ah . . . it's nothing,' he said, and made to wipe it off on his trousers.

'Don't do that. Men,' she muttered, shaking her head. 'Wait there. Don't move.' She threaded her way through the tables, her load of plates carefully balanced, and disappeared into the café.

Alex stood confused. Enchanted. How long should he wait?

It was more than a minute before she emerged, holding a dishcloth in one hand. 'Sorry, there's always someone wanting something. Here, let me sort that out.'

She took his hand in hers, wiping it with the wet half of the cloth. She turned his hand over, drying his palm, then dabbed at the sauce on his cuff.

She grimaced. 'Not much I can do about that. I'm just going

to make it worse. Make sure you soak it as soon as you get home. All right?' She released his hand.

'Ah . . . yeah . . . great. Thanks,' said Alex.

Someone shouted something in French. She flashed Alex a last smile, and turned away. 'Sorry, I'd better get back to work.'

'Ah . . . um . . .' She was gone before Alex could think of anything else to say.

He walked slowly back to the flat. Grinning to himself. He couldn't stop those blue eyes and her smile from intruding into his thoughts at random intervals. Not intruding. They were welcome.

He must have seemed a complete idiot. Why hadn't they ever paid for a translation implant?

Despite that, the next evening he decided that rather than going to his usual bar by the canal he was going to have his drink at her café. He took a seat at one of the outdoor tables, beneath the shade of a large maple tree.

He was disappointed when the waiter who emerged was a middle-aged man who spoke little English, and seemed disdainful of Alex's poor French. He ordered a beer and sat nursing it until what remained was lukewarm. Finally his efforts were rewarded as she emerged from the café looking flustered and tying her apron. She barely glanced at him and said something in French. He looked at her blankly.

'Sorry. You were here yesterday, weren't you?' she said. 'You speak English. It's all a bit rushed today and I'm getting a hard time for being late out of college.'

'No problem,' Alex said. Her smile and her eyes were as bewitching as he had remembered them. 'Could I have another beer please?'

'Of course.'

As she went inside he surreptitiously scanned her. Her name was Emily. She was a worker. A student at a local college, aged twenty.

Alex knew that he was attractive to others – a tall man of mystery, with rock-hard abs and twinkling green eyes. But even after this long he felt like a fraud when he tried to chat people up. They couldn't see it, but inside he was still the fat seventeen-year-old being laughed at and bullied. He had never left that behind. He always worried that at some point people would see through Mike's body to the real him.

Besides, no normal person would go out with a schizo, and certainly not someone as pretty as Emily. She could no doubt have whoever she wanted.

Despite that, Alex abandoned his usual bar and, each evening for the next week, found himself at the same table waiting for Emily to appear, usually late from college. His meals became longer and his tips bigger. He began to worry he was coming across like some sort of stalker. But she seemed to enjoy their snatched conversations. Sometimes he found himself having to leave hurriedly and run back to his house to make the 21:00 curfew. Kate started complaining about the state he left them in, flopping hurriedly into bed. Eventually Alex shyly admitted what was happening, and she alternated teasing with encouragement.

This had been going on for ten days when Emily, after he had settled his bill and was about to head off, lingered for a moment. She looked down at him thoughtfully.

'What is it?' he asked. 'Have I underpaid?'

'The tip you've just given me would pay for two meals,' she said. 'I'm not complaining, but wouldn't it be cheaper if you just asked me out?'

Alex blushed. 'What ... wha ...' he stammered. 'No. It's not that. Um ... I like the food.' Then he added, desperately, 'And the beer.'

She tilted her head and frowned. 'That's just what a girl wants to hear.'

'No. No, I didn't mean ...' He was making a complete mess of this. He had done little else for the last ten days but plan what he wanted to tell her. Now she must think him a fool.

'Why don't we start again, Alex.' She smiled, shaking her head. 'You're quite clueless, you know. It's a good job I find it sweet. Let me make this easy for you. What are you doing tomorrow night?'

Was she asking *him* out? He froze. What should he do? This was going all wrong.

'Honestly?' he said. 'I'll probably be here ordering frites and beer from you.'

'You won't be. Tomorrow's my day off,' she said. 'I've got a better idea. There's a place I know in Little Italy. Handmade pasta that's the best in Quebec, and half the price of anything here. Casa Danielle in Rue Drolet. Will you remember that? We could meet there at six.'

'Sure. I mean – great. That would be wonderful,' he said. Was this really happening? Did she mean a date? She *must* mean a date. A thought struck him. 'You know what I am?' he asked.

'You're not the only one who has been doing some surreptitious scanning.'

'And it's not a problem?'

'Let's not get ahead of ourselves. All I'm suggesting is that we try a conversation that extends to more than you ordering a beer and frites in your atrocious French.' She pulled a face. 'It was cute at first, but it's beginning to grate. How can someone called Du Bois not speak French? As to the schizo thing, you've seen how busy my life is. I struggle to find four hours in the day to devote to anyone, let alone twenty-four.'

'Great,' he said, slightly stung by the comment about his French. He thought he had been impressing her. 'I'll see you tomorrow then. Six o'clock, Rue Drolet.'

'Casa Danielle,' she repeated. 'If you get lost I'll think you've stood me up. I know you're always rushing off by nine, so if it doesn't work out at least we know it will be short.'

That reminded him. He had forgotten the time. It was 20:52.

'I've got to run,' he said. 'Literally. Sorry. See you tomorrow.'

He jumped up and over the low barrier dividing the tables from the cobblestones, sprinting down Rue Charlevoix towards their house. This was going to be a good test of Mike's fitness regime. He raced home, his mind in a spin. He barely made it through the door before dropping out, collapsed in the entrance hall with his keycard in one hand, still wearing his jacket. Kate told him off for that – but forgave him when he explained why.

•

The next two months were the happiest of Alex's life. His four hours each day were spent almost entirely in Emily's company.

She had been right. She was the one who barely had time for him, what with her studies and her job.

She was studying microbiology and hydroponics at McGill University. Alex had never thought about it before, but someone had to programme the vast underground vats that had taken the place of traditional farms. Someone had to develop and tweak the new foods that were constantly being produced to tempt jaded palettes.

One day a week she worked in the experimental hydroponics plants in the converted grain elevators between the canal and the river. On those days she came back tired, with a unique sweet smell clinging to her. Emily no longer noticed it. To Alex it was sometimes the first thing that announced her presence. The thing that made his heart race.

He wanted to pay her to give up the waitressing. He wanted her to spend that time with him, not flirting with customers and dodging the wandering hands of the café owner. But he knew she was proud. He worried that she would react angrily. She might think that he was buying her.

Their time together was snatched, but Emily said that it was no worse than workers who paired, and who then had to find time between everything else in their lives. As the relationship moved on she didn't seem fazed by the fact that he had to leave her bed, or she his, by 8:30 every evening.

She made him more confident, and he found that he could talk to her in ways that he never had talked to anyone else. Against all the odds, this might just work.

The evenings became darker and the trees along the canal turned beautiful shades of red and gold that Alex had never seen before. As they walked along the towpath one evening, hand in hand, he turned to her.

'Emily, does it ever bother you – the others, I mean?'

'I try not to think about them,' she said. 'If I did, I suppose it might. I don't want to share you.' Her grip tightened. 'If you're asking whether I ever expected to date a schizo, the answer's no. Would I take you home and introduce you to my mother? Probably not. She wouldn't understand. She never likes my boyfriends anyway. But if you're asking if this could work long term, then maybe. I don't know. We've only known each other for two months. I didn't choose you with my head.' She leaned into him. 'We shouldn't be thinking about these things yet.'

'You're right.' He turned and kissed her. 'I just don't want this to end.'

'What about you?' she said. 'Have you told the others about me?'

He hesitated. He regretted raising this now. Talking to Emily about the others felt weird. 'I've told some of them. They're all very different. They'd react differently.'

Kate had known from the start. He'd asked her for advice. She teased him about it and asked for details that were more explicit than he wanted to share. 'But it's my body too,' she would say. 'I was there.'

Later he had told Ben and Mike as well. He had to admit that it was partly because he wanted to show off. Him, Alex, with the hot girlfriend. It seemed unreal. Ben was quietly impressed, particularly when Alex shared a photo of Emily. Mike didn't seem all that interested. Alex was sure he'd had more than enough relationships of his own, so this was probably nothing special to him.

But this was different. This was Emily. Alex wanted to tell everyone.

Well, not quite everyone. Not Sierra. He knew what would happen if he did. She would pretend to be happy for him but then make some bitchy remark intended to undermine his confidence. She seemed to take pleasure in hurting people. Besides, as time passed Sierra was getting more and more grumpy about staying in Montreal. She said that she was clean and wanted to return to her old life. If she knew that Alex had a reason for staying she would become even more difficult.

'You never talk about them,' said Emily.

'It's partly to protect myself,' he said. 'To keep my own identity. We may share a body but in some ways we're further apart than anyone can be. They're the only people in the world I can never talk to directly. I guess I also worry that it'd seem weird to anyone else to talk about them. People find schizos difficult to understand.'

'OK,' she said. She snuggled into his chest, her hair tickling his nose. He breathed in her scent. The evening sunlight through the golden leaves made her face glow. 'Enough heavy talk for one night. We should just be enjoying the time we've got together.'

'It doesn't get much better than this,' said Alex. He gestured to the maple leaves lining the canal. 'I've never seen anything quite so stunning.'

'This?' Emily looked surprised. 'This is nothing. Haven't you been out of the city and seen what it's like further north? Hill after hill after hill of these colours. We Québécois tend to forget just how gorgeous it is. We see it every year.' She paused, then said excitedly, 'This is the perfect week to go. Why don't I take you? They owe me time off at the café. We could have the whole weekend.'

To Alex it sounded great. It sounded scary. And he didn't see how it could work.

She stopped walking when he didn't react, and looked up at him. He seemed so serious. 'Don't you want to?'

'I'd love to,' he said. 'I'd love to be with you. It's the others that are the problem. Travel is difficult when you're a schizo. And it's even more difficult for us, after what happened.'

'What do you mean?' she asked.

'It's a bit of a story,' he said. 'Let's sit down and I'll tell you.'

They found a patch of grass under the trees, dappled light flickering over them. Alex sat leaning against one of the maples. Emily lay on her back with her head in his lap. He toyed with her hair while he talked.

'I've never really told you how we ended up in Montreal. It wasn't out of choice. Because we share a body there are rules – protocols, they are called – that are there to protect us, to make sure that we treat the host properly. Probably half the protocols are about how and when you hand over the body after your four hours. The key thing is to keep the host safe. You can't control when you drop out but you can control where it happens. You're meant to be in a locked room, lying down, with food and water available for the next person, because it can be quite disorientating waking up. That first night when you asked me out, I broke all the rules. You remember I had to run back?'

'How could I forget?' said Emily. 'When you ask a boy out and the first thing he does is tell you he was only there for the beer, and then turns and runs away. You're lucky you got it right the next night.'

'Sorry about that. It was all new to me. It still is,' he admitted. 'Anyway, I barely made it home. Kate was pretty cross at first. She comes next in the cycle. Normally I'm careful, unlike Sierra. She just doesn't bother. I've woken in all sorts of places. The worst was a few months ago. I woke up in a pool of vomit with a seagull trying to peck out one of my eyes. It turned out Sierra had been drinking vodka with a Kazakh sea captain, and instead of getting off the ship before it sailed, she had collapsed on the deck in a drunken stupor. The crew thought she'd left, so by the time I woke they were under way to Montreal. Without that I wouldn't have met you, so I suppose I should be grateful. But we were all pretty pissed off at the time. We made it a rule that we don't go anywhere without a majority vote. Any breach of that and it's an automatic fine of a full week's time.'

'What does that mean?' asked Emily.

'Anyone who breaches it loses all their hours for a whole week, and they're shared amongst the rest of us. One week is pretty severe. Time is important to schizos since we have so little of it each day. Very occasionally we trade it amongst ourselves, if one of us needs more time for something. But fines are rare. Normally a fine won't be more than half an hour, or maybe an hour. A week is exceptional. But we were all pretty steamed up about that.'

'Getting away for the weekend might be too much trouble then,' said Emily. She reached up and held the hand that had been stroking her hair. 'That's a shame. It would have been fun.'

'No,' said Alex. 'It would be brilliant if we could do it. Let me see what I can do with the others. I might be able to persuade them. I'll let you know.'

●

Kate, I need your help. Emily wants to go up north for the weekend, into the woods. That means taking you lot with me. I don't want to have to tell Sierra about Emily, but can't really avoid it. What do you think? Alex x.

A. You have to. We could all outvote her, but then she will just cause trouble when we get there. Your choice. Keep it from S or have your dirty weekend. You can't do both. K. x

---

All. I've got a favour to ask. For the last few weeks I've been seeing someone here. Her name's Emily. She and I want to go away for the weekend – up north – but I'll need your agreement. It's a place called Mont Tremblant, up in the woods. There is loads of space to run and walk. You should have fun. I will pay. Please let me know by end of cycle. Thanks, Alex.

Hey, nice one Alex. Fine by me. Kate.

Me too. I've found a ten-mile loop round a lake. M.

Alex doesn't want to be running round a lake, Mike. He has other 'exercises' planned with Emily. It gets my vote. Ben.

Is this why we've been hanging around in Dullsville for so long? I'm bored here. Send me a photo of her Alex and I'll consider it. But only if I like her, and can we agree that after Alex has had his weekend we get out of here for good and go home? Lesnichy has sent me details of two ships leaving in the next month. At least one of them has promised to take us for free. I'm not staying here just so Alex can get his rocks off. S.

Sierra, we are going anyway. Everyone has agreed. But I'd like you to agree as well. Here's a photo of Emily. Please just say yes and be nice about this for once. Alex.

Woah! Does no one else think it's weird that Alex is screwing Kate? Remember Kate at seventeen!? Same hair, same eyes, same body. I'm not sure if this counts as incest but it's weird. I'm only saying what we're all thinking. S.

Shut it, Sierra. We both have dark hair and blue eyes, and that's about it. Stop trying to stir things up. Don't make this bad for Alex. We've had a vote and you're coming. For once in your life try to do something for someone else. I'm in no rush to leave Quebec. If you want to leave get the others to vote for it. Otherwise shut up. Kate.

•

Mont Tremblant was all that Emily had promised, and more. Alex had booked her a suite looking out over the lake, complete with a deck down to the waterfront. They sat watching the sun setting over the rolling hills, as the leaves turned from orange to gold to red. As the first stars began to appear and the temperature dropped, Emily snuggled into him.

'This is stunning,' Alex said. 'So are you. You know I . . .' He hesitated. He'd never told her he loved her. Should he? What if she didn't say it back to him? He waited too long and bottled it. 'You know I think you're amazing.'

She smiled. 'Your chat-up lines may be clumsy, but at least I know you mean them.' She sighed contentedly. 'It's even better from the top of the mountain. It's a shame you can't see it, but the cable-car stops at four.'

'Is that what you did this morning?' he asked.

'Yes. Got the cable-car up and walked back down. It's so peaceful.'

'Did you see any of the others?' Alex had booked himself a rather less-spectacular room on the other side of the hotel. He'd explained to Emily that they needed their own room for when he was not there. He was conscious of the fact that this was the first time that they were all in close proximity, and that she might see 'him' when in fact it was one of the others.

'I saw you – no, I saw Mike, I guess, from a distance on one of the trails. It looked like he had run up and down the mountain. I ducked into the trees until he was gone.'

Alex had known that already.

Almost bumped into your girl this morning, Al. You've done well there. She's hot! And don't worry what Sierra says – she isn't Kate. M.

'Are you all right with that?' Alex asked. 'This is the first time we've had whole days together, and I can't be with you.'

'I think so.' She shrugged. 'I don't know. This is better than I could ever have imagined, but then suddenly you're gone. In Montreal it doesn't matter. I have college, I have my job, and I have my four-hour boyfriend, so I can devote myself completely to each. Does that sound cold? Four-hour boyfriend?'

'Not to me. That's the most I can ever be. Talking of which, your four-hour boyfriend has less than two hours left. There are other things we could be devoting our time to . . .'

She smiled. 'Let's make the most of it then.' She let him take her hand and lead her inside.

Later, as he was getting dressed, she stirred and reached for him.

'Do you have to go already?'

'Yes. I need to be back in my room in ten minutes.' He was loving this, but having to leave her was killing him. 'Don't wake. I'll see you tomorrow.'

She yawned. 'It's such a shame. This place is so beautiful and I don't get to see it all with you.'

He didn't react. He didn't want her to know, but he felt a stab of panic. Emily hadn't said it yet, but was this the regret that was going to come between them? Were all schizo relationships doomed because of this?

He kissed her, resisted her efforts to draw him back in – with difficulty – and left quietly.

He had five minutes to go. On the way to his room he quickly checked his messages.

Cool place, Alex. Love it. You can pay for our next holiday. K x.

_____

The outdoors looks great, but what's with all the bugs? I'll be staying in the hotel, A. Hope you and the girlfriend (!) are having fun. Ben.

_____

So you've managed to find us somewhere duller than Dullsville. Well done, Alex. I've seen a tree. Oh, look, another one. God, this is so boring. They don't even know how to make a decent cocktail. And they seem to think it's odd to be drinking on your own at two in the afternoon. Where are all the people? I haven't even seen Kate's twin – have you told her to hide from me? Please can we just get out of here. S.

_____

S, since you are so bored here I'll do you a trade. Give me your time tomorrow and I'll give you one of mine in Montreal – no, wait, I'll make it two. That's two evenings you can have in the nightlife of the city, instead of sitting here all afternoon drinking bad cocktails. Deal? A.

Emily curled up in a swing seat on her deck looking out over the lake. It was a crisp fall day, but the early-morning mist had burned off the lake. All was quiet except for the rustling and chirping of chipmunks in the woods near the waterfront.

Emily hadn't been this happy in years. Yet there was a troubling feeling she couldn't quite shake. Alex confused her. This was, by some margin, the best relationship she had ever had, but it was also the most difficult. Despite what she had said, could this ever be enough for her? Was this just a summer that she would remember fondly for the rest of her life?

Alex was so sweet. Perfect apart from the schizo thing. What made a person want to live their life like that? Last night she'd thought he was about to tell her he loved her. Did he? Did she love him? And if she did, was that enough? What about the others? They were part of the package.

Something crashed through the woods nearby, and the chipmunks went quiet. She sat up. Maybe it was a deer, or worse, a bear. A dark figure emerged through the trees, pulling leaves from his hair.

She jumped up. 'Alex?' It couldn't be, not yet.

'It's me, don't panic. It's Alex,' he said.

'How?' she asked. 'It's only just gone one.'

'Sorry to surprise you,' he said. 'You weren't answering your door so I came round this way. Sierra is bored out of her mind here, so we've traded time. It does mean you're going to lose me for two nights in Montreal, but it seemed worth it to have a whole afternoon together here. Sorry I couldn't tell you, but

I didn't know that Sierra had agreed until I woke four hours early.' He laughed. 'I hope I haven't ruined your plans.'

'Not at all.' She smiled. 'You just gave me a shock. My plan was to sit here moping until you turned up. But now we can go and do something.' An idea struck her. 'How about the mountain? This is your one chance to see it properly.'

'The mountain?' he asked.

'Yes. You remember I said how stunning it is up there. We can do it while the cable-car is still going.'

'Of course,' he said. 'That would be great. But how long will that take?' He looked her up and down. 'I do have other plans for the afternoon as well.' He grinned and reached for her.

She laughed and stepped back, batting away his hand. 'A couple of hours at most. We've got plenty of time. Let me go and change.'

She went inside, confused and excited. This wouldn't ever happen with a normal boyfriend. Things kept changing with Alex. She dressed quickly. High-cut white shorts that emphasised her legs, and a deliberately tight T-shirt.

When she stepped back out he was standing with his back to her, looking out over the lake. 'Let's go,' she called.

He turned, and stared at her for a moment as though seeing her for the first time. That was what she liked about new love. 'Wow.' There was a sparkle in his eyes. 'You look stunning.'

She knew that look. If they didn't leave now they wouldn't be going at all. 'Come on,' she said. 'Let's go. For once we've got plenty of time.'

He took her hand.

The cable-car was crowded and they were squeezed together

in one corner, Emily pressed into his hard chest. He pulled her tighter, leaning down to kiss her.

'Not here, Alex,' she said softly, but secretly smiling. He was getting bolder. A month ago he wouldn't have done that in front of so many people.

At the top most of the passengers didn't go any further than the viewing platform next to the cable-car. 'Come with me,' said Emily, grabbing his hand. 'They don't know what they're missing.'

They took a trail between silver tree trunks, the sun flickering through a golden-red canopy, their shoes kicking up leaves as they went. The trail began to climb, and after ten minutes they emerged in a clearing at the top of a ridge, with a log cabin in the centre.

'What's this?'

'It's a park ranger's cabin. You can hire them in the summer, but at this time of year they're empty. You won't believe the views from up there.' She pointed to a balcony jutting out from the first floor.

'Can we get in?' he asked.

'Of course. They're left open in case people get lost in the woods and need somewhere overnight. Which does happen. You don't want to be out in the woods in the dark when the bears are foraging. Normally they'll hide from humans, but at night they get much more aggressive.'

She pushed the door open. The ground floor was one large room, sparsely furnished with only a rough wooden table and benches, a log burner, and cords of wood stacked neatly against one wall. There were fire warnings in French pinned to a noticeboard. Steps led to the first floor. He followed her up. Here they were in the eaves of the sloping roof. There was just enough height for him to stand in the middle. Against one wall were a couple of thin mattresses on low bed frames. Opposite them a window gave glimpses of golden leaves and the blue of Lac Tremblant, and next to it a door led to the balcony. Emily pushed hard and it opened with a squeal.

The view had been worth the climb. A sea of endless red and gold dropped away below them, framing the blue of the lake half a kilometre below, continuing up the other side and into the distance. They could have believed that there was no one else on earth.

Emily lent on the wooden rail and took in the view. If things did not work out, and this was all that she was left with from her time with Alex, it would have been worth it. She could hear his soft breath behind her. He pulled her to him and she could sense his heartbeat through her back. His hands ran lightly over her thin shirt. She shuddered, and pushed back.

'Maybe it's time to head down,' she said.

'Why?' he asked. 'Why not here?'

'Here?' she turned, shocked. 'Anyone could come along.' But she was beginning to like this side to Alex. Unexpected, but exciting.

He smiled. 'I don't hear anyone. And you said this place is deserted. No one else even came this way.'

She bit her lip, and hesitated.

Then she took his hand and led him back to the bedroom.

•

Alex woke entangled with a naked Emily. For a moment it felt good, and he pulled her closer.

Then he sat up sharply, cracking his head on the low roof.

'What?' he said, as he blinked in pain. 'What time is it?'

Emily rolled over towards him. 'That was amazing,' she said. 'The best ever.' Then she saw his puzzled expression. 'What is it?' She checked the time. 'It's just gone five. We must have fallen asleep. We're going to have to walk down, but it was worth it. It'll be light enough for another hour. We'll be fine.'

'What . . . what are we doing? Where are we?' asked Alex.

'On the mountain. In the cabin. What is it, Alex? Are you OK?' She sat up. 'You're scaring me.'

Alex looked around. They seemed to be in the attic of a log cabin, with a low sloping roof. Through the only window he could see the lake far below. 'When did we get here? *How* did we get here?'

'On the cable-car, of course. But it'll be shut by now. So we'll have to walk. Don't worry. The bears won't be out yet.' Emily reached over and touched him on the arm. 'Are you all right?'

He shied away from her. He didn't remember any of this. What was happening to him?

Then it clicked. He looked at her through wide eyes. His heart sank. What had *she* done? A burst of anger ran through him.

'What . . . what were you doing here with Sierra?' he asked. His voice was high, accusatory.

She stared at him. 'What on earth do you mean? Are you still asleep? Don't you remember? We came up here together. You traded time with Sierra so we could have the afternoon together. You told me . . .' Her voice trailed off. 'You told me . . .'

She froze, staring at him with her mouth half open.

'*Oh my God*,' said Alex. He slumped backwards on the bed, feeling as though all of his muscles had suddenly collapsed. He was breathing hard. '*Sierra*. Why?'

Emily stared at him, unmoving. 'Alex . . . Alex. It was you. Wasn't it?'

He met her gaze. Then his eyes unconsciously flicked down, brushing over her naked body. She caught his look, and scrabbled at the thin sheet, pulling it up to cover herself. She swallowed hard. For a moment she looked like she was going to throw up.

'Who are you? Don't look at me,' she said, turning away from him.

'It was Sierra,' Alex said. 'Sierra. She lies. It's what Sierra does. She lies about everything. Why did she do this to me?'

'To *you*? It was me she did this to. She . . . she . . .' Emily paused, shaking her head, as if the words wouldn't come out. 'I should have known it wasn't you in the cable-car and . . . out there. I thought you'd changed. That I'd changed you.'

She stared down at the sheet, twisting it hard in her hands. Her fingers were white.

'Why couldn't you tell it wasn't me?' he asked. 'You only had to scan me to know.'

She looked up angrily. 'Who the fuck scans their boyfriend? I trusted you.'

'You trusted Sierra. Big mistake.'

They sat in silence for a moment.

Then Alex said, 'Did you . . .?'

She looked at him. Then laughed bitterly. 'No, Alex, we came here and played fucking tiddlywinks for an hour! What do you think we did? I thought it was you.'

How could Emily have been so naïve? How did she fall for this? It was her fault.

No. It was Sierra's fault. Why had she done this to them?

'Wasn't it . . . different? Couldn't you tell?' he asked.

'Seriously? This isn't about whether you or Sierra is better in bed.'

'But you said it was amazing. The best ever. You must have known it was different.'

'Jesus Christ, Alex. Don't blame me for not realising that you schizo freaks indulge in these sort of games. I don't care if it's you or Sierra who did this.'

'But it was the same body you slept with yesterday,' Alex said. 'I know it was Sierra, and I know it was wrong. But it was still my body.'

'That doesn't make it right. That doesn't make it OK.' Emily's voice dropped to a whisper. She looked down at the sheets.. At her clenched knuckles. 'I didn't agree to this. This . . .' She paused, gulping hard. 'This feels . . .' She coughed harshly, forcing each word out. 'This feels like rape. . . . Why didn't you stop her, Alex? You were meant to protect me.'

Alex didn't know what to say. She was right. He sat uncertain on the edge of the bed. Helpless. The old Alex was back. It wasn't Emily's fault, it was Sierra's. She was the one who had violated Emily. Violated him.

He reached towards Emily, touching her gently on the shoulder.

She jerked round, anger showing through tears.

'Get away!' she screamed at him. 'Don't touch me. Don't ever touch me again.'

'I'm sorry. So sorry. I want to help.' He was starting to cry too. He felt numb. 'I love you, Emily. I'd never hurt you. What can I do? How do we solve this?'

'Stop looking at me. *We* don't solve this. Get out of here. Now.'

'But I want to help. We can find a way.'

'No we can't,' she said angrily. 'I don't know who you are.'

He realised then that it was over. Of course it was. Her shoulders shook and she made no attempt to wipe the tears from her cheeks. He understood – or thought he did. Grief and anger flooded through him.

He slid off the bed, grabbing his scattered clothes. At the top of the steps he turned back. He saw Emily, *his* Emily, beautiful in the setting sun. He wanted to hold her. To make it all better.

'How will you get down?' he asked. Maybe if he'd told her he loved her earlier. Maybe then things would be different. 'I don't want to leave us like this,' he pleaded.

'There is no *us*, Alex.' She spat out the words. 'Get out, now. I don't want to see you again. Ever. You or your freakish friends.'

•

Sierra, you unspeakable bitch!! How could you do this? We can't carry on like this. Drugs I can forgive, but this was just spiteful. Emily accused me of raping her. She thinks this is some sick game we schizos play. She never wants to speak to me again. You narcissistic psychopath. WTF!!!

Mike/Ben, this is just for you. You'll have seen Alex's message to Sierra. He also left me a voice message. It was hard to follow much, between the tears and the shouting. From what I can work out Sierra slept with Emily, pretending to be Alex. It's unbelievable, even by her standards. This is a nightmare. Poor Alex. And poor Emily. No one deserves that.

I've had a quick look, and as far as I can tell it's not a criminal offence under Quebec law, even if it ought to be. That doesn't make it any better, but it does mean we won't get chucked in jail while they work out what to do with Sierra.

We need to get out of here, though. I've arranged transport back to Montreal first thing in the morning – Mike, you're going to need to deal with that. Let's get out of Quebec asap. We can't afford to fly, but let's get somewhere overland if we can. Then we can get a boat. I've messaged Les to see if he can help.

We're going to need to deal with Sierra ourselves. Alex is in no state to talk about it, so let's decide between the three of us first.

God, what a mess!! And let's not forget, Alex needs us.

Kate.

_____

Alex, this is awful. For you and Emily. This is low even for Sierra. I don't understand why she would do it. Doesn't she realise it was wrong? What a bitch. I wish I could give you a hug. You need to talk to someone about this. I know you're focused on Emily, but she isn't the only victim here. Sierra has used you as well. Don't bottle this up. I'm sending you a voice message. This is too much to deal with in writing. Please talk to me. Katie. xxxxx

Kate/Ben, I'm on my way back. We should be in Montreal by 8:00. I don't know if Alex will want to leave, but I agree that we need to.

I've just spoken to a lawyer in Montreal, on a no-names basis. He was pretty cagey, but he said this didn't sound like a crime to him. He said the statute requires force, and trickery isn't the same. He mentioned a case a while ago about someone who fooled women into sleeping with him by pretending to be a famous film star, and he was acquitted. He said it would be all the more difficult to get a conviction where it is different minds in the same body.

It doesn't make it any better. I'm going to propose a vote on putting Sierra into stasis for rehab when we get home. This isn't normal behaviour. She needs treatment. We can force her into rehab for up to three months without needing to involve CGov. Agreed?

It's going to take a while to calm Alex down. There may not have been any long-term potential in this relationship – there never is for us schizos – but that's not how he's going to see it now. Mike.

Alex, so sorry, mate, don't know what to say. I know it's unforgiveable. I don't know where we go from here. I'm going to suggest we put Sierra in stasis for three months. She's ill. We need to get her some treatment. Whether she agrees to it or not. Whatever happens, we've still got to live with her. It's not what you want to hear now, but you are going to have a find a way to forgive her and move on. Sorry. Mike.

Chill, Alex. It's not as though you were going to marry her. She was the one bit of fun I've had since coming to this godforsaken country. I can see why you liked Emily – underneath that prim exterior she was pretty wild. Can we all agree to go home now? S. xxx

KATE

It felt as though someone was sawing off my leg.

I tried to sit up, screaming for them not to touch me, but I couldn't move. I was lying on a cold hard surface, my wrists and ankles tied down. I opened my eyes but there was only darkness. Something was covering my face.

'Help!' I screamed, pulling frantically at my bindings.

Pain coursed through my body again. My back arched and slammed down on to the hard metal.

'Kate, stay where you are. Don't move,' said a voice. 'It's me, Alex.'

To my confused brain that did not immediately seem odd. I had thought the game was over, but maybe it wasn't.

'What? Where am I? What's going on?'

'You're in the medical centre. You got hurt.' He paused. 'And there are other . . . complications.'

'Hold still, please,' said another voice. 'I'm your medical officer. I'm sorry about the pain but I needed to stop the bleeding quickly. In a moment the meds will kick in and you won't feel anything. You need to lie really still and try not to panic. I need to seal the wound. It won't take long.'

My fingernails dug into the palms of my hands. All my muscles were taut. I tried to make myself relax. How had I got hurt? The last thing I remembered was being in the game, pressing the button. Killing Ben.

Was that not the end of the game? Might that mean Ben *wasn't* dead?

'Why can't I see anything?' I asked, trying not to panic.

'You were unconscious,' said the medic. 'We needed to scan your brain for any injuries. The light would blind you, so I put an eye mask on. Try to relax.'

The pain was receding. I was drifting. Was I back in space? Or were the meds just kicking in?

I was losing track of time. For a while I could distantly feel someone poking at my leg. There was the occasional beep or hiss of air, and lights flickering around the edge of my vision.

Then everything went quiet.

'I'm done,' said the medic. 'This all looks fine. There shouldn't even be a scar. She's lost a lot of blood, though. There's a limit to what we can replace, even in an andi. For once it's important that she actually drinks, and gets her fluid levels back up. Make sure she does.'

'OK,' said Alex. 'Could we have a moment alone please? It was a pretty traumatic game, and she almost died.'

So does Alex think the game is over? How can that be? And why are they talking about andis?

'I don't understand why you people play these games,' said the medic. 'Take as long as you need, give her time to come back slowly. She'll be dozy. It's a body, not a machine. I'll be outside.'

'Thanks,' said Alex.

Footsteps came towards me. The bindings on my hands and feet withdrew. Then the footsteps receded, and I heard a door open and close.

I lay still for a moment, then reached up to remove the mask covering my eyes. A hand gripped mine, stopping me gently but firmly.

'Wait, Kate,' Alex said. 'We need to talk first.'

'What? What has happened?' I asked. 'I thought the game had ended.'

'You were hurt. You were unconscious when I found you. You may not be processing this at the moment. But what's happened isn't possible. I don't know what Sierra's done, or how. But I'm here, in our body – Mike's body.' He hesitated. 'And you're here . . . in Amy Bird's body.'

'*What?* Don't be stupid, Alex. That's impossible.'

I sat up, pain stabbing through my head. An arm came round my shoulders, steadying me.

'Take it slowly, Kate. I know this isn't easy, but it's happened. It doesn't make any more sense to me than it does to you. Sierra's done this somehow.'

I reached up and tore off the mask covering my eyes. This time Alex didn't try to stop me.

The first thing I saw was a hand resting on my shoulder. Just above my left breast.

My left breast?

I looked down. I was sitting on the edge of a shiny metal treatment table, in a body that wasn't mine. I was female, small . . .

everything was wrong. My left trouser leg had been cut away, and through it I could see pale white skin. Not my skin. My hands were small, delicate, white.

I reached up to touch the hand on my shoulder. I knew that hand. It was mine.

I flung it off me and jumped down from the table, wobbling as I landed. I turned around. There I was, standing in front of me, staring back at me, a shocked expression on my face. Which was nonsense.

At first my brain couldn't deal with it. Then I laughed.

'This isn't real, Alex,' I said. 'Bird is playing tricks on us again. We're still in the game.' I looked down at my hands. 'It's nicely done. Do I really look like I'm in her body? What's Sierra playing at this time? What do we have to do to end the game?'

Alex hesitated. 'It's real, Kate. The games don't work like this. We know what the goal was – stop the spaceship, and we did that. The game is over. I woke up in an arena, in the usual way. I went to check the other rooms, and found you badly injured. So I brought you here. It shouldn't have been me waking up, though. Ben and Sierra come first in the cycle. So it must mean that Ben is dead, and Sierra is gone.'

Ben dead. I remembered that. Killed by me because Alex wouldn't.

'How can Sierra have gone?' I asked. 'Where? This can't be real, Alex. We're still in a game. If not the spaceship game, then something else.'

'I'm sure it's real, Kate. It all fits. We know Ben shot Bird. She was hurt when we saw her, and her wounds match yours. I carried you here, through the park. No one could have written a game of this complexity in advance, containing the whole park, Bird getting injured, you having the same wounds. And why? If Sierra wants to kill us all she could have done it in the game as it was. It doesn't make any sense for her to put you in her body in the game, and then have me save your life by bringing you here.'

He paused, and took a step towards me, reaching for my hands. I let him take them in his – in mine. Our gentle green eyes looked into mine. 'Kate, you've got to face it. This is real.'

I slumped back against the examination table. Could he be right? I could feel the panic starting to rise again, and my heart was beginning to race.

'But what about Sierra?' I asked desperately. 'Where could she have gone if I've got Amy?'

'I don't know,' said Alex. 'Maybe she's still in here with me and the cycle has somehow got screwed up. If it's the same as happened with Mike then we won't know until the cycle resets tonight.'

'No,' I said. 'This can't be right. What has Sierra done to us? This isn't me.' I pulled away from him and put my head in my hands, to try to shut it all out. But then I hated the touch of the alien white skin on my face. I snatched my hands away.

I hurled myself at him – at me – beating at our chest with my fists. They felt weak, and small. 'Give me my body back!' I screamed. 'Give it back!'

He wrapped his arms around me and pulled me into him. I pushed back but he was too strong. This stupid andi body too weak to escape from him. What was the point of surrendering your humanity for a fake body that was deliberately designed to have no strength at all? I gave up fighting, slumped in his arms.

'Stop it, Kate,' he said firmly. 'I don't understand this either, and I know it's awful. But it's no easier for me. We've got to get out of here and work out what Sierra's done. Together we can solve this.'

I barely heard his words but burst into uncontrollable sobbing. It was overwhelming. His grip relaxed and I felt a hand softly stroking my hair. 'Come on, Kate,' he said softly. 'We'll deal with this afterwards, but let's get out before the medic gets suspicious and decides to report this to someone.'

I couldn't stop shaking, and he continued to hold me, more loosely now.

'Why's Sierra doing this?' I asked weakly. 'This is worse than anything she's done. Worse even than what she did to Emily. She's torn me out of my body and put me in ... in this *thing*. She knows what I think of andis. What any normal person thinks of them. Why's she doing this to me?' I felt numb.

Alex released me. 'Let's discuss it somewhere else. Can you keep it together for that long?'

I nodded and took a deep breath. I blotted my eyes with the cuff of my shirt, trying to find a bit that wasn't splattered with blood. Amy's blood. My blood.

Alex smiled uncertainly at me. 'Come on, let's go.' He put an arm around me and led me out of the treatment room.

The medic was waiting for us. He looked at me closely. 'Is she all right now?'

'She's good,' said Alex. 'Just a bit shocked. It was a rough game. She wants to leave.'

'Physically, she's fit to go,' said the medic. 'I checked the brain scans and it all looks clear. The game booths are a bit too good at simulating wounds, but it all seemed more nasty than it was. Keep an eye on her, though. The main issue is the blood loss. Remember, plenty of fluids. If you have any concerns, bring her straight back.'

'I will,' Alex said. 'Thanks.'

The medic looked at me. 'I do need your sign off,' he said, and handed over a small screen. The text looked blurry to me through my tears, but I could just about make out 'Amy Bird, treatment cost – one month'. So was this to be my new life? Stuck in a stupid andi's body? Living as Amy Bird, not Kate Weston? I sniffed and put my finger on the screen.

'Thanks,' said the medic. 'Good luck.'

I stumbled out of the door, holding on to Alex, holding on to what had been my body for the last twenty-five years.

•

Alex took me to the nearest bar, which made sense. I needed to get some alcohol inside me to dull the shock. Andis don't normally *need* to eat or drink, but they can, and alcohol has the same effect on them as on us.

I didn't bother to look at what Alex had ordered. I downed the first two shots without thinking, as we sat in silence. Alex toyed with his drink.

He poured me a third glass, and eventually spoke. 'How's your leg feeling?'

'It's not my leg,' I said bitterly. '*You* have my leg, Alex, along with the rest of me. Amy's leg is fine.' I glared at him.

He sighed. 'I know this isn't easy, but we need to work out

what's happened and how to fix it. Getting cross with me won't help.'

I bristled. 'I wasn't, but I'm starting to. It's Sierra I'm furious with. It's Montreal all over again.'

Alex sat back and raised his hands. 'Sorry, Kate. Look, I'm not trying to defend Sierra. You know what I think of her. But it's not as bad as that.'

I leaned across the table, banging my glass down. 'Don't you get it? She's ripped me out of my body! I don't see how it could be worse.'

'I'm not trying to diminish what Sierra has done to you. But you were moving to a new body in ten days' time anyway.'

'Not like this! I would have been moving to a body that we had all chosen, with the rest of you. If I'd wanted to be an andi I would have chosen that at seventeen. I didn't. I *like* being a schizo. Sierra doesn't get to turn me into an andi, and then you defend her by pretending it's no different.'

'Sorry,' said Alex. 'All I'm saying is that what she did in Montreal was completely different. Worse.' He took a drink. 'Look, I'm not the one sitting there in Bird's body. I can see you're upset, I would be too. But it's not going to help if we fall out.'

I took a deep breath. I didn't understand why he was defending Sierra. But the alcohol was starting to take the edge off.

'I'm more than upset, Alex. But I agree that we need to work out what's happened so we can reverse it. We don't even know how she's done it. None of this is meant to be possible.'

'Let's take it in stages,' says Alex. 'Somehow she's found a way to subvert the games. She almost certainly killed Mike, but we didn't die. Presumably because she would have died herself. That broke the rules. Then she found a way to get Ben, you and me into the same game, to access three schizo minds from one body at the same time. That broke the rules. And now she has found a way, when the game ends, to dump one of those minds into a different body. Again, that broke the rules. But it seems she can only do all this during the games. That's when our minds have been loosened from the body.' He paused.

'She must have been planning this for some time,' he said. 'Remember, she and Mike were desperate to come to the death park. I said it was a stupid idea, but Sierra persuaded Ben and you to vote yes.'

That was true. I'd been unsure about it, as had Ben. Mike had been confident that no one could beat him, and Sierra and he had pushed us to vote yes. I'd thought at the time that it was just Sierra looking for excitement. Now I realised that there was much more to it than that. I should have trusted Alex's instincts and said no. Then none of this would have happened.

'All right, maybe she has somehow found a way to do all that,' I said. 'When Mike first went missing you suggested he might be Bird. It sounded crazy, but I did a bit of digging and discovered an old government research paper saying that they had experimented with unwinding schizos. It sounds as though it was a disaster. Half the people went mad, and some died. But it said that they were more successful transferring minds back to andis than to humans. They stopped doing it because it was too risky, but maybe not everyone stopped. I'll dig the paper out again and send it to you.' I paused. 'Let's suppose that it's somehow possible. I still don't understand how Sierra would have done this – she doesn't have the skills. Or why. And where she's gone? If she was still with you then it would have been her turn in the cycle, not yours.'

'I'm not certain what happened,' Alex said. 'We don't know if you downloading to Bird was Sierra's plan all along, or if something went wrong. Maybe she didn't intend this. Bird was injured at the end of the game, and left in a hurry. Maybe Sierra was in Bird's body, and needed to get out before she became unconscious. But then where did she end up?'

I thought back. 'I don't see how Sierra could be Bird. They were together in the clip you sent to me of the bar. But when Bird first contacted me she said she had another andi body to take her mind. Most lies contain some truth. Maybe that bit was true, and Sierra always had another body hidden away somewhere. She might have jumped into that body. Did you see anyone else leaving the arena?'

'No, but it took me a few minutes before I came looking for you. Did you see anyone? Do you remember waking in the game booth?'

'No,' I said. 'I remember the game, and pushing the button. Everything after that is a blank until I woke up in the medical centre.'

A waiter dropped some food on our table. I didn't remember ordering. Alex must have done so. There probably wasn't any point in me eating, but it still felt good. Comforting. Some slight link to my humanity. Because whatever they tell you when you're seventeen, no one really believes that andis are human. Everyone knows that they are just a shell to house those who have decided to depart the human race. And now I was one of them.

We ate in silence. It wasn't easy for me as my mind and my muscles didn't seem to understand one another. My balance was off. I lacked the fine motor skills to move food from my plate to my mouth.

Everything about this body was wrong. Colours were different. Sharper. The smell of the food was wrong. If I wanted to lift something I had to tell myself to exert more force than I was used to. Amy's muscles were half the size of Mike's. I hadn't noticed when downing the first few shots, I had been so angry then. But the more time I spent in this body the more I noticed the disconnect between it and my brain.

I realised that that was what meant that Alex was right. That this wasn't a game. I'd played plenty of games where I'd manifested as someone else, as female, as young. They'd always felt perfectly normal. The game mechanics had adjusted to my new body without me needing to. This was different. This was reality. Where the only thing out of place was me.

I pushed these thoughts away. I wasn't ready to face them head on. Not yet.

Having finished his meal, Alex took pity on me, and fed me the last few mouthfuls of my food. It felt strangely intimate. There was concern in his eyes.

I cleared up the mess that I had left on the table and sat back.

'Let's set all this aside for the moment,' I said. 'We need to focus on what we can do about it. I can't stay like this. Apart from anything else, I'll never be able to leave the park as long as I'm Amy Bird. She was purchased here illegally. I need to get back in with you. Back where I belong. If I can't then I'm going to end up stuck here for ever.'

'To do that we need to find Sierra,' said Alex. 'We need to know how she has done this and how to reverse it.'

'I don't understand what she's doing,' I said. 'If she wanted to offload herself into an andi, why not just do it and be gone? Why didn't she just take this body once she had it? None of us would have really cared if she had wanted to spend the rest of her life in a death park. I know you would have been glad to see the back of her. Instead she's probably killed two of us, as well as the dealer, Karl, the other night. And she's presumably stuck somewhere in the park in another andi body.'

'Unless she's found a way of getting out of the park,' suggested Alex. 'Maybe there are ways.'

'Then why not do it with Bird several days ago? These bodies can't be cheap. All she's done is wasted credit on an extra body and made it much more likely you or I might come after her. Or at least report her. What about that?' I said. '*Should* we be reporting her?'

Alex thought. 'I don't like that idea at all. How can we ever prove that Sierra was the one who did all this? We're likely to get chucked in a cell, or stasis, while they try to work it out. When we tell them that Sierra is to blame but that she has somehow managed to run away they'll be all the more suspicious of us. To them, that just isn't possible.'

'So how do we find Sierra? We don't even know what she looks like or what she's called now.'

'No, but we know someone who does,' said Alex. 'If Sierra

had another body stashed away somewhere, odds are that she bought it from Guskov.'

'He's not going to tell us,' I said.

'He's greedy,' said Alex. 'We know that from the fact that he didn't kill Ben. We offer him time for information. He was willing to overlook a murder in return for ten years. Telling us the name of Sierra's new andi is a lot less risky.'

'OK. Maybe,' I said, unconvinced. But I didn't have a better plan. 'How do we do this?'

'We know where Guskov is,' said Alex. 'So why don't we just go and ask him?'

Which was what we did.

ALEX

It was starting to get dark as we walked down the rubble-strewn alley that led to the Death's Head. A drone followed us, no doubt beaming images back to Guskov.

I glanced across at Kate. She had been silent for most the walk. She was still wobbly, and I didn't know if that was from the medication she had been given, the alcohol, or the trouble she was having controlling Amy Bird's body. When the medic had told me to get fluids inside her he probably hadn't meant four shots of single malt.

I was worried about her. She had reacted far more violently to the body transfer than I would have expected.

The Death's Head was busy. We threaded our way through the crowd to get to the bar.

'What can I get you two?' asked the barman.

'Mr Guskov,' I said. 'We need to speak to him.'

The barman paused for a moment, no doubt communicating with someone. Then he nodded to his left. 'Go over there. The door marked PRIVATE.'

As we approached it opened. The doorway was entirely filled by a large figure. Vincent. Or Stas. I couldn't tell the difference.

'I know you two,' he said. 'What do you want?'

'We need to speak to your boss,' I said. 'There's time in it for him.'

'Follow me.' He led us down a long corridor and up some steps to the room where Sierra, and later Ben, had been before us.

Guskov was sitting behind a large desk, and gestured for us to take the two remaining seats.

'Ms Bird,' he said, nodding to Kate. 'My merchandise doesn't usually come back to see me. I wonder who you are now?' He studied her. 'As you'll have realised, scanning doesn't work in here. Perhaps it's better that I don't know who you are.' He looked down at her bloodstained clothes. 'You look as though you have had an . . . interesting day.'

He turned to me. 'Which of you do I have the pleasure of meeting this time? I advised Mr White not to come back. Ms Summers?'

'Alex Du Bois. We haven't met.'

'Delighted,' said Guskov. 'You lot are becoming quite the regular customers. It's the nature of my work that I don't usually get repeat business. Are you back for another body?'

I sat forward. 'We're after information. We're prepared to pay for it. We know that Sierra – Ms Summers – bought the original andi, Ms Bird,' I nodded towards Kate. 'We think that she bought a second one as well. We want to know what it looks like. We're willing to pay you well, five years, if you can tell us.'

Guskov sat back and sucked his lips. 'An interesting proposal,' he said, 'with a certain dilemma for me. As I told your Mr White, I have a reputation to maintain. Part of my reputation is for preserving my clients' confidences. If I lose that reputation I lose business worth much more than five years. On the other hand you, Mr Du Bois, at least in one of your many manifestations, already know the answer to your question. In truth I don't know whether I am talking to Mr Du Bois, Mr White or Ms Summers. Or someone else. I am simply taking your word for it. So I could just be reminding you of what you already know, and getting paid for it.' He tapped his fingers on his desk, the sound echoing round the silent room. Then he looked from Kate to me.

'I'll tell you what,' he said. 'Make it ten years and I will give you what you need to know.' He corrected himself. 'What you know already.'

I glanced at Kate. She nodded. It was a high price but we had already agreed that we would pay whatever it took. 'All right,' I said.

He nodded. 'Vincent,' he said. The andi walked over to me and held out his hand. 'Give him the time and I'll give you the identity in return.'

We lightly touched our fingers.

'Ms Summers told me she needed another andi,' said Guskov. 'Again, she was quite particular about what she wanted. As you can see, young, female, blonde.' It was confirmed by the data that he sent across. The andi looked rather like Sierra when we had first met her.

'Did she say why she wanted it?' Kate asked.

'Don't push your luck, Ms Bird,' said the dealer. 'That wasn't part of the deal. In any event, I never ask my customers what they intend to do with their purchases. I am a sensitive man. I would probably be quite shocked if I knew.

'So, Ms Bird, Mr Du Bois, I think that concludes our discussion. Vincent will escort you out. As ever, it was a pleasure doing business with you. If this leads to trouble it would be best for all of us if you don't mention my name. Wherever you end up. I do have a long reach.

'If, on the other hand, you ever feel the need for another andi, you know where to come.' He chuckled to himself. 'I might start a loyalty scheme just for you.'

•

We retreated to the high-rise to decide what to do. Kate wasn't keen on the climb but I pointed out that Sierra would be looking for us, and we needed somewhere safe to regroup.

We found an abandoned suite on the top floor with a lock that worked. Kate collapsed onto the bed and a cloud of dust erupted around her. She looked exhausted. Quite apart from the difficulty of controlling it, her new body was nowhere near as fit as mine. I had ended up virtually carrying her up the last few flights of stairs.

I walked over to the window, staring out at the lights far below. At night the park looked more desolate than ever.

Kate sneezed and I turned around. 'Bless you.'

'What's the plan?' she said. 'We need to be doing something. If we find Sierra, what are we going to do? Beat the information out of her?'

'If we have to,' I said. 'First we have to find her.'

Kate looked puzzled. 'We know that she has another body, but I still don't understand why. Why didn't she just leave the park in this body? If she can. Why pay for another one?'

'Who knows how Sierra thinks,' I said. 'Maybe she wanted to look like her seventeen-year-old self again. There's a resemblance. Maybe she'd agreed with Guskov to swap Bird for the new andi, so it wouldn't have cost her much. But Ben wrecked that by shooting Bird. Or maybe she was in Bird during the game, panicked when she thought Bird was dying, and jumped to the new andi as fast as she could.'

'Possibly. But that doesn't explain why *I* ended up in Bird. Was she doing that to kill me?'

'We're going to have to find her to get the answer. But in the meantime we have another problem,' I said. 'Read this.'

HIGH PRIORITY, DO NOT IGNORE: ParkGov to Mr Du Bois. We are contacting you as the current representative of your commune. We understand that your challenge today was inconclusive due to a systems failure in the arena. You must accept and complete a challenge by the end of next cycle. If you do not choose a challenge, one will be randomly assigned to you at the start of the cycle.

Kate sighed. 'Again. How do we even do this?' she asked. 'It would need to be you playing the game. Unless Sierra is still in there with you. Which I doubt. But I wouldn't trust her to play anyway.'

'I'm not sure I have the energy for another challenge,' I said. 'We could just leave before midnight.'

297

'You could, I can't. Not in this body, anyway. We need to find Sierra and get me out of this.'

'Then I'd better find an easy one,' I sighed.

'Not that it really matters now, but how much time do we have in credit?' Kate asked.

I checked. 'Not as much as we had, but still quite a lot by park standards. After the ten that we gave the dealer we have 13.4 years left. It's well worth fighting for.'

'All right. You find an easy challenge and I'm going to see if I can get cleaned up. I'm still covered in blood.'

'Last time I tried them the showers were still working,' I said. 'And the printers are still good too, so you can get some new clothes. You need them.'

I was sitting cross-legged on the bed when she emerged ten minutes later. She still looked tired, but at least now she was clean and freshly dressed.

'How are you feeling?' I asked.

'Just wonderful. The best day of my life.' She paused. 'How do you think I feel, you git?'

'You look . . .' I stopped myself. She looked great, but she wasn't going to react well to my telling her that. Not in that body. 'You look . . . better . . .' I trailed off.

She dragged an armchair round and sat opposite me. 'So, what have you been doing?'

'I'm trying to find Sierra. I'm not as good at this as Ben, but I've managed to modify Ben's last search to look for Sierra's new body.'

'Is that it?' Kate said. 'We sit here and hope that she happens to walk past a camera. And that Ben's search routine will recognise her new body? There must be something better that we can be doing.'

'Not tonight,' I said. 'We're both exhausted. You're still in shock. We need to rest. Besides, even if I'm the only one left in this body presumably I'll still drop out at 2:00. When Mike left we still shut down for four hours R & R overnight.'

'All right,' she said. 'We are going to have to come up with a better plan for tomorrow. Sitting here all day and waiting for something to happen is going to drive me mad. If Sierra's found a way to leave the park in her new body I don't want to be the one stuck here for the next fifty years.'

'Fine, but I still need to play a game tomorrow. We have over a hundred challenges now. I'd half expected to have one from Sierra's new andi, but there isn't one.'

'There is another option,' said Kate. 'We could be bold and issue a challenge to Sierra. She'd probably accept it.'

'I'm sure she would,' I said. 'But we know she's subverting the games somehow. It's too risky. We're better off finding her in the real world.'

'You're right,' said Kate. She sounded tired. 'It was a bad idea. I'm exhausted and my brain's not working properly.'

'It's been a rough day,' I said. 'You need to let that body sleep. It's not like a schizo with rest programmed in. You get some shut-eye while I find a game for tomorrow.'

'All right, but wake me if there's any sign of Sierra.'

'I promise.'

I climbed off the bed as Kate slid under the covers.

I dragged the armchair over to the window. I wondered what it was like trying to get to sleep, proper sleep, for the first time in twenty-five years.

I was meant to be reviewing challenges, but there didn't seem a lot of point. Instead I found myself staring out at the darkness. I could see a half-reflection of myself staring back, and beyond that the dim lights of the park.

Four days ago there had been five of us in this body, here for a bit of fun and to try to win some time. Cocky and confident. Now I was on my own. Mike dead. Ben dead. Kate beside me in a body she hated.

And somewhere out there in the darkness was Sierra. Waiting for us.

KATE

I was woken by an alert. It took me a moment to remember where I was. Who I was. How I could be woken like this.

I rolled over and felt Alex lying next to me.

2:38. It wasn't really Alex, then. His mind was shut down while his body simulated sleep. I wouldn't be able to wake him.

I sat up.

Sierra Summers detected. One alert: view?

I was still being copied in on Ben's old alert, which Alex had modified. I was surprised that she was openly going by her real name. How had she even managed that when I was Amy Bird?

I opened the clip.

Sierra was standing at a darkened crossroads, beneath one of the few working streetlights, looking around. She was near the Death's Head. Was that where she had been since the game? Had she been there when we visited Guskov? Had he lied to us? Or was she heading to the bar now?

301

This felt like a trap. Why had she appeared at a time when she knew Alex would be gone? Or did she think that she was safe for this period, that I wouldn't go after her on my own? Did she even know that I was still alive and inside Amy's body? It had all been pretty chaotic at the end of the game, and the andi had been wounded. Maybe she thought she was safe while we slept.

But if we lost her again I lost the chance to get my body back.

I climbed out of bed, trying to be quiet so as to not wake Alex, which made no sense. I dressed quickly. As I did so another alert popped up, showing Sierra entering the Death's Head.

I couldn't count on her staying there until Alex woke up. I left quickly.

It was cold and dark outside. Deserted. There was some light from the moon, but there was rain in the air, with clouds scudding overhead. I kept to the centre of the streets, away from the shadows. I was vulnerable in Amy's weak body.

How was I going to do this? Walking in through the front door of the bar seemed like suicide. I needed to find another way in. As I walked I brought up a map. A jumble of buildings backed up to the bar, behind which was a small park.

It took me a good thirty minutes to get there. I hoped that Sierra was still inside. The park was thinly populated with trees, most half-dead, but providing some cover. I picked my way carefully from tree to tree, trying to stay out of the moonlight.

The nearest building towered a good seven or eight storeys above me. It was in shadow. There was no obvious way in, no doors or windows that I could see. I needed to get closer. To my right was a pile of fallen masonry, which would provide some cover. I scuttled towards it and scrambled up, keeping my head down.

I needn't have worried about Sierra looking out. From close up it was clear that there were no windows, just a blank wall with a small door in the bottom right-hand corner. It was open, swinging back and forth in the wind.

A chance sighting of Sierra. An invitingly open door. This felt more and more like a trap. But what choice did I have?

I slid back down the mound of rubble and approached the door cautiously. I stood and listened, but could hear nothing over the sound of the wind. Eventually I plucked up my courage, slid around it and peered inside.

The building was huge and poorly lit. There were five skylights running the length of the roof, high above. Shafts of moonlight pierced the gloom like dim spotlights. They picked out jumbles of towering machinery and oddly angled walkways.

I stepped cautiously through. I couldn't see enough to stay near the wall in the darkness. This body didn't have the lens enhancements that we did. I needed the moonlight. It was strange that despite being sixty-seven years old, and having time in credit, Amy Bird didn't seem to have thought it worth spending anything on enhancements. Maybe andis were like that. So divorced from their bodies and the real world, so obsessed with their rational minds, that they wouldn't spend time on improving themselves physically.

I wound my way carefully through the debris from one pool of light to the other, trying to stay in the cover of the broken machines that loomed over me. Eventually there was only one skylight to go. I looked cautiously out from behind cover.

I had found Sierra.

She was sitting in the centre of the shaft of moonlight,

cross-legged, facing the door I'd come in through. Her eyes were closed. But I had no doubt she knew I was there. On each side of her, on the edge of the light, was a row of glass-lidded boxes. I couldn't see what they contained, but they looked horribly like coffins.

I stepped out into the moonlight.

Sierra opened her eyes. She looked me up and down. 'Kate,' she said. 'You've aged since I last saw you.'

'I'm Amy, not Kate,' I said. 'You can check.'

She laughed. 'I'm not going to scan you, Kate. I know who you are. I'm the one who put you inside that body.'

'And now you need to put me back,' I said. 'If you want to be an andi for the rest of your life, stuck in this park for ever, then fine. That's not my choice. I want to be back in my body and out of this . . .' I gestured to my andi body. Revulsion overwhelmed me. Each unnatural gesture made me hate this body more.

Sierra shook her head. 'You should be pleased. I've given you freedom. No more four-hour slots. No more worrying about what everyone else has done with your body. You should be thanking me.'

'*Thanking you?*' I took a step towards her, fists unconsciously clenching. 'You may regret your choices, but I don't. I like being part of something greater. When they weren't there I could feel Mike, Ben, Alex – even you. It felt good. This,' I looked down at Amy's body again, 'in this I'm alone. I don't know how you can stand it.'

Sierra blinked, surprised at my outburst. Then she shrugged. 'You'll get used to it. Embrace the positives. You can be with Alex. I watched the game show. I could see something between you. Alex knows you better than you know yourself.'

'I'm not sure what you mean, but it wasn't real,' I said. 'There was nothing between us. It was just a game I was playing to stay alive. Of course Alex knows me. We've been together for twenty-five years. That's all.'

What did Sierra think she'd seen? I shook my head. She was just trying to manipulate me. 'You don't seem to get it, Sierra. I hate this. You screwed Alex and Emily in Montreal. Literally. Now you are doing the same to me. Why?'

'What choice did I have?' she said. 'You bastards stuck me in stasis for three months after Montreal. Do you know what that's like? Being trapped with nothing but your own thoughts? And Alex wasn't going to leave it at three months. He wanted to get rid of me for good. Sooner or later I'd have done something that the rest of you sanctimonious prigs didn't approve of, and he'd have had his excuse to try again. We were never going to live together happily ever after for another hundred years. Either I was going to get rid of you, or you lot were going to find a way of getting rid of me. So I decided to act first.'

To Sierra's twisted mind that might make sense. But how had she managed all this? Ben I could have understood. But Sierra? I'd never seen her apply herself to anything other than the pursuit of an easy life.

'Who was Amy Bird?' I asked. 'How did you do all this? Was Ben helping you? Is he still alive somewhere? And Mike?'

'Ben?' she looked genuinely surprised. 'No. Ben's dead. So is Mike. They didn't give me any help.'

'Who did, then? How did you do all this? There's no way you did it on your own.'

She hesitated before answering. 'Let's keep that as a surprise. You'll find out soon enough.'

What did she mean? 'Why are you still here? You've got what you wanted. You're back to being seventeen-year-old Sierra. Bugger off and leave us alone. What's left of us. I hope you think it was worth killing Mike and Ben for. I don't.'

Sierra grimaced. 'That's difficult. I can't, as you so eloquently put it, just bugger off. I can't get out of the death park in this body. I had to jump here when Ben shot Bird. But I have no status or time. If I leave the park I'll be picked up and erased. So I need Mike's body back. That's where you come in.'

'What do you mean?' I asked.

'I need to get Alex to an arena so we can swap back. But he's not going to agree to that unless I have some leverage.' She pointed to me. 'You.'

'Me?' Was this all a trap from the outset then? 'How did you know I'd even come here?'

'You're not as bright as you think,' she said. 'I knew if I showed myself it would trigger Ben's alert, and you wouldn't be able to resist chasing after me.'

I looked around and laughed.

'How are you proposing to keep me here, Sierra? I've come for you, not the other way around.' I still didn't have complete control of Bird, but I was pretty confident I could take Sierra in her new andi body.

There was a metal rod leaning against the nearest machine. I grabbed it and tested its weight. I would beat the truth out of her if I had to. She had just admitted that it was possible to get back into our body. I needed her to tell me how.

I took a step forward and slammed the rod into the palm of my other hand.

Sierra flinched and stood quickly.

'I wouldn't do that,' she said. She stepped back and held out her hands.

The lids on the glass coffins rose silently. There was a hiss, and smoke rolled out of them into the darkness. An icy wave passed over my feet. What was this?

'When you bastards forced me into stasis, I had mandatory counselling,' said Sierra. 'They told me I was a sociopath – incapable of change. Which is fine. I don't need to change. Before they gave up they kept saying that I needed to face my fears. That I couldn't run away from them.'

As I was wondering what this had to do with anything, I started to hear sounds coming from the coffins. Squelching, coughing, rasping breath. Suddenly something sat upright in the nearest coffin to my right.

I jumped away from it. It was white and indistinct, almost glowing in the moonlight. A dandi, waking up and coated in slime. I realised that this was where Guskov kept his stock. Sierra was reviving them all at once. But how?

'What . . . what are you doing?' I gasped.

'What's your biggest fear, Kate? Being stuck in that andi body for ever? This is part of your therapy. I'm giving you the chance to confront it. My psychologist would say it's good for you. You can run if you like. In fact, I want you to run or there's no fun in it for me. But they will get you.' She paused and grinned at me. 'It's time to face up to your daddy issues.'

How the hell did she know about that? I'd only ever told

Alex. Had he told Sierra?

But I had bigger problems.

The dandis were slowly climbing out of their glass coffins. For a moment I wondered whether I could grab Sierra and use her as a shield. But what would that do? All I had was a metal rod, and they would overwhelm me. I realised that the game had changed. This wasn't about me catching Sierra. This was about me getting out of there alive.

I turned and ran.

Back between the rows of coffins, towards the door where I had come in. Two of the dandis were fully emerged and in my way. They were naked, white, dripping in slime.

I ducked under the swinging arm of one, and pushed the other away with the metal rod. Not hard enough. I cursed my stupid weak body.

The dandi grabbed the rod and I stumbled backwards, felt something touch my back, sliding across my shoulders. I screamed.

I dived away from the touch, between the two dandis ahead of me. I scrambled frantically on hands and knees, slipping on bits of discarded metal. I could hear rasping breath behind me. Close behind.

I grabbed a handle on the nearest machine and pulled myself up. Something slithered across my neck, and a hand pulled at my shirt. I jumped forward, around the side of the machine.

I risked a quick look over my shoulder.

There was a jumble of dandis behind me, shuffling, limbs flailing and uncoordinated, slipping on bits of metal. There was a reason they were known as dumb andis. There was a limit to their AI capabilities. They were getting in each other's way. Even in Bird's weak body I had the advantage of speed. If I could keep ahead of them I could get back to the door before they did.

I darted forward, trying to follow the route from skylight to skylight. Trying to remember how I had got from the door to Sierra. I cut right, round a machine twice my height, then left through a gap between two broken conveyor belts. I cracked my shin on something solid, and stifled a gasp. I could hear the dandis behind me, but I was briefly out of sight. If they had any sense they would be trying to outflank me. Did Sierra have that level of control over them?

Then everything went black.

For a moment I thought that Sierra had somehow blocked the skylights. Then I realised that the moon had disappeared behind clouds. The storm had arrived. Rain started to batter the metal roof high above, echoing round the building.

That worked both ways. If I couldn't see or hear the dandis then they were equally blind and deaf to me.

But time wasn't on my side. I had to get to the door before any of them did. All they had to do was get there first and wait me out.

I pressed on, shuffling my feet forward, arms outstretched, trying to feel my way through the chaos as I waited for my eyes to adjust.

Why was Sierra doing this to me? She knew that I'd never liked andis. Was that why she'd put me in one? Without the others I felt so alone.

A beam of light cut through the darkness to my left. It lit up two dandis just metres away. I ducked under the conveyor belt, trying to calm my breathing. I heard footsteps near where the dandis had been.

'Katie, Katie, where have you gone?'

The light swung towards me, over me, past me. I stayed still. It swung back.

'She's here,' shouted Sierra.

I dived from my hiding place, scrambling through scattered metal. Sierra's torch tracked me until I rounded the corner of another vast machine. I barely stopped myself running into a wall.

I was thoroughly lost now.

The drumbeat of rain overhead wasn't helping, echoing the thumping of my heart. I thought I could hear the scrape of metal ahead, but it was hard to tell.

'Run, Katie, run.' A mocking voice from somewhere behind me.

I needed to know where I was. I could make out what looked like a ladder on the side of the machine to my left. It creaked when I pulled on it, and felt as though it might come away at any moment. But I had no choice. I hauled myself up it and found myself on a metal platform a little above head height. Walkways ran off in both directions. The one to my right ran parallel to what I could now see was the back wall, and ought to bring me out somewhere near the door. I tested it with one foot. It wobbled in a disturbing way.

Despite the cold night I was sweating now. Why did andis sweat? They seemed to have taken all the worst human attributes and not added any improvements.

I stepped cautiously on to the walkway, trusting it would

hold me. I could see Sierra's torch flashing between the machinery in the distance. She seemed to have gone in the wrong direction.

Suddenly there was a deafening crack overhead and the sky-lights were lit up brighter than before. The storm was right above us. For a moment the entire room was picked out in harsh white light as lightening crackled around the building.

I froze. Had anyone seen me? Or were they as deaf and blind as I now was?

Everything was dark again. My night vision was ruined. But in that moment of light I had seen where the door was. Mentally I rehearsed my route. Get to the end of the walkway, drop down a ladder, left round a conveyor belt, right past another of the vast machines, and that was it.

Then I heard a noise from below. Two dandis were shuffling slowly along beneath the walkway, kicking scraps of metal as they went. Their white slimy skins seemed almost to glow in the darkness. Sweat pooled on my face and arms, and down the back of my shirt. It only needed one drop and they would look up. They couldn't miss me.

Without warning I was blinded once again by light. But this time there was no accompanying thunder. It was Sierra's torch.

'She's up there!' Sierra shouted. 'Get her!'

I dived, trying to get out of the light. The metal floor of the walkway collapsed under the sudden weight. I plunged through, dragging one of the dandis to the ground with me. As I struggled to my feet the other clawed at me. I turned and punched him in the face with all that I had.

A blow like that would have knocked him off his feet if I'd

been in my own body. But Bird's puny swipe just rocked him back enough for me to slip past, sliding off his slippery skin, my knuckles aching. I ran towards the door, careless now of making any noise. I could hear movement to my left, Sierra shouting, bodies crashing through the debris that littered the floor. All to the drumbeat of the rain overhead.

I skidded round a pile of metal to see the door ahead of me, still open.

There was a dandi in front of it, staring at me with hollow eyes. I barely hesitated, reaching unseen into the junk pile beside me, and swinging something heavy and metallic into its face. There was a crunching sound and a muted scream, but still he tried to reach for me as he collapsed.

I leaped over his falling body and out through the door. I was briefly blinded by a squall of rain. There was another flash of lightning. Still close, but slightly further away. The thunder took a moment to reach me. I could see the treeline. If I could get amongst the trees I would be safe.

Something hit me from the side. I crashed to the ground, winded, fighting for breath. As I tried to crawl to my feet again, an arm locked around my neck from behind. Hands grabbed me and pulled me up. I twisted and fought to get away, punching and kicking.

But there were too many of them. My wrists were pinned tightly behind my back, and I was lifted until only my toes were touching the ground. The arm round my throat tightened, and I felt as though I was about to pass out.

I was twisted round violently, to see Sierra standing in front of me. She looked at me angrily. The wind was blowing her hair about, the rain plastering it to her scalp. I didn't imagine that I looked any better.

I was gasping for air. Sierra gave a signal and the grip round my throat eased slightly. I gulped a breath.

Sierra was holding a metal rod in one hand. She walked over to me, raising it above her head. Was that wise in the middle of a lightning storm? But it seemed unlikely that a benevolent god was going to strike her down for me.

'Guskov won't be happy that you damaged the goods, Kate. There's at least one in there with a broken nose. Maybe I'll just do the same to you.' She paused. 'Or better still, if you hate this andi body so much why don't we just end it now?' She drew back the metal rod. 'I could drive this through your brain and feel nothing.'

I knew that she was mad enough to do it. I pushed back, to try to get away from her, but the dandis forced me towards her. 'Please, no, Sierra . . .' I hated myself for pleading with her, but I didn't want to die. I knew then that I would rather live in an andi body than die. 'You need me,' I said. 'You need me to get Alex.'

I could see her brain calculating. Then she dropped the metal rod. I went limp with relief. I shivered.

Sierra walked over to me, flicking her wet hair out of her eyes. She put her hands on either side of my face, turning me back towards her. It felt familiar. Intimate.

'You look disgusting, Kate,' she said. She looked up at the sky, opening her mouth and drinking in the torrential rain. Her eyes flashed reflected lightning as she looked back at me. 'At least this is washing some of the slime off you.' She leaned in closer.

Her thumbs pressed on my cheekbones, hurting me. Thunder rolled over us. I couldn't move. Her lips touched mine as she forced herself on me, her tongue flicking between my lips. Then she pulled away.

'You liked that before. Don't pretend anything's changed.'

She was wrong. I held her gaze, then turned from her and spat.

She stepped back and gestured to the dandis. 'Bring her inside. I have my bait. Now let's get my body back.'

ONE WEEK EARLIER

MR GUSKOV

Valya Guskov carefully polished his glasses with a square of silk cloth. He didn't need to wear them, but they were a part of him now. He'd come across them in an antique store twenty years ago, and had decided that they made him look like an intellectual, as well as lending an air of menace. Although now he had Vincent and Stas to achieve the latter.

He looked up at the door. They were late. Not the start he wanted to a new relationship. Still, it didn't look good to seem impatient, so he resisted messaging Vincent. He would give them five more minutes.

They arrived in three.

The man who followed Vincent through the door was tall and graceful, with an easy smile. Not as tall or wide as Vincent. But few were. If Guskov had walked round the desk to greet them the newcomer would have topped him by a good six inches.

He remained seated.

'Sorry, boss,' said Vincent. He was rubbing his knuckles. 'We ran into some trouble in the bar.'

'What sort of trouble?'

'There's an irritating hed, Karl something, who's been hanging around for the last few days. He's barely got any time left. Someone told him that you might give him work, and he seemed to be offended that Ms Summers here is jumping the queue.' Vincent glanced at his bruised knuckles. 'I explained to him that's not how it works.'

'A suitably visual explanation, I trust?'

'Well, he can't see as well as he could. But he understands.'

'Is he worth anything to us?' asked Guskov.

'We could give him a supply of pills. Let him do a bit of dealing. Then, when he's in our debt, we call it in and sell him to an arena.'

'Do it,' said Guskov.

He turned his gaze on the newcomer. 'Sorry, Ms Summers, there's always something to distract me. It is a pleasure to finally meet you. Do have a seat. Can Vincent get you something to drink?'

She smiled, raising a glass that she'd been holding at her side. 'I'm way ahead of you. While your man here dealt with Karl I made friends with your barman.' She sat, crossed her legs, and looked at him quizzically.

'What is it?' he asked.

'The way Les described you I thought you'd be seven feet tall and breathing fire. He didn't seem like a man who was easily scared, but he said you weren't someone to cross.'

'He was right about that. Les and I go back a long way. He knows where a lot of the bodies are buried. A handy man with a shovel, Les, when you're digging through permafrost.' Guskov chuckled at the memory. Then turned to Vincent. 'Go and get the andi.'

Vincent nodded and left.

'So, Ms Summers,' said Guskov. 'Your first day in the park. I'm looking forward to an interesting – and profitable – week.'

'Please, call me Sierra.' She leaned in. 'A handsome man like you – we ought to be on first-name terms.'

Guskov sat back, uncomfortable. 'I'm going to stick with Ms Summers. We don't get many schizos in the park, so it's hard enough getting my head round what you are. The whole sex thing is a bit beyond me. Besides, even if I was so inclined, I try not to mix business and pleasure. Business is pleasure enough for me.'

'Very well.' She shrugged and sat back, sipping her drink. 'Is everything arranged?'

'As we agreed,' said Guskov. 'None of it is difficult. Expensive, but not difficult. You've given me long enough to organise it.'

'So how is it going to work?' she asked. 'The others won't realise that they're being watched? I know you need to make your profit, but they aren't stupid. They'll be suspicious.'

'Trust me. This isn't the first time we've done this. It will be subtle. The show has around one hundred subscribers, all carefully vetted. No one is going to leak. There might be the occasional drone flashing overhead, but mostly we'll be tapping into the ParkGov security feeds. The others won't suspect a thing. My subscribers aren't expecting twenty-four-hour surveillance.

They know there will be gaps. What they're mostly interested in are the games, and who wins. These people are gamblers. They want to bet on which of you survives the week.'

'I can tell you that now. It'll be me.'

'I do hope you appreciate the risks, Ms Summers. I can skew things in your favour in some of the early games – try to make sure you don't all get killed before the week is up. That would be a bit of an anticlimax. But I can't guarantee it. The games are unpredictable. And as I told you before, the risks in the final games have to be real. I'll have some pretty nasty characters wagering very large sums on the final outcome. Some of them are even nastier than me. If they think I've fixed the result there will be unpleasant consequences for all of us. So there's no certainty that you'll win.'

'I realise that,' she said. 'You've told me already. But I know the others well enough that I'm confident.' She took a drink and looked away. 'Besides, the alternative is being stuck with these bastards for another hundred years. I'd rather be dead.'

Guskov raised an eyebrow. He was spared answering as the door opened. With Vincent was an andi. She was dressed in a brown coverall, her skin pale and shiny, her hair still wet. She stared straight ahead.

'So,' said Guskov. 'Here's your andi, Ms Summers. Amy Bird. I hope you like her.'

'Absolutely. She looks perfect. How is this going to work? She's going to need some better clothes, so she looks normal. And we'll need to improve her AI, so Kate will think she's real. You told me she could run a low-level AI with my instructions overlaid. How do we do that?'

'That's not my department,' said Guskov. 'Dr Bernard is the expert. You'll be in touch with him later. He says that controlling dandis is the easy bit. Moving minds in and out of them is much harder. He's going to need your access codes for that.'

'I know. That's all arranged.' She paused. 'You've set up a history for the andi, in case anyone checks? She needs to appear real.'

'Of course,' said Guskov. 'It's all sorted.'

She looked at the andi, and frowned. 'I can't scan her. Has she got the twenty years you promised? I'm going to need that to get Kate interested.'

'We've given her just over twenty. A round number would look odd. I'll be wanting that back. You're getting enough out of me already without extra time.'

'Fine. And what about the second andi? I'm going to need her in a few days.'

'We'll have her by then,' said Guskov. 'We've identified an andi player who fits your requirements and we've been letting her win every game she plays. She's winning big, and starting to believe she can't lose. Tomorrow she'll discover just how wrong she is. Give me a day to liberate the body from ParkGov, clean her up, and you can have her. Two days maximum.'

'Sounds good, Mr Guskov. Les said you were the man for the job. It seems he was right. One week and this will all be over.'

Guskov smiled. 'Indeed, Ms Summers. One week. My audience is waiting. Let's get the show started.'

ALEX

DAY FIVE
06:00–06:05

The bed was empty. Kate was gone.

Sierra had sent me a message, copied to Kate.

Alex, 9:00. Accept my challenge or I start cutting bits off her. S. xxx

Attached was an image clip. Kate, hands tied above her head, hanging from a giant hook, feet kicking inches off the ground. She looked a mess. She was gagged. Her eyes were wide with fear. Sierra was standing next to her stroking Kate's cheek with a knife.

A message from Kate appeared.

Alex, please, come quickly. Sierra is crazy. Kate.

I smiled. It was time to end this.

I accepted the challenge.

KATE

'He's on his way,' said Sierra. 'Punctual as ever. Soon we'll be done with this and I can get out of here.'

We were in a small featureless room with grey walls and no windows. Sierra was sitting cross-legged on the floor, her back to the door. I was slumped in a corner. I didn't know where we were as Sierra had brought me here blindfolded and was blocking me. If this was a legitimate arena I didn't know how she had got me in without questions being asked. Then again, this was a death park. Time could buy you pretty much anything.

I was tired and bruised, my clothes were torn, and I was still dripping with a mixture of slime and rainwater. It stank, a horrible sweet odour that I didn't think would ever leave me. God knows what I looked like.

'You don't need to do this, Sierra,' I said. 'We can find a way of getting you out of the death park. Then Alex and I can sort out the mess that's left.'

'I told you that's no use,' she said. 'I need to leave here in our body, with all the time that we have earned, and with four more lives to come. Besides, I made promises. We have no choice but to play this game.'

I heard footsteps approaching the door, then it opened and Alex stepped through. Followed by Guskov.

Alex rushed over to me and knelt down, brushing a hand through my slimy hair. 'Kate, are you all right?'

'I've been better. And I stink. I wouldn't get too close. What's *he* doing here?' I asked, nodding to Guskov, who stood in the doorway, watching us.

He stepped forward. 'As Ms Summers knows, I have an interest in the game that you are about to play. It is through me that the two of you have your new bodies. The time has come for you to repay your benefactor.'

I didn't follow. Why should I be paying for a body that I didn't want?

Alex turned to Sierra. 'How could you do this? Mike, Ben. And now Kate.' He shook his head.

Sierra shrugged. 'If I'd wanted to talk about my motivation I'd have called my psychologist. He did such a great job last time round. Let's just get on with it.'

'What's the game?' Alex asked. 'Are you actually going to play fair this time? I think you conned Ben into killing himself.'

'I didn't kill Ben,' she said. 'Kate did. Besides, this is one game I can't change. I'm in just as much danger as the two of you.' She looked at Guskov. 'That was part of our deal. The only difference is that we aren't playing for time. If I win, I get my body back and you two are gone for good. If you win you stay alive and you'll have to decide what to do with her.' She pointed to me.

'What do you mean?' I protested. 'If we win I want my body back.'

'Look at yourself, Kate,' said Sierra. 'You aren't in any position to demand anything. You're lucky you're still alive.' She turned to Guskov. 'Let's get this done.'

He nodded. 'Come with me.'

We followed him out of the room and down a corridor which, to my surprise, opened out into the bar in the club where I had met Godfried. This time, despite the early hour, around twenty of the armchairs were occupied. Heads turned towards us as Guskov led us up to the bar. He coughed and looked around, pausing for a moment to acknowledge several of the seated patrons with a nod. A camera drone drifted to a stop just in front of us.

'Good morning all, and welcome. It's good to see so many familiar faces. A particular welcome to those who have travelled from outside the park. Welcome also to those who are watching us remotely.' He turned to us. 'Mr White was puzzled as to why your feeds were being viewed by over one hundred people while you were in the park. This is why. You have, for the past week, been stars of a highly exclusive pay-per-view show. Since you stepped into the park your lives, both inside and outside the game booths, have been broadcast to a carefully selected audience chosen for their discretion and interest in exotic entertainment. That was the deal I made with Ms Summers when she called me several months ago and explained her predicament.' He turned back to his audience.

'Today we have the culmination of our week-long show. I hope you enjoy it. No one is safe. Anyone can die. Real death.

Let me start by reminding you who has got this far. Until recently part of a communal body they have suffered some . . . difficulties since entering the park.' He sighed deeply. 'People have taken advantage of them.'

Yes – mostly him. It seemed that he had screwed us out of twenty years while pretending he didn't know what was going on, and drip-feeding us information.

'Having started in one body our remaining protagonists now find themselves in three. This fine specimen of rippling muscle is Alex Du Bois. Sadly, not one that I created. He was the original host. The other two are mine. First, Kate Weston, although currently going by the name Amy Bird. And second, Sierra Summers.

'As I said, some months ago Ms Summers approached me with a proposition. She had a scheme by which to rid herself of the other four, but needed andi bodies. Given my speciality in that area she was put in touch with me by a mutual friend.

'As we worked through the complexities of the scheme it turned out that she needed a lot more than just dandis. Fortunately our good friend Dr Bernard was able to assist in that regard. His interest and expertise in the workings of the human body are unrivalled. He is particularly adept at moving minds. I understand that he has thoroughly enjoyed the challenges of the mind swaps involved in Ms Summers' scheme.'

I hadn't spotted the doctor sitting on his own near the front of the group. His three-piece suit was at least a size too large, the jacket hanging off him like a sack. On his lap was a battered black leather case, which he clutched tightly. He twitched at the mention of his name, looked around, and raised a hand nervously in the air.

'It is many years now since the good doctor first came to the park. I think that he would agree that he was not well-suited to combat in the arenas. So he came to me for a new body. One of my very first clients. As an android he is always particularly interested in the difference between human and android physiology. He tells me that by far the best way of conducting his studies is live dissection.'

Guskov turned back to us.

'Which brings us to today's game. In return for my assistance, and Dr Bernard's expertise, Ms Summers agreed to make you all stars of this secret show. Sadly Mr Ganzorig and Mr White are no longer with us. If you bet on their survival, commiserations. To those who have complained that they both died in games that were manipulated by Ms Summers, or her andi, I did warn you that this was a contest that was going to take place outside the arenas as well as within. It shouldn't have surprised you that everyone was fighting for an advantage to take into the games.' His smile vanished for a moment. 'Let me make it clear that there will be no refunds.' He looked around the room, and then back at the camera.

'But of course you have the chance today to recoup your losses. I agreed with Ms Summers that the final game would be played here. The winner, or winners, will walk away free from any debt, their body and time intact. They will be free to leave the park. The loser, or losers, will be given over to the good doctor for his medical research. It won't be pleasant.' He sighed theatrically. 'But sadly there comes a time when you have to pay your debts.'

Guskov turned back to Bernard. 'Doctor, come up here.

Don't be shy. Perhaps it will sharpen their minds if you show our players what you have planned.'

The doctor was tall, taller even than Mike. He seemed to uncoil from his seat as he stood, and walked over to us in jerky movements. He paused before each of us, looking us up and down with piercing blue eyes and a thin smile. Despite his shoddy attire there was something awful about him. He had the look of a predator setting eyes on his prey for the first time. And enjoying what he saw. Even Sierra seemed frightened. She stepped back.

He walked over to the bar and carefully placed his black leather case down. He undid a buckle and opened it out. There was a glint of light reflecting off metal. Despite myself I leaned forward to look. And wished I hadn't. Neatly arranged and held in place by leather loops were knives, scalpels, tongs, hammers and other instruments that I couldn't identify.

The doctor turned to us. 'I would particularly like to have her,' he said, pointing at me with a long finger, 'and him,' pointing at Alex. 'It is always good to be able to see how human and artificial bodies react to the same pain stimuli. Despite appearances, the nerve networks are very different.'

I shuddered. He was vile. What had Sierra got us into? This was madness. Was she so sure that she would survive that she would risk his butchery? She had said that this was one game that she couldn't manipulate. Was that just another lie?

I looked at the doctor's knives and calculated what the chances were of grabbing one and fighting my way out. Not high. For the first time I noticed that Vincent and Stas were standing next to the corridor that led to the stairs down to the street. Then Godfried caught my eye. He was seated near them, in the shadows. He met my gaze and pulled a face, nodding in what seemed like an apology for being there.

Guskov stepped forward. 'Thank you, Doctor. So, to the game. You will be able to watch our players' progress here.' He gestured to a large screen over the bar. 'Once it is over, those of you who have an interest may, at no extra cost, stay to watch the doctor's work. No offence, Doctor, but I won't be staying.' He grimaced. 'I must confess to having no stomach for that sort of thing.'

Dr Bernard smiled thinly and returned to his seat, leaving his medical instruments on the bar. Waiting for us.

Guskov continued. 'Our players are in two teams. Mr Du Bois and Ms Weston in one team. Ms Summers in the other. There are two stages to today's game. In the first stage the teams must – separately – escape from a burning ship in the historic New York East River. The first to set foot on North Brother Island wins that stage, and gains a one-minute head start. The second game is set on the island, where the teams will compete against one another. It is a straight race. Whoever wins walks free. Whoever loses . . .' He gestured to the doctor.

Bernard looked across at us, smiling. My skin crawled.

'Given the nature of the games players will have no remote access to information for their duration. Otherwise they might be too easy.' Guskov paused, as though considering whether he had covered everything.

'One final matter. I know that most of you have some time wagered on the outcome of this week's events. It is not too late to back your judgment further, or hedge your bets. Or, for those who lost out on Mr Ganzorig and Mr White, to win something back. I have brought in my associate Mr Godfried to run a book on the final outcome. You will have the chance to place bets until the end of the first game. From then the book will be closed.' I was disappointed. Did that mean Godfried had been part of this all along? That he had strung me along? Had I been naïve to trust him?

'I have said before, and I will say it again. There are no foregone conclusions in any of the games. Just because Ms Summers instigated this does not mean that she has any advantage. One of the conditions I imposed from the outset – for the integrity of the contest – was that both teams are equally at risk.'

I wasn't sure I believed that. How desperate had Sierra been to get away from us to agree to that? Or was she so confident she could beat us?

'So, enough talk. Let's get started,' said Guskov. He summoned Vincent and Stas with a wave of his hand, then turned to us. 'You will be escorted to the game booths. I wish you all the best of luck.'

•

I am standing in the centre of a wood-panelled room. It is sparsely furnished. There is a wooden bed with sheets in disarray, a small chest of drawers, and a writing desk with a fold-down lid.

Alex is standing next to me. There is a mirror on one wall. I glance at it and see an older version of seventeen-year-old Kate looking back at me. I realise that the room is moving, swaying gently from side to side. I look for a window, but there is none – only paintings on the walls.

You are on board the *General Slocum*, a passenger steamboat sailing up the East River, New York. It is Wednesday, 15 June 1904. A Lutheran Church group has chartered the vessel to carry members to a church picnic on Long Island. Twelve minutes ago a discarded cigarette caused a fire to start in the Lamp Room in the forward section of the vessel. The fire hoses are rotten and the life preservers filled with iron and substandard cork. Most of the passengers cannot swim, and most will die. You cannot change events or save anyone. You have fifteen minutes to escape this room and save yourselves by reaching dry land.

I sniff the air, but can't smell any smoke, so the fire can't be too close.

'Let's get out of here,' I say.

'I'll check the door,' says Alex. He walks over and tries the handle, pulling hard. 'It's locked.'

'Don't waste time on breaking it down. It's too easy. We need to find the key. I'll search the bed and the drawers. You check the desk.'

I pull the sheets and blankets from the bed, but see nothing useful. I hear Alex rifling through the desk behind me.

'I know where the key is,' he says.

He is holding up a small metal box, which rattles when he shakes it.

'How do we open it?' I ask.

'There's a four digit combination lock on top. We need to find the numbers. Or I could just try smashing it open.' He raises it above his head, ready to strike it on the corner of the desk.

'No, don't do that,' I say. 'It won't open that way and you will probably jam the mechanism. We need to find the numbers. Quickly.'

'It could be the date,' says Alex. '1904.'

He fiddles with the lock. 'No, it's not that. 15 June, so 1506? Or 0615, as we are in New York.'

'Too obvious, but try them.'

I turn to the chest of drawers. The top drawer is empty. The second contains a man's shirt and jacket. The third contains a journal. I pull it out as Alex says, 'No, neither of those works.'

I take the journal over to the desk and open it. It is filled with closely written manuscript notes in black ink.

'It's a diary of some sort,' I say. 'From 1903. That's last year. But we don't have time to read it all. We need to know what day to look at. Unless there's something loose in it.' I hold it up by the spine and shake it, but nothing falls out.

'Try 15 June. It's the only date we have.'

I flick through until I find the entry for that date. It is short. I read it out.

15 June

Spent the day at home as Gertrude has still not recovered from the lumbago. Doctor Mortimer visited and said that though there is some improvement she needs a further week of bed rest. He provided another vial of tincture of opium. I used the afternoon to continue writing my article on the native *Pomacea* apple snail.

Well that didn't help.

'How long have we got?' I ask.

'Eleven minutes. But it's not just about getting out. We need to beat Sierra to the island.'

I start flicking through the diary at random, but it's hopeless without knowing where to look. Then I have a thought.

'Check the shirt and jacket,' I say, pointing to where I threw them on the floor.

Alex picks them up. He throws me the shirt. The breast pocket is empty. I feel around the collars and cuffs, but there are no signs of anything hidden inside them. There's a label: *Salvini Brothers, Brooklyn*. Again, that doesn't help.

'I've got something,' says Alex. He's holding a piece of crumpled paper. 'This was in one of the pockets.' He unfolds it. 'It's a receipt for some boots from a shop in Queen's.'

'Is there a date on it?'

'It looks like 9 November 1903. I can't see anything else of interest.'

I read the journal entry for that date.

9 November

Winter is early. There was ice on the lake this morning. Dr Mortimer believes that the night air is exacerbating Gertrude's hysteria. He has prescribed bed rest and said that on no account must her windows be left open during the night. I have instructed Charlotte to wake at 1 a.m. and 4 a.m. to stoke the fire. This afternoon's post brought the news that the *Harvard Journal of Molluscan Studies* has declined to publish my article. Went for a bracing walk round the park and stopped for a brandy at the Professor's to drown my sorrows.

'That must be a clue,' I say. 'There are two numbers in here – one and four. We need two more. Was there anything else in the jacket?'

'No,' says Alex. 'We have seven minutes left. Where else is there to look?'

'Check behind the chest and the desk,' I say. 'Pull out the drawers and look underneath. I'll check under the bed.'

There's nothing. Together we drag the mattress off the bed, and turn it over. There is nothing there either, not even a label.

The room lurches to the side, as though we have struck something. I am flung across the room into Alex, who catches me. He holds me for a moment as the room steadies.

For the first time I can hear noise from outside – screams. I can smell smoke. The fire must be close. I look around. Is there a secret panel somewhere in the floor or the walls?

Then I see it. 'The pictures. It's got to be them. Look.'

There are three. The first is a still life of some fruit in a bowl. The second is a painting of a young sailor with a hat labelled *General Slocum*. The third is of a lady lying in bed attended by a physician in a long black coat.

'Check the other two, but I think it's this one,' I say. 'It's linked to the diary.'

I pull the picture of the bedridden lady off the wall and turn it over. I am disappointed. There are some charcoal markings on the back of the frame, but nothing legible. There are no numbers.

'Nothing here,' says Alex.

'It's got to be this one.' I turn it back over, looking for numbers somewhere in the painting.

The sickly lady, whom I think of as Gertrude, is looking up at the doctor with a weary expression. She is holding a small book in her left hand, but I can't read the title and there are no numbers on it. Her right wrist is gripped by the doctor, who appears to be taking her pulse. He is staring at the pocket watch held in his other hand.

An unusually large pocket watch, on which I can read the time: three minutes past five.

'I've got it,' I shout. 'It's the watch. 5:03. We have the four numbers. 1453. Quick.'

Alex picks up the metal box and fumbles with the combination lock. He is too slow. I watch impatiently as he struggles with it. He pulls at the box and for a moment I think I am wrong. Then it opens, and he tips a key into his hand.

'Let's go,' he says. 'We've got four minutes to get off the ship.'

He puts the key into the lock, turns it, and pulls the door open. We step out into chaos.

To our right a fire is raging at the forward end of the ship. Men are throwing buckets of water at it, but it looks hopelessly ineffectual. Black smoke is pouring towards us. Everyone is heading for the back of the ship, to our left. There are shouts and screams, mostly in German.

In front of us a giant paddle wheel is still going round. Through the smoke I can make out an island a few hundred metres away. We seem to be turning towards it. That must be where we need to go.

A man runs screaming through the smoke and fire, his clothes burning. He races to the wooden rail next to the paddle wheel and jumps over. For a moment the wheel seems to pause, and I fear he has been dragged into it. I am right. The wheel resumes and a moment later his crumpled body is lifted up on the other side and flung into the water again.

I feel sick.

'Come on,' says Alex. 'We've got to get off now. We should head for the island.'

'Can you see Sierra?' I shout.

There is no sign of her.

We run towards the back of the ship, as far away from the fire and the paddle wheel as we can get. We elbow our way through passengers – mostly women and children, some carrying young babies. But I know it's not real. We are not here to save them. These people died a long time ago.

When we reach the rail we look down into a scene of devastation. The water is filled with bodies. Some are already face down and unmoving. Others are frantically paddling, trying to stay afloat. There is one small lifeboat in the water, overloaded, with several people hanging off the side, threatening to capsize it. A sailor is standing up in the boat, trying to beat swimmers away with an oar.

As we watch a woman jumps off the rail next to us and disappears under the water. She does not resurface.

I look down at what I am wearing. A heavy ankle-length dress that will pull me under the water if I try to follow her.

'I can't swim in this,' I say to Alex. 'Help me get it off.'

'In a minute. We can't jump in here. They'll grab on to us and drown us. We need to jump as close to the front as we can.' He grabs my hand and starts pulling me against the flow of people, back to the front of the ship.

I can feel the heat from the fire now. The smoke surrounds us and I start coughing. My eyes are streaming. The paddle wheel is still turning, but there is the scream of wood on metal as it does so. Alex stops. 'We can't get any closer. We'll jump in here. If we jump this side the wheel should push us away, not suck us in. Head around it and towards the island as fast as you can. I think they are trying to beach the ship there, but we can't wait to see if they make it.'

I turn my back to him. 'Help me get this off.' Alex fumbles with the buttons down the back of my dress and I step out of it. I am probably scandalising Edwardian society, but what I am wearing underneath – bloomers, a slip and petticoat – is more than I would usually wear to the gym. Alex looks at me for a moment, then quickly glances away when he sees that I have noticed.

He shrugs off the heavy coat that he's wearing and drops it on the deck. 'Come on. Let's go.' He takes my hand and we step up to the rail. The paddle wheel is screaming to our right.

We jump together.

The water is icy and black. I lose my grip on Alex as we plunge down. Struggling back to the surface, I break through gasping for air, the paddle wheel looming above me. I swim as hard as I can away from the ship, dreading being sucked back and ground up.

There is a shout to my left.

'Kate.' I swim towards Alex, arms and legs tiring, coughing up icy water.

'Alex?' I call. Then I see his head through the swells. I grab his arm in relief, then let go as I realise I am pulling him under.

'Which way?' I ask.

For a brief moment we tread water and turn around. There is no one else nearby, although we can hear the screams and shouts of the dying. The ship is moving away from us. The island is closer now. I can see trees and a large building.

Where's Sierra?

Alex points. We strike out for the island. It looks so close now, but I don't know if I have the strength left to make it. Then something pulls at my leg. For a moment I think that it is one of the drowned passengers, risen up to drag me under. Then my other leg snags on something, and I realise that I am tangled in weeds. As I reach down to free myself I hear a shout from Alex. I look up. We are barely twenty metres from shore now, but I can see Sierra crawling through the shallows ahead, coughing up water. I scream at Alex to come back and help free me.

Then Sierra collapses on to the shore. As she turns back towards us in triumph the scene fades.

•

Stage One complete. Congratulations. You have reached safety on North Brother Island. Stage Two is set on the same island in 1953. It will commence in two minutes. Ms Summers, as the winner of Stage One, will receive a head start of one minute.

•

Alex and I are standing in a small grey-walled room, with barely enough space for the two of us. We are dry and dressed in more modern clothes than before. There is one exit, a door with a countdown reading '00:58'.

'Shit,' says Alex. 'We lost. That gives Sierra extra time.'

'We can still beat her. There's two of us and one of her. We have to beat her.' I remember the doctor and his instrument case.

'You're right,' says Alex. 'In the first game I played in the park I got frozen and lost a minute. But I still won.'

There is nothing more we can say. Alex grabs my hand and holds tight. We stare ahead at the numbers as they count down. It seems like the longest minute ever. Alex's grip gets tighter and tighter.

'Zero.'

We both reach for the handle at the same time, and push the door open.

We find ourselves standing in the middle of a dimly lit hospital ward, lined with beds on either side. The door through which we entered has vanished. There is no sign of Sierra.

You are in the Riverside Hospital, North Brother Island, East River, New York. You have twenty minutes.

Twenty minutes to do what? We don't know what the game is.

I look around. The ward is a good hundred metres long, with about thirty beds, half of which are occupied. Most of the patients appear to be asleep. There is an unmarked door at one end, and another opposite marked EXIT. In front of the exit is a desk with a nurse seated at it. Above her hangs an old-fashioned clock with one hand. It is pointing to the number twenty. Grimy windows looking out over the river run down one side of the ward. In the opposite wall, between two beds, is a third door marked SPECIMENS.

Curiously, the ward is overrun with cats. There are cats sleeping on the patients' beds, cats curled up in the sunlight on the window ledges, and several cats prowling the floors. One walks towards us, then hisses and runs away. They are thin and mangy.

'Check the far door,' I say to Alex as I walk over to the nurse. She seems the obvious person to ask. There is a cat sleeping on her papers.

The nurse looks up at my approach.

I smile. 'Can you help us?'

She stares at me, then blinks twice and says: 'Bring me Typhoid Mary.'

'All right,' I say, and look round at the patients. 'Which one is she?'

The nurse blinks again. 'Bring me Typhoid Mary,' she repeats.

So no help there then.

I walk back to Alex.

'Is there anything through the far door?' I ask.

'Nothing useful,' he says. 'There's a walled courtyard with a graveyard.' He glances round at the patients. 'Not the most tactful place to put it, really, right next to the ward. There are more cats out there too.'

'The nurse just keeps repeating that we must bring her Typhoid Mary. Whoever she is.'

Alex rubs his face. 'I'm sure I've heard of her. Haven't you?' I shake my head. 'Hang on, I'll do a search.'

'We can't,' I say. 'Guskov told us we'd have no remote access.'

'I've definitely heard of her,' Alex says urgently. He stares at me as though he can somehow will me to remember. 'She was some sort of plague carrier. A long time ago. Maybe she's being treated here. The game is set in the past.'

'There are charts at the end of each of the beds,' I say. 'We can check the names on those. This shouldn't be difficult. We can ignore the men.'

'All right. You take that side, I'll take this one.'

It doesn't take me long to establish that of the five women on my side none is called Mary. Alex has no better luck. We meet in the middle of the ward to exchange the bad news.

'It was never going to be that easy,' says Alex. 'We need to think about this. Someone called Typhoid Mary doesn't sound healthy. Maybe she's dead, and we're meant to check the graveyard.'

'What, and bring the nurse a decomposing body?' I shudder.

'Unless you've got any better ideas.'

'There's the third door,' I say. 'Let's check that first. And where's Sierra?'

As we approach the specimens room the door opens and Sierra steps out. She looks around the ward, then says to us: 'You'll like it in there. There's one who looks just like Alex used to. Maybe Emily saw him for what he really was.'

'Just ignore her,' I say to Alex. I step round her and into the room.

It's dark and windowless. The stench of formaldehyde assaults my nostrils. Floor-to-ceiling shelves line the walls. There is flickering overhead light, reflecting off glass. As I step closer I gag.

It's an anatomical museum. The shelves are filled with glass jars and bottles, ranging from a few centimetres tall to half my height. Floating in them are body parts, foetuses, and what look like bloated babies. In the largest jar, opposite the door, is the swollen body of what looks to have been a midget or a small child. I'm guessing that's what Sierra called Alex.

Dr Bernard would probably like this place. Few others would. But thinking of the doctor reminds me of what's at stake here.

'This is disgusting,' says Alex, behind me. 'Maybe I'm right, though, and Typhoid Mary is dead and floating in one of these jars. We need to check them.'

Swallowing hard, I step over to the right-hand shelf. I'm trying to breathe as shallowly as possible, but I can taste the acrid air in my throat. The flickering light catches a tall thin jar containing an arm, turning slowly, seemingly beckoning to me.

I need to be methodical about this – and quick. I start in the bottom-right corner and work my way along the shelves. Most of the jars have labels, some curled and fading, peeling off. Surprisingly, several cats have made this revolting room their home. I have to push them out of the way to get to the jars. I straighten the labels, trying to read the faded writing in the flickering light. Most are just descriptions of body parts: *Left hallux – three months* – inside is a tiny floating toe; *Lungs, smoker, fifty-three years* – shrivelled blackened sacs within. Others contain entire bodies: *Foetus, four months* – the exquisite detail of the tiny body brings tears to my eyes.

None have names. For a moment I get excited when I see

an entire head staring at me from a high shelf, the letter 'M' catching my eye. But when I stretch to read the label it says *Male head, twelve years*. Skin falls away from the cheek bones as I move the jar.

This is getting us nowhere. I skim the rest of the exhibits and meet Alex in the middle of the centre shelf, next to the bloated child.

He glances at it and shakes his head. 'Sierra. She'll never let me forget Emily.'

'Just let it go,' I say. 'This is hopeless. Even if Typhoid Mary is in here we have no way of knowing. Let's go and try the graveyard instead.'

We step back into the ward. I'm relieved to be out of that ghoulish room. Sierra is walking along the end of the beds, checking the patient's charts. She looks suspiciously at us as we make our way to the third door. I open it and we step out into a small graveyard, enclosed by high stone walls on three sides and the hospital on the fourth. It is overgrown, the gravestones covered in lichen and at odd angles. Some have fallen over. At a rough guess there are about fifty of them. They are not going to be easy to read. I don't see that we have any other options.

'I'll take the left, you take the right,' I say. 'If we find her I still don't see how we take her to the nurse. Are we meant to dig up a coffin with our bare hands?'

'Let's find her first,' says Alex, brushing the encrusted dirt away from the nearest gravestone. 'We've only got twelve minutes left.'

It isn't easy. Many of the inscriptions are virtually illegible. On others the gravestones have cracked or fallen and I have to turn heavy stones over before I can read what they say. Even if I find one called Mary there's no guarantee it's the right one. This feels hopeless.

It is dirty and hot in the graveyard. About halfway through I pause to wipe sweat from my eyes and step into the small strip of shade next to one of the walls. Alex is kneeling in the dirt, twisting his head to read an inscription, a feral cat brushing against his legs.

The door to the graveyard opens. Sierra looks out. She stares at us for a few seconds, then steps back inside and shuts the door. She clearly thinks we are looking in the wrong place.

I rest a hand on the ivy-covered wall, and something moves beneath it. I brush away the ivy to find a metal plaque, now pinned to the wall by only one rusting screw. It comes off in my hand. I am about to throw it away when the name 'Typhoid Mary' catches my eye. I brush it clean.

'TYPHOID MARY'

THIS PLAQUE COMMEMORATES
RIVERSIDE HOSPITAL'S MOST
INFAMOUS RESIDENT, MARY
MALLON (23 SEPTEMBER
1869–11 NOVEMBER 1938), AN
ASYMPTOMATIC CARRIER OF
THE TYPHOID FEVER PATHOGEN,
POPULARLY KNOWN AS 'TYPHOID
MARY'. SHE WAS A COOK, AND
IS BELIEVED TO HAVE CAUSED
THE DEATHS OF AT LEAST THREE
PEOPLE THROUGH TYPHOID
INFECTION. FROM 1907 TO 1910,
HAVING CAUSED THE DEATH OF
ONE PERSON, SHE WAS HELD
IN QUARANTINE AT RIVERSIDE
HOSPITAL. ON HER RELEASE SHE
RESUMED WORK AS A COOK AND
CAUSED THE DEATHS OF AT LEAST
TWO MORE PEOPLE. SHE WAS
RETURNED TO NORTH BROTHER
ISLAND IN 1915 AND REMAINED
HERE UNTIL HER DEATH FROM
PNEUMONIA IN 1938. HER BODY
WAS CREMATED AND HER ASHES
INTERRED AT SAINT RAYMOND'S
CEMETERY IN THE BRONX.

The last sentence strikes me like a blow. We know who she is now, but she is not buried here. We are wasting our time. We can't take Typhoid Mary to the nurse. Maybe some part of her remains in the specimen room. But I don't see how we can ever identify it.

'Alex.' I call him over and wordlessly hand him the plaque. He skims it and looks up.

'I was right about her. But what do we do now?' he says. 'This is impossible. We only have eight minutes left.'

'It must be the plaque,' I say. 'It represents her. We must be meant to take that to the nurse. There's nothing else we can do.'

The door opens and Sierra steps out, blinking in the sunlight. I hide the plaque behind my back.

'What are you doing?' she asks. 'Have you taken up grave robbing? Have you found her?'

'Find her yourself, bitch,' I mutter under my breath as I edge past her and back into the ward, keeping the plaque out of sight. Sierra hesitates, then follows us. It doesn't matter if she sees it now. If I'm right, the first person to deliver the plaque to the nurse wins.

I walk swiftly down the length of the ward, between the beds and up to the nurse. Cats scuttle away and hiss as I move past, backs arched. I hear Alex and Sierra following. The nurse looks up at me. I drop the plaque on her desk.

'There is it is,' I say. 'There is Typhoid Mary.'

The nurse looks down at the rusted plaque, looks up at me, and shakes her head. 'Bring me Typhoid Mary,' she says.

'This is all we can find!' I shout. 'There is no Typhoid Mary here.'

346

She looks at me blankly. 'Bring me Typhoid Mary.'

'What's that you're hiding?' says Sierra. She reaches round me and picks up the plaque. She skims it. 'Sneaky. But wrong.' She turns and hurries back through the door to the specimens room. That's where she started. What did she spot the first time that we missed? Is there a list of the specimens somewhere? Or is it all a bluff?

We're running out of time.

I pick up the plaque and look about for inspiration. The cat that was curled up on the nurse's desk has been disturbed by the noise. It stands, stretches, and sneezes. There are patches of fur left on the papers where it was sleeping.

I turn to Alex. He is looking up at the clock. 'Five minutes,' he says, his shoulders slumped.

'Alex,' I say. 'What's an asymptomatic carrier?'

He takes the plaque from me and re-reads it. 'It means someone who carries a disease but has no symptoms. Look, it says she died from pneumonia, not typhoid.'

'That's what I thought.' I pick up the cat off the nurse's desk, and thrust it at him. It squirms and jumps out of my hands, leaving me covered in fur. 'Look at these cats. They're all ill. Really ill. Something has infected them. Typhoid Mary isn't a person. It's a cat. We're looking for the one cat in this place that is healthy. The one that is making the others ill.'

Alex blinks at me, but seems unconvinced. 'Maybe.'

'We don't have any other ideas,' I say urgently. 'It's this or nothing. You check in here and I'll check the graveyard. Be quick.'

As I turn back towards the graveyard I see Sierra standing

in the doorway to the specimens room. She was listening. She smiles at me. 'Clever Kate. Thanks for that.' She steps back into the room and I hear crashing glass. Why? Does she know something we don't? If Typhoid Mary is in there then we lose.

Three minutes left.

Alex is racing round the ward, pulling at squealing cats, ignoring the patients that he is waking.

I run the length of the ward, back to the graveyard.

I race from headstone to headstone. I hadn't realised before just how many cats there are. Some have curled up in the ivy clinging to the wall. I drag them out, squealing and fighting, getting scratched for my troubles. But they are all the same, mangy, dying, shedding fur.

I am near the back to the graveyard, tearing the ivy from the walls. A cat is dislodged and falls from above, catching itself on my shoulder, claws scraping the length of my back. I throw it off me and return to my search.

Then turn back.

This cat hasn't run away. It has jumped up on to a headstone and is staring at me, licking my blood from between its claws. Unlike the others this one is healthy and plump with a glossy black coat.

I've found Typhoid Mary.

I need to catch her.

I move carefully towards her, but unlike the others she makes no effort to get away. I pick her up and she settles into my arms, purring softly.

Gripping the cat firmly, I dash back through the door. Alex is kneeling on the floor, looking under a bed. He turns, startled.

The clock above the nurse shows that we are down to the last minute.

I sprint the length of the room, thrusting the black cat into the nurse's arms.

'Here you are. Here is Typhoid Mary.'

The nurse takes the cat from me. It settles on to her lap, purring. She nods. Silently she gestures to the door behind her.

I breathe out for what seems like the first time in ages. I look behind me.

Sierra is again standing by the door to the specimen room. Shocked. Fear in her eyes. She knows what this means.

I step past the nurse and open the door. Alex takes my hand and we walk through together.

•

Stage Two complete
Winners: Mr Du Bois and Ms Bird
Loser: Ms Summers

•

Godfried came to let me out of the game booth.

'Well done,' he said. 'I've not seen the cat one before. It must be new. I didn't get it.'

'But I'm sure you made a nice bit of money out of my suffering,' I said.

'I didn't. The club did, of course. I don't get a choice. Time

349

is all that counts here.' He paused. 'It's all I've got to live for, anyway.'

I wasn't sure what he meant by that, but I didn't really care. He was on their side. It didn't matter why. 'So what happens now?' I asked.

'I guess you're good to go. Guskov always keeps his word.' He grimaced. 'Your friend Sierra – not so good. There will be people who stay to watch, but I won't be one of them. If it's anything like what the doctor has done before it will last for days, and it won't be pleasant. Honestly, I don't know why we let him do this stuff here. But the boss never says no if there's time to be had.'

'The boss . . .' I said. 'So you were scamming me the other day when you pretended you weren't going to tell him about me.'

Godfried shrugged. 'I do jobs for him sometimes. Pass on information if it has value. As I said, time is everything here. Look, I wasn't going to tell Guskov about our meeting. But Doctor Bernard said he'd seen us, so I had no choice. Sorry. Come on – we'd better get back to the bar.'

Alex and Sierra were there already. Alex stepped across to me and grasped my hands. 'Kate,' he said. 'Thank God. We won. It's finally over.'

Sierra was standing next to Guskov. Vincent was behind her, gripping her wrists. She was struggling, but forced up on tiptoe. There was fear and anger in her eyes.

'Fucking Kate,' she said, spitting the words. 'Here to watch me die?'

I didn't want to watch her die. Despite her lies, despite Mike and Ben, despite her attempts to kill us, my overriding feeling was one of pity. How had she come to this? Even after Montreal we had wanted to help her. We had *tried* to help her. But she wouldn't change. I should have realised then that she didn't want to. She couldn't see beyond her own selfish, paranoid worldview. She saw us as her puppets, and when we finally stopped obeying her commands she had to be rid of us.

Even so, she didn't deserve to die at the hands of the doctor. No one did.

Guskov stepped forward, turning to the audience.

'Well, wasn't that fun?' he said. 'Life and death and cats. The end of what I hope was an enjoyable week for all of you. Congratulations to our winners, Kate and Alex. They are free to leave. Commiserations to our loser, Sierra. I hope it's some comfort to know that your time with the doctor will benefit medical science. Those of you who wish to stay may do so. Those of you who won their bets, Godfried will credit your accounts. We will be in touch in a few weeks when we have our next entertainment lined up.'

'Wait,' I said. 'I have your word? Alex and I are free to go?'

He nodded. 'Of course. You won.'

'May I have a moment with Sierra?'

Guskov looked surprised. 'Yes. Say your goodbyes, if you must.'

I walked over to her.

'Just fuck off,' she said. 'I don't need your pity.'

But behind the bravado I could see that she was terrified.

'This isn't right,' I said to her. 'I'm sorry.'

Next to her the doctor's instruments were still open on the

bar. I reached past her and grabbed a scalpel from the case. Before anyone could stop me I plunged it into her ribcage, where I thought her heart would be. It jammed on a bone, jarring my hand. I pushed harder. It sank deeper. I pulled upwards. Sierra gasped.

Her eyes went wide. The andi released her. Her hands gripped my arms. She looked down at the scalpel sticking out of her chest, blood beginning to leak past it. Then smiled weakly.

'Thank you,' she whispered.

She fell into my arms, her grip weakening. Wet, sticky blood was pumping down the front of my shirt.

Her eyes went blank.

I sank to the ground with her in my arms.

Someone grabbed me by the shoulders and pulled me away. Sierra collapsed face down on the floor. Blood seeped out from under her.

I turned, angrily, but it was Stas who held me. I couldn't escape his grip.

Dr Bernard was on his feet, shrieking at me.

'This is wrong! It's too quick!' he hissed. 'I had days of experiments prepared for her.' He pointed at me. 'I want her instead.'

Guskov looked at me. Then at the doctor.

'No,' he said. 'I gave my word. She's free to go.'

'But she killed my ... my ... patient!'

'I promised you the loser,' said Guskov. 'It's not my fault if she didn't stay alive long enough to indulge your sickness. You've already been well rewarded for your part in this.'

The doctor stepped over to the bar, and started packing up his tools. 'Fine,' he said petulantly. 'Don't expect me to ever come back again.'

Guskov laughed. 'Don't be silly, Doctor. We both know that you have nowhere else to go.'

He turned to me.

'Ms Weston, Mr Du Bois. I suggest you leave before I change my mind. This may not have gone as planned, but it has at least been entertaining for my guests. My agreement with Ms Summers is now at an end. This concludes our relationship.'

He paused and studied Sierra's still corpse. Then he looked across at Dr Bernard, who was angrily doing up his instrument case, muttering under his breath.

'Doctor,' Guskov called to him. 'Wait a moment.'

Bernard turned back to him, case clutched in his arms. There was hope in his eyes.

My heart sank. Was Guskov going to give us up?

'Doctor,' he said softly, amusement in his voice. 'Don't leave just yet. You seem to have forgotten one of your knives.'

ALEX

The climb to the penthouse suite in the high-rise was a struggle. Kate was out of it, barely able to drag herself up each flight of stairs. For the second day in a row she was covered in blood. She was shaking. Again, I ended up carrying her most of the way. She hadn't spoken since the club.

When we reached the room she slumped into an armchair, breathing hard.

I went to get her a glass of water. 'How are you doing?' I asked, as she gulped it down.

'Not great. That was awful. Whatever Sierra did to us, she didn't deserve to be tortured to death. I had no choice.'

'You did the right thing,' I said. 'I wouldn't have had the courage to do that. But you took a big risk. Guskov could have killed us both.'

She leaned forward, putting her head in her hands. 'Godfried said that he keeps his word. I trusted that. And she was still Sierra. Whatever she'd done, she was part of us for twenty-five years. She was fun. She gave us perspective. It was grotesque

355

what they had planned for her, even if it was her own doing. I couldn't let her die like that.'

'Don't forget she would happily have handed *us* over to the doctor. That was the whole point of the final game. It was what she had been planning all along.'

'What did we do that made her hate us so? She seemed to be paranoid that we were going to kill her first.' She looked down at herself. 'Sierra's blood. We kill people in the arenas and it feels like nothing. This was different. So personal. You know she thanked me at the end?'

I shook my head. 'That still doesn't make her a good person. It was us or her.'

'I know.' Kate stood. 'I need to get cleaned up.'

She closed the door to the bathroom and I lay back on the bed. I could hear her through the thin door as she turned on the shower. I closed my eyes, trying to shut out what had happened in the club. Sierra had got what she deserved. But Kate was right. It had all been too personal. Too visceral.

It was over. But in some ways it was only just beginning.

Kate emerged ten minutes later, swearing under her breath, her hair dishevelled, wrapped in a towel. To me she had never looked more beautiful.

'What is it?' I asked.

'The bloody printer's stopped working. I'll have to go and find one in another room. My clothes are in no state to be worn again.'

'I'll go find one in a minute,' I said. 'I know your size. First, come sit here. We need to talk.' I patted the bed next to me. My heart was racing.

'All right,' she said slowly. She looked at me, puzzled, and slid carefully on to the bed, pulling down the hem of her towel. 'What is it? You look very serious suddenly.'

I turned to her and took a deep breath. I took one of her hands in mine. She looked down at it, and then up at me, sharply.

'What . . .?' she began.

'Wait,' I said. 'Kate, these last few days have been awful. The worst of our lives. But in other ways they have been the best. I've got to spend time with you in ways that I never thought were possible. Some of it was fun.'

She looked troubled. 'Where is this going?'

'I don't really know,' I said. 'I've never been good at asking people out. I didn't tell you, but it was Emily who asked me out. In Montreal, when we first met.'

'What?' she said. 'What does that matter? There must have been others since.' She laughed. But it was a strained laugh.

'No,' I said. 'Until now.'

Kate shifted back in the bed, away from me. She pulled her hand free.

'Alex, I don't know what you're thinking. Yes, we had a bit of fun. But it wasn't real. And most of it wasn't fun. People died. I *killed* people. I've spent the last ten minutes washing Sierra's blood off me.'

'I know,' I said. 'But we didn't die. We won. And I felt something. Remember the game show. We were good as a couple.'

'That was *a game*, Alex. Nothing more.'

'Are you sure that's all it was?' I leaned in towards her. I could feel her breath on my face. She was breathing fast. One hand was clutching the top of her towel, pressing it to her chest, the other was holding down the hem. Her fists were clenched.

I put a hand on her bare shoulder.

'*No*,' she said sharply. 'What do you think you're doing?'

I hesitated, and her hand struck my chest, pushing me away. Her towel was slipping. I resisted. There was fear now in her eyes as she scrabbled backwards.

'No,' she said again. 'Stop it, Alex! Get away from me.'

Did she mean it? Hadn't she felt what I'd felt when we were playing the games? I hesitated. Then I realised this wasn't going to work. She wasn't ready. I needed to be patient. I was going to ruin everything if I was too quick.

I turned sharply away, and sat on the edge of the bed, my back to her.

'I'm sorry, Kate. This is stupid. Maybe it's the adrenaline. The excitement. I'm not experienced at this.'

I felt her move on the bed and a hand rested lightly on my shoulder. I looked around.

'Alex,' said Kate. 'I'm sorry, but you frightened me. This is wrong in so many ways.'

I nodded. 'I understand. Sorry. We're both in a state. You get some rest. I need to get some fresh air. I'll be back soon.'

I left quickly. I was embarrassed. And frightened. Nothing was going as planned.

KATE

I woke feeling tired and dreamy. It was odd to wake from a real sleep, not the wrench from nothing to sudden existence in a schizo body. I'd never minded it much, but this was somehow more gentle.

I'd moved to another room after Alex left, printed some clothes, and made sure that the door locked. I wasn't sure what had come over him.

Despite that I'd managed to fall asleep for a few hours. There were so many issues that I was blocking out of my mind that one more didn't really matter: my stupid andi body, killing Sierra – not to mention the deaths of Mike and Ben. I'd put them all to one side for now.

I felt sorry for Alex. Deep down he was still the fat teenager being teased by Sierra. In some ways he had never grown up. Maybe his one chance to do so had been with Emily. But Sierra had ruined that.

I'd not heard from Alex. Maybe he was in a bar somewhere, too embarrassed to come back.

Just as I was beginning to worry where he'd got to I received a message.

Kate, sorry about earlier. I don't know what came over me. Not sure where you've gone. If you want to talk, come join me on the roof. I promise to behave. Alex.

It sounded as though he had calmed down. And I was going to have to talk to him at some point.

OK, give me 5. K.

Out of habit I added a kiss, but quickly deleted it. That wasn't going to help. Things had changed.

I skimmed through my messages. Only one was of interest. I had finally received a reply to my anonymous CGov query of two days ago, asking what happened if one member of a schizo died. I was about to put it aside for later. Then it occurred to me that if I ever hoped to get back into my real body there might be something in this that would help. Alex could wait.

Thank you for your enquiry. I am concerned that your query has been posted anonymously, as the idea of a single commune mind being erased outside a government facility is troubling. It would help to understand the circumstances of and reasons for your enquiry.

Nevertheless, in accordance with the Information Protocols I am required to answer. In that regard I can do no better than repeat what was previously posted by one of my colleagues in answer to a similar query.

There followed a link to an older post.

The answers to your questions are as follows:

1. It is not possible for members of a commune to expel one member, whether by majority or unanimous vote.

2. It is not possible for CGov to remove a member of a commune unless the member has committed a crime that requires erasure.

3. Commune members may, if sufficient cause is shown, petition CGov for temporary download into stasis for rehabilitation purposes.

4. If a commune member is removed or erased their time will automatically be shared amongst the remainder of the commune, commencing with the next cycle. In no circumstances will CGov seek to introduce a new member into the commune.

So that was a waste of time. It explained some of what had happened to us over the last few days, but didn't give me any clues as to how to get back into my body.

I went up to join Alex.

•

A stairway led from the end of the corridor to a metal door. I pushed it open and stepped through. The roof was flat with a low wall running around the edge. One half was taken up by an empty plunge pool, now filled with dirt, rotting leaves and bits of rusty metal. A scattering of tables and chairs, mostly upended, filled the other half. Presumably this had once been the hotel's roof garden.

I weaved my way between the debris to where Alex was standing with his back to me. Below us the park was shrouded in low-hanging mist. Just above it, between two high-rises, the sun was setting in an orange blaze.

Alex turned to me and smiled. Whatever madness had been driving him earlier had vanished from his eyes.

'Kate, have a drink.' A bottle of champagne stood on one of the tables, two glasses already poured. He handed me one and took the other. He righted one of the chairs and made an ineffectual attempt to dust it off with his clean hand. 'Please, sit.'

I did so. He pulled up a chair for himself on the other side of the table.

'I wanted to take one last look at the park before we leave,' Alex said. 'To say goodbye to the others.'

'You leave,' I gestured to my new body. 'I can't. I'll be staying here with Mike and Ben. And Sierra.'

'We'll find a way,' said Alex. 'I'm not leaving without you. We'll talk to Guskov again, and pay him to get you out.'

'He made it pretty clear that he never wants to see us again. And the one person who could probably help us would be Dr Bernard. But I rather screwed that up, didn't I? Besides, I want to be back in my own body. Back there with you.'

Alex reached across the table and took my hand. 'I'm sorry. But you need to know that's never going to happen. You remember that old government research paper you sent me? I'm guessing you didn't read it.'

'Not the whole thing. Just the summary. Why?'

'I did. Most of it deals with the risks of moving minds out of schizos back to human or android bodies. But there's more. Some of the schizos that were successfully unwound then decided that it had been a mistake. They wanted to recreate the commune, or start a different one. So they tried it. The success rate for that was zero. Instant madness. It's something to do with taking the minds in and out of bodies too many times.'

'That can't be right,' I say. 'Sierra said it was possible. That was the whole point of the final game, so she could get her body back.'

'Sierra lied to you. Or she didn't know. You don't have to take my word for it. Read the paper when you get the chance. It's buried in the detail – footnote 27. There's no doubt. I'm sorry, but we've got to face the truth. You've gone from human to schizo, then schizo to andi. The odds of a safe transfer back to schizo are non-existent.'

'Fuck.' Why were we sitting here drinking champagne? Sierra had well and truly screwed me this time. 'I'm going to message CGov to ask. Maybe things have changed since then. What have I got to lose by telling them everything?'

'You can't do that. They don't come after andis in the death park. But if you tell them you're here they will. They'll wipe you.'

He was right. 'I could do it anonymously. I did that before, when Mike disappeared. I was trying to find out what happens when one mind in a schizo dies. They're obliged to reply. Look.' I sent him the message I'd just received from CGov.

He went silent as he read. His grip on my hand tightened.

'What is it?' I asked. 'What did you see?'

'Ah . . . it's nothing.' He looked away.

What wasn't he telling me? I knew Alex. I knew when he was lying. There was something in the message that made things worse. I re-read it.

'That's weird,' I said.

'What?'

'The timing of the original post they copied. Look at the date. Just over a year ago. It's the day after we left Montreal. We'd just arrived in New York. I didn't notice before. That's really odd.'

'It's just a coincidence,' he said.

'No, it's not. That's what you saw as well, wasn't it? Why didn't you want to tell me? None of us could forget that day. The four of us had just had a massive row about what to do with Sierra. You wanted to get CGov to put her away for ever. Mike said three months was long enough. I agreed with you that we should refer it to CGov, to let them decide. But Ben sided with Mike. So we didn't have the votes to go to CGov, and Sierra ended up in stasis for three months instead.'

I paused, thinking. 'It must have been one of us who asked the original question about getting rid of a schizo mind. It had to be. Schizos don't die. No one else would ask that question. That's why it was so hard to find an answer anywhere. But it was an obvious question for one of us to have asked at the time.'

Alex hesitated. 'If it was one of us it must have been Sierra. Maybe she wanted to get out. Maybe she was feeling guilty about what she had done to Emily.'

'Sierra? Guilty? We both know Sierra didn't do guilt. And

it wasn't me. It wasn't Mike. He wanted to forgive Sierra. And Ben sided with Mike.'

I looked across at Alex. He still wasn't meeting my eye. 'It was *you*, wasn't it? You were the one who hated Sierra after Montreal. You wanted to get rid of her. Why didn't you want me to know it was you? What else aren't you telling me?'

Why was he lying to me?

'So what if it was me?' he said. 'It was a year ago.'

He was sweating. The hand that I was holding was clammy. What was it that he was hiding from me?

He leaned forward and looked up at me, gripping my hand hard, his eyes imploring. 'Katie, why does any of this matter? You need to accept that you can't go back. Is that so bad? I'm sorry for what happened earlier. I realise you're not ready yet. But if you were back in here,' he touched his chest, 'I'd have lost you again. I don't know if I could bear that. Maybe things happen for a reason. Maybe we were meant to be with one another. Is it so bad you being Kate again?'

'I'm *not* Kate, though, am I? I'm fucking Amy Bird in her stupid andi body. Stuck in the death park. I'm never going to be Kate again. Scan me and I'm Amy.'

I stopped. There was a thought niggling at the back of my brain that wouldn't quite surface. What was it? Something Sierra had said in the storm? No. Something earlier.

What triggered it? 'Scan me and I'm Amy.'

Then it hit me. *No.* Everything suddenly made sense. Instinctively, before I could stop myself, I pulled away from Alex. His grip tightened. He wouldn't let me go. His eyes turned hard. He could see the sudden fear in mine.

He knew.

'Fuck it. Alex. It was *you*.'

'What do you mean?' He sounded puzzled, but his voice had risen. There was a tremor within it.

'Stop pretending. It was *you* all along. Not Sierra. I scan as Amy Bird. But when I was in the medical centre yesterday, when I woke up in this body, you called me Kate. How did you know it was me you rescued from the arena? Why did you even bother to rescue me if you thought I was Bird? You'd have left me to die. You couldn't have known from scanning me. When the medic gave me the bill it came up as Amy Bird. To anyone who looks, I'm still Bird.' My mind was racing. It was all falling into place. 'When I caught up to her in the Guskov's warehouse I tried to pretend to Sierra that I was Amy. She said that she knew I wasn't because she had created me. That wasn't true. Because you knew before then that it was me in Amy's body. But what Sierra said was half true. Only the person who put me in this body could have known. It was you, Alex!'

He looked away. Saying nothing. But his silence was my answer.

'Stop lying to me, Alex. It was you, wasn't it?'

He sighed. Then gave a hollow laugh. 'Typical Kate, with the impeccable reasoning. Worrying away at a problem until you've solved it. That's why we gave you the puzzle games to play.' He let go of my hand and pushed his chair back, eyeing me from a distance. His gaze was predatory.

If I was right, I was in danger alone up here with him. He was between me and the door to the stairs. Could I get past him? Even if I could, where would I go? He was stronger and faster than me.

Was I right? He wasn't denying it. He was just sitting, staring at me. He looked like a dandi stuck in a logic loop.

Eventually he spoke. 'Fuck. Why did I call you Kate?' He paused for a long moment. Then breathed out sharply. Finally he spoke again. 'I ... No ...' He paused once more, as though desperately searching for something. 'No ... I just don't have an answer to that. It was stupid of me. But you were hurt and panicking, and I shouted your name without thinking. Because I love you.'

What?

I looked down at my new body. The slim female with dark hair and blue eyes. 'Which am I – Kate or Emily? Which of us were you thinking of when you bought this body? Can you even tell the difference any more?'

He looked up. His eyes piercing me. 'Kate. You've always been Kate.'

'Sierra was right. In Montreal. You weren't sleeping with Emily, you were sleeping with me.'

'No,' he said. 'Well ... yes. In a way. But Emily was different. She wasn't you. In some ways it wasn't real.'

'You've been planning this since Montreal, haven't you? It wasn't enough for you to put Sierra in rehab for three months. You wanted to get rid of her. That answer you got from CGov told you it could be done. Gods, Alex, it's a long time to hate.'

'It's a long time to love, Kate.'

He sounded like he meant it. But how could he? 'How could you possibly think you were in love with me? How could you think I was in love with *you*? We only knew each other for one day.'

367

'Don't you understand?' he pleaded. 'You need to listen to me. You need to understand. If you knew why I did this you would realise that we're meant to be together. One day with you was all it took. The day we met, you were so kind. Sierra was so horrid. I almost walked away then and there, but you were what kept me there. You shared things with me in a way that no one ever had before. You told me things you wouldn't tell the others. I felt special. You said we were friends. You persuaded me that it would all work out. I didn't realise then that being with you for the rest of our lives meant never seeing you again.'

I stared across at him. 'This is madness, Alex. Look what you have done to us – to me. You ripped me out of my body, then pretended it was all Sierra's fault. You killed Mike and Ben.' I paused. 'No, you didn't. You made *me* kill Ben. And Sierra. Pretending you were too weak, and putting it all on me. You bastard, Alex. It was you who arranged all this with Guskov from the start, wasn't it? You committed us to that final game with the horrible doctor ready to kill whoever lost.'

He didn't reply. I thought back to that day in the canteen, when we were seventeen, when he had first held my hand. When I had tried to comfort him. How had he got things so wrong from that one conversation?

'Why bother with any of this if Emily was me?' I asked. 'If you didn't even love her?'

'It's confusing. I did love her. She loved me. Sierra destroyed that for no reason. She wanted to leave Montreal and Emily stood in her way. It was so petty, and so spiteful. Whatever you say, she was vile. We glossed it over because we didn't want to face the truth. We stuck her in rehab for three months and that made us feel better. But we all knew that she raped Emily, whatever the law might have said. I couldn't live with Sierra for another hundred years. She deserved to die.' He turned to me, his eyes imploring. 'Please, Kate. You have to understand. It might have started because of Emily. For revenge. But in the end this was all done for love. So that you and I could be together.'

'We're not in love. Don't you get it? You killed Mike and Ben. They're not coming back.'

'That was necessary,' he said coldly. 'Mike was always an apologist for Sierra. Whatever she did he had an excuse for her. He always looked down on me as the fat kid. He and Ben were the reason we were stuck with Sierra after Montreal. You and I would have reported Sierra to CGov and had her put away in stasis for ever. But Mike and Ben voted against it. They said three months would change her.'

That wasn't entirely true. Once I had known how Mike and Ben were voting it didn't matter what I did, and I hadn't wanted Alex to be completely on his own. So I'd voted with him. By then it was meaningless.

'This was all their fault,' continued Alex. 'Mike and Ben. If they'd just had the courage to do what was necessary we'd have been rid of Sierra for good. They left me no choice.'

Then I realised the truth about Ben. 'It didn't make any difference what we did in that game, did it? You made me think that *I* had killed Ben, but you and I were always going to live, and Ben was always going to die. If *I* hadn't pressed the button, you would have. All the games you made me play. They weren't about winning time. You were getting off on it. That stupid game show with the intimate questions and us ending up tied together. That pig of a host who felt me up while you just watched and pretended to be outraged. It was all your doing. I was just your puppet. It's sick.'

'I wanted to give us the chance to get close. I knew if you spent time with me, even if it was in the games, you would feel something. The death park was my one chance. To get rid of Sierra, and to get close to you. Once I realised you were all determined to come here it seemed too good to be true. I voted against coming to pretend I wasn't interested – so no one would suspect me.'

'And the dealer, Karl. You killed him as well. It wasn't Sierra or Amy Bird.'

'Did I kill him? He was days away from death. If someone jumps off a building and I shoot him on the way down, did I kill him?' He shrugged. 'Karl and his girlfriend were losers.'

'That didn't give you the right to kill him,' I said angrily.

'I had no choice. Sierra had arranged to meet him but stupidly she hadn't realised that we had taken an hour of her time that day. She never bothered to read half the messages we sent her. So by the time Karl came to meet her, Sierra had dropped out, and it was me Karl met instead. He was an idiot. Didn't bother to scan me.' Alex smiled at the memory. 'He started to tell me that he had seen one of us go in to visit Guskov in the Death's Head a few days earlier, and leave with Amy Bird. He was bright enough to understand how schizos work, which was more than Guskov did. Karl said that if I paid him he would tell me what time he had seen us leave with Bird. Well I couldn't have that, could I? It would have told you all that it was me. So Karl had to be silenced.'

'But that was a complete waste of time when you took one of his pills and left it for us. That's what led me to the club, and finding out about andis.'

'That was a mistake,' admitted Alex. 'I didn't know how andis worked in the park. I assumed Karl was selling recreational drugs. I thought you'd identify it and it would cast more suspicion on Sierra.'

'But why did Guskov haul Ben in, then, and threaten him over Karl's death, if you two were working together?'

'He wasn't happy about me killing Karl,' said Alex. 'He suspected I was double-crossing him. I wasn't able to contact him until after he'd questioned Ben. I told him it was a mistake – that something had gone wrong with my control of Amy Bird. I'd managed to lay enough of a false trail the night before, getting Bird to come to the murder scene, and leaving one of her buttons. So he believed me. But the truth was he wasn't going to stop the lucrative game he was running just for the sake of that waster Karl. Ben was never in real danger. Guskov was just playing with Ben.'

'But from what he said in the club Guskov seemed to think he had been dealing with Sierra from the start. Did he know it was really you?'

'He doesn't really understand schizos. I got in touch with Captain Les after Montreal, once you'd voted to come to the park. I pretended to be Sierra, and said we wanted to get in touch with his cousin. Guskov didn't really care who I was. All he wanted was to have a show for his customers and make a profit. It seemed safer to pretend I was Sierra, in case he let it slip. But he wasn't going to do anything that jeopardised his game, anyway.'

'But why didn't Sierra deny it?' I asked. 'When I saw her in Guskov's warehouse this morning, and when we were in the club, she went along with it all. Was that even Sierra in the new andi's body, or was she dead already? Was that just you controlling the andi?'

'Sierra was in there,' he said. 'But she had no direct control. The andi was running a low-level AI, doing what I had told it to, and drawing on her for memories and behaviour. The feelings and emotions were hers. When I was awake I could give her directions. Dr Bernard fixed all that for me. Sierra could see what was going on, but she couldn't control it. She deserved it. She spent her life manipulating people. Refusing to listen to anything I said. Getting drunk. Leaving us in unsafe places. You've no idea how satisfying it was finally to have complete control over her. To make her do what I wanted.' He smiled. 'Inside she must have been screaming. But for once no one could hear her. It was perfect.'

'She thanked me for killing her,' I said. 'It sounded real.'

'Perhaps that was her at the very end. It was hard to keep her suppressed, especially when her emotions were strong.' He paused. 'Don't you understand? It wasn't enough to get rid of her. This was all for you, Kate, for us. I had to convince you that Sierra was behind all this. So you would be happy to be Amy.'

'It was cruel. Whatever she did in Montreal she didn't deserve that. You made her attack me. She forced herself on me. What were you thinking, Alex?'

'I needed you to believe it. It needed to seem real.'

'Oh, it felt real, all right.' Remembering Sierra's kiss in the rain brought something else to mind. 'Amy Bird – she was you as well? When she kissed me in the castle . . .'

He looked away. 'Yes. Like Sierra's andi after the spaceship game, until you took over Bird's body she was running a low-level AI with a version of me. Doing what I told her to do. It was all part of the show.'

'It was pathetic.' I stared at him, seeing him perhaps for the first time. 'You're pathetic. You're a cuckoo, Alex. Moving between nests. You pretend to be like us. You look like us. But you aren't human. We cared for you, we loved you as one of us. And in return you've pushed us out of the nest one by one.'

He smiled to himself. He seemed oddly pleased with the image.

'So what now, Alex?' I asked. 'Are you going to push me off this rooftop and empty the nest entirely?'

'You?' He looked at me in astonishment. 'I could never hurt you Em— . . . Kate.' He tried to cover his slip. Too late. Anger coursed through me again.

'You don't even know which one of us you claim to love. You never loved either of us. All you wanted to do was kill Sierra and fuck me. Well you've managed the first, but the second is never going to happen. I'd rather die.'

'But, Kate . . .' he stuttered. 'This was all for you. For us.' He looked away and bit his lip, staring past me. The sun had almost gone now, the sky and the mist blending to a fiery red. He seemed entranced by it. 'I did it for you, Kate. Whatever you say now, we both know there's something between us. You know this could work if we give it a chance.'

Did he seriously believe that? 'You're delusional,' I said.

373

'There was never anything between us. We had five minutes holding hands twenty-five years ago, and I felt sick for most of that time. You were sweaty and creepy and needy. I was just trying to be nice. I told you things about me to calm you down. Not because I felt anything for you. There is never going to be anything between us. You've destroyed our lives for nothing. The others are dead. I'm stuck in this body and can't get out of the park. Is it true what you told me earlier? That I can't go back?'

He nodded. 'I thought it didn't matter. I knew you didn't like andis, but I thought you'd come round. There's no way of getting you back in here. I'm sorry I screwed up so badly. This seemed perfect. You and me, together at last. But it's all messed up. All because I shouted your name out of love. Now you're in a body you hate. But I'm still sure we could make it work. You just need to give me a chance. With time you'll realise that you love me too.'

'That's never going to happen,' I said furiously. 'You're broken inside. More twisted than Sierra, even. After twenty-five years you're still just the sad fat boy who held my hand for too long. I wish I'd never tried to help you. I felt sorry for you then, and I pitied you after Montreal. But pity isn't love. It's disgusting what you've done. You've killed my friends. I'd never love you if we lived another hundred years. I never want to see you again.'

'Truly?' he asked. There were tears in his eyes. 'Why?' He reached across the table again and before I could stop him had grabbed my hand. I tried to pull away, but he put it to his lips, kissed it lightly, then let it fall.

I snatched it away from him, and stood. I threw my glass at

his feet, where it shattered in a mix of champagne and shards. He flinched backwards.

'I'm leaving,' I said. 'Did you really believe that you were going to charm me with this? With some egotistical story of how you ruined everyone's lives? It's vile. I don't know how I'm going to get out of the park, but I'll work it out myself. Whatever happens, you're on your own.'

He looked up at me and smiled sadly. 'I always was, Kate. I realise that now. Schizos are the loneliest people of all. It was foolish of me to think I could change that.'

ALEX

I watch her leave.

The metal door bangs shut, and I hear her footsteps fading down the stairway. The silence creeps back until I feel as though I am the only person left in the world. The only monster.

Kate. Emily. It doesn't matter any more. I was never good enough for either of them.

Emily hated me at the end. No doubt still hates me.

And Kate thinks I'm pathetic. A pathetic, killer cuckoo. A strange image to be left with.

The sun is almost gone. I pick up my champagne glass and walk over to the edge of the roof. The mist shines red below, as if on fire. My entire adult life, the only sunsets I ever saw were when we went to Montreal. The one place where, briefly, I was happy. I remember the last sunset. Stumbling down a mountainside, half-dressed, barely able to see for tears in my eyes. The red of the trees and the sky merging into one. Leaving Emily.

I may have got everything else wrong, but that bitch Sierra got what she deserved. I'm only sorry that it wasn't my hand on the knife.

I step up on to the low wall that runs around the edge of the rooftop, knocking back the last of my drink. Unlike Kate, I'm not going to waste it.

I let the glass fall, and it tumbles end over end until I lose sight of it.

It's starting to rain and I don't fancy getting wet.

I step forward and the mist rushes towards me.

Kate is wrong. I'm not a cuckoo.

Cuckoos can fly.

EPILOGUE

Kate sat back in her chair, arms folded. The man standing in front of her was sweating. He might cry at any moment.

It was early morning. The club bar was empty apart from Kate, the tearful man, and Vincent standing threateningly to one side.

'Let me understand,' she said. 'For the past three months you've been selling methylphenidate – *our* methylphenidate – and instead of taking our generously agreed ten per cent, you've been skimming off an extra chunk for yourself. How did you think we wouldn't notice?'

'I'm s-sorry ... so sorry. It was a mistake. I'll pay it back.' He glanced sideways at Vincent. Then back at Kate. 'I promise it won't happen again. Please ... please don't give me to the doctor. Tell Mr Guskov I'm sorry.'

Kate paused for a long moment, and stared at him. Letting him think. The mind is the best torturer. When he looked as though he was about to collapse, she spoke. 'The doctor's gone. We don't do that any more. You'll pay back what you stole from us – doubled. By my calculation, that's just over three weeks. Since you're feeling generous we'll round it up to a month. Plus a three-month fine for stealing from us. Four months, to be paid to my associate,' she nodded to Vincent, 'before you leave. Don't let there be a next time.'

'Thank you . . . thank you. I promise it'll never happen again.'

'Take him away.'

Vincent winked at her over the man's shoulder, then grabbed his arm and led him towards the exit.

Kate winced as they stepped on the patch of floor that had once been covered with Sierra's pooling blood. It was a year ago – exactly a year – and the ground had long since been scrubbed clean. But she could still see it. Could still feel the doctor's knife scraping along Sierra's ribs. Could still hear Sierra's gasped 'thank you'.

She always avoided that part of the bar.

They had been less fastidious in cleaning up the mess left by Alex's twenty-storey fall to the concrete roadway beneath the high-rise. Eventually, the rain had washed even that away.

Kate visited less often now, but still went there occasionally when she needed to think. To remember. There were no graves to visit. No memorial to either Sierra or Alex. Their bodies had long since been recycled. Ruined beyond repair, at least there was no risk of Kate ever bumping into them in the park, housing different minds. Nor was there any memorial to Mike or Ben, who hadn't even died in the real world. They lived on now only in Kate's memory. Which was ironic. Five minds become one.

There was a low wall near the bottom of the high-rise.

Sometimes, when she needed to, Kate would sit there, staring unseeing at the patch of ground where she had found Alex. His body – their body – broken and bloodied, covered with a thin layer of settling concrete dust. The body that Mike had spent so long creating, destroyed in a final act of selfish guilt. Destroying all their carefully earned time.

Leaving her stranded in the park. For how long, she still didn't know. If Alex had really loved her, would he have done that?

Footsteps interrupted her musings. Godfried threaded his way through the plants and armchairs. Carefully avoiding stepping on the place where Sierra had died. She hadn't said anything, but he'd noticed.

'Are we done?' she asked.

'That's the last of them. We took two years in fines. I like this new system of yours. Less blood and more income.'

'Let's hope the boss is happy with it,' said Kate. 'Sometimes I think he still prefers the old ways.'

'What matters to Guskov is the bottom line,' said Godfried. 'That's looking pretty healthy these days, and there are fewer corpses to dispose of.' He walked over to the bar. 'Can I get you something?'

'At nine in the morning? I've told you before, God, it's not good for you.'

He laughed. 'And I've told you before, that's not what's going to kill us. Live a little.' He brought over a bottle and two glasses, setting them down on a low table. He sank into the chair next to her and handed her a shot. 'You need this today. Where I come from, we have a tradition. One year on we go back to the graves of our friends, our loved ones, we take a bottle to loosen our memories, our tears, and we remember them. I didn't know your friends and they don't have any graves. But I'm all there is.'

She looked at him in surprise. He had remembered. She took the glass. 'Thanks.'

She knocked it back in one. The fiery liquid coursing down her throat. A warm glow spreading to her fingers and toes. *Her* fingers and toes. She no longer thought of them as Amy's. People change. Sometimes because they have no choice.

She handed the glass back to him for a refill.

'Why don't you leave the park, God? You aren't stuck here like me. You could go at any time.'

He paused. Thinking about the question as he filled her glass.

'I don't really know. I like it here. The world out there is just a little too perfect. Too ordered. It's hard to break the rules. Everything is decided in advance – even how long you're going to live. Here things are different. Here you can live. Despite the games it somehow feels more real. Maybe that's why people come here. To take risks they can't take in the real world.' He drained his glass and sat back. 'I don't see myself leaving.'

'I'll be out of here as soon as I can. The boss has promised he's got people on it. Even after we got rid of the doctor. That's the only reason I'm working for Guskov.'

'I wouldn't be so sure,' he said. 'You like the park. And this is where your friends are.'

'Dead friends.' She tapped the side of her head. 'They're still here. They'll travel with me wherever I go.'

'And new friends.' He leaned across and tapped his glass against hers. 'Here's to the next year.' He smiled. 'I'm willing to bet that, whatever the boss discovers, you and I will be sitting here in a year's time doing the same. And you know that I only take bets I'm sure I'll win.'

Kate smiled back. Maybe he was right. Maybe she needed this place. For now.

They sat in companionable silence, nursing their drinks as she remembered the others. Their absence had left a void in her. Something missing that she couldn't quite explain. Something she still missed.

Eventually Godfried spoke. 'If we're going to do this properly we need to talk about them. Remember the good times. I can't do that. You need to tell me.'

Kate held out her glass.

'Give me another drink, God. Then shut up.'

ACKNOWLEDGEMENTS

My wife, Julie, still hasn't entirely forgiven me for writing the first draft of this book without telling her. So I should start by thanking her, not just for the support in getting *Five Minds* finished, but also for putting up with that sort of behaviour for more than twenty-eight years.

Julie was the first person to read the book, and without her enthusiasm and encouragement it would have died there. Her comments were rather kinder than one of my other early readers, who responded with the somewhat double-edged, 'It reads really well – doesn't sound like you at all.'

At the time I naively thought that all I had to do was finish it, find a publisher, and I'd see it in bookstores in a matter of months. Then I learned about agents, editors, submissions, structural edits, line edits, copy edits, cover design, and everything else that goes into taking an idea from an author's mind and making something that a reader can hold in their hands.

Two years on, here we are.

At some point in the process I realised that this had ceased to be just my book, but included and depended upon the contributions of many others. Without them it wouldn't exist.

With hindsight I realise that my agent, Max Edwards, should not have been the third person (after my wife and one son) to read the book. But he saw enough in my 55,000-word manuscript to take me on, and then (together with Alice Skinner) did a lot of the heavy lifting necessary to turn it into something we could present to publishers. I owe Max more than I can say. Thanks also to everyone else at Aevitas Creative Management who has supported me in this.

Perhaps Max's greatest contribution was finding my superb editor, Miranda Jewess, who turned *Five Minds* into what it is now. She gently explained to me that characters fighting for their lives wouldn't talk like a fifty-year-old lawyer making submissions to a High Court Judge. She not only trimmed my language, but forced me to ensure that the jigsaw fitted together in a logical and coherent way. Brainstorming ideas with Miranda was invaluable.

Thanks to the many others at Viper and Profile Books who have helped along the way, in particular: Graeme Hall, Penny Daniel, Flora Willis, Rachel Nobilo, Drew Jerrison and Niamh Murray.

Thanks also to my meticulous copy editor, Sam Matthews.

I did, belatedly, realise the importance of non-family first readers. I appreciate just what a commitment this involves. Some of them have read the evolving drafts as many times as I have. Thanks, in no particular order, to: Taryn Tomlinson, Lottie Chesterman, Mimi Steward, Charlotte Peach and Geoff Steward. I realise that your criticisms – however hard to take sometimes – were justified and have made this a better book.

Finally, I am grateful to my family for living with me through this. Not just Julie, but also our sons, Elliot and Caden (aka Zog). This book was finished during the first Covid-19 lockdown, and many hours were spent with them tramping through the Surrey Hills on our government-prescribed exercise, debating character motivations and potential plot holes.

Thank you, all.

ABOUT THE AUTHOR

Guy Morpuss spent thirty years as a practising barrister and QC, working on cases involving everything from drug-taking cyclists and dead Formula 1 drivers to aspiring cemetery owners. His favourite books have always involved twists on reality and playing with the consequences, which led to him secretly writing his debut novel about five people sharing one body. Readers who want to know whether they have the temperament to be a commune are encouraged to go to guymorpuss.com, where they can undertake a short and painless personality test, or even visit the Death Park for themselves. Guy lives near Farnham, England, with his wife and two sons, and when not writing he can usually be found walking or running in the Surrey Hills. His next novel, *Black Lake*, will be published by Viper in 2022.